W9-CPB-419

THE MOST ROMANTIC HOLIDAY OF THE YEAR

Passion and romantic intrigue are in the air on Valentine's Day! In these six heartwarming holiday love stories, the sparks fly and passions ignite amidst all the romance of Valentine's Day. Cupids and red hearts, lace-edged cards and bouquets of flowers, lavish balls and secret admirers set the scene for A VALENTINE'S DAY TREASURE.

So celebrate the holiday and give yourself this very special valentine. Let bestselling Regency authors Janis Laden, Georgina Devon, Violet Hamilton, Valerie King, Irene Loyd Black, and Teresa DesJardien take you to a Valentine's Day in an age where love and romance are the order of the day!

ZEBRA'S HOLIDAY REGENCY ROMANCES CAPTURE THE MAGIC OF EVERY SEASON

THE VALENTINE'S DAY BALL (3280, $3.95)
by Donna Bell

Tradition held that at the age of eighteen, all the Heartland ladies met the man they would marry at the Valentine's Day Ball. When she was that age, the crucial ball had been canceled when Miss Jane Lindsey's mother had died. Now Jane was on the shelf at twenty-four. Still, she was happy in her life and accepted the fact that romance had passed her by. So she was annoyed with herself when the scandalous—and dangerously handsome—Lord Devlin put a schoolgirl blush into her cheeks and made her believe that perhaps romance may *indeed* be a part of her life . . .

AN EASTER BOUQUET (3330, $3.95)
by Therese Alderton

It was a preposterous and scandalous wager: In return for a prime piece of horse-flesh, the decadent Lord Vyse would pose as a virtuous Rector in a country village. His cohorts insisted he wouldn't last a week, yet he was actually looking forward to a quiet Easter in the country.

Miss Lily Sterling was puzzled by the new rector; he had a reluctance to discuss his past and looked at her the way no Rector should *ever* look at a female of his flock. She was determined to unmask this handsome "clergyman", and she would set herself up as his bait!

A CHRISTMAS AFFAIR (3244, $3.95)
by Joan Overfield

Justin Stockman thought he was doing the Laurence family a favor by marrying the docile sister and helping the family reverse their financial straits. The first thing he would do after the marriage was to marry off his independent and infuriating sister-in-law Amanda.

Amanda was intent on setting the arrogant Justin straight on a few matters, and the cozy holiday backdrop—from the intimate dinners to the spectacular Frost Fair—would be the perfect opportunities to let him know what life would be like with her as a sister-in-law. She would give a Merry Christmas indeed!

A CHRISTMAS HOLIDAY (3245, $3.95)

A charming collection of Christmas short stories by Zebra's best Regency Romance writers. *The Holly Brooch, The Christmas Bride, The Glastonbury Thorn, The Yule Log, A Mistletoe Christmas,* and *Sheer Sorcery* will give you the warmth of the Holiday Season all year long.

Available wherever paperbacks are sold, or order direct from the Publisher. Send cover price plus 50¢ per copy for mailing and handling to Zebra Books, Dept. 3641, 475 Park Avenue South, New York, N.Y. 10016. Residents of New York and Tennessee must include sales tax. DO NOT SEND CASH. For a free Zebra/Pinnacle catalog please write to the above address.

A Valentine's Day Treasure

Janis Laden•Georgina Devon•Violet Hamilton
Valerie King•Irene Loyd Black•Teresa Des Jardien

ZEBRA BOOKS
KENSINGTON PUBLISHING CORP.

ZEBRA BOOKS

are published by

Kensington Publishing Corp.
475 Park Avenue South
New York, NY 10016

Copyright © 1992 by Kensington Publishing Corporation

All rights reserved. No part of this book may be reproduced in any form or by any means without the prior written consent of the Publisher, excepting brief quotes used in reviews.

If you purchased this book without a cover you should be aware that this book is stolen property. It was reported as "unsold and destroyed" to the Publisher and neither the Author nor the Publisher has received any payment for this "stripped book."

First printing: January, 1992

Printed in the United States of America

"The Gilded Cage"
Copyright © 1992 by Janis Laden
"A Ring for Remembrance"
Copyright © 1992 by Alison Hentges
"The Bay Leaf Legend"
Copyright © 1992 by Violet Hamilton
"A Play of Hearts"
Copyright © 1992 by Valerie King
"Tattered Valentine"
Copyright © 1992 by Irene Loyd Black
"A Valentine Bride"
Copyright © 1992 by Teresa DesJardien

CONTENTS

The Gilded Cage

by Janis Laden

Alexandra Rutledge stood at the stern of the *Star of India,* heedless of the long blond tendrils that whipped across her face in the wind, and watched the great port of Calcutta recede. She could not believe Papa had actually done it! He had sent her away from India, her home for thirteen of her twenty-one years! She was meant to travel for endless weeks on Captain Hawkins's three-masted merchant vessel, and then for unknown days in a northbound coach over the wintry English countryside to her aunt's home in Yorkshire. Her aunt and uncle, Sir Horace and Lady Hartcup, had ofttimes over the last few years extended an invitation to Alix, but Papa wouldn't hear of it. There were plenty of eligible men in Calcutta, he'd said; he'd wanted his little girl with him.

Papa wanted her no longer. He had been so eager to be rid of her that Aunt Hartcup would have no more warning than the missive Alix carried, and it would be full winter when she arrived; there would be no time for her body to adjust gradually to the cold and alien English climate. She shivered even now at the thought and felt her eyes well up.

"That fop is hardly worth your tears," drawled a contemptuous voice to her right. Alix jumped. She had not heard him approach.

She stiffened and turned, chin high, to regard the man her father had chosen to convey her home. Derek Muldaur, Viscount Weddington, was tall and muscular with jet black hair, deep blue eyes, and full, intriguing lips. He was exceedingly wealthy, well-respected by men, desired by women. And he despised Alexandra Rutledge.

"I do not believe you are sufficiently well-acquainted with me to vouchsafe any comment regarding my emotional state, my lord," she said dismissively and whirled round to leave him.

His hand reached out and clamped down on her wrist. "You'll have to do much better than that, Miss Rutledge. I am not one of your foppish flirts to slink away, tail between my legs, when you administer the slightest set-down or flick of the fan. And as we are to be at very close quarters for weeks on end, I suggest that your emotional state *is* my concern. This is not a passenger ship, as you well know, and it will not do at all for you to turn into a watering pot before we are half a day's journey from port. Nor will I have you attempting to set up some flirt among the officers on board ship. This is not some soiree at Old Government House in Calcutta. Do I make myself clear?"

Now we are even, Alix thought, biting her lip. Now I despise you quite as much as you hate me. She lowered her eyes to their entwined hands. He was squeezing her too hard, and yet there was a curious warmth to the feel of his large hand encircling her wrist. She ignored it and kept her voice cool. "You are hurting me, my lord. Pray give me back my wrist."

The Viscount Weddington cursed under his breath and let her go.

Alix paced the length of her small cabin, alternately fuming and impatiently brushing back tears. How dare he speak to her that way! Odious man! And whyever had he taken her in such dislike? They had only met fleetingly at various routs and balls in Calcutta, but from the first she had seen unmistakable contempt in his eyes. Indifference she might have understood— although it was rare for a man to look at her without *some* interest, for after all, there weren't *that* many ladies in Calcutta—but Weddington's obvious disdain left her at a loss. Why, before this week, they'd rarely exchanged a word, never even danced together!

And then Captain Peregrine Granger had asked Papa if he could pay his addresses to her. Papa had refused him peremptorily and raked Alix over the coals for once again encouraging the attention of "some demmed court card." No daughter of his was going to marry some useless fribble. Granger was worse, according to Papa, than the last coxcomb who dared to aspire to her hand or the one before that. He was very disappointed in Alix. Perhaps it was the climate. Or the spicy food. She kept developing *tendres* for all the wrong sorts of men. She must leave for England at once. Perhaps his sister would have better luck with his chuckleheaded daughter. After all, Winifred Hartcup had a reputation for just this sort of thing, did she not?

And so Papa had asked the Viscount Weddington, who was soon to sail for home for the first time in some ten years, to escort Alix. He had consented, not troubling for a moment to hide his dislike of her, nor that he was in full agreement with Papa on the lack of worthiness of Captain Peregrine Granger.

Oh, blast! Alix thought. It was all so humiliating, so infuriating, so—she paused and realized for the first time that she was far more crushed by Papa's disapproval, far more humiliated at having to be sent away like some wayward child than she was devastated by the loss of Peregrine Granger.

He had never, of course, gotten to the point of making her an offer, nor had she ever really decided whether she would have accepted him. Captain Granger was amusing, of course, and all that was handsome, with thick blond hair and the kind of broad shoulders that looked most dashing in uniform. He danced admirably, he made her laugh, and he was quite smitten with her, but as to whether she wanted him for a husband . . . in truth, she did not know. For all she had flirted and danced her way through countless entertainments over the last three years, she had never seriously considered what she wanted in a marriage partner. She supposed that she'd simply assumed she would one day be swept off her feet. Papa had never said anything to counter that notion, merely that to attract an eligible *parti* she must always be in her best looks and at her most charming, just as her late mama had done.

Indeed, with servants always underfoot and her days crowded with social engagements, Alix had little time for rumination of any kind. And at all events, Papa did not hold with excessive cogitating or solitary pursuits among females.

And so she was most confused and hurt and vexed that, having done all that Papa wished, she had been exiled over the matter of Peregrine Granger. Why, Papa had not even given her the chance to refuse the captain! And Alix realized now, for the first time, that she would have done just that. Captain Granger had not, after all, swept her off her feet.

Derek Muldaur, Viscount Weddington, had watched with decided pique as Miss Alexandra Rutledge sashayed toward the companionway of the main deck. He did not like the way her hips swayed in that subtle, tantalizing way, the pale aqua muslin of her dress clinging where it oughtn't to cling. He did not like the way her small, perfect, pointed nose had quivered with indignation as she spoke, nor the way her hair, the color of rich golden honey, had whipped in wild abandon about her face as the wind blew. And he most especially did not like the way her wrist had felt when he grabbed her. It had been a mistake. He had never touched her before and had been unprepared for the rush of heat he'd felt. He did not welcome it. And he'd been unprepared for how delicate, almost fragile, her wrist felt. True, she was small, perhaps five foot three to his nearly six feet, but still he hadn't thought . . .

Blast! He did not welcome fragility in a woman. And he did not welcome the task at hand. The last thing he wanted to do on his long-awaited voyage home was to play nursemaid to a spoiled, pampered ninny-hammer who was mooning after the likes of Peregrine Granger. Alexandra Rutledge was everything he despised in a woman. She reminded him of his bubble-brained older sister, who'd never had a thought in her head beyond what to wear for the next evening's entertainment and who had wed the first titled gentleman who turned her head with pretty compliments and had sufficient funds to keep her in gowns and jewels.

And Miss Rutledge, with her easy charm and sparkling, green-flecked hazel eyes, reminded him of his late mother, who had blithely run his father's fortune into the ground. Not that his father had been a particularly prudent man. He hadn't. But once he died, his mother had ignored all the warnings of her man of business and her only son, then but fifteen years old. She had continued her profligate lifestyle—wardrobes had to be of the first stare, his sister had to be properly launched in Society, each house had to be fully staffed—until there was nothing left. Whereupon she promptly died, four years after her husband, leaving her son with two mouldering estates, a grand but shabby London house, and a mountain of debts. And so Derek had sold the London house and one estate to pay the debts and upkeep on the other, Greenvale, his principal seat in Herefordshire.

And he'd set off, at the age of twenty, to India to make his fortune. And he had. He'd been gone ten years, and he'd amassed a great amount of wealth. Enough to have had his man of affairs buy back Weddington House in London when it came on the market last year. Enough to look forward to restoring Greenvale to its former glory, to pouring money into the land, where it belonged, and to taking his rightful place in society.

Derek felt the spray of sea foam on his face and inhaled deeply the tangy air. It had been ten years of hard work and exile in a burning, forbidden land. Ten years in which he'd evaded eligible gentlewomen like Alexandra Rutledge, who knew naught but how to dance and flirt and count a man's money. Not that there were that many women in India, but more seemed to be coming every month. They were all cosseted even more than in England, isolated from the native population, waited on hand and foot by a multitude of servants, and accustomed, because of their relatively small numbers, to being the center of masculine attention. In such an environment had Alexandra Rutledge come of age.

And Derek had the dubious honor of escorting her home, having been unable to refuse her father. Martin Rutledge had been his friend, occasional business partner, and a school friend of his father's. And so Derek would see Miss Rutledge to English shores, then convey her north to her aunt in Yorkshire.

He smiled now, leaning on the railing, as he recalled what Martin Rutledge had said about his sister. "Doesn't set foot in London, don't y'know, but up there in Yorkshire she's the *grande dame.* Quite the matchmaker, m'sister. Don't know if anyone in Yorkshire gets shackled without her say-so. She'll see Alix hitched by summer, I make no doubt."

The Viscount Weddington was perfectly content to leave the matter of Alexandra Rutledge to the immensely capable Lady Hartcup.

Alix wore an evening gown of rose satin for her first dinner on board the *Star of India.* Her hair was caught up in a topknot and her mama's ruby pendant nestled, as always, at her throat. The food at the captain's table was surprisingly good and the company, save one, pleasant enough. The chief mate was a tall, gangly young man who stammered and actually blushed upon greeting her. He could vouchsafe no further conversation during the four-course meal, but he cast several hesitant looks in her direction. She answered these with a smile calculated to put him at his ease.

Captain Hawkins was a husky man of medium height and middle years, who had a definite air of command when dealing with his men. With Alix he was a bit more reticent, though clearly pleased with the novelty of having a lady on board.

The Viscount Weddington was *not* pleased and took no pains to hide it. He treated Alix with the sort of scrupulous civility that was rather off-putting. He addressed few remarks to her and his expression remained impassive all the while. Captain Hawkins attempted to draw her into the conversation, but did not know quite how to do it. Papa would have said that he was not in the petticoat line, but Alix found his attempts to explain the intricacies of the new steamships rather endearing.

She understood nary a word but vouchsafed that the *Star of India* at full sail was of a certain far more beautiful than any steamship could be.

"Surely these great sailing vessels will always rule the seas, Captain," she said, and the captain, in between bites of minted peas, agreed wholeheartedly, adding that steamships could not travel such great distances.

Conversation lapsed after that, for Lord Weddington glowered at her and Captain Hawkins looked from her to the viscount in some confusion.

To fill the silence and to set the dear man at his ease, she asked about the ship. "Just how large *is* it, Captain? I began to do a bit of exploring today, but I own I saw not the half of it!"

" 'Tis a twelve hundred ton merchantman, Miss Rutledge, with thirty-eight guns and over two hundred in crew," he said with quiet pride.

Alix's eyes widened. "Two hundred! My goodness me! Where have they all been hiding?"

Captain Hawkins chuckled. "They each have their own tasks, my dear, and apply themselves diligently, if they know what's good for them. Feel free to continue your explorations on the morrow, but do stay off the magazine deck."

It was then that Alix remembered about the thirty-eight guns. She nervously sipped her wine, then asked, "Ah, Captain, you do not really mean to *use* those guns, do you?" The captain's brown eyes crinkled up. He reminded her of Papa when he was relaxed at the end of a day.

"No, no, my dear." He patted her hand comfortingly. "We do not expect to use them, though on the high seas the possibility is always there. But besides that, the *Star of India* is nine years old, and we have only just come out of a war two years ago. She needed her guns then, believe you me."

Much relieved, Alix smiled at him, and the remainder of the meal passed in amicable conversation. The chief mate, too shy to do more than mumble a few monosyllables, followed the discourse, however, and laughed with them several times. Only the viscount seemed discomposed. In truth, by dinner's end he appeared to be clenching his jaw. He looked daggerpoints at Alix and she feared the captain had noticed.

Oh dear! Whatever was Lord Weddington so het up about? Surely he must see that at such close quarters ease of conversation was most desirable. Would he wish her to be a veritable rudesby, hardly deigning to speak to the captain at all?

She was to have her answer soon enough. After dinner she left the gentlemen to their port, drew her shawl about her, and made her way to the main deck.

"What are you doing here?" the harsh voice demanded not ten minutes later.

She whirled round. "I am watching the moonlight as it pours over the ocean. Do you make it a habit to sneak up on people, my lord?"

"Watching the moonlight!" he echoed, ignoring her question. "Have you taken leave of your senses? To stand here in the dark of night, quite unaccompanied—I cannot think what you are about, Miss Rutledge!"

He was in high dudgeon, but very handsome for all that, his dark hair tousled by the breeze, the strong planes of his face illuminated by the moonlight. His coat was unbuttoned, revealing a broad chest and muscular thighs encased in close-fitting pantaloons. Alix resolved that she would no more be discomposed by his very masculine looks as by his temper. She drew herself up.

"Why, as I told you, I am admiring the view. And I own it is quite unexceptionable for me to do so. I am disturbing no one, and the weather is quite lovely. Just the right amount of breeze—"

"Miss Rutledge!" he interjected, striding toward her. "The

weather is much beside the point, as you know full well."

"And just what is the point?" she queried, determined to maintain her imperious pose despite the fact that he stood just a foot away and quite towered over her. And indeed, she was not afraid. His proximity was causing quite an odd sensation in her stomach, but it was not fear.

"The point, Miss Rutledge," he fairly growled, "is those two hundred-odd crew members you were so curious about, men who will not see another woman for months. You are not a schoolroom miss. It should be perfectly obvious what a danger it is for you to move about the ship unattended."

"Surely you jest! Why—"

"You will not go anywhere without me or your maid. Where is she, by the bye? Why did she not escort you to dinner?"

"Because I sent her to see about her *own* dinner!" Alix snapped. "She was hungry."

"Such concern for the welfare of your servant is a bit late is it not?"

She raised a haughty blond brow in question. Derek watched her perfect, patrician nose quiver ever so slightly and her rosebud lips purse in indignation. He told himself he had not the least desire to kiss those lips.

"Would you care to explain that remark, my lord?"

"Only that I find the custom of taking Indian servants away from their homeland deplorable, Miss Rutledge."

Her hazel eyes flashed. "Sita begged me to take her with me, not that it is at all *your* concern, Lord Weddington. She is of mixed blood. There is no place for her in India."

"There will be no place for her in England either," he retorted.

"She will have me," Miss Rutledge countered with her chin in the air, and then gathered her skirts and began to excuse herself.

He blocked her way but did not touch her. "Not so fast, Miss Rutledge. I repeat that you will not go about alone on this ship, and you will cease forthwith this blatant attempt to set up a flirt with the captain!"

"I did no such thing!" Her beautifully rounded breasts rose and fell in indignation. He told himself he was not growing warm at the sight.

"No?" he sneered, then tossed off in a falsetto voice, " 'Just how large *is* the ship, Captain? You do not mean to *use* the guns, do you?' What the deuce do you call that if not—"

"I call that being pleasant, my lord, something of which you can have no notion. And now, if you will excuse me, I wish to retire. You will oblige me by recalling that you are neither my father nor my guardian. You are merely my escort, and you *have* escorted me on board ship. You need not concern yourself with me until we disembark on English soil. Good night, Lord Weddington!"

With that, she stormed off; Derek strode right after her. "You will allow me to *escort* you, ma'am," he said with a note of command.

She did not demur. He walked beside her, careful not to touch her, until they reached the narrow passageway leading to her cabin, and then he preceded her. He opened her door and found himself in something of a quandary. The cabin was in a corner, so that in order to let her pass he had either to enter her small cabin or flatten himself against the wall opposite her. He chose the latter course and knew immediately that it was a mistake. For she could not help but brush against him, her breasts grazing his chest, her thighs rubbing against his, her sweet scent assailing him. And all the unwelcome fires he had been carefully banking all evening flared up within him.

For one instant their eyes locked in that dim passageway, and he knew that she felt the same unwelcome fire.

"G-good night, my lord," she stammered, and disappeared.

Lord Weddington did not have a good night at all.

Her encounter with Lord Weddington outside her cabin so unnerved Alix that she resolved to stay as far from him as possible. He infuriated her, odious man that he was, and yet that feel of him against her had engendered within her a rush of warmth and ripples of sensation such as she had never before experienced. They were not at all unpleasant and left Alix most confused.

They were the sort of sensations that made her think very unladylike thoughts, such as what his sculpted lips would feel like atop hers, what his arms would feel like about her waist. She flushed even now at the mere notion and wondered whatever was wrong with her. Why, she disliked his lordship mightily! And she had liked Peregrine Granger well enough but had never once wondered what his lips would feel like . . .

Clearly the most prudent course was to avoid Lord Weddington, and in the days that followed, Alix did just that. She kept Sita with her whenever possible, not, she told herself, to obey his odious lordship, but to give him little reason to approach her and censure her. She befriended the chief mate, who became more and more at ease with her, the second mate, who liked to tell stories of his travels, and the surgeon, who liked to play chess when he was not in his cups. Unfortunately his predilection for gin kept him in that state more often than not.

It was only at night, at the captain's table, that she encountered Lord Weddington. He was stiff and formal and disapproving with her, much to the bewilderment of Captain Hawkins, with whom she got on famously. Lord Weddington escorted her to her cabin after dinner each evening. They walked in silence and by some unspoken accord they never touched. He no longer preceded her down the narrow passageway but watched her go and open her own door.

She wondered if he had found their brief contact that first night as unsettling as she or if he had sensed, as she did, that palpable tension in the air between them. His rigid bearing and clamped jaw gave no indication, and, of course, she could not ask.

Thus continued this rather uneasy state of affairs for some weeks until the weather changed. It had been fairly mild since they'd left India, growing cooler as they went farther south, to be sure, but such rains as there were had been light, the seas obligingly calm. But then they rounded the Cape of Good Hope and the very next day dawned bleak. By lunchtime the sky had darkened and the sea was churning ominously. Sailors were scurrying everywhere, securing the rigging and battening down the hatchways.

The ship rolled and rocked most uncomfortably, and Alix felt rather queasy. Sita, when she came to help Alix dress for dinner, looked decidedly green, and Alix sent her to bed, accomplishing her toilette by herself. At all events dinner was a hurried affair, the gentlemen talking of nothing but the approaching storm.

The squall hit sometime in the middle of the night. Alix was jolted from sleep when the ship lurched violently, nearly tossing her from her bunk. She burrowed under the blankets, listening to the raging storm and trying to calm her unsteady stomach. She lay there, praying that the *Star of India* could hold her own, when she heard a faint moaning sound. At first she thought it was the wind, but then she realized it was coming from the adjoining cabin, where Sita slept. It was little more than a closet, really. These rooms, she'd recently learned, were usually occupied by the chief mate. Sita's cabin served as his office.

Gingerly, Alix lowered her legs to the floor, drew on her wrapper, and lit a taper. She staggered as she made her way to the adjoining door, for the ship pitched perilously. The first thing that hit Alix as she opened the door was the stench. Poor Sita had been sick in her bed. She was curled up now, clutching her stomach and rolling as the ship rolled. Alix called to her; Sita moaned and was sick again. Alix reached for the basin.

And thus began the nightmare. Alix bathed the little maid and held the basin again and again. But she could not move Sita enough to strip the bunk, nor could she find clean bedsheets in either cabin. The basin had to be emptied, and she needed more than a pitcherful of water. And she wondered if there was some tonic that Sita could drink to ease her stomach.

Clearly Alix needed help. She made her way back to her own cabin and hastily donned the simplest dress she owned, one that buttoned down the front. She twisted her hair up, put on her half boots and cloak, and ventured out toward the sick bay. She most sincerely hoped Mr. Lambert, the surgeon, would be sober; he wasn't. He was, in fact, lying in no small distress on the floor of the dispensary, whimpering incoherently. Alix tried to help him stand up, but he cried out in pain. She finally realized that he must have fallen and injured his leg, for it was bent nearly beneath him at a most odd angle. She hoped it was not broken. She tried unsuccessfully to maneuver him a bit to ease the pain and finally gave up.

She bit her lip, feeling helpless. She hesitated about going up to the main deck where the storm would be raging and likely most of the crew at work. But what choice had she? She did not even know where Lord Weddington's cabin was, nor if he would be there. Of a certain the captain would not be in his.

Seeing no help for it, she made her way to the main deck, clutching bars and banisters wherever she could and still being thrown from side to side and once falling down completely as the *Star of India* lurched in the waves.

Nothing below had prepared her for the reality of the squall up on deck, however. The rain pelted her in sheets, drenching her in minutes even as the wind ripped her cloak up and around her body. Men were running about, shouting, climbing the masts, hurrying to obey orders. A particularly fierce gust of wind caught her unaware, tossing her viciously against the starboard railing. She hung on for dear life as the ship pitched high up and then plummeted down. Her stomach plummeted as well; she could not stay here for long.

She pushed her thick, wet hair from her face so that she could see. Surely one of these men could be spared a moment to help her. But no one came near enough to hear her call out, for the roar of the storm was fierce. Finally she left the safety of the railing and tumbled across the deck, clutching a bulwark here, a coil of rope there, anything to steady herself against the buffeting winds. Several sailors to whom she called didn't hear or ignored her, and when she tried to grab one by his sleeve, the wind pushed her back. She fell against one of the derricks, and was certain she would be black and blue by morning.

And then she saw Lord Weddington, hauling a coil of rope up over the railing and peering over the side of the ship. She hurried toward him and shouted above the din of the storm.

"Lord Weddington! Please! I need—"

"Miss Rutledge! What the devil!" He grasped her shoulders, his face suffused with fury and something else which she could not name. "Have you no sense, woman? We've just had a man overboard! Do you want to be next?" he railed.

Her eyes widened. "Overboard! Is he—"

"We've got him." The ship pitched again and his strong hands steadied her. It occurred to her fleetingly that he could easily have been safe and warm and dry below. He was not a crew member. Instead he was here, drenched, doing his share and perhaps more. "Now, get below, dammit!" he snapped. "This is a killer storm! What did you think you were about—"

"I need help! My maid is ill and Mr. Lambert—"

"Your *maid is ill??*" he echoed, the familiar mask of disdain descending onto his face. He dropped his hands abruptly, causing her to lose balance for a moment. "Well then, you'll just have to tie your own ribbons for a while, won't you, Miss Rutledge?" he sneered, and then strode away, leaving her shaking with rage and humiliation.

He hadn't even let her finish! He had jumped to the most odious conclusion, had been willing to believe the worst of her. He—

Her thoughts were interrupted by a blast of wind, felling her against the railing, followed by the roar of a huge wave. She watched in horror as it rose up and crashed over her, flooding the deck and knocking her down. She gasped for breath, struggling to her knees as the wave receded. She pushed her hair back from her face and saw the viscount advancing toward her. She rose shakily to her feet and glared coldly at him. He stopped in his tracks. Good, she thought. She did not want his help. Not anymore.

If necessary, she would do what needs must be done without any help at all. She was *not* helpless, despite what Lord Weddington might think, despite the fact that she'd never before been called upon to be particularly useful. Squaring her shoulders, she went below.

The next thirty-six hours passed in an agonizing blur for Alix. She nursed Sita, emptying the basin countless times and lugging pots of water in and out of the cabin. And every time Sita was calm, she went to the sick bay. The sailor who'd gone overboard had been brought in shivering, chilled to the bone, and not long after he was showing signs of fever. There was, of course, no one to nurse him; all hands were needed on deck. The *Star of India* was fighting for her life.

She did contrive to locate the first mate, who set Mr. Lambert's broken leg while Alix poured gin down his throat. And then he disappeared, leaving her with two patients besides Sita.

By mid-morning the storm showed no signs of abating, and another sailor was brought into the sick bay, suffering as wretchedly as Sita from *mal de mer.* Occasionally one of the crew came by to lend a hand, but then the ship would pitch violently and some officer would shout for him and he would disappear. Lord Weddington did not come.

Day became night. Alix was dizzy from fatigue. She was starving but so queasy she could keep down nothing save weak tea. She had no idea if anyone else was eating. She'd seen naught of the captain or the viscount. Her back ached from bending over bunks and carrying basins, but she had no thought to stop or lie down. She could not, after all, leave a man with fever alone, nor allow anyone to lie in his own sickness.

It was dawn on the second day before the sea calmed. The ship righted itself and someone, she could not say who, came to take over the sick bay. And only then did the full measure of Alix's exhaustion hit her. She could barely move one foot in front of the other as she walked toward her cabin. The companionway loomed before her. How was she to ascend those steps? She looked up and there, at the top, was the last person she wanted to see.

It was all too much. She felt the blackness close in on her even before she fell, sinking into blessed oblivion.

Derek cursed audibly as he raced down the stairs, too late to catch her. He lifted her from the floor and stared down at her incredulously. What the devil was she doing here and in such a state? She'd been walking all bent over. Her dress was soiled and wrinkled, her eyes rimmed by purple circles.

Dear God, she was lighter, more fragile then he could have imagined. He carried her to her cabin, laid her gently on her bunk and went in search of her maid. The girl was in her own bunk, half moaning, half asleep, quite obviously sick. He left her and went back to Miss Rutledge, removing her boots and unfastening the top buttons of her dress, noting absently the ruby that always nestled at her throat. But today the smooth skin of her neck looked much too white. She was cold, shivering, and he did not need a doctor to know she was going to be ill. He covered her and rubbed her hands, calling her name until her eyelids fluttered open. But she closed them again and he did not know if she was aware of him.

He tried unsuccessfully to get her to drink. She shuddered more violently, and he covered her with more blankets. She whimpered in distress. " 'Tis all right, Miss Rutledge, you'll be fine now," he soothed, but she gave no indication of having heard.

And still he had no notion of how she had come to this pass until, perhaps an hour later, Captain Hawkins came to the cabin to report all he'd heard from the crew. And then he withdrew, leaving a stunned viscount behind him.

Derek gazed down at her pale face and a wave of remorse hit him. She'd been here all alone, nursing her own maid, for pitysakes! And the others! He'd had no idea! He remembered her coming to him, the first night of the storm, telling him that her maid was ill and something about Mr. Lambert. And he'd assumed . . . Hellfire! She'd asked for his help and he'd denied her, certain it was of herself she'd been thinking.

Now her beautiful face was taut with the strain of exhaustion. God only knew the last time she'd slept or eaten. He could not credit how this woman and the most accomplished flirt in Calcutta could be one and the same. His own mother would never have done what Miss Alexandra Rutledge had. Nor would his sister, nor any other woman of his acquaintance.

The shivering gave way to fever, as he'd feared it would. He stayed with her all morning, bathing her brow and trying to spoon a bit of broth into her. The surgeon was still indisposed, but the captain and chief mate each came to inquire after her. She remained oblivious.

Derek was not oblivious. Every time he touched her, he was made aware, again, of how soft and delicate she was. He deliberately forced from his mind that other time he'd touched her, the first night on board ship. He would not think of how this fragile, feminine body, brushing against his, had made him feel. He tried instead to remind himself how much he disliked fragility in a woman.

He was much relieved when Sita rose from her bed in the early afternoon and took over the nursing. Such close proximity to Miss Alexandra Rutledge was not a good idea. But back in his own cabin, he could not keep her image from his mind. He returned to check on her after dinner and found the maid in not much better state than her mistress. He thought fleetingly about the impropriety of his nursing Miss Rutledge. But what choice had he? Sita was near collapse; there was no other woman aboard. The surgeon could not move about, and of a certain Derek could not allow any *other* man to see to her. Her father had entrusted her to *his* care, after all.

And so he sent Sita to her own cabin and pulled a chair to Miss Rutledge's bedside. She grew hotter and cried out in delirium. Derek bathed her face and throat and forearms. Sita had dressed her mistress in a delicate white lawn nightdress. Everything about Miss Rutledge—Alexandra—was fragile and fine-boned. Why had she driven herself to such a pass? What had she been trying to prove, and to whom?

Alexandra. Such a big name for a small woman, he mused. The nickname her father used, Alix, suited her, he thought. And when she called out again, he murmured the name and spoke soothing words of nonsense.

It was well past midnight when the fever broke. Alix suddenly began thrashing about and sweating profusely. Derek abandoned his chair and sat down on the bed, trying to hold her still. "Alix, 'tis all right," he whispered. "You are going to be fine."

She stopped thrashing. "Papa?" she rasped. Derek wondered why he felt such a sharp stab of disappointment that she did not know him.

"No, 'tis I, Derek, Lord Weddington."

"Derek," she echoed softly, a golden note in her voice, as if she were testing the sound of his name. He did not know why that sound should make his breath become suddenly shallow, but it did.

And then she began to shiver anew. He covered her to the chin with blankets, but it did not seem to help. "So-so cold. I'm so c-cold," she kept saying. She reached for him, as if to draw him close, and he realized she hardly knew what she was about. She was out of her mind with fatigue and illness.

And he had to help her, though he knew it was not wise, nor at all proper. He had long since taken off his coat and waistcoat, and now he lowered the blankets and gathered her close, her chest pressed against his, his arms clamped around her back. She burrowed into his warmth, stopped shivering, and sighed contentedly.

Derek was far from content. She might feel only welcoming warmth, might not even fully realize who held her. But the warmth he felt was not welcome, and he knew very well whom he held. The fires that he'd banked so carefully all day and night flared dangerously as her breasts, small and round and perfect beneath her nightdress, pressed against him. Long, honey-gold tendrils of her hair spilled onto his fingers; her sweet scent engulfed him.

His heart beat erratically; his blood pounded. Damnation! He wanted her! A woman who represented everything he despised in women, a woman who had confused him utterly by her unprecedented behavior during the storm, a woman who just now needed his care, not his passion. And a woman who at all events was completely off limits to him by virtue of his gentleman's code of honor—blast it all! *This* was the woman he wanted!

Derek Muldaur clenched his jaw and steeled himself to endure. But then, minutes later, she raised her head and gazed solemnly up at him. "Alix?" he questioned softly. He was not certain she knew him.

Her rosebud lips parted. He told himself they did not look at all inviting. "Thank you," she breathed, but made no move to free herself from his embrace.

Let her go, Weddington, he told himself. She does not know what she is about. She is no longer shivering. If she does not have the sense to pull free, you must. Illness and the confines of the ship might excuse this highly improper situation up to a point. But now, now there was no excuse.

Only that she fit so well in his arms and that it felt so natural to lower his head, to seek her mouth with his. Her lips were dry from the fever but soft and yielding. He brushed them with his in a featherlight caress and felt an equally light pressure and the hint of her tongue, inching out between her lips.

It was enough. His body tightened immediately. It was like putting a torch to dry timber. If he did not let her go now he was like to dishonor her!

Abruptly, he disengaged himself from her, setting her back against the pillows. Her hazel eyes looked like fathomless pools of confusion, hurt, and. desire. Dear God, she couldn't possibly know what her eyes held, could not know what affect she had on him! She was still not in her right mind, else she would never have permitted that kiss, would she? She was a lady. Besides, she did not like him any more than he liked her!

He backed away from the bed, aware of a charged silence between them, and stayed away until her eyes finally closed in sleep. And when Sita came back not long after, he beat a hasty retreat.

The next time he saw her, her door was open and she was sitting up in bed. She wore a pink bed jacket, her hair coiled upon her head. Her color was good and her eyes held their usual sparkle. Too much sparkle. Sita sat near her; at the foot of the bunk sat Captain Hawkins and the chief mate, each with perfectly moonstruck, rapt expressions. Having male visitors in her chamber was not at all the thing, but he supposed the circumstances *were* a bit exceptionable. That did not, however, excuse the way she was flirting with them, giggling, fluttering her long eyelashes just so, causing two otherwise reasonable men to make utter cakes of themselves.

"Good afternoon," he said stiffly as he entered the cabin, his eyes flitting from the men to Alix. She was the shallow, heartless flirt once again, using men as sources of amusement until the day she chose one to be her source of funds. He'd known, of course, that her behavior during the storm was out of character. It was not disappointment he felt at finding himself correct, he told himself. His eyes hardened.

Alix heard the disapproval in his voice, saw the coldness in his blue eyes, and knew that last night, yesterday, had been an oddity. The storm had thrown everyone off kilter. Lord Weddington—Derek, she recalled—despised her as much as ever. His care, his gentleness, his . . . warmth had been a response to her illness, not to her. So be it.

"Good afternoon," she returned equally stiffly. The smile had left her eyes, Derek noted, and her chin rose fractionally.

If she recalled last night, if she'd even been aware at the time, she gave not the slightest indication now.

Even when the others departed, leaving them alone, her eyes did not soften but were cool and remote.

"Stay away from those two, Alix," he commanded with a note of contempt in his voice. "They are not in your league."

Her hazel eyes flashed with anger for just a moment. "Really?" she said in that haughty, drawing-room tone of hers. "I own I cannot *think* what you mean . . . Derek!" Her patrician little nose quivered slightly; her rosebud lips were pursed in arrogant dismissal. But she had called him Derek.

He wanted to wipe that look of cool composure off her face. He wanted . . . he wanted her lips again, under his. Damnation! He knew what she was, and their dislike was mutual.

So be it.

The remainder of the voyage passed uneventfully, if tediously. He and Alix treated each other in the same distant manner as before the storm. They rarely spoke, and they never, ever, touched. The only remnant of that night in her cabin, the only reminder that it had, indeed, happened, was in their manner of address. He called her "Alix," though he knew it was improper and imprudent. But that was the way he thought of her, and that is what came out of his mouth. She called him "my lord" in company, but when they found themselves alone, he was "Derek." And that was how he realized that she recalled that night and had not been so very much out of her mind, after all.

The exigencies of traveling together in the confines of the ship were child's play compared to the torture of the journey north from Bristol to Yorkshire in his new traveling coach. There was no place to go, no way to distract himself, no one else with whom to speak. There was only Alix, sitting across from him in a form-fitting traveling costume, her green-flecked, hazel eyes luminous as she stared out the window, wisps of her golden hair falling about her face as the day wore on. Alix, looking good enough to eat, except that her perfect little nose turned high in the air and her eyes looked haughty whenever they locked with his.

But every so often, when she was unaware of his scrutiny, he caught a very different expression in her eyes. It was a mixture of sadness, wistfulness, and yearning. Was she thinking of her father, of India, of that fribble Granger? Did she ever think of what happened that night in her cabin? Sometimes it seemed as if it had been another woman in that bed. How could she be so unaffected by it? What manner of woman *was* she? And what the devil was wrong with *him*, that he could think of little else, the sensations she'd aroused in him always near to the surface, his frustration mounting with each hour of travel?

There was something else he saw in her eyes in unguarded moments, a certain vulnerability that he found most disconcerting. It reminded him of the woman who had shivered in his arms in the aftermath of the storm. It did not remind him of a woman who assumed she could have any man—and all he could provide—with the mere flutter of her eyelash.

If his thoughts were disturbing, he found conversation with her even more so and avoided it as much as possible. He also avoided touching her, although there were times when it could not be helped. If there were no coachman or ostler to hand, he had to help her in and out of the coach. It should have been the most simple and casual of gestures. It was ludicrous that he should feel such a jolt of heat when his hand held her gloved one or touched the small of her back.

It was ludicrous and unwelcome and dangerous. And furthermore, Alix felt it as well. Try as she might to hide it, she jerked at his touch. Jerked as if touched by fire. So, he'd been wrong. She was not unaffected. That only made the whole damnable coil that much worse!

They'd been traveling for two days. They would likely not arrive in North Yorkshire for another two. He gritted his teeth and stared out the window.

Alix was counting half-timbered houses. She did not know how else to distract herself. Never in her life had she been so aware of a man, of his size, his scent, his every breath. And his touch. Dear Heaven, every time he touched her in the most nonchalant way, it all came rushing back to her. That night in her cabin, his chest against hers, his arms enfolding her, his lips. . . . She felt a flush of humiliation every time she pictured that scene, recalled virtually asking him to hold her. She had surely been out of her mind with illness.

But that did not excuse her shameless behavior. And that kiss—why, she had responded to it! She had felt bereft when he set her down and backed away from her. And it was all the more humiliating because she knew that that interlude only added to his contempt for her.

She could not wait to arrive at Aunt Winifred's home! They had been traveling north for three days now. It seemed to be getting colder by the minute. She was not at all used to the climate. It was only the beginning of February. Winter in Yorkshire would last a long time still. Dear God, it was even starting to snow. She fervently hoped their journey would not be delayed! When counting houses and smokestacks and church steeples failed to distract her, she set herself to thinking about her aunt and all she'd heard of her over the years.

Alix had lived in England for the first eight years of her life but had only vague memories of infrequent visits to Yorkshire. Sir Horace and Lady Winifred Hartcup rarely ventured from the north country and never went to London, where Alix and her parents had spent most of their time. Alix remembered her aunt as a beautiful woman who favored purple chiffon and her uncle as a man who laughed a great deal and liked cigars. Everything else she knew of them came from Papa's stories and the letters from Yorkshire which he read to her regularly.

Mama had succumbed to the fever just two years after their arrival in India. Papa was inconsolable, and that was when he began to correspond with his sister. But he refused repeated offers to send Alix back to England. Alix was hard put to understand why. Papa spent little time with her and called her a hoyden for doing things Mama had always permitted, like running wild with the native children and dirtying her hands with clay as the potters worked. Papa, she came to understand, wanted her to be a lady like Mama had been. And so gradually Alix stopped running and learned to keep her hands clean, her hair just so, her face smiling no matter what she felt. And then Papa would invite her to come and visit him in his office, and when she was older to preside at his dinner parties. And everyone would say she looked like Mama. Papa would swell with pride, and Alix would feel an inner glow.

But she was always curious about her aunt, for Papa seemed to hold her in affection, and she did not seem at all like Mama.

Although Papa did not say so in so many words, Winifred Hartcup sounded suspiciously like what Papa would call an eccentric. She never troubled about fashion, never gave a fig for Almack's or the patronesses or the London Season. Having no children of her own, she had fired off two of her nieces from Arden Chase in Yorkshire and seen them wed in short order. Her aunt was, in fact, considered to be the premiere matchmaker in Yorkshire. Many a parent had come home distraught after their daughter's unsuccessful Season, only to have Lady Hartcup swoop down and assure them she knew of just the right eligible connection. And so, many never troubled now to stand the expense of a London Season. They simply went to Lady Hartcup.

And the height of Lady Hartcup's season was her grand ball, given every year on . . . Valentine's Day! Goodness me! Alix thought. Today was the third of February. She would arrive on her aunt's doorstep just days before the ball! Alix's heart sank. Surely arriving unexpectedly at such a busy time would not endear her to her aunt and uncle.

Derek watched the light snow fall with a sinking heart. He'd hoped to arrive at Arden Chase on the morrow. But if the snow continued. . . Blast! He could not take much more of this. And it was deuced cold. He and Alix each had a hot brick, but his was barely warm by now. His gloved hands were chilled, and he did not know how much good the rug across his knees was doing. And if he were uncomfortable, Alix looked worse. Her body seemed stiff with cold as she huddled beneath her rug, hands hidden in the folds of her pelisse. They were neither of them accustomed to the weather, nor had adequate clothes. It would make sense for them to sit together on one seat, using both rugs, warming each other . . . No, dammit! It would make no sense at all.

By midmorning of the next day he was not quite so certain. Even he felt near to frozen now, the hot breakfast he'd eaten but a distant memory. The snow was still falling steadily, more heavily. The carriage plodded slowly on. Had it not been for the snow they should have arrived at Arden Chase any time now. Instead, they were somewhere in the middle of Yorkshire; he could barely discern landmarks for the snow.

All he knew was that as long as the roads were passable, he meant to keep going in the hope that they would arrive by nightfall. He did not relish another night in some tiny isolated inn with Alix, the maid and valet riding in the luggage coach notwithstanding. And he was eager to go home to Greenvale. He had no wish to find himself snowbound in Yorkshire, neither at an inn nor Arden Chase.

He wanted the nice, safe distance of half of England between Alexandra Rutledge and himself. Besides, it was the fourth of February. Martin Rutledge had mentioned in passing that his sister gave a ball on the fourteenth every year—for Valentine's Day of all things! Apparently it was taken quite seriously up here in the wilds of the north country. Lady Hartcup even followed the ancient tradition of holding a Valentine lottery, whereby unattached ladies and gentlemen were matched by lots. The local superstition was that whoever one drew for the lottery dance was one's true and predestined mate!

Derek had no intention of being around to witness that bit of provincial fustian, nor to allow any grasping mama to dream of titles and untold wealth because he happened to draw her daughter's name in some damned lottery! No! He clearly had got to be gone well before the fourteenth, and every extra day made it that much easier for Lady Hartcup to ask him to stay.

In the meantime, Alix was shivering, though she was trying to hide it. Her lips looked blue, and he suspected her hands were like ice. Yet she had never once complained, he marveled.

"Alix," he heard himself say, " 'tis very cold. Why do you not come here? We'll be warmer if we sit together beneath two rugs."

Alix tried to keep her eyes from widening. He'd barely spoken to her the entire tedious journey in the coach, and now. . . . How she longed to take him up on his offer. It *was* so frightfully cold. It was all she could do to keep her teeth from chattering. But she remembered the last time she was cold on board ship and the way he'd warmed her, then looked upon her with contempt afterwards. No, she did not need his warmth.

"I thank you, Derek, but I own I am right," she managed to say between lips that were stiff and probably blue.

Blast the chit! Derek thought. This was no time to be on her high ropes. Did she not realize she was like to become ill? Why, she was too slight, too delicate for such harsh weather . . .

He waited until after they had partaken of a cold repast from the hamper wedged next to her feet. He'd watched her attempt to eat a chicken leg without removing her gloves, to down the brandy he forced upon her through chattering teeth. But the brandy did not turn her lips from blue to pink. He asked her again to come to him, for the hamper prevented his moving to her seat.

"No," she began, "I am f-fine, D-Derek."

"Oh, hell fire!" he muttered and, reaching his arm across the aisle, he grabbed her and hauled her peremptorily onto his seat.

He had her tucked beneath his arm, both rugs covering them, before she could vouchsafe any objection. And when she tried, he put his gloved hand to her lips. "Hush. It is best," he said.

He laced his hands with hers and moments later removed all gloves. Gradually, her hands and his began to warm. Her shuddering began to subside, her small body relaxing against his. Of its own volition, his hand stroked her back. She felt so good, so utterly feminine. He remembered another time when she had shivered with cold. His body began to warm in places he'd had no intention of warming.

Her head rested at his shoulder. This time she did not look up, which was all to the good. Her lips would be turning pink again, and he might be tempted. . . . He must not! It would be completely dishonorable! It was all wrong. *She* was all wrong for him. How could a woman who was so very wrong feel so very right in his arms?

Alix told herself that what she felt was simply the relief from the unending cold. The warm sensations deep in her body had naught to do with who was holding her! The hand that caressed her back had no magical properties, could not cause ripples of pleasure such as she imagined she felt. She had no urge to lift her head to study the strong planes of his face, to gaze into his deep blue eyes. And she did not want this man, who made no secret of his disdain, to kiss her again!

He was an odious man; it was wrong for him to hold her. Why, then, did she feel not only warm but safe and secure, as if, for the first time, all was right with the world?

It was almost late afternoon by the time they arrived at Arden Chase. Derek was not quite certain how they had made it, but he was eternally grateful. He'd held Alix close until they'd turned onto the road leading to Arden Chase. He'd not kissed her, not spoken to her. Yet she'd clasped his hand tightly all the way.

He was more than happy to deliver her to Lady Hartcup. He would take his leave within the hour; he'd seen an inn not too far back. He feared that if he stayed longer he'd be obliged to stay the night, and they might well be snowed in by morning. He had no intention of allowing that to happen.

He had not reckoned, however, on Winifred Hartcup. She came floating into the entry lobby—indeed, there was no other way to describe it—on a cloud of purple silk. She was a singularly beautiful woman, for all she must have seen more than fifty summers. Her extraordinary hair, light brown streaked with gray, was piled high atop her head in a series of rolls and twists reminiscent of the wigs of the last century. She talked nonstop from the moment she saw them, hugging Alix, welcoming them both, ordering the butler to take their things, and quickly reading the sealed letter Alix produced from her reticule. Her green eyes went from Martin Rutledge's letter to Alix and Derek and back. She tucked it neatly into her pocket.

"How perfectly splendid that you both have come just now!" she exclaimed. "Not but what you must be frozen to your very bones! 'Tis a miracle you contrived to arrive at all, what with this blizzard—for I am persuaded that is what this storm is—upon us. Well, you are here now! That is all that signifies."

And before either Alix or Derek could vouchsafe more than a word or two, Lady Hartcup had slipped an arm through each of theirs and led them to the Purple Saloon. A cheerful fire burned in the grate, and everything else in the room was purple. Derek's protestations that he needs must take his leave in short order were blithely ignored as, with almost magical speed, tea was brought for Alix, brandy for him, and a tray of warm biscuits and watercress sandwiches was produced. He had to admit to himself that the repast was most welcome, and he was gratified to see Alix's color return to normal. But he was careful not to meet her eyes, and he had not touched her since they'd separated in the coach. Nor would he. Ever again.

The feel of her against him was still vivid in his mind. He had got to take his leave straightaway. It was on the third try that he finally succeeded in capturing Lady Hartcup's attention.

She flashed wide green eyes at him. "Leave? Now? Dear boy, whatever can you mean? Why, 'tis near dark, the roads nigh impassable." She put a hand to her full breast. "You cannot mean that you prefer to pass the duration of the storm in that ramshackle village inn rather than here at Arden Chase?"

"Not at all, Lady Hartcup, but only that—"

"Well, thank Heavens! You much relieve my mind! Your luggage has already been brought to your rooms, dear boy. I make no doubt you will find them most commodious, but you must tell me if you lack for anything. Oh, I do hope you have brought your formalwear with you?" At his curious expression she added, "For the ball, of course." She did not say which ball, as if it were completely unnecessary.

He began a most forceful protest when they were interrupted by the arrival of a man he knew immediately to be Sir Horace. He was tall and thin, with a shock of white hair and laughing gray-green eyes. He removed his lit cigar from his mouth and bussed his wife on the cheek, quite oblivious of his audience. Lady Hartcup made the introductions while she poured him a cup of tea.

"Thank you, Win, my love," Sir Horace said warmly before welcoming his visitors heartily. Then he settled back with a bemused expression which Derek did not understand until it was too late.

"Thank you for your hospitality, Lady Hartcup," Derek began again. "I shall be grateful to stay until morning. After that—"

"Dear boy, absolutely *no one* is so formal with me! You may call me Lady Hart—near everyone does—or Auntie Win, if you wish. Now, no more fustian from you! I am persuaded you must be fagged to death from weeks of journeying. I would be a poor hostess, indeed, to turn you out after only one night's rest. Another biscuit, dear boy? Well, and the weather being what it is, 'twill not be safe at all events. As to the ball, why it is only ten days away! I am sensible of the fact that you are eager to go to your own estates, but what is ten days after ten years, after all?" She reached over with a plate to catch the falling ash from her husband's cigar. "I am persuaded dear Alix would be so much more comfortable with someone she knows here. And it would please Sir Horace and me so very much. Is that not true, dear heart?" She turned to her husband, who, with admirable composure, kept a straight face as he agreed.

Derek wondered whatever had happened to male camaraderie but realized there would be no help from that quarter. Martin Rutledge had described his brother-in-law as a man who loved his wife, his lands, and his cigars, in that order. Derek had no reason to doubt him. His hostess kept up her cheerful monologue for some minutes, directing questions at Alix and him, demanding no answers, and refilling tea cups. She called her husband "dear heart," or was it "dear Hart"? at least four times, and he'd lost count of each "dear boy" and "dear girl."

He never did agree to stay until the ball. He was certain of it. And yet, by the time a maid came to take the tea things, his hosts seemed to be assuming he would. Too weary to argue, he told himself that tomorrow was another day.

And then, for the first time, he glanced at Alix. "Lady Hart, I fear the journey has been rather arduous for Alix. She is much in need of a hot bath and a good long rest."

Lady Hart, for an unprecedented minute, was silent as her eyes swept from him to Alix. Then in the blink of an eye she had summoned servants, given orders, and established her guests in their chambers.

And Alix decided, as she gratefully sank into a steaming hot tub, that she would never understand the Viscount Weddington. He spoke little to her, at times barely masked his contempt. And yet he had warmed her in the carriage, and he was the only one to note, just minutes ago, that she hardly had strength left to hold her teacup.

Derek's contempt was back full measure by dinnertime, however. The evening meal had been held back an hour that Alix might rest, and now she felt much refreshed. She wore a low-cut gown of seafoam green gauze and watched Derek's eyes narrow in that familiar look of disapproval. Truly, there was no pleasing this man, nor, she assured herself, did she have the least desire to do so!

Besides their hosts, there were three other people at table. Signor Antonio D'Orsini, a handsome Italian gentleman of middle years, intense black eyes, and silver-tinged black hair, was here to paint Auntie Win's portrait. It was to be unveiled at the Valentine's Day Ball. He sat at Alix's right. Derek, at the foot of the table, sat to her left. On his other side sat Miss Isabel Sykes, here with her mother for the ball. They had come down from Northumbria early as a precaution against the weather. Mrs. Sykes appeared pleased as punch at the arrival of new guests, especially since Derek seemed quite taken with her tall, dark-haired daughter.

Determinedly, Alix turned her attention to Signor D'Orsini. He was a most interesting man, and she found the notion of painting a portrait, using a live model and working with oils, quite fascinating. She had always been relegated to painting landscapes with insipid watercolors, as befit a young lady. As soon as Signor D'Orsini began to talk, she listened avidly.

Derek glanced about the table with extreme displeasure. Alix was at it again. Wearing that shockingly low-cut gown, she was using all her wiles on D'Orsini. But she did not know with whom she was dealing. D'Orsini was no tame puppy, no society fribble, to be led around on her leash. Before she knew what she was about, he'd have her in his studio for a "private viewing" of his work. Oh, Derek knew his type well, and Alix, innocent temptress that she was, did not. It was as well that the snow would keep Derek here for a few days. He would need to keep an eye on Alix, for Lady Hart, from her place next to her husband at the head of the table, seemed quite unaware that anything was amiss. But *he* had not brought Alix halfway across the world to have her seduced by some middle-aged Latin Lothario!

Having little choice at the moment, Derek turned his attention to Miss Sykes. She was tall for a woman, just a few inches shorter than he, with incisive gray eyes and a face that he supposed was pretty. She asked him what he thought of the future of the East India Company, and he found himself smiling. Here was a woman of sense, a woman whose interests went beyond the latest fashions in *La Belle Assemblée.* When they had exhausted that topic, Miss Sykes began speaking of the Luddite riots and machine breaking in the northern factories. After a time Derek began to feel he was dining with a pamphleteer or some overearnest member of the Commons. Miss Sykes did not smile much, he noted, and though she had comely features and curves in all the right places, there was no feminine softness about her. She was, he decided, a lady in need of a husband, not a woman in need of a man. There was, he realized, quite a difference.

Lady Hart, though she conversed with Mrs. Sykes across from her, spent most of the meal exchanging mooncalf looks with her husband. It was quite extraordinary, given their ages. As was the fact that she sat beside him, not at the foot of the table as was proper. She laughed now at something Sir Horace said and struck him playfully on the wrist. And that was when Derek realized that Alix looked very much like a younger version of her aunt. He found the thought most disquieting.

At the conclusion of the four-course meal, a footman set a large bowl of fruit down before Sir Horace. "Well, new fruit from the north, I see, Win love," he said thoughtfully, fingering a shiny red apple. His eyes swept the table and came back to his wife.

She picked up a hothouse orange. "Yes, dear heart," she replied, "but I do think the tropical fruit is far more sweet and succulent."

"Ah," he said, as if comprehending some profound thought, "so you have noticed."

Derek wished he knew what the devil they were talking about!

The snow was still falling relentlessly by the next morning. Restless, Alix wandered into the library, intent on finding something of interest to read. Papa had not kept an extensive library in Calcutta and in any case did not hold with females being too well-read. Still, Alix had read most of Shakespeare's plays and had dog-eared Papa's English translation of Homer. Here at Arden Chase, however, the selection was vast, and she stood for some time perusing the shelves, unable to choose.

"I doubt you'll find anything to interest you here." Derek's acerbic drawl startled her. She turned as he sauntered into the room, closing the door behind him.

Ignoring his tone, she smiled. "Indeed, I am unused to so much choice. It is quite a library, is it not?"

"Quite." His smile was mocking. "But I daresay you would do better to pay a visit to Lady Hart's sitting room. I am persuaded she would have a selection of fashion magazines and Nora Tillington novels for you."

She blinked in disbelief. Was that all he thought her willing or able to read? Did he think her such a ninnyhammer as that? Had he always, or was it merely by comparison with Miss Sykes and her scintillating discourse upon the subjects of the East India Company and the Luddite riots? But no, Derek's low opinion of her went back much further than last night, to the very beginning.

Now, with the width of half the room between them, she willed her eyes to remain dry. The Viscount Weddington had accused, tried, and convicted her before they'd ever exchanged ten words. He'd never given her the opportunity to discuss anything of moment with him, never endeavored to learn the first thing about her. Yes, he thought *La Belle Assemblée* the sum total of her literary accomplishments. He thought her a shallow, heartless flirt. Had he not made that eminently clear?

And she thought him insufferable and overbearing, his occasional gentleness, charm, strength notwithstanding. "Thank you for the suggestion," she said with sweet sarcasm. "And here I'd been hoping to find a Nora Tillington novel sandwiched between Homer and Virgil!"

She whirled round, grabbed a volume of Renaissance poetry that she'd espied before, and made for the door. His large hand clamped her upper arm, forcing her to turn to him. When she did, he released her as if he'd been burned. Indeed, her arm still felt his warmth.

"Not so fast, Alix, if you please. There is something I would say to you."

She lifted a brow in what she hoped was a show of haughty impatience, and he went on, "You are playing with fire, Alix, in the form of Signor D'Orsini. He is not some moonstruck halfling like the *Star of India's* chief mate, nor some tame fop to dance to your tune. You think to entice, but you will be the one ensnared."

"I beg your—"

"Have a care, Alix. I know his type. You are no match for him." He stood just a foot away, towering over her, his face rigid with command and disapproval.

She would not be cowed; she drew herself up. "I see I am not the only person you have judged and convicted with no evidence whatever. It would seem Signor D'Orsini and I have something in common. Good day to you, Derek!"

She heard him curse as she snapped the door shut behind her. But her satisfaction was short-lived, for as she sat in her room reading the sonnets of Shakespeare and Sir Philip Sydney, she found her mind wandering. She was not the shallow creature Derek painted her, was she? True, she knew little of the internal workings of the East India Company, for all it had been a household word most of her life. But she had little interest in it, nor had Papa ever tried to discuss it with her. True, she flirted—she was brought up to do just that—but she was not heartless. She did not callously toy with men. And surely a woman who cried over seventeenth-century love poems could not be shallow and heartless.

That was why she was crying, was it not? It was not because, having decided what she was *not,* she did not precisely know what she *was.* She had always thought she was a dutiful, well-loved daughter. But apparently that was not so. And she was considered a most charming lady, but that did not add to her credit, it seemed, at least not with . . . with a man whose opinion meant nothing to her!

She went back to reading, "Then hate me when thou wilt; if ever, now . . ."

It was after luncheon that she wandered, quite by accident, to the door of Signor D'Orsini's studio. She had been aimlessly wandering the upstairs east wing corridor, when she espied a door partially ajar. Once at the threshold she was assailed by a pungent odor, odd but strangely familiar.

"Ah, signorina, come in, come in," Signor D'Orsini called, and when she hesitated, he came to take her hand, drawing her inside.

She took it all in at a glance—the pots of paint, the myriad brushes, the model's chair, now empty, and the easel by the window. And suddenly, long-dead memories came rushing back to her. Another roomful of brushes and paints, another painter, who had come to paint Mama's portrait. They were still in England then, and she remembered the painter allowing her to watch him work, instructing her, giving her some oils with which to work.

She did not know what she said to Signor D'Orsini, but she became that little girl again, eager to see, to feel textures, to learn. And once again she had a willing teacher. He spoke of color, technique, light, and darkness.

"We must find you an easel, *cara,*" Signor D'Orsini said. "I think you want very much to have a brush in your hand, no?"

"Oh!" She smiled uncertainly, "Oh, but I—I would not know where to begin. It's been so long since—"

"We begin here, *cara.* With paint and a brush. But first, you must see the portrait of Lady Hart. It is almost done, and as you will see—*magnífico!*" His eyes twinkled as he darted to the now-covered painting.

"I should love to, signor, but I believe Auntie Win wants to surprise everyone at the ball."

"*Sí, sí,* but for you, I make an exception. It will be our little secret, *cara.*"

His words sent her back again in time. Packing to leave for India and wanting to take her precious oils with her, but knowing that Papa would not approve. He thought Alix spent too much time at her easel and the paint so hard to remove from ladylike fingers. Watercolors should be fine for a girl. And Mama had squeezed her hand and begun packing the pots of paint. "It will be our little secret," Mama said.

And it had been until Mama died, then Alix had a governess, one who only approved of watercolors and landscapes. She was scandalized when she caught Alix trying to paint one of the native children in oils. So was Papa, and while he never forbade her from painting with oils, from spending blissful hours a day at her easel, she was aware, nevertheless, of his disapproval. He would catch the telltale smudges of color on the pads of her fingers and frown, or sniff the odor of paint remover when she greeted him in the evening and say, "Not a very ladylike scent, is it?" And he wouldn't quite hug her.

Alix could not say when she had put away her paints for the last time—it could not have been more than a year or so after Mama died—but she had. And had forgotten all about it until now.

Signor D'Orsini whipped the cloth off the easel and Alix stared, open-mouthed, at the magnificent portrait of her aunt. It was not only that the painting looked just like her—her beauty and charm were faithfully rendered for posterity—but it was much more than that. He had captured the very essence of Lady Hart. One could almost hear her voice, see her move, know what she was thinking just from the portrait. But most telling of all were the deep green eyes.

"Signor, it is brilliant," she breathed in awe. "And the eyes—I feel as if I can see into her very soul."

"Yes," he said quietly.

"And her expression. She is thinking of Sir Horace, is she not?"

He chuckled. "You are very observant, *cara.* But come, it is your turn."

And before she knew what he was about, he had put a brush in her hand, a smock across her shoulders, and a canvas before her. For the next hour he talked of color and brush strokes and line and light. Her abstract lines began to take the shape of a tree. The simplicity of it embarrassed her, but she realized that Signor D'Orsini was watching her, not the canvas.

And then, quite abruptly, he stopped her. "You come back tomorrow. Same hour. We begin in earnest."

"Begin?"

"Your lessons, *cara.*"

Too stunned to say a word, Alix allowed him to usher her out.

She was even more stunned the next afternoon when Signor D'Orsini led her through his studio to a rear door which opened onto a small chamber. The chamber contained a small cabriole-legged table, a chair, and a very large window in front of which stood an easel with an empty canvas. Pots of paint sat on the table, waiting.

"I do not understand," Alix said. "For—for me?"

Signor D'Orsini smiled. He really looked most dapper when he smiled. "But of course, *cara.* Every artist needs his own place. I will be nearby to help you. But here you will concentrate, alone, no?"

"Signor, I—I am more grateful than I can say. But I fear you will be disappointed. I am not an artist—why, you have not even seen my sketches!"

"Signorina, *I* am an artist, a portrait painter. I see faces, *your* face. I do not need to see sketches."

"I will never be able to capture in a portrait—"

"You do not start with portraits, *cara,* nor with faces. Here," he handed her a pencil, "you will sketch. You begin with a living being—a tree or squirrel or bird."

Alix thought for a moment, gazing out at the unrelenting snow. Then she smiled. "There is a bird in a cage in your studio. Might we bring it in here?"

"Ah, Lady Hart's canary. She will not mind, I am certain. She liked to watch the little bird during her sittings, but I do not need her to sit any longer."

Alix thanked him with tears in her eyes and then haltingly asked if this new endeavor might remain a secret between them.

"For as long as you wish, *cara mía,*" he said softly. Then, kissing her hand, he withdrew.

Alix gazed at the pots of paint, the empty canvas, the pencil in her hand. Taking a deep breath, she began.

On the afternoon of their first full day at Arden Chase, Derek had wondered where Alix was, for he did not see her in any of the public rooms of the house. 'Twas merely idle curiosity, he told himself. Lady Hart, when he asked, blithely assured him that Alix must be resting and then corralled him into a discussion about where the orchestra had ought to be placed for the ball.

The infernal ball seemed to be all anyone at Arden Chase could talk about. His valet had already had an earful in the servants' hall. It seemed that the Valentine's Day lottery was a much-cherished tradition in many parts of the north country and with it came the belief, to which Martin Rutledge had alluded, that whoever one drew in the lottery was one's predestined mate. Lady Hart had elevated this tradition to a grand affair with her yearly ball. So ubiquitous was the belief in the lottery as fate that servants were invited from miles around to their own lottery and dance in the servants' hall.

The question that sprang to Derek's mind, given Lady Hart's penchant for matchmaking, was whether it was fate or Lady Hart who made the lottery matches. Derek's valet had been unable to ascertain such information, though the twinkle in his eye told Derek he'd wondered the same thing.

When Derek very delicately put the question to Lady Hart, she looked at him as if he'd gone mad. "*I?* Whatever can you mean, dear boy? Now tell me, shall I use the formal dining room or the drawing room for the supper buffet? The dining room is closer, you must know, and so much simpler, but a trifle small, perhaps. These little affairs do seem to grow in number each year, do they not?"

Derek murmured a nonsensical reply and went off in search of Alix. Where had she been for the last hour? Her maid had not seen her; clearly, she was not resting. No one, least of all a woman lately returned from the tropics, would venture outside on such a day. And come to think on it, that Latin portrait painter was also conspicuously absent. He, of course, could well be in his studio. Alix would not be *there,* would she?

He was unable to follow up that irksome question, however, for he was waylaid outside the Purple Saloon by Mrs. Sykes and her statuesque daughter Isabel. He must come in for a moment; there was such a cheerful fire in the grate! Was it not exciting to be a part of the preparations for the ball? Mrs. Sykes wanted to know. Dear Lady Hart had asked her to help with the flower arrangements!

Was he acquainted with any of the local gentry? Miss Sykes wanted to know. She had it on good account that there would be at least one marquis and an heir to an earldom in attendance, although they did not live in the immediate vicinity. The highest persons of rank were the Baron and Baroness Rossmore, but they, unfortunately, would not be in attendance. The baron, it seemed, was on a diplomatic mission on the Continent, and the baroness was soon to be brought to bed with her first child. Did Lord Weddington know that the baroness was sister to the Duke of Marchmaine?

No, he did not, although he did know the duke, a fact which he declined to mention. He wondered whatever had happened to the East India Company and the Luddite riots. He was beginning to miss those topics of conversation, and by the time he was able to extricate himself from the informative ladies, it was time for tea. Alix dutifully appeared and was decidedly vague about how she'd spent her afternoon.

On the second day, with the snow still falling and his determination to escape before the ball becoming a dim memory, Derek learned a bit more about local Valentine's customs from his resourceful valet. It seemed that if a young man had been paying court to a certain young lady or merely gazing at her from afar with mooncalf eyes, he set his hopes very high that the lottery would fall out in his favor. And to demonstrate his belief that it would, that his heart and fate were in tandem, he might purchase a special token to give his lady love if they were, indeed, matched by the lottery. For a second time Derek wondered at Lady Hart's hand in all this but was wise enough not to ask again.

His wisdom did not lead him to Alix's location during the long afternoon hours, however. But his valet's resourcefulness did provide him with the third floor location of D'Orsini's studio. He set off straightaway and found the large, airy chamber with little difficulty, its door slightly ajar and the aroma of paint drawing him. He peered in and saw D'Orsini intent on his work. The studio was otherwise unoccupied. Feeling slightly foolish and greatly peeved, Derek silently slipped away. Where the deuce was Alix?

He was merely concerned for her, Derek assured himself. Of a certain he did not miss her company. Why, a good book would be far less troublesome!

By the third blissful day of painting in her very own studio, her fourth day at Arden Chase, Alix had run out of excuses for Derek as to her afternoon activities. The snow had finally stopped, but the drifts were so high that he would never believe she'd gone out of doors. And her need to rest was wearing thin. She was thankful he had not tumbled onto the truth of her whereabouts. For while she could not know what his reaction to her artistic endeavors might be, she had no doubt of his feelings on the matter of any association with Signor D'Orsini.

She tried to ignore his looks of faint disapproval at table or in the Purple Saloon during tea, and concentrated instead on all the talk of the upcoming ball. Truth to tell, she was not looking forward to it. Not that she did not enjoy a ball—she quite adored to dance—but rather it was the accompanying lottery that accounted for her sense of unease. And not merely the lottery, but the staunch insistence, both above and below stairs, that the lottery had a direct connection to one's fate. How could any lottery determine the fate of Alexandra Rutledge when she did not even know *herself* of late?

And then there was her niggling suspicion that Auntie Win had more to do with the lottery than she let on. Alix thought she preferred the fate theory. She knew Papa must have commissioned Auntie Win to find her a husband, but she was not ready for one just now! And the Valentine's Day lottery aside, Auntie Win had cast enough speculative glances at Alix to tell her she was busily cogitating upon all the eligible gentlemen of her acquaintance.

Her aunt had been gazing with equal speculation at Derek and Miss Sykes. Indeed, those two had been engaged over the past days in several conversations of great moment. Even now, as the footmen began serving dinner, they were engrossed in a discussion of the Corn Laws. It would be no wonder if Auntie Win decided they should suit. Why that was a lowering thought Alix could not say. It was not as if she wanted Lord Weddington for herself! They had not two civil words to say to each other. She was only too happy to answer Signor D'Orsini's questions about the colors of the Indian landscape. She might know little of India's business, but its mountains and vegetation had impressed her as exceeedingly beautiful.

The second remove of stuffed game hens, braised asparagus, and poached turbot was now being served. Derek had turned from Miss Sykes to address a remark to Auntie Win across the table. He did not precisely ignore Alix, but the chilly look in his eyes told her that, his absorption in Miss Sykes notwithstanding, he had noted with displeasure her tête-à-tête with Signor D'Orsini. And what right had he to pass judgment on her? They had no connection whatever! Nor did she care a rush what he thought!

Still, it was most disheartening to watch him be so attentive to Miss Sykes and all that was charming and affable with her aunt and uncle, when he had only disapproval for her.

"Ah, but of course you must have the waltz, Lady Hart," Derek was saying in response to her aunt's query. "And I would be honored if you would save one for me."

Auntie Win smiled prettily. "And so I shall. That is," she turned to her husband, "if it is all right with you, dear heart."

Sir Horace gazed pensively at Derek and then Auntie Win. "Very well," he said at length. "But I will have the first waltz and the lottery dance, whatever it be."

Derek's eyes widened almost imperceptibly, but Alix knew he was surprised, as was she. Auntie Win had asked and received permission. Both she and Sir Horace had been quite serious. Alix had not thought her uncle a possessive man. Derek's lips curled into a smile of approval, and Alix realized that he, too, would be a very possessive husband. Somehow she did not think Captain Granger would have been. He would have expected Alix to be gay and gracious and grant dances to whomever she chose. She had always thought that kind of freedom within the married state most desirable. Now she was not at all certain.

Signor D'Orsini interrupted her reverie, leaning over to ask her if she would save a waltz for him. She smiled her consent and squelched the wish that it was Derek who had asked her.

On their fifth day at Arden Chase the news was all over that the butcher's wagon had contrived to make it to the service entrance. The roads were passable, if only barely. Yet with the ball only five days away, Derek knew well that he could not leave. It was not only that he had impulsively bespoken a waltz of Lady Hart. It was not only that it would have seemed churlish if, after partaking of his hosts' hospitality, he left so soon before an event so obviously dear to their hearts. It was also that he had not yet accounted for Alix's whereabouts each afternoon, and he could not in all good conscience leave her under the same roof with that damned portrait painter. At the least not while Lady Hart was so preoccupied with the ball.

Derek did not know what Alix was about, encouraging D'Orsini so, but he meant to find her, no matter what, this very afternoon and have it out with her. He had watched them last night, Alix smiling, her eyes shining as she hung on the Latin's every word. And D'Orsini looking as though he could eat Alix for dessert. Blast her! For all her beguiling ways, she was a veritable innocent. She was accustomed to dealing with gentlemen who knew the rules. D'Orsini did not look like a gentleman; he looked like he made his own rules.

Today, as every day, when Derek made a cursory check of the artist's studio, he was surprised to find it empty. He did not understand it; with the ball rapidly approaching he was under the impression that D'Orsini was spending every spare minute on the portrait. Curious, he took a step inside. His eyes took in the haphazard array of paints and brushes and the covered easel at the window. Where was D'Orsini? Was the portrait completed? Somehow he would have thought he'd have heard if it were so.

"No, no, *cara!*" The Latin's voice pierced the stillness of the room. But where the devil—his voice seemed to be coming from another chamber, toward the rear of this. Slowly and silently Derek moved forward. "Remember your shading, *cara.* Remember that the background spaces are just as important as the foreground," D'Orsini said, and then there was silence.

Sí, sí, caríssima! That is exactly what I mean!" exclaimed the artist in ringing tones. *"Brava! Brava!* Now a bit more here, like this," he added, just as Derek reached the heretofore hidden doorway.

The door was ajar, and Derek stared, wide-eyed and furious, at the sight that met his eyes. The room was just large enough for a chair and table, a hanging birdcage, an easel at the window, and two people. D'Orsini and Alix stood before the window, gazing at some canvas on the easel. Derek could not see the painting, though he could clearly see the artist and Alix. They would have seen him had they troubled to look up. But they were intent on the painting, and each other. The blackguard D'Orsini was standing just a hairsbreadth from Alix, close enough to have one hand on her slender shoulder, the other clasping hers as it wielded the brush.

Derek felt his jaw clench. His hands balled into fists at his sides. The damned Latin was "instructing" Alix in the finer points of shading with oils. And she, the little gudgeon, was being taken in! Did she really think D'Orsini believed in her artistic abilities? Did she not realize what else he would soon be instructing her in?

"I do hope I'm not interrupting," he drawled from the doorway, his cold voice belying the politeness of his words.

He heard Alix gasp, but D'Orsini merely raised an eyebrow and slowly let his hands slip from Alix. "Ah, it is Lord Weddington. Good afternoon." He made an elegant bow, looking perfectly at his ease. Alix was anything but. Her face had stiffened; she seemed suddenly tense. And well she might! When he got through with her . . .

Derek became aware that the artist was regarding him with an expression of faint amusement. It disconcerted him for a moment; he would have expected the man to be highly peeved to have his little seduction scene interrupted. It was obvious the Latin was far more clever and subtle than he'd given him credit for.

With a most casual air, D'Orsini divested himself of his smock. "Well, signorina, I think we finish for the day, no? I leave you in the capable hands of his lordship. Do not forget to clean your brushes the way I taught you. Your servant, Weddington."

Alix waited until the door to the outer chamber closed, signaling D'Orsini's departure, before draping a cloth over her canvas and silently moving to the table to clean her brushes. Derek was amazed that D'Orsini had actually left them alone. Just what sort of deep game was he playing? And why was Alix not chattering away, trying to defend her reprehensible behavior?

He watched her methodically, almost lovingly, clean and put away the brushes. He felt a pang of remorse for the crushing disappointment she would suffer when she realized that both D'Orsini and her artistic promise were false. But there was no help for it. Someone had got to bring her to her senses; it was obviously going to have to be he.

"Alix, we have to talk," he finally said, his tone gentler than he'd intended.

"Oh?" That perfect little patrician nose quivered haughtily.

Exasperated and not a little piqued, he spoke more sharply. "Yes, 'oh'! And you know perfectly well why. Just what the deuce do you think you are doing, closeted in a room with D'Orsini? And today is not the first day, is it?" He had advanced as he spoke and stopped just before her at the table.

"No," she said defiantly, "it is not."

Lord, he wanted to shake her! How could she be so brazen? But he also wanted to kiss her. She looked adorable with her rosebud lips pursed just so, her golden hair escaping the confines of its topknot, her small body enveloped in a smock much too big for her. D'Orsini's smock, damn his eyes! Derek kept his hands resolutely at his sides.

"Have you not a care for your reputation? And if not that, have you no more sense than a schoolroom miss?"

She drew herself up. "If you are so concerned for my reputation, Derek, then of a certain I must not remain here with *you*. Now, if you'll excuse me . . ." She started to turn away, and he grabbed her shoulders and spun her round. He ignored the rush of heat and . . . protectiveness induced by the feel of her slender shoulders.

"Hellfire, Alix! Do you not understand what that man wants from you? He does not care a hang whether or not you can paint, I do assure you! When you finally accept, or spurn, his dishonorable advances, you will see which 'talents' of yours really interest him!"

Alix fought back tears, even as she wished bitterly that his touch did not warm her so thoroughly. "Thank you for . . . edifying me, Derek," she managed to say. "I have obviously reached one and twenty years without having more sense than a peagoose." She bit her lip; she *would not* cry.

But fearing that very thing, she twisted out of his grasp, turned her back, and shrugged out of her oversized painting smock. Then, without a word, she walked through the door to Signor D'Orsini's studio and to the cupboard where she hung her smock.

She was going to cry. Damnation! He hadn't meant to make her cry. And suddenly he knew there was more here than met the eye. He had cut her deeply, and it was not just to do with the damned painter. He followed her, coming up behind her and putting one hand gently to her shoulder. "What is it, Alix?" he asked softly.

She whirled round. Through her tears he saw fire in the hazel eyes. "You know naught about Signor D'Orsini! You simply make accusations, having no idea what manner of man he is. And . . . and you know even less about *me!*" she cried. "Nor did you ever trouble to find out!" With that she turned and ran for the door. Suddenly he felt like crying himself. What had he done?

She could hear him come after her and increased her pace. She must reach the corridor; he would not pursue her outside the studio. She must not let him see that she had turned into a watering pot; it would only increase his disdain. But, of course, she was no match for him. He caught her several feet from the door, grabbing her upper arms and pulling her back against his broad chest.

"Don't run, Alix," he whispered into her ear, flooding her entire body with unwelcome ripples of heat. "Tell me. Tell me what I do not know, what I've never, in all the time we've spent together, troubled to find out."

He had never spoken to her this way before, with that infinitely gentle yet oddly compelling note in his voice. But still, she would not tell him what he wanted. How could she, when she barely understood it herself? She had been one person in India and here . . . here she felt as if she were becoming someone else entirely.

She shook her head and tried to pull away. He only held her more tightly, then slid his hands up and down her upper arms.

"Please," he murmured. "Tell me about India, about Captain Granger. Tell me about what you are painting. Tell me about Alexandra Rutledge."

If his warm breath had not been caressing her ear, if his hands had not been stroking her in a manner strong yet gentle, she might have been able to resist his entreaty. As it was, she did not move save to bow her head. And she gave into the urge to tell him who Alix Rutledge was, and in the telling, perhaps come to understand it herself.

"When Mama died," she began in a threadbare voice, "I was ten years old. I remember feeling so alone. Papa was always busy working. There were few English girls my own age, and the governess Papa engaged was a most formidable woman. Papa had never paid much attention to me, but as long as I had Mama, it hadn't mattered all that much. Now, suddenly, it mattered a great deal. I remember thinking I would do anything to see Papa smile at me the way he had used to smile at Mama."

Alix moved out of Derek's grasp then and went to stand at one of the large windows that overlooked the now completely white east garden. She wrapped her arms around herself and continued, well aware that Derek had neither moved nor spoken. "You will think me to have been a perfect ninny, even for a child, but that is how it was. Pleasing Papa, winning a smile, perhaps a hug at the end of the day, became the most important thing in my life."

She leaned her head against the window, welcoming the feel of cold glass against her face, which burned with unshed tears. "Papa did not like me playing with the native children, so I stopped. He said I was a hoyden to ride my pony astride, so I rode sidesaddle. He did not like to see my hands dirty from the potters' clay, so I ceased my puerile attempts to fashion spittoons. And he did not approve of oil painting as a pastime for young ladies." She sighed, heedless of the slow tears trickling from the corners of her eyes. She heard Derek's footsteps as he came up behind her, but she did not turn, nor, having started to speak, did she stop.

"Once he and my governess caught me painting one of the native boys in oils. Young ladies, I was informed, painted landscapes, with watercolors. He did not forbid me to use the oils I loved, you must know. It was enough to know he would not smile at me if he caught the telltale smudges on my fingers." She felt the tears now and impatiently brushed them away. "Later I learned other ways to coax a smile out of him—a certain giggle of my own, a certain turn of phrase. When I was older and became Papa's hostess, I found the other gentlemen reacted in much the same way. It was very pleasant to banter with gentlemen, and flirting, once I'd come out, was more of the same."

Now she turned around and ignored her moist eyes as she looked up at Derek. "Only by that time I had forgotten that there was any other way to be. My conversation consisted of commonplaces, my thoughts of gowns and parties."

"Alix," he began, but she forestalled him.

"No!" She sidled away from him and went to lean against the back of the model's chair. "You will think me a veritable nodcock and will despise me all the more, but you asked, and so I am telling you. I—I became everything Papa wanted, you see. But somehow, the gentlemen who paid me court were not what he wanted. Least of all Captain Granger."

"Did you love him?" Derek's voice seemed to come from far away, for all he stood perhaps ten feet from her.

She tried to smile. "No. But it would not have made a difference if I had, would it? He was not what Papa wanted."

He stared at her with the width of half the room between them and wondered when anyone, himself included, had last paid the slightest heed to what Alix wanted or needed. What *he* wanted right now was to enfold her in his arms, just to hold her. She looked achingly beautiful, vulnerable, in a pale yellow muslin gown that was far too thin for the Yorkshire winter. The softly rounded neckline exposed a small, tantalizing glimpse of her smooth white throat. Yes, he wanted to hold her, to kiss the hollow where her ruby pendant nestled as always. But one look at her proud little face told him that was not what *she* wanted. Not now. And, of course, she was not finished speaking. There was more to tell, the part that damned *him*. . . .

Alix took a deep breath and went on. In for a penny, in for a pound, she reminded herself. She spoke of the storm, of how it had been the first time she could ever remember being completely without servants, of how it had actually felt good—not that she would wish anyone ill—but it had felt good to do something useful for a change.

She moved to the grate and stared into the flames, hardly aware now of what she was saying. "I do not know when the full extent of my stifling existence truly hit me. Perhaps after the storm, perhaps here at Arden Chase. Or no—I must amend that—it did not hit me. It has simply grown, an awareness that I can no longer escape." Alix frowned, speaking slowly, for indeed, she had not put words to the fledgling thoughts before. "I—I cannot go back to being the creature that Papa helped me become. For though she was not as shallow and as heartless as you seemed to think her, she was, however, a creature without substance, without a will of her own."

She sighed, too drained now even for tears. She went to the covered portrait of Auntie Win and fingered the top. Derek did not move, did not say a word. Yet she was vividly aware of his presence. The air was charged between them. "As to Signor D'Orsini, he has been kind to me. I do not know if I have any talent in this direction. He has made no pronouncements upon the subject. He has only seen my desire to paint. A desire, I might add, that I had completely forgotten about until the day I walked by and smelled the paint through the open door. I do not expect you to understand this—this need I have to paint. But Signor D'Orsini does, and for him, it is enough."

Derek felt a lump in his throat. He pushed it down by sheer will. "Are you . . . in love with him, Alix?"

She smiled then, a smile of joy and wistfulness and the sadness that comes of pain. "Only in the way a pupil loves the teacher who has opened a new world for him and in so doing, has shown him a part of himself. And I think he is beginning to care for me a little, like—like the daughter he never had." She raised her chin and her voice became more forceful. "And even though I know that my being here with him undoubtedly offends all notions of propriety, I take leave to tell you that at this point I simply do not care a rush."

She gathered her skirts and he knew she meant to leave. "Alix, wait, I—"

"No, Derek, there is really naught—"

"Oh, there you are, my dears!" Lady Hart's voice jarred him. "Come children, 'tis time for tea." Her tone was breezy, but her sharp eyes swept from Derek to Alix, and he wondered for a moment how long she'd been out there and how much she'd heard. The thought was not comforting, nor was the fact that he'd not had the chance to say aught, nor to hold Alix, even for a moment.

The truth was, Derek had had no idea what to say to Alix. She was right; he'd not known anything about her. Or rather, he'd known a mass of contradictions which he'd refused to acknowledge: the consummate flirt, the selfless nurse, the fragile woman whose mere touch inflamed him. And now, after a nearly sleepless night, he still was not certain of what to say to her.

The sun had just risen. Derek had no desire to go out of doors, and yet he felt the need to move about. Suddenly, he knew exactly where he wanted to go. He dressed himself hurriedly, not caring to alert his valet as to his intentions, and made his way into the corridor and up to the third floor.

He did not know why, but he wanted, *needed,* to see what Alix was painting. Her little studio had an eastern aspect, and he silently padded to the easel, slowly and carefully drawing the cloth away from the canvas. And then he held his breath and just stared, mesmerized.

The background was still only penciled; there was much left to do. He thought it was a rendering of the solarium in her father's house in Calcutta. She had already painted part of the golden brown Indian landscape beyond the archways framing the room. But what drew his eyes was the finished part of the painting, the focal point, which was something that had not been in her father's house. It was the very gilded birdcage that hung right here, in this tiny studio. And inside the gilded cage, Alix had painted Lady Hart's yellow canary. But Alix's rendering was not at all like the original, and it was the differences which drew him.

The cage in the painting was disproportionately large and far more ornate, its gilded bars beautifully detailed with floral designs. And the canary! It, too, was large, exquisitely detailed, and Derek marvelled at the delicacy that Alix was able to achieve with oils. But there was something more, something intensely compelling about the little bird, and he finally expelled his breath as he realized what it was. The golden feathers of the head had been very cleverly painted in a series of swirls and curls such that they actually resembled a woman's hair. The wings, a paler yellow, seemed to fall in the folds of a woman's gown, similar to the gown Alix had worn yesterday.

And the face. The beak had been shortened, curved, and reddened, the hazel eyes painted with green flecks. It was subtle, yet unmistakable. Alix had painted the face of a woman. And not just any woman. For if he had any doubts about whom she had painted, he had only to look at the ruby red dot at the base of the throat.

It was uncanny. He himself had thought of Alix as a fragile little bird. And she had painted herself as just that—a beautiful, delicate, golden bird. A bird locked in a gilded cage. Derek wondered if Alix realized what she had revealed with this painting. Did she even understand the feelings that led to it? She mightn't, but Derek certainly did. She *was* a fragile little bird, imprisoned in the gilded cage of her father's love and protection. She'd had all that wealth could provide, all but the freedom. The cage door was locked; there was no way out. And when she'd left India, he himself had seen to it that she remained imprisoned. He'd done it with accusations and assumptions, with contempt rather than love, but he'd kept her in her cage all the same.

It seemed that Signor D'Orsini might be the one to open it, though Alix seemed unaware of that. She said she loved him as a teacher, but could that love, that gratitude, not turn into something else? Derek was surprised at the fierce stab of jealousy that thought engendered. And yet he was not at all surprised; he was simply willing for the first time to call the emotion by its proper name. He had wanted Alix since that first night on board ship. He had not forgotten the intense wave of heat he'd felt brushing against her in that narrow passageway. Nor had the heat lessened each time he was imprudent enough to touch her.

He still wanted her. But he wanted more, much more, than her heat. He wanted her smile, her softness, her delicate beauty, her sensitivity, her goodness, even her vulnerability. The last thought astounded him. He had always seen vulnerability as a weapon females used to keep men at a disadvantage, to drain them of their strength, their common sense, their funds. Of a certain his mother and sister had done just that. But Alix was not at all that way. She did not *use* vulnerability; she *was* vulnerable, fragile, a woman in need of a man's protection.

Did he want to be that man?

Suddenly Derek threw the cloth over the exquisite painting and backed away, out of her studio, and D'Orsini's, and into the corridor. He attained his own rooms and paced his bedchamber floor.

Did he want to be that man?

He did not know. He simply did not know. He did not want D'Orsini to be, that was certain, nor some Peregrine Granger type who could never be man enough for her. Would there be someone at the ball?

The ball! The infernal thing was but four days away. He'd been counting the days, eager to be gone from here. Now they sounded like a countdown to some dire event. For there was that damned lottery to consider, with Lady Hart and fate working hand in hand. And to which man would the lottery give Alix? Would she give credence to it? For if she did, it would be far too late for Derek Muldaur, Viscount Weddington.

Did he want to be that man?

Derek laughed in self-deprecation at the very arrogance of the question. For it was not only what *he* wanted, but what Alix wanted. And it was a fair guess that she hated the very sight of him by now.

Damnation! He had got to speak with her . . .

Alix evaded him all morning, disappearing round corners or fobbing him off with the myriad preparations with which Lady Hart needed help. And then it was time for luncheon and after that Alix disappeared again. He knew she was painting and waited till it was nearing teatime before ascending to the third floor. This time he knocked loudly on the door of D'Orsini's studio and, finding it empty, marched unabashedly to Alix's smaller chamber.

He greeted both Alix and D'Orsini warmly. The artist smiled and left him alone with Alix quite as if it were the most natural thing to do. Alix, however, was not smiling. He leaned against the doorjamb with a casualness he was far from feeling and watched her methodically clean her brushes. When she twisted to remove her smock, he stepped forward to help her. She stiffened but did not pull away.

"Alix, we needs must talk," he said from behind her.

"This was not well done of you, Derek. We have nothing more to say to one another." She moved away to hang the smock in the cupboard, then whirled round to face him. "You have twice interrupted me with Signor D'Orsini. You have made your point. I am fully sensible of your disapproval. But I remind you that it is none of your concern! Good afternoon, sir!" she fumed, and started for the door.

He could not later say whether it was the fire in her hazel eyes or the way her perfect little nose quivered or the way her breasts rose and fell beneath her jonquil muslin gown or simply that he could act faster than he could speak and knew he had got to detain her.

In truth he did not think at all but strode after her, grabbing her, spinning her round, his hands on her shoulders. And even then, he might have had sense enough to start talking, except that she started struggling to free herself. And so naturally he pulled her closer and felt the familiar warmth overtake him. And as she struggled further, all the soft, rounded parts of her wriggled against all the hard, muscled parts of him, and he was lost.

He brought his mouth down onto hers, his lips hard and demanding. She went rigid, her lips resolutely pursed together. But only for a moment.

His hand stroked her back and his mouth softened on hers, coaxing, teasing, his tongue tracing the line of her lips before thrusting between them. He felt a shudder go through her, and she swayed to him, opening her lips, inviting him in.

His entire body burned; he felt as if he were on fire. His tongue tasted her sweetness, his hands caressed her softness. He could not pull her close enough, could not get enough of her! By God, how he wanted her!

No! Alix told herself. She must not let him do this to her, must not let him make her feel this way. Her body was aflame! She was clinging to him, her hands creeping round his neck. He was plundering her mouth, sending ripples of the most intoxicating sensations through her body, and she was allowing it! She must stop him! He would despise her even more for behaving in such a wanton manner. For this embrace was like no other they had shared.

But his hands were so warm, gentle and yet frenzied as they massaged her back, her hips, and now her breast. She heard someone moan and realized it was she. He kissed her throat; his lips seared her skin. He was making her feel things she was certain no lady should ever feel and, God help her, she wanted him never to stop!

It was her unbridled response that brought him to his

senses. Her arms were clasped to his neck, her soft body molding to his, her tongue dancing with his. She was an innocent. She did not know what she was about any more than she'd known when he'd kissed her in her sickbed, aboard ship. She did not know what would happen in very short order if they did not stop. But *he* knew! Dear God, what was he doing?

Resolutely, he pulled his mouth from hers, put his hands to her shoulders, and pushed her from him. Then he dropped his hands and stepped back from her. She stared at him, trying to catch her breath even as he willed his own body to calm down. The air between them crackled with tension and he watched the smoky look of desire in her green-flecked hazel eyes give way to a shadow of hurt and then finally to sparks of anger.

She had been right, Alix thought in despair. She had behaved like a lightskirt and given him a disgust of her. But her mortification rapidly turned to anger. How dare he! How dare he take such liberties, bring her to such a pass, and then push her away! Without further thought, she swung her right arm up. "How dare you!" she cried, aiming straight for his cheek.

He caught her hand midair and forced it down, then held her upper arms in a harsh grip.

"Don't *you* dare, Alix," he growled. "Don't you dare pretend you didn't enjoy that, didn't want it as much as I did!"

He pulled her close again, his mouth seeking hers.

"No!" she gasped, and wrenched herself from him.

He gazed at her through smoldering deep blue eyes. She turned away, trying to squelch her tears. How *could* he humiliate her so? She wrapped her arms about her suddenly chilled body.

"Why do you hate me so much?" she rasped.

She heard his sharp intake of breath and his voice, when he spoke, was very soft, with an odd note she could not place. "Alix, Alix, you are wrong. Very wrong. I do not hate you. I—I admire you greatly."

He did not know if she would believe him. He supposed she

had no reason to.

She raised her head, still not looking at him. "You mock me, sir," she said coldly, and started for the door.

This time he did not make the mistake of going after her, of touching her. Instead he began speaking. Rapidly.

"Again I beg to tell you that you are wrong, Alix. Just as I was wrong about many things."

She stopped a hairsbreadth from the door but did not turn to face him. He kept talking. "My father died when I was fifteen, Alix. He had not been a prudent man with his fortune, and whatever he left, my mother and sister dissipated in short order."

She finally turned and looked across the room at him, a slight frown of puzzlement marring her smooth brow. And as he continued speaking, she came to sit on the green brocade sofa. Pacing before her, he told her of his mother's profligate nature, of the way his sister wed the most wealthy, titled man who offered for her, of their frivolous, flirtatious, helpless demeanor. He spoke of India, of how he'd enjoyed his work but passionately missed Greenvale. She said not a word, merely gazed from him to the fire in the grate and back again.

And then he came to the hardest part. "You have something of the look of my sister, and especially of my mother. She, too, had hazel eyes, though without the green flecks of yours, and blond hair, though yours is the color of rich honey and hers was more a dull flaxen. You are smaller, more dainty than Mama was, or than Chloe will ever be, and your smile is much sweeter, but still, there is some resemblance. I used to watch you in Calcutta, across the crowded drawing rooms and ballrooms. I would see you laugh and flick your fan just so, flutter your eyelashes, and all I could think was—well, I am afraid I drew many parallels, jumped to many conclusions—"

"Which you brought with you onto the *Star of India,*" she interjected quietly.

He sighed and came to stand before her. "Yes, Alix. And I am sorry for many things that have transpired between us. We have, I think, been dealing at cross purposes." She was staring down at the hands in her lap just now, and he sat down next to her.

Very gently, he lifted her chin with his forefinger. Even that light touch warmed him too much. He let go the moment she raised her eyes to his. "But I am not sorry I kissed you just now, Alix. And if you will be honest with yourself, you will admit that you are not sorry either."

He watched her flush red and wondered what the devil was wrong with him. To have kissed her, touched her, a lady of quality, in such a manner was bad enough, but to expect her to admit—

She jumped up and darted to the window, her back to him. He rose and went to the chimneypiece, keeping his silence. He would give her a moment to compose herself.

Oh, dear God, Alix thought. He must think her little better than painted Haymarket ware! Surely a gentleman who had any respect for a lady would not kiss her, embrace her, in the manner in which he had! Nor, having done so, would he remind her, several times, that she had been so lost to all propriety as to respond to the embrace, to return the kiss.

She had responded to him that night aboard ship as well, but then she'd had the excuse, however paltry, of illness. Now . . . Good Heavens! How could she face him? Why, she was persuaded that even a betrothed couple did not behave in such a shocking manner! And they were most definitely *not* betrothed. She was certain it was the furthest thing from either of their minds!

At the least, she reminded herself, all that he had told her of his family explained much. It had been an apology of sorts for his unwarranted assumptions about her. He was not, after all, an odious, insensitive man. But he . . . he was a libertine! He had offered her insult, then compounded it by throwing her response in her face!

And why on earth had she allowed herself to succumb to him like some . . . some bit of muslin? Because, a little voice at the back of her head answered, whenever he holds you, touches you, it feels so right . . .

No! It was not right! How could her body betray her so? Was she, indeed, a wanton? Oh, dear. She could not even speak of it.

But Derek awaited a reply. She turned round, squaring her shoulders. "I thank you for what you have told me of your family, Derek," she said evenly. "Indeed, I hope that now we can go on with a modicum of peace and civility between us. Now, I, ah, am persuaded 'tis near to teatime. I—I'd better go and freshen up."

What the devil? Derek thought, striding toward her. What farrago of nonsense was this? She was fobbing him off, talking of a modicum of peace. What had all that to do with what had transpired between them just moments ago? Somehow, he had got to set that to rights.

"Alix," he began. "I—"

"Alix, dear, are you there?" trilled an all-too-familiar voice.

Derek stopped in his tracks and bit back an expletive as Lady Hart sailed into the studio trailing yards of purple lace. "Alix! I thought I'd find you here! And you, too, Weddington? How delightful! Well, now, I am working on the servants' fete, you must know. Tell me, dear girl, how old is your maid?"

"My maid? Sita? Why, nineteen," Alix replied, much befuddled.

"Ah, splendid. Then perhaps she will agree to be part of the lottery below stairs. You must know that several of my friends have Indian servants—young men who came here years ago as pages—and you never know but what the lottery might bring about a perfect match! If you do not mind, that is, dear girl, for I daresay you will have to find another maid. One of the young lads is first footman to my friend Mrs. Carstairs over in Giggleswick, a bit far to—"

"Of course I do not mind, Auntie Win," Alix interrupted, and Derek refrained from asking whether they weren't jumping the gun just a bit.

"Well, that's settled then. Come along now, children, 'tis time for tea. You'll be happy to know the roads are finally passable and we have two new guests. Captain Watson of the

Horse Guards and Mr. Benchley. He's a widower, you must know, but young, and very well to pass."

Another captain, Derek muttered to himself minutes later as his eyes scanned the Purple Saloon. What *was* it with Alix and men in uniform? Here she was, flirting shamelessly again, hardly aware of it. Captain Watson was all but falling at her feet and the widower, Mr. Benchley, looked ready to pounce. D'Orsini, interestingly, had taken it upon himself to distract the miffed Miss Sykes. Good Lord! Was he to spend his entire life fending off Alix's admirers, protecting her from them, or *them* from *her* as the case might be?

He nearly dropped his teacup. What the devil was he thinking? Why, that she needed a man's protection, of course. *But did he want to be that man?* He asked himself that question over and over through the tea hour, and again as they sat at table for dinner. Two more guests had joined them, the Honorable Mr. Appleby and his sister, Clarissa, from east Yorkshire. Mr. Appleby joined the ranks of Alix's swains, though Mr. Benchley decided to divert himself to Miss Sykes.

Alix looked delectable in a peach satin round dress, the corsage of which was cut exceedingly low and trimmed with tiny rosettes. She was polite with Derek, but no more. And she refused to meet his eyes. He did not know if she was piqued or embarrassed over what had transpired between them this afternoon. She did not flutter up at him, nor tinkle with laughter while engaging in banter with him. All of that was reserved for the others. Derek did not like it one bit, for all he knew it was his own damned fault.

But as the evening wore on and he watched her closely, he saw that she seemed uncomfortable. There was a kind of a desperation to the way she parried the various bon mots thrown at her. She was, he realized, playing a part, one that she no longer enjoyed. She clearly needed rescuing from such situations.

Did he want to be that man?

A syllabub was served and with it, as always, a huge bowl of fruit. Lady Hart selected an orange and as she peeled it her shrewd eyes scanned the table, coming to rest on Alix for a moment. Then she separated a wedge and bit into it. "The tropical fruit is rather tart just now, dear heart," she said to her husband.

Sir Horace chuckled and patted her hand. "Merely needs to ripen a bit, Win, my love. A few more days should do it."

Lady Hart smiled enigmatically. Derek wished he knew what the *devil* they were talking about. He had a strong feeling it was not fruit.

When the gentlemen joined the ladies for coffee in the drawing room, Captain Watson and Mr. Appleby vied for the place beside Alix on the sofa. Appleby won and sat a damn sight too close. He peered down at her, affording himself a most ungentlemanly view of that part of her bosom that rose above her décolletage. Hellfire! Did Alix not even realize what the man was about? She could not be that much of an innocent! Someone had got to take her in hand!

Did he want to be that man?

Yes, dammit! He nearly shattered his delicate china teacup as he slapped it onto its saucer in answer to his own inner question. Yes! He wanted the right to protect her, take care of her, love her.

Love her? Did he . . . love her?

He looked across at her now, at the silky honey-blond ringlets that caressed her face, at her soft, green-flecked hazel eyes, at her perfect patrician nose and her rosebud mouth. He thought of the way she felt in his arms, soft and warm and right in a way no woman had ever felt before. He thought of her courage during the storm aboard ship, of her fragility, her extraordinary sensitivity and talent. He thought of the blazing heat that flared between them at the slightest touch.

Did he love her? Yes, by God, he did! He loved her as he had never thought to love a woman. *He wanted to be the man!* He wanted her to be his and his alone.

But he had no idea how she felt about him, or whether she

would, given all that had transpired, be receptive to his addresses. And then there were Lady Hart and that damned lottery with which to contend. There were four days left until the ball. Obviously, he would have to plan his strategy carefully.

The next morning dawned clear and sunny enough so that even a man who'd spent ten years in India was willing to venture forth, the snow drifts notwithstanding. At first Derek thought to ask Alix to come driving with him but decided it was probably still too cold for her. He must find another way to be private with her.

And then another thought struck him. He did not know how the Valentine's Day lottery would fall out. But he *did* recall hearing, from his resourceful valet, that a gentleman hoping to be paired with a certain lady might purchase a gift for her, perhaps to encourage "fate" to find in his favor.

The lottery be damned! Derek would give her the gift no matter what. He would give her something that in some way symbolized his regard. He would give her . . . Ah, yes, that would answer! He would see about finding a jeweler straightaway, one who was able to execute a commission on very short notice.

He went in search of Lady Hart, seeking the direction of just such a person. And it occurred to him, as he scouted the ballroom, the Purple Saloon, and finally the kitchens in search of her, that it would be well to have a word with Lady Hart about the lottery. He, of course, did not put much credence in it, but Alix might. And Lady Hart, upon whom Martin Rutledge had settled the task of finding Alix a husband, certainly did. Yes, a word would be wise, for he suspected his hostess and "fate" were rather thick as thieves.

But when he found her, as directed, in the larger of the two kitchens serving Arden Chase, the conversation did not go at all as planned. He asked if there was a jeweler in the vicinity who might oblige him.

"Why, of course, there is, dear boy. For when would you

need it?" she asked in all innocence.

"For the ball, dear lady," he replied dryly.

Her face lit in a smile. "Splendid, dear boy!" she exclaimed, her extraordinary, multilayered haircomb bouncing rather precariously in her enthusiasm. "So, you've finally decided, have you?" she murmured.

But before he could vouchsafe a reply to that enigmatic statement, she held up her hand. "No, do not tell me, dear boy. 'Tis one of the rules, you must know. Mustn't tempt fate, must we?"

Oh, mustn't we? he muttered inwardly as she gave him the direction of the jeweler's shop, warning him that he was rather busy at this time of year. Making heart-shaped lockets, no doubt, Derek thought uncharitably. He had something very different in mind.

Derek had been gone all morning, which Alix decided was just as well. She really had no notion of what to say to him. She knew he thought her terribly brazen after what happened in the studio yesterday. And despite all that Derek had told her afterwards, he still had looked dagger points at her as she conversed with the other gentlemen last night. She supposed she could not blame him, for she had been almost tongue-tied with him. She had felt like the veriest schoolroom miss, unable to meet his eyes.

For the plain paradoxical truth was that she found it easier to converse with strangers than a man who confused her so much, caused her to behave in a manner that no lady ought. She hoped he would not seek her out in her studio again today. She did not want to be private with him. He might . . . might touch her again and then her body might . . . betray her again. Oh, dear! Even to think about it was not at all the thing! Whatever was wrong with her? She did *not* want to see him again!

And yet, when he had still not returned by nuncheon, she felt a pang of disappointment. And when Captain Watson took her arm to lead her into the dining room, she could not squelch the thought that it was Derek's arm she wanted to feel entwined with hers.

More guests had been arriving all day, and Auntie Win organized activities for the afternoon. There were carriage rides for the hearty and parlor games for the rest.

Alix begged off and headed for her studio. She spent the afternoon quite engrossed in the background of her painting. She barely heard Signor D'Orsini when he said he was finished for the day. And she did not hear approaching footsteps in the outer chamber—which was why she gasped upon hearing that familiar voice, the voice that made her think of large, gentle hands and warm, full lips. "Good afternoon, Alix," Derek said from the doorway.

Startled, she threw the cover over her canvas. It was an instinctive reaction, like protecting her innermost thoughts and feelings. Derek noted it and raised his brows, but he did not question her, nor make a move toward the easel. Perversely, she wondered if he was simply not interested. He was not, after all, convinced that she possessed any artistic abilities, though at the least he was no longer berating her for spending time with Signor D'Orsini.

He stayed where he was while she cleaned her brushes. But when she turned to remove her smock, he was right behind her. His hands merely grazed her shoulders, she told herself. There was no reason for her to feel such ripples of warmth! She pulled away from him as soon as she could and sidled past him to go hang the smock in the cupboard. When she turned back round he was right there again, towering over her, his body blocking her escape.

"Alix," he began softly, "I thought we might take a walk to the picture gallery. It is too cold outside for you, but we can have a fine stroll indoors, I believe."

"A stroll?" she echoed, once again finding herself nearly tongue-tied. He hadn't touched her, but his nearness, the intensity in his deep blue eyes, the strength evident in every plane of his handsome face, the proximity of his sensual lips, all warmed her far too well. She swallowed hard and tried to back up. But of course, there was no place to go.

"Yes, a stroll," he murmured. "I wish to speak with you and I make no doubt that if we stay here we shall be interrupted within a very few minutes."

What did he want of her? Merely to speak, or—or to lead her into some dark secluded corner, to—No! He could not think to offer her such insult again, could he? And she would not melt in his arms again, would she?

"Will you come?" He lifted a finger and stroked her cheek lightly, just once.

Her skin burned in its wake. Dear God, she could not be alone with him again! She would disgrace herself!

She jerked her head back. "No, please, Derek! I—I cannot!" And with that she squirmed away from him and fled for the door.

Horrified at himself, he let her go. What had he done? He wanted to court her, to begin wooing her. Instead he had frightened her, perhaps offered her insult where none was intended. He should never have touched her. Something explosive happened between them every time he did. He would not make this mistake again, would not seek to be private with her again. At the least, not until the ball . . .

Dinner was unbearable. She could hardly face Derek. She behaved like a wanton whenever she was with him! Undoubtedly, that was why he wanted to be private with her! At dinner, however, he did not attempt any tête-à-tête with her and was merely civil. But with Isabel Sykes and Clarissa Appleby, he was all that was charming. Clarissa's brother, the Honorable James Appleby, was once again most particular in his attentions to Alix. He was a slender man of medium height, thin blond hair, and gray eyes. As he had last night, he sat too close to her when the gentlemen joined the ladies in the drawing room. He peered down at her in such a way as to make her wish the bodice of her forest green gown buttoned up to her chin. When he leaned over and whispered in her ear, his breath did not warm her as Derek's did. She repressed a shudder, which caused Mr. Appleby to ask if she was cold and to arrange her muslin shawl more firmly about her shoulders. Alix only felt colder.

And then, unwittingly, her eyes flew across the room to Derek. The look of fury and contempt she saw in his deep blue eyes chilled her to her very core. Did he not realize she did not welcome these attentions? How had she made such a muddle of things with him? Suddenly, she could bear it no longer—not Mr. Appleby's proximity, nor Derek's anger, nor the cheerful chatter of everyone else. She had to seek the privacy of her own chamber.

Pleading fatigue, she bid everyone good night and made to leave. Mr. Appleby, however, was not to be deterred. He insisted on accompanying her above stairs and brushed aside her protestations that it was not at all necessary. She did not want his company, but, short of making a scene, she did not know how to stop him.

She dared not look at Derek as Mr. Appleby led her from the drawing room, his hand at the small of her back. She did not like his hands, she decided. They were very long and thin, barely dusted with blond hair. They lacked the strength of Derek's hands, which were larger, more solid, sprinkled liberally with black hair. Nor did she like the feel of James Appleby's hand at her back. But as she tried to inch away, he followed.

He did not leave her even when they reached the door to her chamber. She bid him a perfunctory good night, only to have him grasp her hand and bring it to his lips in a lingering kiss. She felt a wave of revulsion at the feel of his wet, thin lips on her skin. It was all she could do not to snatch her hand back. When he finally released her, she realized that he had maneuvered so that he stood very close to her, with her back against her door. Just so had Derek stood—was it only this afternoon?—and she had wanted to melt in his arms. But she did not want to be anywhere near Mr. Appleby's arms!

"My dear Miss Rutledge," he said into the silence of the dimly lit corridor, "I understand there is to be waltzing at the ball. May I ask you to save the first for me?"

Alix swallowed. The thought of being held close by Mr. Appleby fairly sickened her. "I—I'm sorry, Mr. Appleby, but I—"

"Miss Rutledge's first waltz is bespoken, Appleby," came a familiar voice from the darkness. There was no warmth in it now. "I believe she has the first set of country dances free, however."

Mr. Appleby whirled round just as Derek stepped into the light cast by a nearby wall sconce. Derek looked menacing, a lock of his thick black hair falling onto his brow, his blue eyes hard, his jaw rigid. He towered over Mr. Appleby, who mumbled something about the country set being fine, and beat a hasty retreat.

For endless minutes she and Derek stared at each other, neither of them moving, the air between them vibrating with unnamed emotions. Finally she could bear the silence no longer.

"Th—thank you, Derek. I did not want to dance the waltz with him, but I did not know quite how to refuse."

"I realize that, Alix. But you must have a care never to find yourself in darkened corridors with the likes of James Appleby." He spoke quietly, but there was an unmistakable steel in his voice. Was he angry at Mr. Appleby or at her?

She nodded slowly. "I know that, Derek. I did not wish to be—that is—"

"I know," he said, his voice softening. He stepped closer to her but did not touch her. Her breath became shallow. Her back was to her door, and they were in a darkened corridor . . . "And now, you must give credence to my lie, Alix. You must reserve the first waltz for me."

"I—I should like that very much, Derek," she replied breathlessly, and then he smiled.

It was a soft, intimate smile that caused the oddest sensation in the pit of her stomach. She swallowed hard. He was no longer angry. He no longer looked menacing. But there was a look in his eyes, an intensity, that was far more dangerous.

She wanted to reach up and brush that lock of black hair from his face. She wanted to fall against his broad chest and feel his arms enfold her . . .

No! She must not allow herself to—

"Alix," he whispered, and raised his hand.

She must not let him touch her! she thought wildly. But he merely put his hand on the wall near her head. Still, it was too close. He was too close. She could not trust herself, or him.

"G—Good night, Derek," she stammered, and fled into her room.

"Hellfire and damnation!" Derek muttered to himself as her door closed firmly shut. He'd done it again—frightened her, nearly offering her insult, even though this time he'd not even touched her! What the deuce was wrong with him? He had vowed to stay away from her. He had got to give her time!

And yet, he'd been unable to keep himself from following her tonight. He'd known well enough what Appleby was about. And when he'd seen him corner Alix, put his mouth to her hand, and seen Alix fairly cringe in response, he'd wanted to kill the man and carry the woman off and claim her for his own. Indeed, Alix had looked relieved when he'd sent Appleby to the rightabout. More, she'd looked as if she wanted to fall right into his arms. It was all he could do not to grant her unspoken request, but he did not want to overset her further.

But if he'd had any doubts on the matter, he'd learned one thing this night. Piqued with him over that kiss though she might be, frightened though she was, the look in her eyes moments ago had spoken volumes. She was *not* indifferent to him! But he did not think she was as yet aware of that most interesting fact. He would give her time to refine upon the matter. He would give her until the ball. And that night, come what may, he would stake his claim. And nothing, neither Lady Hart and her lottery, nor Alix herself, would stand in his way!

Alix was shaking as she stumbled to her bed. What manner

of wanton woman was she that she could not be anywhere near Derek without wanting to touch him, to have him . . .

Oh dear! Her face flamed even now at the thought. She wanted him to be here now, in her bedchamber, to hold her and never let her go, to kiss her . . .

Did that make her a wanton? She had not, she reflected, wanted Mr. Appleby near her, had, indeed, been repulsed by his kiss of her hand. Nor had she liked it when Captain Watson patted her hand.

It was only Derek she wanted.

Did that make her a wanton? Was not a wanton indiscriminate with her favors? Surely she was not that! But how then to explain the way Derek made her feel?

Just moments ago, when he had rescued her from Mr. Appleby, she had wanted him to hold her, but more, she realized, she had wanted to know that he would always protect her from the James Applebys of the world.

But, of course, he could not do any such thing. Only a husband could offer such protection. And he was merely asking for a waltz, not her hand! Nor did she wish to give it to him! She did not love him, after all.

Did she? Startled by the thought, she rose from the bed and began pacing the floor. Was *that* why she felt so . . . right in his arms? No, it could not be! She did not even know what love was all about. And it must not be! For he did not love her.

He had never indicated anything of the kind. True, his voice had been very gentle tonight, even this afternoon, when he asked her to stroll to the picture gallery. But what had that to say to the matter? she admonished herself. That had merely been a prelude to what he really wanted—to kiss her and . . .

No, he did *not* love her. He had merely made it plain that he liked kissing her, and that was not at all the same thing. Why, men liked kissing their mistresses, but they rarely loved them, and they most assuredly did not wed them! And Captain Granger, who had wanted to wed her, had only kissed her perfunctorily on the hand.

Perhaps kissing and . . . and embracing the way she and

Derek had done had naught to do with love and marriage. Which thought brought her full circle. She *was* a wanton!

She had simply got to avoid being private with him. Somehow, she must get through the next few days, until the ball. After that, he would leave. She told herself she did not feel desolate at the very thought.

It was, in fact, a simple matter to avoid Derek the next day, for Derek quite assiduously avoided her. And what with his evasiveness and Auntie Win's request for help with decorations and the placement of chairs and tables for the ball, the day passed rather quickly. She was not at all surprised when he did not appear in her studio as she cleaned her brushes.

She suppressed a pang of disappointment. She could not face Derek, could not risk being alone with him. And yet the ball was only two days hence. He would leave after that. Suddenly, she could not bear the thought of not speaking with him before he left. At the least, she reminded herself, they would have their waltz together. They might speak then, and she would feel his arms around her one last time . . .

She squelched the tears that threatened and wished that the ball was still weeks away. It was not only Derek's imminent departure that discommoded her. There was also the matter of Auntie Win's lottery. Alix was persuaded the lottery had little to do with fate. It was mere chance, after all. Chance aided, perhaps, by Auntie Win. No one would or could say for certain, least of all Auntie Win. Yet, Alix could not escape the ubiquitous talk at Arden Chase about all the matches that had come about as result of previous Valentine's Day lotteries. And how would she feel when Derek's name was drawn with that of Isabel Sykes's or Clarissa Appleby's? When her own was paired with Mr. Appleby or Captain Watson or some other gentleman?

She would feel a misery such as she had never known before.

Somehow, Derek got through the next two days. Alix, he was pleased to note, looked as blue-deviled as he felt. Yet he did not once approach her, nor did she come near him. He would wait until the ball. It would not hurt to allow the romantic atmosphere of Lady Hart's Valentine's Day Ball to help advance his cause.

And romantic atmosphere she did create, Derek marveled on the afternoon of February fourteenth. With the help of all her houseguests, whose aid she had blithely enlisted in a mad whirl for two days running, Lady Hart had transformed the ballroom.

Red hearts were intertwined with reams of purple and pink lace, all of it draped ceiling to floor, festooning every pillar and window, the orchestra dais and, of course, the two huge lottery drums. The effect should have been absurd, but together with the myriad fragrant blossoms being arranged about the huge room, it was instead . . . magical.

Indeed, some kind of strange magic was in the air. He had lost track of the names of the numerous house guests. But the men and women all eyed each other with a kind of expectant curiosity. Captain Watson had attached himself to a giddy chestnut-haired schoolroom miss. Mr. Benchley, the widower, had not left Miss Sykes's side in days. Even the servants were in a fever pitch of excitement. Derek wondered what "fate" would have to say to all this.

As to himself, he had kept his resolve to stay away from Alix. But the jewel he'd ordered rested even now in his coat pocket. He was quite pleased with it.

Alix dressed with care and trepidation for the ball. One could not escape the mood of expectation at Arden Chase, the feeling that something momentous would transpire this night.

But would it happen for her? She knew she did not want the lottery to pair her with anyone but Derek. But what would she do if it so transpired? What would Derek do?

She bit her lip as Sita wound yellow silk rosettes through her hair. And then she picked up her reticule and her fan, squared her shoulders, and made her way down the stairs.

It was magical, she thought two hours later, standing amid the throng in the crowded ballroom. The myriad candles twinkling in the crystal chandeliers, the red satin hearts, the hothouse flowers—and most of all, the air of expectancy about the guests. Everyone was waiting for the lottery. Everyone except Alix. But she determined to put it out of her mind, for the orchestra struck up the strains of the first waltz.

Derek had not come near her all evening. It had been all she could do not to go to him. He looked achingly handsome in a black velvet coat, charcoal waistcoat and white satin knee breeches. His black hair, full and wavy, gleamed, and his blue eyes smiled down at each of his dance partners.

And now he was walking toward her, his tall, broad shoulders blocking her view of everyone behind him, his eyes boring into hers with an intensity she did not understand.

He swept her into his arms, into the steps of the dance. Her skin felt heated at his touch. It had been days since he'd held her. It shocked her now to realize how very much she'd missed it. She looked up at him, wondering what he was thinking.

But his blue eyes were unfathomable. He was regarding her piercingly, unsmilingly. Instinctively, she stiffened.

"Relax, Alix," he murmured. "I am not going to eat you. People are watching, my dear. Can you not at the least pretend you are enjoying this?"

He smiled that intimate smile again, and she nearly melted in his arms. The feel of him holding her, spinning her about the floor, was intoxicating. She dared to sway to him, and he pulled her closer. She inhaled his spicy, masculine scent and reveled in the warmth of his strong arms. She smiled up at him.

"That is better," Derek whispered, and had to keep himself from lowering his head and kissing her rosebud mouth. Oh, to feel her again so close to him! He had been aching for her all night, watching as she danced with every man who had scrawled his name on her dance card, waiting for his turn. And he had vowed that this was the last night of his life that he would wait his turn with Alexandra Rutledge.

She had never looked more lovely, her hair curled in soft golden ringlets about her face, her hazel eyes luminous, her gown of pale yellow crepe lisse molding sensuously to her shapely form. The more he held her, the more he wanted her. He reminded himself that they were on a very public dance floor and that there was much unresolved between them.

Her head rested at his shoulder. He allowed his hand to creep up her back in a soft, surreptitious caress. He felt a shudder go through her and knew, with a sense of great satisfaction, that it was not one of revulsion. Ah, Alix, my love, he thought, we shall have our reckoning soon.

Moments later she raised her head. "Derek?"

"Yes, Alix?"

"I am not pretending."

He felt a certain tension leave his body, a tension of which he'd not been aware. "That is good, Alix. And, Alix?"

"Hmmm?"

"Sometime after the lottery, no matter what happens, I would speak with you. Do you understand?"

She nodded, but the confusion in her eyes told him she did not understand. No matter. It would not be much longer now.

It was time at last. Auntie Win ascended the platform on which stood the two lottery drums, one for the men and one for the women. A hush fell over the crowd. Alix thought Auntie Win looked resplendent in a swirling gown of deep violet velvet. Her magnificent hair, piled almost a foot atop her head, was threaded with matching ribbons. Sir Horace stood next to the platform beaming up at his wife.

She began by speaking of the Valentine's Day tradition in Yorkshire, of the long history of the lottery, of how it had been forgotten in these parts and then revived here at Arden Chase some fifteen years ago. And then she named some of the couples who had been brought together over the years as fate and the turn of the lottery drums worked hand in hand.

Unwittingly, Alix's eyes searched, and found, Derek's. She looked quickly away. Was that—was *he*—what she wanted? She did not know.

Signor D'Orsini appeared at her side. He was one of the few unattached gentlemen of Auntie Win's acquaintance who had declined to have his name put in the drum. He had told her that he was well past his salad days and that when he wanted a lady, he would go after her himself. Alix thought that lady would be very lucky, indeed.

"You are anxious, signorina?" he asked.

She smiled ruefully and nodded. "Silly, I know. After all, there can be little meaning in the turn of a drum."

He chuckled softly. "Never underestimate Lady Hart, *cara.* And always look to your *own* heart."

And with those enigmatic words he blended into the crowd. Auntie Win went on explaining that this year, for the first time, the lottery dance would be a waltz. Following the dance there would be the unveiling of Auntie Win's portrait, and then the gentlemen would lead their partners into supper.

The crowd applauded loudly but quieted as soon as Auntie Win stepped behind the two lottery drums. Two figurines, a shepherd and shepherdess, had been pinned to the lace beneath each drum. There was a dramatic trumpet blast as Auntie Win began turning the drum above the shepherd. She closed her eyes and put her hand inside. There was absolute silence from the crowd assembled on the dance floor.

"The Honorable James Appleby!" Auntie Win announced, and everyone broke into applause as Mr. Appleby came forward to stand next to the lottery platform. And then a hush fell over the room. If possible it was more silent than before as Auntie Win turned the second drum. Alix held her breath. Please, not me, she prayed.

"Miss Lucinda Farnsdale," announced Auntie Win.

Alix breathed a most unladylike sigh of relief as Miss Farnsdale, a gregarious girl who was quite pretty except for a decided squint, moved forward. Mr. Appleby's face was stony. Alix decided that Miss Farnsdale, no milkwater miss, would probably deal quite well with him. The couple moved off and the crowd quite forgot them as the trumpet sounded again.

And so it went as name after name was called. Isabel Sykes was paired with the widower, Mr. Benchley. They both seemed pleased as punch. Captain Watson drew a schoolroom miss who gazed at him in awe. But Derek's name had not been drawn yet, and neither had hers. Those who had been called and those not participating stood to the rear of the ballroom. Those still awaiting the sound of their names remained in front. Their numbers were dwindling. Alix could hardly credit how very nervous she was, her entire body tense. Why, the lottery had no significance at all, she kept telling herself. And yet, with only about eight people left, she could barely draw breath.

Derek stood a few yards from her. She stole a glance at him. His stance was rigid, his eyes front. What was he thinking?

Another trumpet blast. Auntie Win closed her eyes, put her hand into the first drum.

"Derek Muldaur, Viscount Weddington!" she announced.

Derek marched forward. He did not look at Alix. He assumed a casual stance, but Alix could see his jaw clench. She forced her eyes back to Auntie Win, who was spinning the second drum. Alix's heart stopped beating; her breath simply didn't come. Time seemed suspended as her aunt closed her eyes and put her hand inside the drum. Alix closed her own eyes and prayed.

"Miss Alexandra Rutledge!"

Her eyes sprang open. Her heart began to pound. She could not believe it! However had it happened? She heard the applause ringing in her ears, but still she could not move. Her eyes flew to Derek. He was smiling at her, a very warm smile. Was he pleased? Suddenly, she wanted so very much for him to be pleased.

She took a deep breath and walked forward on limbs that were frightfully unsteady. Derek extended his hand to her, and she grasped it as if for dear life. He drew her close and in full view of everyone, kissed her hand, lingeringly.

"Hello, Alix," he said at length, almost as if they hadn't seen each other in years.

And then he drew her aside so the lottery could continue. And when it was over, Auntie Win signaled for the waltz, and Derek took her into his arms. It was different this time. He did not speak, did not allow her to speak. He merely gazed at her through eyes that were a very deep, warm blue, and then pressed her head onto his shoulder and pulled her very close. She did not know what the lottery meant. Was it Auntie Win's doing? Was it fate? She did not know what tomorrow would bring. Would Derek leave as planned? For the moment, it did not matter. If the first waltz had made her feel heady with sensation, this one was pure heaven. She closed her eyes and gave herself up to it.

The dance ended all too soon. Derek kept her close at his side as Auntie Win's incomparable portrait was unveiled to great applause and "oohs" and "aahs" from the crowd. Alix was pleased that Signor D'Orsini received several new commissions. And then everyone began moving toward the supper room. Derek took her arm and gently, inexorably, led her in the opposite direction.

"Ah, Derek, the supper room is—"

"I know," he said softly. "Supper can wait."

A tingling sense of expectation suffused her as she allowed him to lead her to the library. Candles danced in the sconces and a cheerful fire burned in the library grate. He closed the door quite resolutely and came to stand before her. He did not touch her, but he might well have, for all her every nerve ending was aware of him. She lowered her eyes.

"It is customary, you must know, for a gentleman to give a gift to the lady who has been chosen for him in the lottery. And if," he moved closer and put a finger under her chin, forcing her to meet his eyes, "and if the gentleman has one particular lady in mind, he might buy a very special gift, to help fate along, as it were."

She swallowed hard. He was so close, his eyes so intent, his voice so compelling. He dropped his finger from her chin and reached into his coat pocket, withdrawing a small, black velvet case.

She gazed at him wonderingly. His smile was intimate. "I would have given you this regardless of the outcome of the Valentine lottery, my dear. But I am very, very glad that fate and I are in accord."

He held the box out to her and her eyes filled with tears. "For me? Derek, I—"

"Open it," he said gently.

Her hands were shaking as she did so. There, on a bed of black velvet, nestled an exquisite gold pendant on a gold filigree chain. She sucked in her breath, amazed. Then very carefully, she picked the pendant up. Why, it was a perfect miniature recreation of . . . of the gilded cage she had painted! But here, on the pendant, the delicate little bird was perched on the *outside* of the cage, and there did not seem to be a door. At the bird's neck was a small, beautifully faceted ruby.

Derek watched the myriad expressions cross her lovely face. "Derek, you—you saw my painting," she rasped, looking up at him.

"Yes." He smiled ruefully. "Forgive me, my dear. It was the morning after you'd told me about your papa. I had to see it, because somehow I knew that I would truly come to know you if I did. Has—has D'Orsini told you yet how talented you are?"

She shook her head. "He said that I would find out for myself soon enough." She lowered her eyes again to the pendant.

He knew she was overcome with emotion, but he did not yet know what she was thinking. He schooled himself to patience. He had waited this long . . .

"Derek, the—the bird is outside the cage," she said in some puzzlement.

Now he gently took the pendant from her hands and reaching round, fastening it at her nape. The gilded cage nestled just above her bosom, just below the ruby at her throat. The effect was stunning. He let his hands slide from her nape to her shoulders. His eyes held hers. "Yes, Alix. The bird is outside, where it belongs. It is free now."

The look in her hazel eyes told him she still did not understand. Derek took a deep breath. It was time to say what had been in his heart for days. He stroked her soft cheek with his right hand. He felt her fire and knew he had to wait. That would come later.

"I have come to love you very much, Alix. And I wanted you to know that I would never keep you in that cage. If you want to paint or make clay pots or—or bring the Valentine's Day lottery to Greenvale, it would be fine with—What? What is it Alix?"

To his utter horror, two huge teardrops trickled from her eyes, followed by a veritable flood. What had he said? Had he so misjudged—? "Oh, Derek, Derek!" she cried, her hands creeping up onto his lapels. "You—you understood! I hardly knew myself what I was painting, but *you* did!"

He grasped her hands and held her tightly She was gazing at him in wonder, through her tears. But she still had not told him what he wanted to hear. She pressed her lips together as if to stem her tears or—or to keep from saying something he would not want to hear. Dear God, no . . .

"Derek, I did not know," she paused to sniffle loudly, "until this moment, how—how very much I love you."

"Alix!" He grabbed her now, his hands around her back, and pulled her close.

"I love you, Derek!" she exclaimed, and began to laugh through her tears. "I love you so much!"

"Oh, my heart!" he rasped, "my sweet, sweet heart!" And then he bent his head and began to kiss her. He strove for gentleness, but he caught fire the moment his lips touched hers. He kissed her deeply, drinking of her sweetness. His hands caressed her every curve in a frenzy he tried desperately to restrain. She moaned and yielded and molded her body to his, and he knew he had to stop, lest they end up on the floor right here in the library!

Somehow, he summoned the control to ease them apart. He could hardly breathe; her face was flushed, her hair tumbled.

"Derek, what is wrong?" She looked suddenly overset. "Do you—do you think me a . . . wanton?" she whispered.

"A wanton? Good God! Whatever put such a notion into your head?"

"That day when you kissed me in the studio, you pushed me away and I—I thought I had given you a disgust of me. And now—"

"You thought—Oh, my love!" He began to chuckle and wrapped his arms about her and hugged her tightly. "We have been dealing at cross purposes, I fear. I pushed you away, as you put it, because I feared that if I did not, I would not, *could* not, stop at all!"

"Oh!" she exclaimed, and then an impish look lit her hazel eyes. She wound her arms around his neck. "Truly, Derek?"

He grinned. "Truly, my sweetest heart. And that would not do at all until we are wed, you must know. Alix, you *will* marry me, will you not, and come home with me to Greenvale? I suddenly have lost my desire to go there at all, unless you come with me."

"I believe I had better marry you, Derek. For I would not wish to be accounted a wanton, and I do like kissing you so very much, you see."

He let forth a bark of laughter. "I am so very glad, Alix. So very glad."

And then his expression grew serious, as did hers, and he gently took her beautiful face in his hands and bent his head again.

"Two weeks," came that all-too-familiar voice. Derek jerked his head up in time to see Lady Hart sail into the room, followed by Sir Horace. "You'll have to wait two weeks until the banns are read, children dear!"

Derek did not even trouble to ask how she even knew banns were in order. He put his arm about Alix's shoulder, smiled reassuringly, and turned them both to face their hosts. Lady Hart—Auntie Win, Derek amended—was looking smug as the cat who'd swallowed the cream. Sir Horace was grinning, holding an unlit cigar in his left hand and bouncing a hothouse orange in his right.

"As I said, Win, my love, very ripe, this tropical fruit. Sweet. Only needed a few more days," Sir Horace said smugly.

Enlightenment dawned and Derek's lips twitched. "You may wish us happy, Sir Horace, Auntie Win. You, my dear ma'am, are a premier matchmaker."

Auntie Win's green eyes widened with innocent surprise. "I? Whatever can you mean, dear boy?"

"The lottery, Auntie Win," Alix put in. "You cannot mean to say it is truly fate."

"Oh, but of course 'tis fate, my dear. Fate is never wrong. As to matchmaking, it is a singular talent, I will own, and they say it, er, runs in families. Sisters and brothers, that sort of thing." Auntie Win's eyes twinkled.

"Papa!" Alix exclaimed, at almost the same time that Derek spoke.

"Martin?"

Lady Hart let forth a peal of laughter. "You do not think he would have subjected Alix to a winter voyage on a cargo ship for no good reason, do you?"

Derek roared with laughter and pulled Alix even closer as a wide smile suffused her face. "Oh! Papa! He—he knew! He was not casting me off! Oh, Derek, how I wish he could be here for the wedding!"

"That would take months, Alix!" Derek exclaimed, aghast.

"Oh, I know 'tis not possible. Two weeks is quite long enough," she said matter-of-factly, unaware of the barely suppressed grin on her uncle's face.

But even two weeks seemed a lifetime to Derek, especially with a woman who liked kissing so very much. "Ah, you know, Sir Horace, Auntie Win, I really do need to return to Greenvale straightaway. Perhaps a special license might be more the thing," Derek ventured.

Auntie Win looked shocked. "A special license! I should say

not! Why—"

"Come now, Win, my love," Sir Horace interjected. " 'Tis plain as pikestaff the boy cannot wait to, er, go to Greenvale. He's waited ten years, after all."

"All my life," Derek murmured, turning to Alix, drawing her into his arms.

"And all *my* life," Alix echoed, as she pulled his head down, and did what she liked best, quite oblivious of her scandalized aunt and her much amused uncle.

A Ring for Remembrance

by Georgina Devon

Carolly Stanhope-Jones caught up with her small charge just as six-year-old Alicia skittered to a halt on the main staircase landing. Alicia's heart-shaped face beamed with mischievousness.

"Minx!" Carolly said, smiling as she scooped the child up in her arms. "What am I going to do with you?"

"Love me, Caro, just love me," Alicia said, wrapping her arms around Carolly's neck.

The fresh smell of clean hair and warm child engulfed Carolly, making her heart contract painfully. Alicia was the child she would never have. Years ago, she'd thought to have children of her own, a golden-haired daughter or a black-haired son. She pushed the self-pity aside.

Turning to leave, Carolly's attention was diverted by the front door opening and someone stamping booted feet on the foyer tiles below. She glanced down at the newest guest for the Aldeboroughs' Valentine's Week house party.

Her breath caught. Her pulse galloped like a runaway horse. She felt the color leave her face. Instinctively, her free hand crept to the small bump in the fabric between her breasts, then fell away. She squeezed Alicia tighter.

"Caro . . ." Alicia protested.

Darting a look at Alicia, Carolly kissed her absentmindedly on the cheek before returning her gaze to the man. He was handing his many-caped greatcoat and beaver hat to the hovering butler. Underneath he wore a bottle green coat, buff breeches, and a pristine white shirt, the cravat done neatly and simply. His blue-black hair was cut short as a Corinthian would wear it.

He looked every year of the thirty Carolly knew him to be. He was still rangy, but his shoulders were filled out. And there was a frown between his eyes, eyes she knew were dark brown. In her memories he always smiled.

Alicia twisted to see what Carolly was looking at. In her high, child's voice, she said, "Ohh, Caro, isn't he handsome. I hope he's the one Elizabeth's to marry."

Embarrassment suffused Carolly at Alicia's words. The man looked up and smiled at the child, his countenance lighting. His gaze flicked over Carolly, dismissing her as quickly as he'd responded to the innocent exuberance of the girl. Then he followed the butler to the sitting room.

Pain ripped through Carolly. He had acted as though she were invisible. Had he forgotten her so easily?

Many times over the past seven years she'd envisioned their meeting again, and each time had played differently through her mind. Never had she imagined that his eyes would be void of recognition.

She squeezed her eyes shut to keep the tears from falling. The anguish was worse than anything she'd ever experienced. It was greater than when he'd first left her, more intense than what she'd felt when his promised letters never came. Once, she'd thought nothing could hurt her as deeply as finally admitting to herself that he wasn't returning to her.

She'd been wrong.

"Caro," Alicia said, putting her palm on Carolly's cheek, "let's go play."

Carolly forced herself to focus on the child in her arms. Alicia needed her. Alicia loved her. Alexander Phillip Staunton, Marquis of Claybrooke, could make merry with the Devil himself for all she cared now.

Carolly sighed with release as she sank onto the window

seat of the third-floor alcove. She rested her head on the many-paned glass and watched her breath fog it. With her forefinger, she drew designs: a snowflake like the ones clinging to the outside, a gnarled tree limb, a heart broken in two.

Realizing what she'd done, she scrubbed away the offending picture. She sat back, shivering in the cold emanating from the window. The wide hallway was uncomfortably chilly, too. She pulled the shawl tighter around her shoulders and leaned her head back against the dark oak paneling of the wall, wishing for a fleeting instant that she hadn't come.

But this was the only opportunity she would have to get away. Alicia was resting before dinner and the house guests were dressing.

Why did he have to come back into her life after seven years? Why, when she had finally eradicated him from her mind and heart?

Footsteps echoed hollowly on the wooden floor. With a start, she turned and peered into the dimness of the hallway. Who could possibly be walking around up here? She was the only one who ever came to this part of the house.

In the poor light she could make out *his* shoulders and the way *his* body moved as he paced toward her. What was he doing? Had he come looking for her? Or was he searching for a way to escape the memories of his past just as she was?

She knew when he realized she was present. His body stiffened.

Stopping next to her, he nodded. "Pardon me, ma'am. I didn't mean to intrude on your privacy."

He was the only person she knew who would understand that she was here for solitude. Anyone else would think her shirking her duties. The realization that the old bond of perception still existed softened the fact that he wasn't acknowledging her or their past relationship.

Well, then, neither would she. She rose and curtsied as was proper with someone of his rank. "Milord."

He smiled wryly at her. "News travels quickly in a country house."

She couldn't help smiling at his understatement. "News travels quickly in any house, milord. Especially when a marquis is involved."

"I suppose it does," he replied, studying her more closely. "You were on the landing this afternoon with the little girl?"

Her fingers clenched in the folds of her gown. The smile left her lips. Their commitment to each other had meant so little to him that now, only seven years later, he was having difficulty placing where he had seen her last—scant hours before.

Somehow, around the constriction in her throat, she managed to say, "Yes, I was."

"The governess?"

"Yes." It was a bald answer, but all she would vouchsafe.

"I'm Alex Staunton," he replied. "Your young charge is very engaging, but I imagine she's a handful."

He smiled at her, and her heart warmed—as it always had—making it easy for her to reply. "Alicia is a darling, but she tends to speak her mind."

He chuckled, a rich gravelly sound. "I've never known a child who wasn't brutally honest. That's their charm." Then, looking beyond her shoulder at the winter scene outside, he added with a cynical tinge in his voice, "That and their innocent enjoyment of life."

What had happened to him in the past years to disillusion him so? The Alex she had known was idealistic, believing there was good in everyone, not just children. She wanted to reach out and comfort him, much as she would have done for Alicia. His eyes, piercing and impersonal, focused back on her, forestalling any gesture she might have made.

"But enough of childhood and innocence. It's all transitory." He seemed to mentally shake himself. "I've intruded on your privacy enough. I was looking for some privacy of my own when I stumbled onto you. It's my experience that before long many of the guests here will soon wish themselves elsewhere. No one tolerates being cooped up in a single house with other people they don't know well. Or know too well. The snow and sleet that have been coming down since I arrived will only exacerbate people's nerves the more."

Even though she agreed with his assessment, her hackles rose at the implication that her employers, the Aldeboroughs, would be unable to properly entertain their guests. And for him there was always Elizabeth.

Carolly sat back down, lifting her chin only slightly. Purposely, she watched him as she said, "Well, milord, I know the Aldeboroughs have planned many activities. It shouldn't be hard for persons with breeding to keep themselves occupied." Meeting his stare with one of her own, she saw him withdraw at her sharp words.

"Your point is well taken, ma'am. I begin to feel less sorry for you in your dealings with Alicia."

Surprise at his plain speaking gave her pause. When she finally decided to retort, he was moving away.

She shrugged. Defending her employers had been the right thing to do. The Aldeboroughs treated her as a member of the family. She couldn't repay their kindnesses by allowing someone else to disparage them in any way, not even Alex.

But she sighed nonetheless. Her first real meeting with Alex and they parted on a hostile note. Rising, she headed for the stairs and her room. If she were to take Alicia down after dinner, she must change into her best frock. No matter that it was another gray kerseymere that was less worn than the one she had on.

That evening Carolly sat composedly on the Egyptian settee in a corner of the drawing room. Alicia sat beside her, a bright butterfly in her yellow muslin dress with her body in constant motion. Carolly took the child's hand and squeezed lightly, sympathizing with Alicia's excitement at being allowed to watch the adults.

Across from them, the roaring fire for his backdrop, stood Alex. The orange glow of the flames haloed him, showing to advantage the formal black evening dress he wore so well. A single lock of hair fell across his wide brow, bringing Carolly bittersweet memories of all the times she had brushed that errant strand back.

Beside him stood Elizabeth Aldeborough, the daughter of the house. His attention was focused on her. Carolly couldn't blame him. Elizabeth was a beautiful girl, all golden and pink, and with a sweet disposition.

They appeared deep in a conversation that Carolly couldn't hear, but she could guess what it was about from Elizabeth's animated features and the slow, provocative smile that curved Alex's lips. He was courting her former charge.

"Caro!" Alicia's excited squeal broke into Carolly's melancholy.

"Yes, dear," Carolly said, keeping her voice free of emotion with an effort.

"Elizabeth is bringing *him* here!"

Him could only be Alex. Carolly looked up with both anticipation and dread. They were coming: Elizabeth with her hand on his forearm, her blond head tilted back as she looked up at the tall man; Alex with his dark head bent down to hear what she was saying. Carolly felt as though a giant hand was squeezing the air from her lungs.

"Caro," Elizabeth said, her eyes twinkling, "I want you to meet someone special." Her adoring gaze returned to the man standing closely by her side. "Alexander Phillip Staunton, Marquis of Claybrooke. Alex, this is our governess, Carolly Stanhope-Jones. Caro to us."

"Pleased to make your acquaintance," he said, in tones that were deep and resonate.

Even with her disillusionment, Carolly couldn't stop the tingles from running down her spine at the sound of his voice. He had always been able to make her react this way. Her lips curved sardonically at her weakness.

Carolly rose from her seat and curtsied. "Milord."

"Don't stand on my account, Miss Stanhope-Jones. It's not as though we are at Court or even in London."

Neither in word nor look did he give away that they had already met in the alcove. His dark, chocolate brown eyes twinkled at her, inviting her to share with him the heady secret in spite of the acrid note on which they'd parted.

He had never held onto his anger once the cause for it was past. It had been an endearing trait to the young Carolly and still had the power to charm her now. She bit her lip to stop the smile that came so readily for him. Once she might have entered willy-nilly into his little game—and had done so many a time—but no more.

Instead, she mumbled, "Yes, milord," and sat abruptly, her eyes downcast to hide the beginnings of anger at him and at her own response to him. How dare he refuse to acknowledge their past and in the next instant try to rekindle the camaraderie that had once been theirs. How dare she be so weak as to almost succumb to his blandishments.

"And this," Elizabeth continued blithely, "is my sister Alicia. She's all of six and very much in awe of you, Alex."

Alicia bounced off the settee and bobbed a deep curtsy. Her grin was so huge that dimples showed on each cheek. "Pleased to meet you, milord." She looked disparagingly at her older sister. "And I'm not in *awe* of him."

Very solemnly, Alex took her offered hand and lightly squeezed it. "My pleasure, Miss Alicia."

Alicia continued to babble, telling him everything about her day from the moment she woke up until the present. In confidential tones, she finished with, "Soon I shall have to retire. Caro is very strict and makes sure that I'm in bed by eight. I tried to talk her into letting me stay up late because you're here, but she won't listen." She cast a sideways glance at her governess. "Milord," she wheedled, "perhaps you could make her let me stay?"

He laughed outright.

Carolly's heart ached at the sound, as familiar to her heart as though it were seven years earlier. All the fury of minutes before turned to ashes in her mouth.

"Miss Alicia," he finally said, his mouth straight once more, but a decided glint still in his dark eyes, "you're a charming little baggage. However, I shan't put Miss Stanhope-Jones in such an uncomfortable position. I'm sure that she's right and eight o'clock is a perfect bedtime. But I will look forward to talking with you tomorrow."

Why couldn't he have been arrogant and officious, Carolly thought as he made a bow to Alicia and then another one, equally polite, to her. His manner and charm were still the same, which only made it harder for her to maintain her anger. And without her fury at his mistreatment of her, there was nothing to protect her foolish heart from him.

As soon as his back was to them, Carolly rose and took Alicia to make her curtsy to Sir Walter and Lady Aldeborough.

"My dear Carolly," Lady Aldeborough said, her apple red cheeks and magnificent bearing attesting to the beauty she'd been and the handsome woman she still was, "I saw Elizabeth introduce you to Claybrooke. He's such a handsome man and *so* well-mannered. I do *so* fervently hope he comes up to scratch."

Carolly grinned at Lady Aldeborough's usage of cant. It never ceased to amuse her when her mistress fell into the sporting tongue of her sixteen-year-old twin sons.

"Harumph!" Sir Walter's eyes followed the movement of his daughter and her hoped-for beau. "Claybrooke's an exceptional match, marquis and all, but can't say as how I entirely approve. Man's got a past."

The breath caught in Carolly's throat. Did they know? It all happened so long ago. She thought no one knew. And it wasn't as though the daughter of an Oxford don was grist for the gossip mill.

Lady Aldeborough laid a hand on her spouse's arm. "Now dear, not so loud. And it's not as though his past is sordid, only sad."

"Sad past's usually a sordid past, ma'am."

Carolly's curiosity was thoroughly piqued. She looked questioningly at them, even as she sent Alicia toward the cake table with a little push.

In a conspiratorial whisper, Lady Aldeborough said, "I don't suppose it would hurt to tell you, Carolly. It's not as though everyone in this room doesn't already know. They are too polite to mention it." She paused, her gaze seeking her subject who was once more lounging against the fireplace. Then, in hushed, dramatic tones, she pronounced, "Lord Claybrooke has lost his memory."

"I beg your pardon?" The question was automatic. *Lost his memory.* Carolly felt as though the earth had opened up beneath her feet and swallowed her whole, leaving her in Stygian darkness with no hope of finding her way out.

"Yes!" Lady Aldeborough breathed. "In the Peninsula." Her eyes rounded and her full lips puckered. "It's so terribly sad. The poor man. They found him wandering after Salamanca. It was days before he even remembered who he was. Later, his memory of his childhood came back, and he knew his name and all, but it seems he couldn't recollect the last five years of his life, the time he spent at Oxford and the time he spent in the army. And that was six years ago and he still doesn't remember. *So* sad."

Everything fell into place at once for Carolly. Through some miracle of self-control, she kept herself from crumbling into a sodden heap as the anger that had sustained her evaporated to be replaced by devastating comprehension of just how truly finished her past love affair was.

Alex hadn't deserted her and then forgotten her. A twist of fate had erased her from his mind, and there was nothing she could do to change that.

In spite of her attempt to remain outwardly unmoved, something must have shown, for Lady Aldeborough said comfortingly, "My dear Carolly, I know how horrible it sounds. Believe me, I was equally appalled when I first heard."

Carolly looked dazedly at her employer, trying desperately to gather her scattered thoughts. There was no reason for her, the governess, to be distraught by the Marquis of Claybrooke's memory loss. "Yes, ma'am. It is terrible, but he doesn't seem to be suffering."

"Harumph!" Sir Walter interjected. "Should hope not, since he seems bent on asking for Elizabeth's hand."

The reminder of Alex's impending betrothal was a double

blow to Carolly's already raw emotions. She couldn't help but turn to stare at Alex, the source of all her happiness, all her sorrow.

He was bending forward, listening to an elderly lady seated near the fire. The discussion must have been serious, for his face was solemn and intense, accentuating the sharp angle of cheekbone and the jutting strength of chin she remembered so well.

He had looked like that when he proposed.

Carolly slammed memory's door shut. Blinking away the tears that insisted on forming, she found that her emotional stamina was depleted beyond endurance. She had to get Alicia and get out of there.

Gathering the child up, Carolly ushered her out of the room and up to the nursery. With a minimum of fuss, she got Alicia into bed and read the evening's story. Then she sang a lullaby softly, as was her habit.

The mantel clock chimed twelve before Carolly realized that Alicia was in the Sandman's arms and that she could go to her own room. Rising from the chintz-cushioned chair by the dying fire, she pulled her woolen shawl tighter around her shoulders. Then she went through the connecting door to her own room where midnight's chill lay like a mist.

She should go to sleep also, but her mind and emotions were in a turmoil. So much had happened that day, and all of it had turned her world upside down.

Like a wraith in her gray kerseymere gown, she moved to stand in front of a tall mirror. It was silvered in places, but still a luxury for her. Picking up a brace of candles, she studied her reflection.

A tall, angular woman with eyes the color of pewter stared out at her. The eyelids were heavy and thickly fringed with mouse brown lashes. Her full, pouty lips turned down, but the remnants of laugh brackets faintly showed at the corners. She looked tired, almost haggard.

How did Alex see her? It was something she didn't want to contemplate. Alex probably didn't even notice her next to

Elizabeth's beauty and youth.

Carolly twisted away from her reflection and clenched her teeth to keep from uttering a despondent moan. She would *not* be so self-pitying.

With long strides, she went to the unadorned oak wardrobe. Using equally efficient movements, she divested herself of her gown and put on a plain, white wool sleeping shift, ignoring the ring hanging on a chain around her neck. Then she quickly got into bed.

It was no use. She couldn't sleep. Her mind refused to stop churning, and her emotions defied her every attempt to rule them.

Strange how time changed everything, she mused. Just seven years ago she would never have imagined that the woman in the mirror could ever be her. At seventeen, she'd been loved deeply and completely by a man whom she trusted with her very soul. She'd almost been beautiful.

Then Alex's father had stepped in and separated them. She and Alex had vowed that their time apart would not be for long and that until they were reunited each would write the other of their undying love.

A bitter laugh escaped her tight throat.

What foolish children they had been. The golden glow of their everlasting love had sustained her through the initial separation. It supported her when her father called her a whore and disowned her, sending her to the parish poorhouse. Even when Alex's promised letters never arrived, although she wrote each day and begged for the paper to write on and the pence to post them, her belief in his love gave her strength.

Eventually, she convinced herself that his betrayal no longer mattered. She made a life for herself without him, and she was content. She had a family who treated her as one of their own despite her position, and she had a child to love with all her heart. Alicia received all the love Carolly had once lavished on Alex, all the love Carolly had once hoped to give children of her own.

Then Lady Aldeborough's revelation. Like an old wound

torn open again, the knowledge of Alex's memory loss was a gaping hole in her heart. Until that moment, she hadn't realized that deep in the part of her self where all hurts were buried she had secretly nurtured a small seed of hope that some day, some way, he would return to her. And now, in the cold darkness of her lonely governess's bed, she must finally admit to herself that Alex was never coming back for her.

Turning her head into the pillow, Carolly allowed herself one tear of despair. No more. Fate had stepped in and irrevocably separated them. Where there was no memory of love, there could be no love. She must accept that and go on with her life—as she had already done once before.

But it was hard, so very hard.

Dressed for the day, Carolly paused, then pulled the chain from under her bodice. No longer able to resist the temptation, she gazed long and hard at the small golden ring hanging suspended from the golden links. It was Alex's christening ring. A plight of his love.

She should throw the thing away; it brought too much pain. Even when the two years of waiting had expired and Alex hadn't come for her, she hadn't been able to rid herself of the ring. She still couldn't.

She moved to undue the lock but instead found her fingers tucking the ring safely back under her gown.

"Carolly!"

A small whirlwind rushed into the room and wrapped herself around Carolly's legs.

"What, sweetheart?"

Carolly bent down to embrace a just-awakened Alicia. When Alicia's small sleep-rosy face lifted to her, Carolly couldn't resist the urge to kiss the child. Alicia was her world.

"Carolly, today I get to talk with the marquis." She paused and uncertainly entered her eyes. "Do you think he really meant what he said last night? That he's looking forward to seeing me again?"

Stroking the hair back from Alicia's forehead, Carolly said,

"I'm sure of it, sweetheart." The Alex she knew had been a sincere person. She didn't think that part of him had changed. And even if it had, she didn't think his honor would allow him to disappoint the child. And if it did, then she would quickly set him straight!

"Oh, Carolly, I'm so excited!"

Carolly laughed, her mood lightened just by Alicia's presence. "Then you'd best get back to your room and let Nanny get you ready for the day."

"Oh, yes," Alicia said, bounding back the way she'd come.

Carolly watched the child disappear behind the door to the nursery. A little bit of sunshine went with Alicia. Still, she wasn't going to allow herself to mope. In fact, she would go down to the breakfast room to eat. Lady Aldeborough had been very adamant that she was to continue on as though there wasn't a houseful of guests, and that meant eating breakfast with anyone who was up early.

At first, Carolly had intended to keep to herself until after the Valentine Ball and all the guests were gone, but now she readily admitted that the last thing she needed was solitude. It would allow her to dwell on thoughts best avoided.

Entering the breakfast room, Carolly stiffened at the sight of a broad, brown-clad back. She should have remembered that he rose early, too. If she moved quietly enough, she would be able to leave before he realized anyone was here.

Just at that moment, he turned to face her. Carolly's shoulders tensed from the strain of having to face him so soon. She'd hoped to avoid him for the rest of the house party, but that had been foolish, considering that every evening she would have to take Alicia to spend time with the guests.

His voice still full of early morning roughness, he said, "Good day, Miss Stanhope-Jones."

"Milord." She made a dip of a curtsy, stiffening her spine and lifting her chin. There was no retreating, and she refused to act as though he intimidated her in the least.

He smiled wryly at her. "It appears that we are the first to rise."

"Yes, milord," she mumbled, making her way to the side table where the covered chafing dishes were. If anything, it was harder to speak to him knowing about his loss than it had been yesterday in the alcove when she'd simply been mad at him.

"May I serve you some kippers?" he asked, suiting action to words before she could reply.

Her immediate thought was to tell him not to put things on her plate. Fast on its heels was the memory of their first meeting. Ostensibly, he'd come for tea, but really it had been to discuss antiquities with her father. She had served tea and cakes to him, plain Alex Staunton then. He had taken his plate and promptly put the last scone onto her nearby plate and handed it to her. Surprised, she looked at him, truly looked at him. The warmth and appreciation in his dark eyes sparked her own response. Love at first sight? It had felt like it at the time.

He put the kipper on her plate, pulling her thoughts back to the present. It was all she could do to mutter, "Thank you," her chest tight with unshed tears that she'd thought she had banished last night.

Before she knew it, they were seated next to each other at the long table that seated twenty. What could she say to this man?

"Miss Stanhope-Jones, where's your charge? I'm looking forward to seeing her today."

Carolly stopped her spoon of soft-boiled egg in mid-air. "Alicia will be thrilled to hear that, milord. She was as excited as a puppy today because she'll get to see you."

He chuckled. "I'm flattered. It's been my experience that children are oftentimes more critical than adults." He took a sip of black coffee. "And between us, please, no formality. I'm Claybrooke to everyone else. There's no reason the same can't apply to you."

"I . . . I." She didn't know what to say. Somehow, through all her agonizing over him, it had never occurred to her that he would tell her to call him by his title. She wasn't sure she could. When she'd known him, he'd been the younger son. Claybrooke was his father's name and should have been his older brother's, but his father and brother died from smallpox within days of each other. At the time she heard the story, it had been all she could do to keep herself from writing to him with her sympathy.

As though taking pity on her, he added, "But if you find Claybrooke too much of a mouthful, I answer to Alex. I would have said it first, but you strike me as a woman who stands on formality. I didn't want to offend you."

For the first time that morning, she gazed fully at him. Even though he was smiling at her, almost as though the whole conversation was a large joke, she could see that he was tired. Dark circles ringed his eyes and lines of exhaustion bracketed his mouth.

Unconsciously, she found herself returning his smile even though it hadn't been her intention to do so. What she truly wanted to do was smooth the black hair from his forehead and find out why he wasn't sleeping well. Instead, she said, "Milord, your given name is entirely too personal for a governess to use when addressing a peer of the realm. But I'll try to use Claybrooke."

"Good," he replied, as though he honestly felt that way.

Her discomfort began to ease.

"Oh, here you are, Claybrooke," Elizabeth Aldeborough said, entering.

Elizabeth's bright, golden beauty made Carolly feel as though the sun had risen in the small confines of the breakfast room. The young woman reminded Carolly of Alex's reason for being there, causing Carolly's heart, that most treacherous of organs, to contract painfully.

"Please excuse me," Carolly said, unable to remain and watch the lovers. "Alicia is sure to be ready for lessons by now." She rose and nodded briefly at the marquis and then smiled warmly at Elizabeth.

Without looking back, Carolly left. Reaching the stairs, she mounted them with determination. In none of her soul-searching of last night or the last seven years had she considered that she and Alex might simply be on friendly terms if they met again. She didn't know whether to be happy or sad at the possibility.

That evening, Carolly and Alicia were late arriving in the drawing room. Carolly tried valiantly to suppress her amusement over the cause for their tardiness. Alicia had spent the better part of thirty minutes trying to decide between her blue velvet and purple wool frocks. The child was determined to impress the marquis.

"Oh, Caro," Alicia trilled from her perch on the settee, "the marquis is looking our way."

Carolly turned to see if Alicia was correct or merely allowing her wishes to carry her away. It was true. Alex was taking his leave of a dowager, but his gaze kept returning to their corner.

He was magnificent: broad shoulders and narrow hips were accented by a leanness that she found immensely attractive. Had always found attractive. His lips curved up at the corners, lighting the craggy planes of his face and making him seem approachable. He was headed their way.

For the first time in the six years she'd been with the Aldeboroughs, Carolly wished she had a gown that was more becoming to her brown hair and wan complexion than her regimented, governess gray wool. Even the small lace trim on the high neckline that she'd saved two months' wages to purchase didn't seem as elegant and becoming as she'd thought when she had painstakingly sewn it on.

"Ladies," he said in his deep voice.

He bowed over Alicia's extended hand, but his eyes looked at Carolly as though he could see beyond her cool exterior and into her very soul. Carolly flushed to the roots of her tightly pulled-back hair. Did he know how ugly she felt in her drab costume? Did he know that more than anything, she wanted to look attractive to him as she once had? It was too humiliating to meet his eyes when his opinion mattered so much and should not matter at all.

"Ohhh," Alicia enthused, "I was so hoping you would come over, Lord Claybrooke."

The child fairly squirmed in her seat, providing a focus for Carolly's disjointed thoughts and emotions. She couldn't help but take pity on Alicia's extreme case of hero worship.

"Call me Alex," he said to Alicia in perfectly solemn tones.

When Carolly searched his face to make sure he truly meant for Alicia to be so familiar, she was caught by the twinkle in his eyes. He really liked Alicia. Anxiety Carolly hadn't realized she felt flowed out as her clenched hands relaxed in her lap. Alex wouldn't hurt or disappoint Alicia.

With a gentle smile for the two, Carolly rose and excused herself. She would give them time to get to know each other without the distraction of another person's presence. She would also give herself time to regain her equilibrium. It shouldn't matter to her what Alex Staunton thought of her.

When she returned to collect her charge, Alicia piped up. "Carolly, Alex and I are agreed that we are best of friends." She paused before adding in an awed voice, "I've never had a boy for a bosom beau."

Carolly couldn't keep from chuckling at Alicia's ingenuousness. A deeper rumble from Alex drew her attention from the child. He was amused by Alicia also, but his eyes held a special warmth that Carolly remembered seeing in them long ago. It discommoded her and made her nervous.

"If you will excuse us, milord," she said hastily. "It's past time for Alicia to leave."

She hastened the child from the room. But even as they reached the nearby door, Carolly could swear she heard him say softly, "Call me Alex, please."

His request followed her up the stairs and into Alicia's room. The child was so excited about her newfound friend that she was difficult to calm down enough for sleep, but eventually Carolly's patience won and Alicia fell into slumber.

Gently, so as not to awaken her, Carolly brushed back Alicia's stray curls before bending down to kiss the child's flushed cheek. She knew Alicia would be tired in the morning, but it would be a good sort of tired, the kind of exhaustion brought about by a surfeit of happiness.

Leaving the nursery, Carolly decided that she needed some calmness and privacy where she could be sure no one would come looking for her. She needed the retreat of her third-floor alcove. However, this time she collected a heavy shawl before making her way from the nursery wing to the North wing where the alcove was.

Carolly turned the corner and halted. Instinctively, she knew someone was there. Covering her single candle with one hand, she strained her eyes to see in the dim hallway. Someone was in the alcove. Like herself, this person had brought a single candle that illuminated his face and threw a larger-than-life shadow on the wall to his left.

It was Alex. But why would he come up here? Why wasn't he with the rest of the guests who had all moved to the music room after she and Alicia left?

Stepping back behind the corner, Carolly leaned back against the wall, closing her eyes to block out the sight of him. She knew why he was there. He needed solitude—just as she so frequently did. That was one of the first traits they had realized they shared.

And because of that shared need, she could not intrude on him, no matter how much she might want the comfortable familiarity of her alcove. With a soft sigh of resignation, she opened her eyes and turned back the way she'd come. She would lock her door and not answer if a servant knocked. It was better this way. She wasn't capable of any more emotional intimacy with Alex.

The next day, Carolly studiously avoided any place or gathering where she might encounter Alex. She required time and distance to place her awakening emotions into perspective. While she knew they would never be lovers again, their many similarities, coupled with his overtures of friendship, hinted that they might conceivably become friends. She wasn't sure she could do that.

Meanwhile, as troubled as she was about Alex, Alicia still

needed her love and care. Alicia was a very active child, and just because there was a foot of snow on the ground didn't mean the child should be without physical activity. Carolly convinced Alicia to play tag with her in the ballroom. They were chasing each other around the room when Alex's voice intruded.

"You ladies have been avoiding me today."

They both turned startled faces towards him. Carolly was speechless, wondering how he had found them and whether she dared to stop the game and take Alicia back to the nursery. But Alicia had other plans.

"Alex!" Alicia launched herself at him, and luckily, he caught her. "Play tag with us. You can be It."

Putting his hands on his hips in mock affront, he stated, "Me, It? Oh, no. If I'm to play, someone else must be It." He turned a mischievous and inquiring look on Carolly. "Miss Stanhope-Jones, for instance."

Carolly pretended equal indignation at his suggestion. "Me? I think not."

"You two are so funny," Alicia said between giggles. "But you can't fool me. I know you're only make-believing."

"Not I," said Alex.

"Nor I," added Carolly.

That only sent Alicia into fresh peals of laughter. When she paused for breath, she gasped, "Then I'll be It."

"Good," Alex said. "But first, you must tell me the rules."

Since Alicia was unable to speak because she had started laughing again, Carolly explained. "The ballroom is the boundary; you may not leave it. If you're tagged, you're It. Wood is safe."

Before either of the adults could move, Alicia sprang at them, tagging Alex. Her young face alight with enjoyment, she danced away, caroling, "Alex is It. Alex is It. Catch me if you can."

With an exaggerated growl, he charged after the child, not quite fast enough to catch her, but close enough to keep her moving. The two circled the room, Alicia shrieking her enjoyment and Alex saying, "I'm going to get you!"

Carolly stood firmly planted next to a 'safe' wooden table that was pushed against the wall. The two were having so much fun, she had no intentions of doing more than watching and shouting encouragement to Alicia when Alex got too close.

After thirty minutes both participants were panting and mopping perspiration from their foreheads in spite of the coolness in the large room.

Realizing that the players were getting overly warm, Carolly said, "That's enough for now, Alicia. Lord Claybrooke probably has other things to attend."

Both turned startled and disappointed countenances her way. Carolly grinned ruefully but stuck to her guns.

They reached her, and Alicia clung to Carolly's hand while Alex performed a mocking bow of submission. If his eyes hadn't been brimming with amusement when he finally straightened, Carolly would have thought him angry at her termination of the game.

"Alicia," Alex said, affectionately ruffling the girl's hair with his fingers, "do you know how tag began?"

Carolly just stared at him, wondering why it should matter to a six-year-old, but recognizing the old Alex in this question. Myths and religion had been his passion at Oxford. He and her father had stayed up till dawn on many an occasion debating the origin of modern traditions and superstitions.

Alicia was thrilled to keep her idol with her as long as possible, no matter what she had to endure to do so. "No, Alex. Please tell me."

Carolly almost laughed out loud at the girl's blatant adoration. Had Carolly asked the question, Alicia would have indicated no interest whatsoever.

Alex smiled down at Alicia and drew her closer to his side where he wiped a smudge from her nose with his handkerchief. "Do you believe in magic, Alicia?"

She nodded her head.

"Then you'll believe in this." He lowered his voice and drew her into the circle of his arm. "Long ago, ancient people—people who lived before our grandparents—believed that witches were real. They also believed that some trees had magical powers and could protect them from harm. Tag is supposed to be people running from witches, and having wood as 'safe' is supposed to represent the magical trees that can protect against everything."

Alicia's eyes widened with wonder and not a little bit of fear. But she stood bravely.

Carolly smothered her sigh of exasperation. It was a nice tale and typically what she remembered the young Alex doing, but Alicia was going to have difficulty sleeping tonight.

Briskly, Carolly interrupted. "Well, milord, that's a very interesting story, but Alicia must return to the nursery for her lessons."

He must have sensed her displeasure, for he quickly added to their retreating backs, "I'll give Alicia a little wooden figure I have with me. She can sleep with it at night and it will protect her from all evil."

Both females turned to stare at him.

Alicia was delighted at the idea of a gift from Alex. "Thank you, Alex," she trilled, her step becoming light and bouncy.

Carolly looked at him with dawning respect. He had grown since she knew him. Before it would have never occurred to him that his tale might have frightened the child. "Thank you, milord. That's very considerate of you."

His answering smile was enough to melt Carolly's bones, let alone the barriers she was so carefully erecting against his charm. When she noticed the tired droop of his heavy eyelids, the wall of her resolve crumbled a bit more. Why wasn't he sleeping? And why couldn't she put him and his problems out of her mind? He was no longer her concern.

Carolly leaned back against the wall of the alcove, her feet on the seat and her knees pulled up so that her arms rested across them. Three days ago Alex arrived and her world became topsy-turvy.

She turned to look out the many-paned window. A full moon shone on the snow-covered lawn, turning it to silver. Cold and pristine, the landscape resembled her life. That wasn't quite true.

With a sigh, she looked away. She had Alicia to love, and possibly, just possibly, she would have Alex for a friend. Playing children's games with them yesterday, he definitely seemed to want a friendship with her. But did she want friendship with him, the man she had once loved with a passion that ruined her? She didn't know.

"Miss Stanhope-Jones?"

Him! With a jerk of her complete body, she looked up. She'd been so absorbed in her thoughts she hadn't heard him. Never taking her eyes from him, she hastily put her feet on the floor and smoothed back the strands of hair that had come loose from her tight bun. He set his candlestick down near the seat, and his features changed from hesitant to amused. A chuckle started deep in his throat. It sent little shivers of pleasure coursing through her veins.

"No need to straighten your hair. It's only me and, besides, you're perfectly presentable."

"Milord," she breathed, "I wasn't expecting company."

Chagrin chased the laughter away from his face. "I know." He paused, his eyes flitting to the vacant spot beside her and then back to her. "Would you mind if I joined you?"

Was this an even more blatant overture of friendship? How could she refuse him? "Of course not, milord."

He sat down, careful not to brush her skirts with his thighs. "Do you find it that hard to call me Alex or Claybrooke? I find that having come into the title late, and with no expectations of ever doing so, that 'milord' always makes me wonder who's being spoken to."

"Oh, dear," she said, beginning to relax because of his shared insight. This was the Alex she remembered, and it was impossible for her to be stiff and formal with him no matter what the past had been. "I hadn't thought how awkward it must feel to be called by a name that has never been yours."

"Deuced awkward, take my word on it."

He grinned at her, a lopsided curving of his lips that quickened her pulse. That, combined with his familiarity, made her feel diffident, and she could feel the heat rising from her neck into her cheeks. "Well, since I'm to call you Alex, please call me Carolly."

"I would be honored, Carolly."

There was such warmth in his regard that she began to wonder if friendship was all he offered. The idea made her even hotter, and her hands curled in her lap to still their urge to reach for him. She was being silly.

Taking a deep breath, she said, "Now that that's over, what brings you here tonight? Everyone is still in the drawing room playing charades, and I would imagine that your absence is being noted."

He sighed and turned away from her inquiring gaze. "I'm sure that you're correct about my being missed, but to tell the truth . . ." he turned back to her, all solemnity, "I don't give a fig. I told you once that long before the party was over people would be chomping at the bit to leave."

When he didn't continue, Carolly finished the sentence for him. "And now, after only three days, you're ready to depart."

His nod of agreement sent hope surging through Carolly. Perhaps he didn't intend to offer for Elizabeth after all. Perhaps, she didn't have to contemplate spending the next twelve years of her life watching him with another woman. Remorse followed quickly as she remembered Elizabeth. The young woman would be devastated if Alex didn't offer for her. Carolly cared too much for her former charge to want her unhappiness, even at the expense of her own.

"However, I have an obligation to the Aldeboroughs."

Once more, he turned from her so that she couldn't read the emotions behind his words. But she didn't need to. He had as much as told her that he intended to ask for Elizabeth's hand.

"We all have obligations." Her voice was as void of emotion as she could make it, but something in it must have registered with him.

Turning eyes full of sympathy and compassion on her, he asked, "And what have your obligations been, Carolly, besides raising another woman's children?"

His question totally nonplussed her. Did he somehow know about them? She didn't see how it was possible since the only people who knew, their fathers and his brother, were all dead. Still, flustered as she was, it was impossible to respond properly. "I . . . I . . . that is to say. . . ."

He put his hand over one of her clenched fists. Heat and sparks skittered up Carolly's skin from the contact. "Pardon me, Carolly. I didn't mean to pry."

Without conscious volition, she yanked her hand free. She regretted it immediately as he jerked away from her, his jaw twitching. But she couldn't undue her action. The feel of his skin against hers had been both exciting and debilitating. Temptation lay down that avenue. She dared not risk it.

She tried calming herself by counting to ten backwards. "I'm sorry. You took me by surprise. That's all."

He regarded her with skepticism, and she hoped he would change the subject. It was rapidly becoming harder for her to keep an emotional distance from him.

"I overstepped the bounds. My apologies." He stood, his back to her, and strode down the hall, pivoted, and strode back. "It's just that I find it very easy to talk to you." He shrugged. "I feel as though I've known you for a long time, and that's something I've experienced with very few people."

She watched him, wondering what he was trying to do. She didn't think she could take much more of this without breaking down, and that was something she wouldn't do. Yet, even as she tried to withdraw from him, his features took on a ravaged look that pulled at her heart.

Rising, she moved to him and laid a hand briefly on the fine wool worsted of his jacket. As ephemeral as the touch was, she could feel the tight bunching of his muscles.

"Alex," she said softly, unsure of what to say. "Alex, I'm sorry I flinched. It was nothing you did. It was me. I'm not used to being touched—except by Alicia," she finished with a wry smile.

"Ah, Alicia," he said the name slowly, letting the unease flow from him at the same time.

His eyes met Carolly's and she stood transfixed. His look held such tenderness and suffering that for this small moment in time, she let herself believe that it was seven years before. His palm came up and cupped her face.

"Your eyes are beautiful, Carolly. They're so large and lustrous. The exact shade of gray as the sky before a storm." He rubbed his thumb along her jaw. "Someone has hurt you badly."

Mesmerized by the rough feel of his thumb along the sensitive line of her face, his words were a distant, faint echo in her mind, muted by the physical awareness his touch and closeness evoked. Flames licked along her skin, traveling downward until they became a fire in her stomach.

"Do you want to tell me about it?" he asked, his voice deep and rough with emotion.

"Wha . . . ?" What was he saying? She was like a dreamer awakening from her heart's desire.

"Can you trust me enough to tell me what has hurt you so badly that it's dulled the bright promise of your eyes?"

Comprehension crashed in on her. She pulled away, twisting on her heel so that her stiff back faced him. Tears threatened to spill over. He was so sympathetic, and his words were so poetic—as they'd always been. *Always been.*

"What are you trying to do?" she asked, all her hurt and confusion in the words. "I'm a governess. You're practically engaged to Elizabeth. Why are you pursuing me and asking me questions that no one else would even care to?" She turned back to confront him, her tears held in check by determination only. "Why?"

Emotions she did not associate with him—puzzlement, uncertainty—flowed across his face.

"I don't know."

Two days later his words continued to reverberate in her thoughts. *I don't know.*

Carolly stared through the window at the full moon. It cast silvery crowns on the trees and shrubs below, creating mysterious shadows where none existed during the day.

Pulling her feet up onto the cushion, she hid her face in her cupped hands on top of her knees. She knew Alex wasn't interested in her romantically, but she wasn't one of the family, no matter how much the Aldeboroughs might make it seem she was. Therefore, Alex should not be prying into her private life. He shouldn't even care about it.

Her thoughts were interrupted by his voice.

"Carolly?"

She lifted her head to look at him. Standing several feet away, he seemed almost hesitant.

"Carolly, may I please sit down?"

It was déjà vu, except that this time he sat in the small space between her still-raised feet and the opposite wall before she could tell him not to.

Instead of answering his question, she asked one of her own, the same one that had been circling in her thoughts for what seemed to have been forever. She had to have an answer to it so she could go on with the life she had carved out for herself.

"Why?" she asked, referring to his familiarity with her.

His hands were on his thighs, and she could see the indentations where his fingers pressed tightly. Was he under as much strain as she was?

He didn't pretend to misunderstand her, only cleared his throat before speaking. "I don't know, but . . ." His eyes locked with hers. "I feel as though I've known you forever."

She gasped, one hand rushing to her chest and the small mound made by the ring under her garment. Had his memory returned?

"I know this sounds forward," he said, his knuckles white, "but it's not meant to be. I . . . would like to be your friend, and I don't feel that way about many people."

"Friend?" It didn't surprise her. For a while now, she'd thought he was trying to be friends. But there were other people involved, too. "What about Elizabeth? Is it fair to her to spend this much time with me?"

He shrugged, but his gaze shifted from hers. "Elizabeth's having an enjoyable time with the other guests. She and young FitzWilliam are singing a duet this very moment. But that's only an aside." He looked back at Carolly. "I'm not ashamed of anything you and I have said or done."

His denial of anything compromising between them made Carolly's question of fairness to Elizabeth seem almost presumptuous, as though she wanted something unseemly to be between herself and Alex. Her skin hot with embarrassment, she put both feet firmly on the ground. "I didn't mean to imply that there was anything improper between us, only that I'm the governess, not a member of the family or another guest. Friends of the family don't usually ask me the sort of question you did, nor do they seek out my company."

He smiled ruefully at her. "I realize that, but then they probably don't find you as restful and soothing as I do, either. The first time I stumbled across you in this alcove I knew that you and I had something in common. Watching you and talking with you has only confirmed my first impression."

How could she deny him this? Even on the periphery of the entertainment as she'd been, she'd still sensed a distance in him, an aura of not truly belonging to the house party. And he was only asking for friendship. There was nothing dishonorable in that.

Taking a deep breath, she said, "I suppose there's nothing wrong with a friendship. And you're right. We do share a need for solitude." She smiled tentatively at him, warmed by the look of deep appreciation and almost relief that her words evoked in his expression. "I use this time to regain strength sapped by dealing with large numbers of people."

"That's exactly how I feel."

At his words, she could almost feel the bond of shared emotions between them. They were in such accord that her original misgivings began to slip away. Everything would be fine.

Convinced of the rightness of what they were beginning, Carolly returned his regard without subterfuge. Staring into his eyes, she watched his pupils, already dilated from the sparse lighting provided by one flickering candle, enlarge until no brown showed. All she had to do was lean forward and she would lose herself in their depths. The realization brought her up short.

They just were friends.

"Is something wrong?" he asked, his voice heavy with concern as he touched her arm briefly with his fingers.

The physical contact shot through Carolly like lightning through a black night. It brought her mental picture of them as friends into sharp focus. He hadn't meant anything by the touch, only comfort. She was the one taking every gesture, every word out of context.

"No," she finally managed, "nothing's wrong." But even as she said the words, she knew that if fleeing wouldn't make her look cowardly, she would do so. She needed time to adjust to the idea of him as something less than a lover.

"That's good," he said, leaning back against the frosted windowpane. "Brrr. This glass is like ice." He sat back up. "It reminds me of the winter I spent in Spain." His complexion darkened, and his eyes took on a haunted look that accentuated the lines of tiredness bracketing them.

"You fought in the Peninsula." She meant it as a plain statement of fact, an opening for him to elaborate on what it was that caused him pain.

"Yes," he said, rubbing his eyes. "I lost my best friend there." He laughed, a harsh, hurtful sound. "And I can't even remember how." He rubbed his eyes, looking more tired by the second. "But I don't want to burden you with my ghosts."

"Please." Now it was her turn to offer comfort: that was part of friendship. "I want to know."

He turned to her, his chin made sharp and his eyes made into dark, expressionless holes by the erratic flickering of the candle on the floor at their feet. But she could sense his suffering. He was a very lonely man.

"Are you really interested?" he asked, his voice deep, almost breaking on the last word. "I doubt if it will do either of us any good for me to continue."

Speech couldn't convey her sincerity. Laying a hand on his shoulder, she nodded. When he didn't break the contact, her heart swelled with the knowledge that she was helping him. She met his eyes squarely and honestly. "I want to hear it all."

He looked away from her into the darkness around them. "I don't know which is worse, knowing John's dead or not being able to remember it." He sighed, glanced at her and then away again. Bleakly, he continued. "Occasionally, I have nightmares. I never remember them, only that they've something to do with the time the French caught us. But since arriving here, the dreams have been every night. I'm almost to the point where I don't want to sleep for fear of another nightmare."

Now she knew why he always looked tired. He was visiting his own personal hell each time he went to sleep. Carolly longed to take him into her arms and soothe away his pain, but she knew how futile the attempt would be. Instead, she released his shoulder and took the fist he'd clenched in his lap. She held on tightly to him.

His lips thinned. "There isn't much more to tell. Needless to say, we were caught." Pain cracked through his voice. "I don't remember how or when. We were tortured. I know that because when they found me wandering several days later I bore the evidence of beating . . . and more."

His head bent forward, and the fist in her hand tightened until Carolly thought he would break away from her and lash out at something—anything.

"God, I wish I knew what happened. I couldn't even tell John's widow how he died." The choked sound of an aborted curse escaped him. "Perhaps it's just as well."

It was worse than she'd ever imagined. "I'm sorry, so sorry." It was all she could say—and it was so little. Blinking rapidly, she tried to keep her tears from falling.

He didn't need her pity.

For long minutes they sat there.

Finally, he cleared his throat. "Yes, well, the physicians tell me that while memory loss is unusual, it's not uncommon in someone who wants to forget something that was very painful. The last doctor I saw even went so far as to say that if I truly wanted I could regain my memory, but that I would have to want it very badly." He sighed. "I don't know of anything that could make me want to remember the hell my nightmares only hint at."

"I can certainly understand that." Even though it meant that he would never remember their love, she didn't want him to go through the trauma of reliving what had happened to him and John.

"Do you really understand?" He searched her face, his own relaxing as she sat calmly allowing him his scrutiny. "Yes, I believe you do. You're the first person to do so. Most seem to have a morbid curiosity. They want to know what could be so bad that a man would block out five years of his life to forget it. I lost the four years I spent at Oxford and the first year of my military time." He freed his hand from her hold and briefly touched her cheek with one finger. "You're a true friend."

Yes, she would be his friend, knowing she could never be his wife. Somehow, through her own agony, she managed to smile at him.

"Well," he said with forced lightness, "I've burdened you with my woes for long enough. It's late and, as you've made clear, you're not a guest who can sleep as late as you wish. Please accept my apologies and my gratitude."

He lifted her hand from her lap where it had fallen when he'd fleetingly caressed her cheek. Like the dappled touch of sunlight on a just-opened rose, his lips met her skin. Then, without another word, he left.

Watching his retreating back, Carolly finally let the tears flow, cleansing herself of his pain and her own foolish hopes. He needed a friend, and she would be it.

Perched precariously on the top step of a twelve-foot ladder, Carolly carefully basted the swaths of multihued pink silk together in loose gathers so that, hopefully, the material would drape in filmy waves. Under her breath she whistled a jaunty tune.

"Good Lord! What are you trying to do, break your neck?"

"Oh!" Carolly squeaked. Startled by Alex's angry words, she lost her balance, swaying dangerously, her arms windmilling out.

"Damn!" Alex cursed.

Carolly fell backwards. In the split seconds before hitting, she wondered who would finish decorating the room for tomorrow's Valentine Ball. It had to be perfect for the announcement of Elizabeth's betrothal.

With a heavy thud, she landed against something that gave under her weight. Shocked by the sense of her stomach lodging in her throat, Carolly lay for long minutes trying to gather her scattered thoughts back together.

"Carolly, are you all right?" Alex asked, his voice anxious, his hands moving over her arms to feel for any breaks.

Sensations rushed over Carolly as she realized where she was—cradled in Alex's lap, the two of them practically prone on the floor. Everywhere he touched her sparks flared, all of them spiraling into the furnace of her stomach. Her muscles clenched and her skin sensitized to the point that if she didn't escape his concerned ministrations immediately she was afraid that she would disgrace herself by kissing him.

"Carolly," he said, his voice husky.

Looking at him, she was caught by the yearning in his eyes. The hint of passion she saw in him combined with the feel of his body beside hers, rekindling desires she'd long ago thought damped down to ashes. Her body responded, flaring hot and bright, bringing back memories of their last time together. They'd been a half day's distance from Gretna Green, spending their last night on the road in a tiny inn. It was their first and only experience as lovers.

A small sob escaped Carolly's parted lips. She knew that if she didn't get away from Alex's touch she would disgrace herself by leaning into him. Awkward in her urgency to quit him and the need he aroused in her, she tried to untangle her skirts from his legs. Tension made her fingers ineffective as she picked at the material.

"Oh, dear," she murmured.

"Let me," Alex said, his eyes never leaving her face. "I'm well aware that my yelling at you is the cause of this."

Their skin met as he tried to help her undue the twist of her skirts. The actual touch of flesh to flesh weakened Carolly's barriers, and she melted into the hard planes of his chest, her eyes questioning his. She saw passion and caring and. . . . She didn't dare to hope for more.

His lips lowered to hers, and Carolly thought her heart would burst with yearning for him. It had been so long. So very long.

"Here you are," Elizabeth's cheery voice said from the double doors across the massive room.

Galvanized into action, Carolly sprang away from Alex, struggling to get to her feet. The abrupt, disjointed movement sent her sprawling on her knees; thankfully, away from Alex.

"Elizabeth," Carolly gasped, trying again to rise, "I . . ." Finally standing, she took several deep breaths and forcibly calmed herself, patting her hair into place where it had fallen in tendrils after being rubbed against Alex's lapels. "I was on the ladder and, clumsily, I lost my balance. You know I've never had a head for heights. It was really quite stupid of me to have attempted hanging the silk and ivy in the first place." Carolly stopped to draw in air. She was babbling and she knew it, but seemed unable to stop. "I should have gotten a footman."

"Oh, no, Carolly. Are you hurt?" Elizabeth asked, moving rapidly across the parquet floor toward them.

Elizabeth's genuine concern sobered Carolly's sense-drunk emotions better than any cold water could. "No, dear," Carolly said, calmly, allowing the younger woman to embrace her.

Smiling gently, Carolly patted Elizabeth's back, knowing the girl needed the reassurance of touch. Elizabeth had always needed the concrete. It was a characteristic Carolly had loved in the young Elizabeth and still liked in the woman Elizabeth had become.

Alex clearing his throat reminded Carolly of his presence and what had just transpired between him and her. Carolly noticed that he looked more tired than normal and—yes, she would not deny it—resigned. Shame flooded her cheeks, bringing heat that made the cool room seem like a furnace to her. She had blatantly pursued him while they lay on the floor. He must be wondering how he would be able to avoid her advances after he married Elizabeth.

Carolly turned sharply away from his regard, disgust at her weakness replacing her initial shame. They were friends. He had made that clear, and she had thought herself accepting of that fact. She *had* to be.

Friendship was all she could have from him, or she must leave the Aldeborough family. Leave Alicia. She had already lost the greatest love of her life. She didn't think she could survive losing Alicia, too. Surely, even fate couldn't be that cruel to her.

Carolly slid inside the ballroom through the side door leading from the service hall. She still wasn't comfortable being here for the Valentine Ball, but neither could she bring herself to miss it. Seeing and hearing Alex's betrothal to Elizabeth would be the final nail in the coffin of her love for him. She would never allow herself to love another woman's husband.

Looking around the room for Alex, she noted the clumps of guests, the group of musicians just starting a quadrille, and the bouquets of trailing ivy catching up the swaths of silk that ranged from palest pink to deepest blood red. Elizabeth's pink muslin gown would show to advantage against the decorations. Carolly was glad for the younger woman. She wished her former charge only happiness.

Couples began to form on the dance floor, giving Carolly more room to move about without having to thread her way through people. She went to the punch bowl and dipped herself a glass. The room was stuffy, and her anxiety made it difficult to breath.

Once again she scanned the room, wanting to find Alex: to watch him from afar; perhaps to dream one last time about what might have been before he went forever beyond her reach.

He was across the room, Elizabeth a laughing, slim nymph at his side. They were a striking couple. He was tall and thoroughly masculine in his black silk coat and knee breeches, his dark hair gleaming in the candlelight. Elizabeth was a petite vision of pink and blond loveliness. It was obvious they were in love.

They were both people Carolly cared greatly for, and she was honestly happy for them; truly happy that they each had found someone to love and cherish for the rest of their lives. Still, her chest hurt, and she knew all her talk of accepting Alex's friendship had been nothing but a sham. She wanted more than his friendship. She wanted his love—and that belonged to Elizabeth.

Blindly, Carolly looked away. She put down her half-empty glass of punch. It hit the corner of the table and crashed to the floor. The shattering crystal was a sharp burst of noise resounding in her ears.

She fled the room without a backwards glance.

Instinctively, Carolly made her way through the servant's hallway to the stairs, and from there to the third floor and her alcove. Reaching her haven, she collapsed onto the seat like a rag wrung dry.

More than anything, she wanted to cry and purge herself of the unbearable pain, but the tears refused to come. Her eyes remained dry, burning with emotions too powerful for her to easily contain.

Her chest heaved, and the ring suspended around her neck

on a thin gold chain slid into the hollow between her breasts, reminding her of its presence. She drew it out, the dull glint of fine gold against her palm a magnet drawing her gaze.

For years it had been her only reminder of him. It had been the engagement ring she never got. She had even convinced herself that it could substitute for the promised letters that never came. What a fool she was!

She squeezed her fingers shut, hiding from sight the symbol of all her lost dreams. The hard edges of the ring cut cruelly into her skin, just as the sharp sword of her love for Alex cut into her heart.

Eyes closed, head leaning forward onto the frosted windowpane to cool her flushed brow, she shivered. She pulled the Indian shawl she wore closer, trying to ward off the physical discomfort, knowing even as she did so that the soul-deep cold she felt could never be abated.

It had been a mistake to go to the ball. The sight of them together had ruined all her tightly held illusions. She had deluded herself into thinking that she could be friends with Alex. She knew differently now. She still loved him with the same intensity that had propelled her to Gretna Green with him seven years ago. There was no way she could water that passion down to mere friendship. She didn't want to.

Carolly took a deep breath. She was stronger than this. She had to be. But she wasn't.

Even when Alex was Elizabeth's husband, Carolly would never be able to stop loving him. She must leave, even if the price for her weakness was losing Alicia.

Tomorrow she would give Lady Aldeborough her resignation. Tonight had proven completely that she would never be able to remain there after Elizabeth married. Carolly couldn't bear the continual strain of knowing that at any moment Elizabeth and her new husband might visit.

Damn him! Damn her own foolish heart!

"Carolly . . . Caro? What's wrong?"

Alex! She jerked around, her eyes aching from unshed tears. "You! Go away!"

Instead of leaving, he sat beside her, crowding her against the wall as she tried to keep from touching him. "Go away," she hissed.

"No." He took her free hand into both of his. "I won't leave you alone like this."

She tried to pull away, but he only held tighter. It was more than she could bear. Averting her face from his study, she said in an agonized whisper, "Must you take my pride as well?"

"I don't understand, Caro." He massaged her cold flesh with his warm fingers. "I thought we were friends."

The pain caused by his use of Alicia's pet name for her gave Carolly the strength to deny him. "We are *not* friends. Never have been. Never will be. It was nothing but a foolish woman's fancy." She forced herself to look him in the eye. "And now, will you please go."

"I can't."

Had he slapped her, he couldn't have devastated her more.

"Can't? Or won't?" Bitterness seeped from her words, as blood from a mortal wound.

"Can't, won't. . . . Caro, it doesn't matter." He laughed, a wrenched sound that twisted his full lips. "I need to say something to you. If, after you hear me, you decide that you still can't stand to have me around," he paused and took a deep breath, "I'll leave. But not until then."

She stared at him, noting the lines of strain around his eyes and mouth that hadn't been there yesterday. Even in the throes of her own heartbreak, she could not find it within herself to send him away without first trying to comfort him.

He took her silence for assent. "I'm glad we aren't friends, Caro. I want more."

"What?" she said with a strangled sob. "What about Elizabeth?" One day he wanted friendship, the very next he didn't. He was shredding her heart. She wrenched her hand from his hold and surged upward.

Alex grabbed her shoulders and pulled her back down. The entreaty was gone from his voice, replaced by resolve. "Elizabeth means nothing to me."

Stunned, she sat unmoving. "Nothing? Then why—"

"I never, by word or deed, compromised Elizabeth. Neither did I tell Sir Walter that I would offer marriage to Elizabeth when I accepted his invitation." A rueful grin crooked his lips. "She's dancing with FitzWilliam right now. I don't think she'll be hurt when I don't propose."

What was he saying? Could she have been wrong about Elizabeth's feelings for him? More importantly, why was he telling her this? In her confusion, the anger began to ebb from her. Eyes wide and uncomprehending as she studied his ravaged countenance, Carolly forbade her errant heart to hope.

He took a deep breath. "Carolly, I couldn't ask it before. I thought you cared for me only as a friend, but when I held you in my arms, when I saw your face while I was dancing with Elizabeth tonight and found you here and so distraught. . . . I'm beginning to think differently." He cupped her chin in his palm and forced her to meet his eyes. "I think you care for me. I hope so."

Did she want to believe the words he said? Could she stand to go through the agony of the last seven years again if he turned false? Could she stand the exquisite pain of hope again? No. She tried to twist her face from his grasp, and her hands went to his shoulders to push him away.

"Leave me be," she gasped. "I don't know what sport you're playing now, but it's monstrously unfair of you."

He caught her hands where they pressed against him and slowly, coercing her every inch of the way, raised them to his lips for his kiss. "I've done this badly. My only excuse is that I never expected to experience the glory of love. It was something I thought never to find."

She stilled, her attention riveted on him, her ears straining to comprehend his last words. Was there truly a chance for them again, after all these years? His eyes met hers fully, the dark brown of his turning almost golden with warmth and . . . love. Carolly felt the cold lump that had been her heart begin to melt under his regard.

Alex grinned ruefully at her. "I want the chance to know

you better. I want to see if perhaps there's a future for us."

Could he truly mean what he was saying? "You want to . . . ?" she trailed off, still unable to allow herself to completely hope.

"I want," he said, slowly and deliberately, "to give you a chance to know me better. I want to court you."

The world, so dark when she'd fled the ballroom, began to take on a golden haze for Carolly. The chill that she'd begun to think permanently rooted in her bones started to dissolve. Still, after so much time and so much hurt, her heart craved more reassurance.

"But why? Why me, a governess with no looks and no future?"

Not speaking, he drew her closer until their lips were separated only by the air they breathed. Trepidation and anticipation held her motionless in his gentle embrace as his mouth met hers.

Sparks of fire licked along Carolly's nerves, melting her doubts. Her body molded itself to him: the thrust of her breasts flush to his chest, the curve of her shoulder cupped within the hollow of his, the placement of her hand around his neck to hold him close. It was as though the seven years of separation had never been.

When they finally parted, she knew all the love she felt for him was shining from her eyes, plain for him to see. She didn't care.

Leaning back in Alex's arms, Carolly reveled in the look of contentment and joy lighting his features. For the first time since his arrival at the Aldeboroughs, he looked like the young man she'd sacrificed so much for. It no longer mattered that he couldn't remember their youthful love. He loved her as a mature man. With a sigh of contentment, she nuzzled into the warmth of his embrace.

With his finger, Alex traced the curve of her brow, down the side of her face to her chin and up to her parted lips. Tingles of delight radiated from where he lightly tickled her skin. It felt so good to be in his arms again, so right.

Carolly looked up at him with eyes full of her love and basked in the promise of love she saw in his eyes. Never, not even as a runaway bride-to-be had she felt this contentment that seemed to reach to her very soul.

"I love you, Caro," he murmured.

She lifted her lips for his kiss, but just as he bent down to take her mouth with his, his gaze wavered. His attention riveted to the small gold ring lying on Carolly's breast where she'd dropped it when he arrived. His look of fulfillment turned to puzzlement as he reached out and closed his fingers around the piece of jewelry. In a quiet voice, he asked, "Where did you get this?"

Carolly met his scrutiny without flinching. Should she tell him? She couldn't lie, and neither did she want to. "You gave it to me."

The words fell between them. Alex's face twisted into a frown. Wordlessly, he set her from him, even as he continued to hold the ring with the fingers of his left hand.

Carolly felt him tremble where his flesh rested against her bosom. She took his hand and raised it to her lips.

In a voice hoarse and ragged with strain, he asked, "When? I thought it lost."

His face was white and pinched. The warmth was gone from his eyes, leaving them bleak. He seemed a man facing the worst devils of his existence. How she wished she'd removed the ring before dressing tonight, instead of allowing vanity and her heart to overrule her caution. Had she taken the thing off, there wouldn't be this new division between them. But there was no going back. She had to see this through, no matter what it did to their newly burgeoning love.

"You gave it to me when we parted seven years ago."

"Why?"

The bald word was all the more poignant because of the anguish Carolly saw lurking in the depths of his eyes. Suddenly, she realized that Alex was afraid of the answer even though he asked.

She took a deep breath to steady her nerves. "You gave me your christening ring as a reminder that your love for me would never die. It was a promise that you would return when the waiting period was over."

"My God," he groaned, pulling her tightly to him and burying his face in her hair. "I loved you before and then I forgot you along with everything else. It's no wonder I'm in love with you after only a week. My heart must have remembered even though my mind did not."

His self-reproach was more than she could bear. Raising her face, she kissed him softly on the lips. "It doesn't matter, Alex. Once it did. No more."

Fiercely, he said, "It matters to me. That I could have left you, promising to return, and then forgotten you. I know things weren't easy on you or you wouldn't be a governess in another woman's house."

She raised her hand to his cheek. "My father disowned me after you left, but I've survived. My life has been good. Don't castigate yourself for something that was none of your doing. I understand about your memory loss."

"Do you?" he asked, his mouth twisting. "Then you understand more than I do. How could I have loved you, known you loved me—and not remember any of it?"

"We were children, Alex," she said softly, aching to lessen his self-recrimination.

"Were we lovers?" he asked harshly. "Did I love you and then forget you?" He groaned. "Did I?"

Should she tell him? She must. He would find out soon enough if they wed, and she wouldn't have him thinking she had ever given herself to another.

Barely above a whisper, she said, "Yes."

His grip on her tightened to painful intensity. "My God! When? How?"

She endured the pain of his hold, knowing he didn't realize how he held her. "We were less than a day from Gretna Green. It was our last night. You asked for separate rooms, but there were none. Then you intended to sleep on the floor, but I wouldn't let you. I loved you—love you—and I intended to share myself with you completely."

Choking on the words, he asked, "Did we . . . Were we lovers?"

She nodded, knowing the pain this was causing him, but knowing she couldn't keep this from him.

He stood, his back to her, his voice agonized. "I have to remember it. I need to remember everything."

"Alex," she said, sensing that something momentous was about to occur, "please, sit down."

Looking over his shoulder at her, he smiled lopsidedly, sadly. "I'm not losing my mind, Caro. No, just the opposite. I feel that I'm getting my mind back after years of wandering in purgatory."

"What do you mean, love?" she coaxed.

His eyes took on a faraway luster as though he gazed at a scene distant in time or space. She couldn't tell which. Standing, she went to him, wanting to be nearby for whatever was about to happen.

Hesitantly, he began. "We were on a scouting mission. In the hills. Some fleeing Spanish peasants—resistance fighters, really—had told us the French were just over the rise."

He paused and Carolly could see the beads of perspiration forming on his forehead. She knew even without him saying so, that his friend was with him.

"It was night and so cold our spit froze. Not a good night to be skulking about in enemy territory. There wasn't a cloud above. The sky was so clear, the stars lighted our way. And there was a full moon, too, but we had no choice. It was risk two lives or risk fifty." His eyes squeezed shut as though what he saw was too painful to endure, but then he opened them again, shaking his head slightly.

"The French caught us. They tortured John first, hoping to make me reveal the location of our troops." He stared straight ahead, a single tear winding its way down his cheek. "I remember it all, Caro."

She took him into her arms. "My love, my love. It's over

now. There's nothing you can do to change the past. Let it go."

Then slowly he turned to look at her, his voice barely above a whisper. "Why didn't you write?"

"I did. You didn't answer."

Shock, anguish, guilt flitted across his face. It tore her apart to watch the realization hit him that their separation had started even before he lost his memory.

He dragged in a breath, his eyes searching hers. "I wrote you every day, Caro. I put all my fears and disgust at the war on paper for your eyes. And I put all my love and hopes for our life together. That was all I had over there."

"Oh, dear God," she whispered, clinging to him. "My father had disowned me. After I left, he probably destroyed all the letters you sent to his house for me. Alex, I never stopped writing you until the two years were up. I sent the letters to your father to be franked since I didn't have the money to pay for sending them. I don't know . . ."

Dawning comprehension eased some of the pain from his face. "My father." He took her into his arms and held tightly. "He never intended for us to wed."

"But all the expectations, all the hurt and dashed hopes." She gulped, refusing to shed the tears that were so near the surface from all the emotional upheavals. "All the time."

"I know, love," he crooned, stroking her hair. "I could damn my father to hell and back, but it won't do either of us any good. It won't bring back our lost time."

She looked up at him and saw all the love and devotion in his eyes that had been there seven years ago when she'd bid him farewell. "You're right, Alex. The past is over. It's time for both of us to be courageous. We have the future."

Alex took a deep breath, his gaze never leaving her. Reflected in his eyes, she saw, mingled with the pain of memories, more love than she could have ever hoped for. It was as though the love he'd felt for her as a youth had combined with the love he felt for her as a man.

His lips took hers in a kiss that was gentle and yet deeply passionate. A kiss that promised eternity. Twining her arms around his neck, Carolly clung to him as her world spiraled out of control.

Much later, the candle gutted, Carolly's world firmly centered in the man still holding her, she murmured for the first time in seven years, "I love you, Alex Staunton. I love you with all my heart and soul."

Rising, he pulled her up with him. "Now that you're in my life again, I intend to see that you stay here. We're going downstairs right now and have Sir Walter announce our betrothal to the Polite World at the Valentine Ball."

The Bay Leaf Legend

by Violet Hamilton

"For this was on Saint Valentine's day,
When every bird cometh to choose his mate."

Geoffrey Chaucer

The Pump Room appeared very thin of company this damp February morning, but Annabel Maitland was not disappointed in the depleted ranks. Her attention was fully occupied by the young officer resplendent in his regimentals intent on persuading her to grant him a coveted favor.

"Remember you have promised me the first dance tomorrow evening at the Fitzherberts' ball," he insisted, gazing at her with flattering expectation. Annabel smiled, pleased by his insistence but not prepared to surrender easily. Colin Armistead was a young man upon whom many girls smiled, for he was a handsome figure in his uniform of the Fifth Northumberland Fusiliers. Tall, with burnished chestnut hair brushed into the windswept style, he had the disciplined carriage of the soldier which made him appear taller than his average height. And with expressive blue eyes in a tan smooth face, the lieutenant had become the object of many a young woman's dreams since his arrival in Bath some months ago.

But it was Annabel who had early attached him and to whom he had proved most faithful. His manners were pleasing and his conversation beguiling. Annabel could not understand why her grandmother, Lady Clifton-More, found him untrustworthy and unacceptable.

"Never credit a man with a cleft in his chin," that astute guardian had warned Annabel several times. Annabel, gazing now at the offending characteristic, thought it only enhanced Colin's charm. She did not believe that Colin's assiduous pursuit of her was prompted by her fortune. She believed in his sincere avowals, his desire to make her a devoted and loving husband.

Annabel was not inexperienced in flirtation. Since leaving Miss Augusta Sinclair's fashionable seminary in Cheltenham more than a year ago, she had enjoyed light romantic passages with various young men who frequented Bath's Assembly Rooms and the most acceptable neighboring manor houses. From her debut in society, she had taken, casting any rivals quite in the shade. A slight graceful girl with a mop of blond curls, a winsome smile, and a merry manner, she was not a beauty in the common mode. Her most arresting feature was a pair of heavy-lashed deep sapphire eyes, almost too large for her elfin face. Her effortless ability to captivate an eager bevy of gentlemen puzzled other misses who yearned for her success.

Most of the attention accorded her she accepted modestly, but not with any seriousness. Colin Armistead was the first of her admirers to touch her heart. She found him both exciting and vehement in his professions of love, a combination of qualities difficult to ignore. His handsome stalwart figure crossing the room to greet her whenever she put in an appearance at a gathering brought a blush to her cheek and a stirring of her heart she could not deny. Already some of her most ardent swains had begun to drift toward less bewitching girls, believing the lucky devil Armistead had secured the prize.

If only Grandma was not so stubborn and difficult, Annabel sighed, she and Colin could become engaged, and then be married in a splendid ceremony in the Abbey with all her friends and few relatives rejoicing. But because her grandmother refused her consent, they might have to elope to Gretna Green, a scandalous prospect. Lady Clifton-More was chaperoning Annabel and superintending her Bath season at the request of her son-in-law, Annabel's father, Gen. Richard Maitland, career officer and widower, who was serving with Wellington on the Peninsula. Annabel longed for his return, confident her father could be won around, that he would be delighted to bestow his daughter on a fellow officer. She considered, too, the dreaded possibility that Colin might soon depart for the Peninsula, leaving her behind. Until her father returned, she had no recourse but to try and persuade her grandmother, of whom she was fond, that Colin would make Annabel an admirable husband.

All these troubling thoughts chased through her mind as Colin continued talking, but Annabel scarcely heeded his inconsequential words until she was brought up short by his hand on her arm.

"I will not be put off much longer, Annabel. You must decide soon or it will be too late, and the regiment will be posted abroad. Since your grandmother has seen fit to disapprove of me and your father is away fighting, what other recourse do we have?" Colin pleaded, irritated by her distracted air.

"This is hardly the place to discuss the problem, Colin." Annabel did not want to elope to Gretna Green. She was quite sure she loved Colin, but to steal off to the border, creating a scandal and causing her grandmother grief, was not behavior she could countenance. For the moment she was seriously annoyed with Colin. "You must be content with tomorrow night's dances." Then, remembering that she had half-promised the first dance to Charles Fitzherbert she frowned. Charles, a long-time friend and lately somewhat more, would be hurt. Really, her life was becoming too complicated.

"Why are you looking so sad? If some cad has made you unhappy I will call him out at once," Colin insisted, only half in jest. Before Annabel could reassure him, they were interrupted by a dark-haired girl who glided up to them intent on attracting Annabel's notice.

"How intriguing, Annabel. Colin is threatening to fight a duel in your behalf." Her tone was light but ironic as if ridiculing such dramatic emotion.

"He was only funning, Susan," Annabel hastened to put matters right.

"I wonder," Susan said, casting an enigmatic look at the officer who was bowing over her hand and murmuring pleasantries, belied by the cold cast to his eyes.

"I am sorry to break up your tête-à-tête, Annabel, but Mama wants to leave, and since she promised your grandmother not to let you out of her sight, I am afraid you must accompany us."

"Of course," Annabel agreed politely, but convinced Susan had made the decision for some reason or other. Mrs. Pettigrew, a vague indeterminate woman, was completely dominated by her strong-willed husband and managing daughter. Annabel turned to Colin and bid him a cool farewell, unwilling to make any further commitments under Susan's watchful eye.

"Until tomorrow evening, then, Annabel." Colin bowed and stood gravely to one side as Susan took Annabel's arm and walked away.

"Really, Susan, you were almost rude to Colin. I had no idea you disliked him, hardly anybody does," Annabel whispered artlessly to her companion.

"Charles Fitzherbert does," Susan replied sharply, but before Annabel could pursue this intriguing thought they had reached Mrs. Pettigrew's side. That lady was nodding her head silently as one of her cronies told her some long story about a servant's transgressions. Susan waited a bit impatiently and finally, as the tale wound to its inconclusive end, said briskly, "Here is Annabel, Mother, so now we can be on our way."

"Our way, why . . ." Mrs. Pettigrew trailed off, catching the admonitory eye of her daughter. "Yes, yes, we must be going."

As the trio left the Pump Room, Colin's were not the only eyes which followed them. Bath matrons and their daughters enjoyed exchanging *on-dits* over morning coffee and chocolate, and the current gossip centered around Colin Armistead's chances with Annabel. Several of his fellow officers drifted up to talk to him, wanting to know if he had made any progress with the fascinating Miss Maitland. Colin had made no secret of his intentions and at every occasion acted the devoted lover, but Annabel showed more restraint. Bath's closed society had an avid interest in such affairs.

Annabel disliked being the object of gossip but in her modest way rather enjoyed her success as a reigning belle in Bath's circumscribed society. Puzzled by Susan's brusque attitude, and rather hurt, she wanted to ask what her friend had meant by her reference to Charles Fitzherbert, but she realized that Mrs. Pettigrew's presence made this unwise. For all her deceptive meekness and vague airs, that lady had a penchant for gossip which made her a poor recipient of any but the most casual comments.

Susan Pettigrew and Annabel had been schoolmates at Miss Sinclair's seminary, and these shared experiences had formed a bond between them, although Annabel did not wholly understand Susan's moods and strange reticences. Lady Clifton-More regretted that her intermittent attacks of painful arthritis had forced her to rely on Mrs. Pettigrew's eager offer of chaperonage for Annabel. Edward Pettigrew, manager of the Marquess of Bath's estates at Longleat, had a certain position in Bath society, but Lady Clifton-More found him rather too ambitious. She could find nothing to criticize in Susan's manners, but she felt that perhaps the daughter had inherited many of her father's characteristics, rather than her mother's submissive airs. Annabel's grandmother, like many ladies of advanced years, sighed for the great days of Bath, when Beau Nash and Ralph Allen had served as social arbiters of the community with dignity and grace. Although too well-bred to voice her regrets, she implied that Bath had been inundated with social climbers and parvenues who had no idea at all of how to go on. Privately she included the Pettigrews among the despised lot even if she refrained from criticizing them outwardly.

Coming out of the Pump Room into the colonnaded Stall Street, the trio of ladies waited for the Pettigrew carriage, although Annabel would have preferred to walk the short distance to Charlotte Street. But Mrs. Pettigrew found exercise fatiguing, pleading the poor state of her health which Bath's reputed waters had done little to improve.

Annabel chatted politely to Mrs. Pettigrew while Susan remained obstinately silent. Was she regretting her rebuff to Colin or was she just generally unhappy?

"Have you a new gown for the Fitzherbert Ball?" Annabel asked her friend as the carriage rolled through the crowded streets.

"I am wearing a new eau de nile satin. Papa created when he saw the modiste's bill," Susan admitted, then added, "Of course, it little matters what we lesser guests wear as you will have every gentleman in thrall. We could look like veritable houris and escape notice."

"Really, Susan, that is no way to talk—such shocking language. What will Annabel think of you?" Mrs. Pettigrew worried a great deal about what people thought and was inordinately proud of her daughter's friendship with Annabel Maitland. Rushing into speech to prevent any further solecisms by Susan, she asked, "And what are you wearing, Annabel? Really, girls today are so bold. Everyone used to wear white to balls until they married, but now I would not be surprised to see a scarlet gown, and the decolletage is shocking."

"Well, my gown is a cream silk with a rose silk gauze overskirt. Not too audacious, I believe," Annabel informed Mrs. Pettigrew, hoping her teasing would not be taken amiss.

"I am sure it will be lovely. Your grandmother has such wonderful taste." Mrs. Pettigrew, having paid her dues to the august Lady Clifton-More, retired again into vague inattention.

It was just as well that the carriage had arrived at its destination, a fine pedimented cream stone residence in a row of similarly impressive houses. Thanking Mrs. Pettigrew politely and bidding Susan a cheerful farewell with promises to meet at the ball, Annabel skipped up the stone steps to the house, turning to wave goodbye as the carriage lumbered away. She could not help wondering if the Pettigrews were now having a coze about her. Really, she was becoming a most unpleasant person, she reproved herself, and gave Willoughby, the butler, one of her most winsome smiles when he opened the door.

"Your grandmother would like to see you, Miss Annabel," the stately major-domo informed her. Though a most august person, more terrifying than a duke, Charles Fitzherbert believed or at least had said to Annabel, Willoughby could not resist an indulgent smile for the girl he had known since she was in leading strings.

As he took her bonnet and pelisse, Annabel looked up at him and asked anxiously, "Is she angry with me, Willoughby?"

"I don't believe so, Miss Annabel. I just think she wants a chat, lonely as she is, not getting about with her arthritis." The butler disdained idle chat about his betters, but he could never resist Annabel and was often betrayed into relaxing his strictures. He discouraged any talk below stairs about his employers and their friends. Annabel often wondered if her grandmother's standards would not be so strict if she had not been afraid of lowering herself in Willoughby's eyes. But no, sighed Annabel, her grandmother feared nothing.

On learning that Lady Clifton-More was settled into the morning room, her first day downstairs in a week, Annabel rushed to greet her.

Seated by the fireplace in a small informal, flower-decked room, at first glimpse Lady Clifton-More looked like a tiny little doll, with her white hair beautifully coiffed in the rather elaborate fashion of some twenty years past and her delicate unlined complexion. But beneath the smooth brow were a pair of shrewd azure eyes and the firm chin which Annabel had inherited. Across her knees lay a light mohair rug and across her shoulders a wisp of pink cashmere to ward off the

February chill, but aside from these obvious protections she gave little evidence of illness, only a fragile deceptive air which invited sympathy.

"Dear Grandmother, how nice to see you up and about. Are you feeling more the thing?" Annabel asked, crossing to her side and giving her a light kiss on the forehead, the only salute Lady Clifton-More accepted.

"Yes, indeed. I became quite tired of my bedroom and finally prevailed on that old dragon Tyler to allow me downstairs. She really is impossible," explained Lady Clifton-More. Annabel, knowing the true devotion that existed between mistress and maid, discounted this complaint. Tyler, her grandmother's abigail, had been with her for fifty years and ruled her with stubborn insistence.

"And what news from the Pump Room? I suppose you had a rendezvous with that Armistead boy?" Lady Clifton-More said somewhat irritably. "I should have known that Pettigrew woman was not up to keeping an eye on you."

"She could hardly prevent me from talking to officers in the Pump Room, Grandma. Be reasonable. And I don't understand why you are so haughty about Colin. He's a perfectly acceptable escort. Lots of girls envy me his attentions." Annabel argued persuasively, determined to talk her grandmother around to seeing Colin's virtues.

"Other girls are not heiresses, and their stupidities are not my concern, nor my responsibility. I know your father would disapprove heartily of you flirting with a line officer from an inferior regiment," was the response, storm signals gathering in the searching eyes.

Annabel laughed, although her own temper was rising as it always did when her grandmother criticized Colin. "Papa approves of army officers. After all, he is one himself. You really are a frightful snob, Grandma," she reproved with spirit, bracing herself for her grandmother's reproof.

But Lady Clifton-More surprised her by sighing sorrowfully and patting Annabel's hand gently. "Come, my dear, sit by me. We have some time before luncheon, and I will tell you why I find Colin Armistead a disturbing young man. I know you young things believe we old fossils have forgotten all about love, romance, and all the delights that tomorrow's festival celebrate. But that's not true. I should have explained my reasons for frowning on Colin's attentions before this, but the reminder is painful to me."

Surprised, Annabel raised an eyebrow in inquiry but said nothing, pushing a nearby hassock close to her grandmother's chair in order to hear her confidences.

"You probably do not remember your grandfather very clearly, child. You were so small when he died, more than fifteen years ago," Lady Clifton-More began.

"Oh, but I do, Grandmother. I remember a tall, white-haired gentleman who always had sweetmeats in his pockets patiently answering my questions. He had such a kindly way with him. Much less fearsome than Father."

"Richard was always kind and patient, especially with me, and at times I must have taxed that patience. We grew up together, rather like you and Charles, and he taught me how to fish, to look for wildflowers and badger sets, to ride my first pony. But then he went away to school, Eton and then Oxford, and finally on a Grand Tour of the Continent. Napoleon, of course, had not begun his conquests then and the Capets were still on the throne. Although he was only four years older than I was, he seemed very grown-up, worldly, and experienced. I had almost forgotten him, however, by the time I made my debut, and then there were so many new exciting young men that Richard no longer was the model by which I measured my beaux. I may say, a bit immodestly, that I had a certain success during my first season." Lady Clifton-More paused, recalling those long ago exciting days.

Annabel, squeezing her hand, interrupted to assure her. "Grandmother, I know you were an Incomparable. Mother was, too, I understand. And in London which is so much more demanding than Bath." She sighed, for she had rather wished for a London season.

"Nonsense, child. Even in London you would have attracted much attention. But, unfortunately, girls feted and made much of, if they happen to have a certain popular type of looks, become spoiled. In their innocence, too, they are not alway the best judge of character and can be influenced by flattery and tall tales, as well as by a handsome figure. I certainly was naive. And when Richard returned and began paying me attention, I treated him badly, finding him boring and prosy. I was vastly enamoured with the Earl of Anglesea's younger son, ignoring all my parents' warnings. He was a dashing sort, rode like a demon, danced divinely, had a commission in the Queen's Guards, and in his uniform cut a very romantic figure. I thought he was perfect and dreamed of an idyllic union with him, despite my parents' disapproval."

"Oh, dear," murmured Annabel, certain now of what must be coming.

"Yes. What my parents knew, and I did not, was that he was a wastrel and a womanizer, that the Angeleseas were under the hatches, and that Percy needed to make a good match if they were not to be rolled up. Like his father and grandfather before him, and his older brother, he was an inveterate gambler, wagering vast sums he did not have on horse races, cards, whatever bet was offered. Then there were tales that he had seduced a girl of impeccable position and abandoned her, but of course I believed none of this."

"You were prepared to stand by him no matter what others said, determined to rescue him from his follies," Annabel concluded shrewdly, still a bit amused at her grandmother's attempt to point a moral.

"My dear, I was desperately in love. Richard had proposed, after securing my parents' permission, and they wanted me to marry him, but I would have none of it. If I could not have Percy, I would wed no one, I vowed. I must have been a sore trial, stubbornly clinging to my faith in Percy although I could not help but be aware that there was some truth in my parents' accusations. Richard never criticized Percy, nor my willfulness in not seeing what he was, although he knew all about him."

"Well, the older generation always expects the younger to abide by its advice, not realizing that one has to experience one's own troubles." Annabel hoped her grandmother would take these words in good part. She saw exactly where events were heading.

"Yes, I know." Lady Clifton-More eyed her granddaughter wryly. She knew what Annabel suspected, but she had not yet finished her tale.

"I agreed to elope to Gretna Green with Percy, a shocking decision, for any girl who was married over the anvil was considered no better than she should be. But I was deaf to all arguments and completely under Percy's spell. We set off from the Landownes' ball well after midnight. I was in my ball gown, both scared and thrilled by this adventure, not really understanding what I had undertaken. Percy was bosky, and the carriage he had hired was driven by a ruffian of the worst sort. We stopped along the Great North Road at a rather seedy inn." Lady Clifton-More hesitated, frowning. She had come to the most humiliating and painful part of her story. She disliked revealing her foolish behavior to her granddaughter, but if it helped Annabel see that she was in danger of suffering a similar unhappy fate, she must force herself to continue.

"I had realized that it could take three or four days to reach Scotland, but somehow I had expected that Percy would behave with perfect propriety, would not dream of trying to consumate our union before the wedding. I realized that just being alone with him was enough to compromise me, but I thought he would act the gentleman. I did not understand his real nature, especially when he had taken too much drink and was thwarted in his demands. Until that night at the inn, he had always treated me with the utmost respect."

"And suddenly you saw his true colors." Annabel had been determined not to be swayed by her grandmother's story, not entirely believing it, for she knew why she was hearing these confidences now. But despite her suspicions she was touched by the pathetic picture of her grandmother alone with this rake in a disreputable inn, completely at his mercy, and beginning to see where her reckless ignorance had taken her.

"Well, yes. Looking back on it I can quite see how melodramatic the revelation must have seemed, but at the time it was ghastly. After I had repulsed his advances and insisted on retiring to a chamber of my own, he stormed out in a passion, leaving me alone and frightened with no comfort. But that was not the worst. I sat there, ignored and apprehensive for about two or three hours, wondering what was to become of me, when suddenly Percy appeared with a tavern wench and ordered me out of the room. Of course, I did not completely understand what he had in mind, but he soon made it clear. If I would not grace his bed, this agreeable lass was not so reluctant, and I had better clear out immediately if I didn't want to witness how a man and maid answered the urges of their bodies."

"Oh, Grandmother, how dreadful! What a hateful man." Annabel was shocked and embarrassed, but her grandmother appeared to be neither, intent on telling her story with every bit of sincerity and honesty she could summon.

"Yes, it was most shaming. I really was such a silly widgeon. I had no idea what to do. My disillusionment with Percy had happened so suddenly. I think I grew up in about two hours that terrible evening. I remember standing in the middle of the room, looking at the pair of them and thinking how sordid it all was. They were both the worse for drink, the girl disheveled and giggly, Percy surly and frustrated. Looking back on it I can see that all three of us must have cut the most ridiculous of figures," she confessed, the distressing confrontation as clear in her mind as if it were yesterday.

Annabel, at first amused at what she thought of as a morality tale, was disgusted and outraged by what her grandmother had faced in that tawdry inn. She did not know how to express her shock. But her curiosity triumphed. She had to know what had happened.

"What did you do, Grandmother?" she asked, her eyes wide with anticipation.

"Nothing. I was rescued from my dilemma by your grandfather. Richard and my brother Harry arrived just as Percy was about to throw me from the room. They burst into the room in a fury of anger, intent on wresting me from Percy's arms. They were a bit taken aback at the scene which met them, but my relief was so great I burst into sobs and threw myself into Richard's arms. You notice I turned to Richard, not Harry, which was most significant. Of course, Percy was at a great disadvantage, being both bosky and in the wrong on every count." She chuckled as she thought of her erstwhile lover in such straits.

"I hope your brother or Richard horsewhipped him," Annabel said fiercely, appalled that her gentle little grandmother had endured such a frightful experience.

"No. But Richard called him out, even though I assured him Percy had not actually taken my virtue. And I was always grateful that Richard never questioned the truth of that. Of course, just the fact that I had been alone with Percy for several hours was enough to ruin me, as Percy had mentioned."

"Did Grandfather meet him at dawn in some distant field and kill him?" Annabel urged, quite pleased at this outcome.

"He would have, I think, but Percy was afraid to meet him. He fled to the Continent in disgrace and stayed there for years, for his family would not have him back. Poor Percy," Lady Clifton-More sighed, remembering happier days with that tarnished rogue.

"And no one ever knew what had happened?"

"Well, Richard and I announced our engagement some days later. He and Harry had managed to smuggle me home, so that no one knew I had not left the ball with my parents, who really treated me with great forebearance. All Richard's doing, I am sure. And, of course, they were thrilled that I had chosen him as a husband."

"Did you fall madly in love with him because of the romantic rescue?" Annabel asked, hoping for a dramatic volte-face.

"Alas, no. I was very grateful, of course, and I had always quite liked Richard even if I thought him a bit stiff at times.

That all changed after we were married."

"I don't see why." Annabel was puzzled and rather disappointed by this tame outcome of her grandmother's incredible elopement.

Lady Clifton-More smiled and then, deciding that she must make her granddaughter understand, continued, "I fell in love with Richard after we were married. He was the kindest, most obliging of men, always eager to promote my happiness and always behaving as if I had granted him the most precious gift by agreeing to accept him as a husband. I saw what several of my friends endured in marriages which many of them entered into because of passionate love. Their husbands gambled, drank, and kept mistresses, ignored their wives for months at a time, banished them to the country if they protested about their affairs, spent their money, and even abused them. Marriage is not always a happy fairy tale, you know. It's much more apt to be an indifferent accommodation or even misery. I knew how fortunate I was. I shudder to think what would have been my future with Percy—abandoned, betrayed, insulted, no doubt. Instead I had my loving, wonderful Richard, who never once referred to that miserable night in the inn on the Great North Road."

Lady Clifton-More's eyes misted over. Her Richard had been dead more than a decade and she missed him every day, but never more than now when she could have relied on him to keep Annabel from making a grievous error in the marriage stakes.

"I know you have told me your story, Grandmother, because you do not want me to suffer a similar disillusionment, or worse. But I cannot believe that Colin would act in that dreadful way." Annabel's voice was concerned. She believed her grandmother only wanted to spare her pain, keep her safe, and probably wed someone of whom she approved. Annabel could not fault her for that, but she was not prepared to abandon Colin because of an episode which had happened half a century ago.

"I never dreamed Percy was such a weak, dissolute, selfish man either. Unfortunately, when we are young and first make our come-outs, we see gentlemen at their best, in carefully arranged situations under rigid chaperonage. Today, girls have far more freedom than we did, what with riding, picnicking, and dancing all under a more relaxed social code. Still, a man's true nature rarely emerges under these circumstances. Percy had always played the gallant suitor to me. And girls are so influenced by a handsome figure and pretty speeches."

"Well, I will promise you that I have no intention of eloping to Gretna Green with Colin Armistead. I think it's a shabby way to behave, and besides, I would miss all those bride clothes, presents, and a lovely wedding in the Abbey," Annabel said lightly, attempting to dispel her grandmother's fears. "All I am asking you to do is to receive Colin and try not to be prejudiced against him because he may remind you of the poisonous Percy." Annabel thought she would press her arguments while her grandmother was gripped by her memories of her own youth. She might regret these confidences later and return to an intransigent attitude.

"Thank you, Annabel. You are so much more sensible than I was. I trust you to behave levelly. You know your father is depending on me to keep you safe. I could not face him if you ran off to be married. He would be deeply wounded at such an action."

"Grandmother, I know I am a trial to you, and when you have been feeling so wretched, too. I will admit I am quite taken with Colin Armistead, and he seems to like me, too, but I would never cause you unhappiness and shame Father by eloping. You may rest easy on that score."

Lady Clifton-More smiled, relieved and slightly embarrassed that she had confided in her granddaughter. But she was shrewd enough not to press Annabel, nor to suggest that Charles Fitzherbert might fulfill the role Richard had played in her own romance. Let Charles do his own wooing. All she wanted was Annabel's assurance she would not hastily decide on that upstart lieutenant. She should have told Annabel before now about Percy, for the child had a sympathetic heart and a true affection for her grandmother. She would say no more on the matter.

"Now I am quite exhausted by all these revelations, child. And I suppose you want to ride out on that restless mare of yours. Do you good to get some exercise. I don't want you cooped up here trying to entertain me. I feel the need of a short nap, so be off with you," Lady Clifton-More ordered, wanting to put matters on a more prosaic footing.

"You are a darling. And I am glad I had Richard for a grandfather. He was a darling, too." Annabel gave her grandmother a gentle kiss before running from the room, leaving behind a tired but satisfied old lady.

Annabel enjoyed her ride, despite the presence of the groom her grandmother insisted upon accompanying her. She had a great deal to think about. Her grandmother's story of that pathetic romance with the dastardly Percy had touched her, and she understood the parallel between that situation and her own. Although she could not imagine herself in such a situation with Colin, it was sweet of her grandmother to confide in her at a great deal of cost to her pride and self-respect. Yet Annabel still believed that Colin was sincere, eager to claim her as his bride because he was about to go to war. She could not credit that her main attraction for him was her fortune. Still, she did not regret her promise to her grandmother not to elope. Tomorrow evening at the ball she would tell Colin they must wait.

After she returned from her ride, Annabel rang for her maid, Dorrie, and resolutely put her misgivings from her mind.

Dorrie, a country girl who had adapted very quickly to the more sophisticated environment of a luxurious Bath town house, had not lost her village memories, nor her faith in old legends. Small, rosy, and buxom, with bright eyes and a tongue that rarely stopped, she chattered away to Annabel as she arranged her bath. Once in the water, Annabel could not escape Dorrie's babbling. The abigail was full of information about tomorrow's festival, St. Valentine's Day.

"That bold carter's boy sent me a valentine card, all blue and gold, most handsome, and I bet cost him more than a penny. Not that I am supposed to know the sender, but we have been walking out some, and who else could it be?" Dorrie tossed her head coquettishly as she laid out Annabel's chemise and her dinner dress, a yellow silk.

"Valentines are never signed, Dorrie. You might have a secret admirer," Annabel teased as she soaped her shoulders and then slithered down beneath the sudsy water.

"Ooh, miss. Wouldn't that be something? Maybe I'll find out tonight. Some of us, Mary and Lizzie, are thinking of going to the churchyard. If you run around the church twelve times and all the time say these special words, the name of your husband will come to you. Wouldn't want to run around the Abbey. It will have to be St. Michael's," Dorrie decided firmly.

"You don't really believe all those old tales, Dorrie," Annabel scoffed as she rose from the bath to take the towel Dorrie proffered.

"Oh, miss, it doesn't do to make fun of the legends." Dorrie was horrified. "I'd rather run around the churchyard than do that nasty business with the hard-boiled egg. You take the yolk out and fill the space with salt, then you have to eat the whole bit, shell and all. Then you'll dream of your lover. Ugh."

"Where do you hear these fables, Dorrie. I never heard of Valentine myths." Annabel laughed, but she found Dorrie's tales intriguing and distracting. "Can't you tell me a spell which would be easier? I don't want to run around the churchyard, nor do I want to gobble eggshells."

Dorrie looked at her mistress a bit enviously, thinking what a lovely figure she made in her silk chemise. Then, recalling her duties, she carefully lifted the yellow gown and dropped it over Annabel's head, turning her around to smooth down the fabric and then fasten the small pearl buttons at the back.

"Well, my old mum did tell me a nice bit of magic. You

need bay leaves."

"Not so difficult to get. There's a bay tree in the back garden here," Annabel said idly as Dorrie brushed her hair.

"Well, let me see, now. You pin four leaves on the corners of your pillow and another in the middle. You might dream of your sweetheart, and if you do, you'll be married to him before the year is out." Dorrie thought about this for a moment. "Yes, that's the ticket, much nicer, and bay leaves smell fine."

"Oh, Dorrie. It's all nonsense, these fancies. You mustn't put your faith in them. Probably you haven't met your husband-to-be yet. Perhaps I haven't either, and maybe we will neither of us marry. All these aids to romance are just so much hum."

"Oh, never say that, miss. And, of course, you'll marry, a fine lady like yourself with all the gentlemen after you, officers even, although I don't set much store by soldiery in general. They're a faithless lot. A noble gentleman with a comfortable property and a fine carriage—that's what you should have, Miss Annabel," Dorrie hinted slyly. There had been lots of talk in the servants' hall about Charles Fitzherbert's interest in Annabel. The servants, aware of the various social gradations, preferred the earl's heir to any dashing foot officer. Dorrie knew all about Colin Armistead and disapproved, with native good sense, of his suit.

Annabel, in no doubt that Dorrie had her own sources of information about Annabel's beaux, wondered why Colin was frowned on below stairs as well as above. His manners were all that could be desired, but the Clifton-More household had its own ideas about who was a fit and proper mate for their Miss Annabel. She found their interest endearing if at times annoying.

"Well, good luck to you in your dreams and spells, Dorrie. But I wouldn't rely on any magic to catch a husband," Annabel advised as she clasped her mother's pearls around her neck and took a critical look at herself in the cheval mirror.

Though Annabel resolutely ridiculed Dorrie's credulous tales of Valentine spells and magic potions, she could not completely discount them. An aura of myth and magic surrounded Valentine's Day, and Annabel was romantic enough to admit that under the festival's spell one might suspend sensible belief. She did not really credit that chanting a spell, swallowing a potion, or indulging in some arcane practice would reveal the name of her husband. Only a ninny would choose a husband in such a goosish fashion, but Dorrie's notions could not be completely dismissed.

During an amicable dinner with her grandmother followed by a spirited game of piquet, Annabel managed to banish all thoughts of myths and legends. By unspoken agreement, Lady Clifton-More and her granddaughter did not discuss the question of Colin Armistead, nor did either of them refer to the dowager's earlier confidences. Annabel did not want to mar the serenity of her grandmother's first meal downstairs in a fortnight and thought those memories of her youthful indiscretions had best be ignored. If Annabel found her grandmother's story touching, she did not wholly accept that it matched her own situation. But she did not want to quarrel with her grandmother, of whom she was truly fond, nor cause her any embarrassment. And Annabel had been moved by her story and the courage it had taken to reveal it, knowing the revelation was offered to help her beloved granddaughter.

So, the two enjoyed their evening, and Lady Clifton-More took a certain delight in besting Annabel at the card table. They bade each other an affectionate good-night and retired to their chambers early, Lady Clifton-More reminding Annabel that tomorrow would be an exciting and tiring day, culminating in the Fitzherbert ball.

Dorrie was awaiting Annabel to help her off with her frock and brush her hair, but Annabel, with a great deal to think about now that she had some privacy, dismissed her abigail quickly. She was in no mood for more wild legends. Wrapped in her warm dressing gown, she sat by the fire to think about Colin. Obviously, from what he had said this morning in the Pump Room, he would not wait much longer for her answer. Did she love him enough to elope to Gretna Green, to become an object of gossip, to disappoint her grandmother, to cause her father unhappiness? Annabel truly loved her august parent, was proud of his reputation as one of Wellington's most fearless and dependable officers. She must not cause him any anguish, fighting as he was far from home in who knew what discomfort and peril. Perhaps, now that she and her grandmother had this new understanding, Colin would be content to wait, to court her in established fashion.

Yet despite her assurances that she was not the naive innocent her grandmother had been all those years ago, Annabel had been influenced by Lady Clifton-More's tawdry tale of love betrayed. Could Colin, who seemed so open, so sincere, so decent, behave in such a fashion? Oh dear, it was such a coil, and as Annabel prepared to get into bed, she still had not decided what to do. About to snuff out her candle, she noticed the pillows arranged on the large fourposter, and she laughed. Dorrie would not be gainsayed. Her abigail had pinned four bay leaves to each corner of the pillow and a large one square in the middle, determined that her mistress would have the opportunity to dream of her destined husband.

If Annabel would not take Dorrie's story seriously, her abigail was determined to make her. Too tired to dismantle the careful arrangement, Annabel decided to humor Dorrie. She had a niggling suspicion that there might be some validity to her abigail's convictions. At any rate Annabel quickly fell into a deep sleep, in no way incommoded by the bay leaves. Whether it was her grandmother's tale about her sad little romance, Colin's pleas, or her own indecision and doubts, Annabel passed a troubled night, tossing and turning, victim of the most distressing dreams.

She found herself running desperately down a long avenue lined with lime trees, trying to reach a figure who appeared to be Colin although he was shrouded in shadows. The longer she ran, the more he receded into the distance, and then, just when she felt she was making headway, a woman muffled in a cloak loomed before her holding out a restraining hand. Strangely Annabel believed the woman bore some resemblance to Susan Pettigrew. And Susan tried to stop her. Annabel managed to shake her off and resume her struggle toward Colin, but just as she approached him, he turned, and she saw it was not Colin at all but Charles Fitzherbert. For some reason she found this comforting and threw herself into his arms which closed about her with sympathy and support.

She awoke then to find her pillow drenched in tears. While not a real nightmare, the dream frightened Annabel. She did not want to dream of Charles Fitzherbert. Fond as she was of him he excited little passion in her breast. Much too prosaic, too humdrum, not at all the man who should figure in her dreams. Dorrie's spell had not turned out well at all. To dream of Charles Fitzherbert as her knight was too ridiculous. Annabel, puzzled, irritated, and disappointed, refused to take the dream seriously, thinking that the strange smell of the bay leaves had inspired the weird dream. She would have some strong words for Dorrie in the morning. Resolutely she turned over and dropped off once more into sleep, this time a restoring and calm rest which held no more mysteries.

Annabel awoke to a bright morning and chided herself for the foolish imagination which had provoked her dream, now only dimly remembered, although she had not forgotten the unease which she had felt on the earlier awakening. But today would be a busy one, and she had no time for musing over improbable fictions. Dorrie arrived with her chocolate and found her mistress in a determinedly cheerful state of mind. Still, there was that in Annabel's manner which prevented her abigail from questioning her. No mention was made of the bay leaves as Annabel dressed, except just before she left the room for breakfast.

"Please remove the bay leaves, Dorrie. You had no business putting them on my pillow without my leave." Annabel spoke a bit sharply, but then as if repenting of her ill temper, smiled at her abigail in forgiveness. "It's such a nice day I cannot be cross, but you are a widgeon."

Dorrie, left alone to straighten the room, wondered if her mistress had indeed dreamed of the gallant officer or of someone nearer home, but she knew it was worth her place to ask Miss Annabel any questions. The kindest of girls, Annabel Maitland could be quite firm and cool when the occasion demanded it, and Dorrie feared she had incurred her mistress's displeasure. She herself had passed a dreamless night, to her disappointment, and conceded that Miss Annabel was probably correct, the whole business was a hum.

Lady Clifton-More disliked breakfasting in bed, and whenever she was physically able insisted on coming downstairs for the morning meal. So Annabel was not surprised to see her grandmother presiding at the table when she arrived in the dining room. Giving her a kiss on her forehead, Annabel sat down and proceeded to eat a hearty meal.

"You look quite chipper this morning, Grandmother. I am happy to see you have recovered from your last bout of illness," Annabel said, noticing that her grandmother did, indeed, look good, her color excellent. Her hands, which tended to be useless from the arthritis were flexible.

"Yes, thank goodness. I do hate being ill. And I am considering accompanying you to the Fitzherberts' this evening. It's been a long time since I felt up to any social occasion. I think the spirit of Valentine's Day must have eased my old bones."

"Capital, Grandmother. Just the thing to cheer you up. You might even dance," Annabel replied merrily. "And it's going to be a lovely day, bright, sunny, even warm for February. I am going on a long ride this morning, I think. I need the exercise."

"Not by yourself, dear. Be sure that one of the grooms accompanies you," Lady Clifton-More insisted, always mindful of the proprieties. Young women did not gallop heedlessly around the countryside.

"Yes, of course," Annabel promised. They chatted casually about the evening ahead and finished their breakfast in harmony. No mention was made of Colin Armistead, and Annabel was relieved that her grandmother did not bring up his name. As she finished the last rasher of bacon on her plate, the butler entered to announce a caller.

"Mr. Charles, milady," he intoned, and close on his heels their visitor entered. Charles Fitzherbert apologized for making such an early call. In his hand was a charming nosegay of pale pink rosebuds tied with matching ribbons.

"For you, Annabel." He offered the flowers tentatively, laying them down by her plate. "I hoped you might wear them this evening."

"Thank you, Charles. You are kind." Annabel smiled at him but made no promise. It was difficult not to smile at Charles, an appealing young man of average height with tanned regular features, a shock of chestnut hair, and a pair of direct gray eyes. He was dressed in riding clothes. It was obvious that he had stopped by on his morning ride to deliver the flowers.

"Will you have a cup of coffee, Charles?" Lady Clifton-More asked graciously. She was extremely fond of Charles, having known him since his birth. "I suppose you could not wait to escape all the preparations at home for the ball this evening."

"Well, Mother does seem distracted, and Pa rode off early to the Home Farm. I did offer my services, but she suggested my absence was preferred to my presence," he laughingly agreed. "I don't know why she gets in a pother, for she is an accomplished hostess and has planned for every contingency. I am sure it will all go off with a bang." He sat down next to Annabel, casting her a look of admiration. "You look lovely this morning, Annabel. I hope you are anticipating the ball. I know all your partners are. I want to put in an early request for as many dances as you will give me, three at least."

Annabel remembered with a pang of guilt that she had half-promised him the first dance, and then with dismay realized that she had promised Colin the first dance as well. Oh, dear. Perhaps the best idea was to grant neither of them the privilege. She smiled, but remained silent.

"Annabel has decided to take a ride this morning. She hates taking a groom, so if you act as her escort I can rest easily," Lady Clifton-More insinuated. She encouraged Charles's courtship, but she realized that if she made too much of Charles, Annabel would obstinately demur, as she did immediately.

"Oh, Grandma, I am sure Charles does not want to wait about for me to change," Annabel protested, knowing full well what her grandmother had in mind.

"Not at all, Annabel. I am at your service. Actually I was hoping you might want to ride. It's a nice warm day, not at all like February. Please come," he begged, turning to her eagerly.

Seeing no way of avoiding the inevitable, Annabel conceded graciously, excusing herself to change into her riding costume.

"I will not be long," she promised, hurrying from the room. Charles rose to hold the door for her and then returned to his seat, eyeing Lady Clifton-More with an air of determination.

"I wanted to speak to you, Aunt Lucy. Since Annabel's father is abroad and will probably not be home for ages, I must apply to you. It is probably no surprise to you that I love Annabel and want to make her my wife. Of course, I would not speak to her without securing your permission. I do hope you look kindly on my suit." He spoke eagerly, with a sincerity and a fervor that brought a smile to Lady Clifton-More's face. She admitted that she had always wanted this match and knew that General Maitland would not object. Only Annabel had to be persuaded.

"You know it is one of the dearest wishes of my heart that you wed Annabel, Charles. And her father would approve, I know. It is Annabel you must persuade. Of course, you must be aware that you have rivals."

"That puppy Armistead for one. Girls are always susceptible to a uniform. It isn't as if I hadn't wanted to fight myself, but Pa said he could not spare me. And Mother created terribly when I hinted I wanted a commission, being the only son and all." Charles spoke with a certain amount of bitterness. He had dearly wanted to join Wellington but had surrendered reluctantly to his parents' protests and fears.

"Yes, I know, dear boy. Unfortunately, there is a certain

glamour to the uniform, and then, too, Annabel has known you all her life. A perfect basis for marriage, I happen to think, but girls her age are always attracted by novelty allied to a handsome face and practiced words. I suspect Colin Armistead has designs on Annabel's fortune as much as he desires her love and affection. I dislike him exceedingly, but my words of warning have fallen on deaf ears, I fear. Opposition always increases determination in the young. I only hope she does not let him persuade her into some foolish decision which could ruin her life and bring her unhappiness." Lady Clifton-More confided her deepest forebodings to the young man she favored. Charles represented all her dearest wishes for Annabel, with his honest temperament, his consideration, his solid worth. They were not qualities which were apt to inspire a romantic young woman, but they were of incalculable importance to a happy marriage.

"I know, Aunt Lucy. She thinks I am a dull dog and I guess I am, but I do truly love her and would take the utmost care of her always. And the parents want this match, too. If only there was some real impediment she might look on me more kindly. I should be a scapegrace, a rake, or a ruined gambler with a score of mistresses. Then she might look with more favor on me," he admitted with gentle humor. "I wasn't even sent down from Oxford."

"And you won that First, too. Not at all the thing, Charles, to display such rectitude and unobjectionable behavior. And you have never flirted with another girl. Perhaps if Annabel had some competition," Lady Clifton-More suggested wickedly.

"I know, I know, Aunt Lucy. A hopeless case and a very prosy fellow. What do you suggest?" he asked with an endearing smile, wanting to enlist the help of this cooperative and charming old lady who had always treated him so kindly.

"I wish I knew what to tell you. I wish I had some magic spell to cast over the pair of you, but I fear we do not live in a fairy-tale world. So often we rush toward disaster despite the best intentions. I did myself," she recollected sadly.

"You, Aunt Lucy? I cannot imagine it." Charles looked shocked. Surely this gracious lady could not have ever behaved foolishly or with impropriety.

"Like Annabel I was apt to mistake dross for gold, but that is another story. Perhaps she will tell you one day. I can only suggest you put your case and assure her of your devotion. She would be a ninny to turn you down. Good luck."

"I will ask her tonight. It seems suitable at a ball on Valentine's night," Charles said with decision. He had dallied long enough. He could not take the chance of waiting longer, for some other chap would surely win what he was too faint-hearted to dare. And he could not bear for Annabel to wed another.

"Thank you, Aunt Lucy." He leaned over and gave her a kiss as Annabel appeared, dressed for their ride. If she wondered about their conversation, she asked no questions, and the pair went off to the stables talking easily about the evening ahead.

Lady Clifton-More, rising from the table, watched them depart with every hope that Charles would win her granddaughter, but afraid that Annabel, who was so willful, so independent, and so sure of young Colin Armistead, might make the wrong choice and live to regret it. She could not bear for her beloved granddaughter to suffer at the hands of a greedy, ambitious, and faithless husband.

For the moment husbands were not in Annabel's mind. She was content with enjoying the springlike morning and the movement of her mare as they cantered briskly down the road toward the open country.

"What a relief to get out into the country. I was at the Pump Room yesterday and it seems so stuffy and tedious. I really need a good gallop to blow away the megrims," Annabel confided to Charles as their horses trotted eastward toward the Avon River. Charles, a trifle surprised by this criticism of the venerable assembly where Bath's social life ebbed and flowed, raised an eyebrow but wisely said nothing. He knew only too well how capricious Annabel could be, enthusiastic one moment over some pursuit, abandoning it the next when its novelty palled. It was true she had always loved country pursuits despite her success as a town belle, another reason he thought she would settle well on the Fitzherbert acres. They talked about past adventures, hunting, chasing Farmer Green's cows, fishing, and a host of shared experiences from their childhood days.

So engrossed were they in their memories as they rode companionably toward Bath's limits, they failed to notice a group of red-coated officers gathered in Argyle Street. But Colin Armistead and his companions recognized the popular Miss Maitland and her escort.

"Ho, Colin, me lad, you are not the only pebble on that beach," jibed Rory O'Brien, a red-faced and portly Irish captain whose rough humor caused his fellow officers to hail him as the regiment wit. Of a careless but kindly disposition, he had little spite in his nature, but liked to gossip about the ladies.

"Don't be cheap, Rory," Colin reprimanded the captain. "I won't discuss Miss Maitland." He spoke sharply, warning the officers he would entertain no jokes on this delicate subject. He seemed indifferent, but he had recognized Charles Fitzherbert, and he didn't like the idea of that gentleman squiring Annabel one bit.

The irrepressible Rory was not so easily silenced. "That's Charles Fitzherbert, rather a good sort for a lord's only son and very plump in the pocket, too. Any girl would look happily on him, to be sure, having a sensible regard for her future."

"A fine place that Woodley Park," added the third officer, referring to the Fitzherbert estate. "Lots of fine acreage goes along with it."

Colin, whose popularity with the ladies, and especially Annabel Maitland, had not endeared him to less fortunate officers, sensed their enjoyment of this setback. Let them snicker now, but he would win the prize in the end and then they would not be laughing. To illustrate his indifference to Charles Fitzherbert, Colin merely shrugged and offered in an offhand fashion, "Annabel tells me they are childhood friends. He's rather a dull chap. Not up to much, I gather." And he dismissed Charles as a rival. His companions, realizing that this complete confidence meant Colin had no doubt secured the lady's affection, were impressed.

"Ah, you're a downy one," Rory O'Brien said in admiration, clapping Colin on the back and the trio continued on their way to the Argyle tavern which was their destination.

Colin might not have believed that Charles was up to much, but if his rival had heard the officers' conversation he would have been both disgusted and angry. Annabel's name was not to be bandied about street corners by shabby officers in a line regiment. And he would have called the perpetrators to account for their coarseness.

But happily he knew nothing of this conversation, being totally occupied with Annabel. He was concerned with forming his proposal and wondered if he had the patience to wait until this evening to chance his hand. Now they were alone and not apt to be disturbed, while this evening his chores as host would keep him busy, for Charles usually sought out the less attractive girls who lacked partners and did his duty by them. And, of course, Annabel was always besieged. He had better pin her down to dances now, for although she could be unpredictable, Annabel had a definite sense of honor. If she promised him three dances, she would hold to that promise.

He wanted to ask her about Colin Armistead, too, but hardly knew how to broach the matter of that young man's intentions and his prospects. So they trotted along silently until they reached the open country across the river where they could let the horses out for a good gallop. After about fifteen minutes brisk run, Charles pulled up, indicating he wanted to talk—just what Annabel had feared. She knew he would press her about the opening dance that evening, and she also suspected that he had more important matters than dances on his mind.

"That was glorious. I had a very restless night and felt out of sorts this morning, but this lovely day has quite blown away my depression," Annabel said brightly. Indeed, it was an exceedingly warm morning for February with more than a hint of spring in the air—a deceiving day, for winter would return without doubt. But for the moment she was determined to enjoy it.

"You really love the country, don't you, Annabel?" Charles said, preparing the ground carefully as he jogged beside her.

"Yes, although I would like to spend a season in London. But Grandmother is not up to such a move. And Father will be away for many months, I fear. Not that he would be much use in chaperoning a season for me." Her tone was a bit wistful.

"Your husband might take you," Charles suggested.

"Ah, yes, but as yet, I do not possess that fortunate commodity," Annabel joked.

"You could have," Charles insisted, then hesitated as if unsure as to how to proceed. Then, deciding that he must take his chances, he rushed into speech. "You must know how I feel about you, Annabel. I would be honored if you would become my wife. I know I should wait to speak to your father, but he might not be home for months, years even, and your grandmother has indicated that she favors my suit. Of course, I know you must have had many offers—you are so popular—and there isn't a girl in Bath to equal you."

Charles's sincerity made up for a certain lack of grace in his proposal, and Annabel was touched by his diffidence. Still, she had no answer to give him. He waited patiently, braced for a rejection, which stirred Annabel's sympathy if not her heart. Suddenly she remembered her dream. Dorrie was right after all. The first eligible man who had crossed the threshold this morning had offered for her. She had not realized how difficult it would be to refuse Charles.

"Oh, Charles, I am fond of you. We have shared so much, but I wonder if fondness is enough. And I am not sure I want to marry yet. I have seen nothing much beyond Bath," she said gently, her luminous eyes full of compassion, willing him to understand.

"Is there someone else, Annabel?" he asked, knowing there must be but reluctant to have her name a rival.

"Well, there is an officer stationed here with the Fifth Northumberland Fusiliers. Colin Armistead. I suspect you know him. He is coming to the ball tonight." She hated hurting Charles, but it was foolish to hold out false hopes.

"Have you accepted him?" Charles asked sadly.

"No, of course not. Grandmother disapproves, and I would not wed without her consent what with Father away fighting. I could not be so cruel."

"You know I only want your happiness, Annabel. If this fellow can make you a good husband and you love him, I will be terribly disappointed, but I understand. I realize I must seem a dull chap alongside a serving officer. And you have known me forever, which means there is no excitement or mystery. I can only offer a very prosaic life when you might be following the drum, seeing the world."

Annabel wished Charles would press his case with a little less understanding and more force, but she appreciated his tact and honesty. She could not help but remember all they had shared, and the safety and security he represented was not to be despised. But she yearned for excitement, passion. If Charles felt more than devotion and affection, he did not evidence it, she observed tartly.

"If I were sure I loved you as a wife should, dear Charles, you know I would not tease you or flirt just to satisfy my consequence. But I just don't know what I feel for Colin or for you. I am all muddled up," she confessed with an engaging grimace.

"I was a fool to ask you now, but I was afraid if I did not declare my intention some other fellow would win what I was too cowardly to ask. Annabel, your happiness means a great deal to me, and I will honor your wishes. But please decide nothing in a hurry. I will always be here, you know," he pleaded, not knowing whether to be totally cast down or reassured a bit by her indecision.

"If you could only see your way to accepting me now," he

The Publishers of Zebra Books
Make This Special Offer
to Zebra Romance Readers...

AFTER YOU HAVE READ THIS
BOOK WE'D LIKE TO SEND YOU
4 MORE FOR *FREE*
AN $18.00 VALUE

NO OBLIGATION!

ONLY ZEBRA HISTORICAL ROMANCES
"BURN WITH THE FIRE OF HISTORY"
(SEE INSIDE FOR MONEY SAVING DETAILS.)

MORE PASSION AND ADVENTURE AWAIT... YOUR TRIP TO A BIG ADVENTUROUS WORLD BEGINS WHEN YOU ACCEPT YOUR FIRST 4 NOVELS ABSOLUTELY *FREE*

(AN $18.00 VALUE)

Accept your Free gift and start to experience more of the passion and adventure you like in a historical romance novel. Each Zebra novel is filled with proud men, spirited women and tempe tuous love that you'll remember long after you turn the last page

Zebra Historical Romances are the finest novels of their kind. They are written by authors who really know how to weave tales of romance and adventure in the historical settings you love. You'll feel like you've actually gone back in time with the thrilling stories that each Zebra novel offers.

GET YOUR FREE GIFT WITH THE START OF YOUR HOME SUBSCRIPTION

Our readers tell us that these books sell out very fast in book stores and often they miss the newest titles. So Zebra has made arrangements for you to receive the four newest novels published each month.

You'll be guaranteed that you'll never miss a title, and home delivery is so convenient. And to show you just how easy it is to get Zebra Historical Romances, we'll send you your first 4 books absolutely FREE! Our gift to you just for trying our home subscription service.

BIG SAVINGS AND FREE HOME DELIVERY

Each month, you'll receive the four newest titles as soon as they are published. You'll probably receive them even before the bookstores do. What's more, you may preview these exciting novels free for 10 days. If you like them as much as we think you will, just pay the low preferred subscriber's price of just $3.75 each. *You'll save $3.00 each month off the publisher's price.* AND, your savings are even greater because there are never any shipping, handling or other hidden charges—FREE Home Delivery. Of course you can return any shipment within 10 days for full credit, no questions asked. There is no minimum number of books you must buy.

4 FREE BOOKS

TO GET YOUR 4 FREE BOOKS WORTH $18.00 — MAIL IN THE FREE BOOK CERTIFICATE T O D A Y

Fill in the Free Book Certificate below, and we'll send your FREE BOOKS to you as soon as we receive it.

If the certificate is missing below, write to: Zebra Home Subscription Service, Inc., P.O. Box 5214, 120 Brighton Road, Clifton, New Jersey 07015-5214.

FREE BOOK CERTIFICATE

4 FREE BOOKS

ZEBRA HOME SUBSCRIPTION SERVICE, INC.

YES! **Please start my subscription to Zebra Historical Romances and send me my first 4 books absolutely FREE. I understand that each month I may preview four new Zebra Historical Romances free for 10 days. If I'm not satisfied with them, I may return the four books within 10 days and owe nothing. Otherwise, I will pay the low preferred subscriber's price of just $3.75 each; a total of $15.00, *a savings off the publisher's price of $3.00.* I may return any shipment and I may cancel this subscription at any time. There is no obligation to buy any shipment and there are no shipping, handling or other hidden charges. Regardless of what I decide, the four free books are mine to keep.**

NAME

ADDRESS APT

CITY STATE ZIP

( ) TELEPHONE

SIGNATURE (if under 18, parent or guardian must sign)

Terms, offer and prices subject to change without notice. Subscription subject to acceptance by Zebra Books. Zebra Books reserves the right to reject any order or cancel any subscription.

GET
FOUR
FREE
BOOKS
(AN $18.00 VALUE)

AFFIX
STAMP
HERE

ZEBRA HOME SUBSCRIPTION
SERVICE, INC.
P.O. BOX 5214
120 BRIGHTON ROAD
CLIFTON, NEW JERSEY 07015-5214

continued, "we could announce it at the Valentine's Ball tonight. Think how suitable it would be." A twinkle in his eye, he displayed a certain levity that Annabel had never noticed before. "Mother would be ecstatic. You know what a romantic she is. One reason for the ball is she expects all sorts of star-crossed lovers to come together under her auspices."

"We are hardly star-crossed lovers, Charles." Annabel did not want to admit that she was rather charmed by the thought of Lady Fitzherbert playing good fairy to troubled lovers.

"I am willing to be star crossed if that will insure I am your lover, Annabel."

Charles surprised her in this mood. Returning to his normal sober, sensible humor, he concluded, "I am mean to badger you, Annabel. And I would not want a reluctant wife. I must know I am your first and only choice for a husband, the man you love above all others. Nothing less will do."

"Thank you, Charles. You are a perfect, gentle knight, as Chaucer would say, and I am a goose to be so unsure. Any girl would be fortunate to claim you as a husband."

"But I don't want any girl, only you, Annabel." Charles reined in his horse and Annabel's mare, too, stopped. He reached across and raised Annabel's chin with one hand. "Just promise me that if you decide I will do, you won't be missish and shy and will come and tell me what I want to hear."

Annabel touched by his consideration, his obvious sincerity, smiled warmly. "Of course I will, Charles. You deserve the very best."

"And I still hope to get it," he smiled back, enchanted by her merry face and honest reaction. Annabel would not let him dally, hoping for a favorable answer while she flirted with other men. She was too decent for such behavior and Charles knew that if she ever agreed to be his wife she would be loyal, supportive, and loving. That was her nature and one of the reasons he loved her so.

"Thank you, my dear." He took up his reins and said briskly, "We'd best let the horses out again. It's a bit chilly in this east wind." And he spurred his mount into a canter while

Annabel, relieved to have brushed through the encounter so easily, followed his lead. Charles might not be exciting, but his solid worth was very reassuring, and his tolerance for her shilly-shallying was more than she deserved.

The rest of their ride passed in easy comradeship, no further reference to Charles's proposal troubling Annabel. Although she appreciated Charles's delicacy in not pressing her for a decision, she wished he had been more ardent. She knew if she refused him he would accept his congé with grace and no recriminations. His gentlemanly attitude could not be faulted. If she were in trouble or despair, she knew of no one to whom she could turn with more reliance than Charles, but he certainly did not cut a dashing figure of romance. And on this Valentine's Day that was what she craved. They parted at the Charlotte Street house with amity, Charles not even insisting on the privilege of the first dance. Annabel, a little piqued at this omission, bade him goodbye with a certain coolness. He did not seem offended.

Lady Clifton-More had accepted the Fitzherberts' invitation to dine in a small group before the ball, somewhat to Annabel's surprise. She hoped her grandmother was up to all this jollity. But that dowager, once her mind was made up, seldom surrendered to either Annabel or her maid's pleas that the outing might tax her energies. She had decided to attend this Valentine's Ball and her will would not be gainsayed.

Annabel donned her new gown, the cream silk with the rose gauze overskirt, with satisfaction. She knew the soft hues emphasized her creamy complexion as did the lustrous pearls which she clasped around her neck. Lady Clifton-More believed pearls were the only suitable jewels for young girls, although she herself favored a stunning display of diamonds with her magenta satin gown. Both Annabel and her grandmother complimented each other on their gowns when they met in the hall to await the carriage that would carry them to Woodley Park.

"This is only your second ball, Annabel, so I am sure you

are excited. I hardly count the gatherings at the Assembly—mere parochial affairs. I understand that the Fitzherberts have invited guests from London for the great occasion," Lady Clifton-More informed Annabel as they settled into their carriage for the twenty-mile drive ahead.

"Oh, dear. I hope I won't be intimidated," Annabel replied, only half in jest.

"I understand the Fitzherberts are entertaining Lord and Lady Coristand and their daughter Clarice. She's supposed to be one of the Incomparables this season, but you have no need to worry about any rival, my dear. You look charming," Lady Clifton-More said slyly. She had no idea whether or not Charles was interested in Clarice Coristand, but it did Annabel no harm to think she might have some competition. The girl was apt to take Charles for granted.

"I shall enjoy meeting her," Annabel said demurely, refusing to be drawn, although she understood her grandmother's attempt to cause a little diversion.

For the rest of the journey they discussed what they might expect from the ball, the guests, the dinner, the decorations. Lady Fitzherbert had a reputation as an inspired hostess, and her infrequent invitations were to be prized. No mention was made of Colin Armistead. Annabel wondered if her grandmother knew he had received a bid to the ball along with other officers of his regiment. There was not much which escaped Lady Clifton-More, even when she was confined to her room with her indisposition.

Theirs was not the only carriage to travel slowly up the long driveway to Woodley Park, a long stretch of winding road leading to a pleasant but not overpowering Jacobean house on a slight rise. Built by a pupil of Inigo Jones in the late seventeenth century, Woodley Park was designed of mellow red brick in a modified Palladian style with four stone pillars supporting a pediment over the central bays, a comforting not overpowering house of great charm. Although the evening had drawn in and darkness enveloped the house and park, large flambeaux lit the entranceway, reflecting the hospitable scene.

Waiting for their carriage to approach the steps, Lady Clifton-More looked out of the window with pleasure. "Such an attractive estate, not too pretentious but solid, rather like the Fitzherberts themselves."

"I doubt if Lady Fitzherbert would enjoy being called solid for she certainly is an elegant creature." Annabel chuckled thinking of their hostess, a very stylish if somewhat fey lady with a kind heart and a generous nature.

Finally, the Clifton-More carriage reached the marbled entrance, and the ladies were helped to alight by their coachman. Inside the great hall, with its double flight of stairs rising to right and left, they were received by the Fitzherbert majordomo, a portly man of great dignity whom Annabel had known since she was a child.

"Good evening, Andrews. I take it we are not the first arrivals," Annabel asked as she surrendered her cloak.

"Not at all, Miss Annabel. Good evening, milady," he greeted Lady Clifton-More deferentially, allowing Annabel a small smile. Andrews was not unaware that Charles had a deep interest in Miss Maitland. He led them toward the drawing room and announced them impressively. Lady Fitzherbert had recently refurbished the rather musty Gothic furnishings of the large well-lit room but had not followed the current craze for Egyptian and Chinese motifs inspired by the Prince of Wales. Instead, she had decorated with graceful Sheraton and Adam pieces, pale rose damasks and swagged silk draperies. She had not sacrificed comfort for elegance, and the effect was most attractive. The room was filled, for Lady Fitzherbert had augmented the local guests with a large London party. Annabel was happy to see that her gown did not suffer from comparison with those of fashionable ladies from Town. Their hostess welcomed them cordially, looking quite the mode herself in a sapphire blue silk with a lace tunic and a delicate necklace of sapphires. Her blond hair dressed in a Grecian style showed little gray, and her blue eyes sparkled. She was tall, slender, and very ebullient, a distinct contrast from her sober son and husband. Annabel had always found her fascinating.

"Ah, Lucy, you are looking very distinguished this evening, and Annabel is sure to set all tongues wagging with her beauty. You will have a full dance card in no time, my dear, and Charles will have to move smartly if he hopes to secure your hand. But come and meet our guests." Lady Fitzherbert steered them toward a group by the fireplace where Annabel at once noticed a sultry brunette with a haughty nose in a gown of cerise silk which was cut daringly low.

"I want you to meet our dear Bath neighbors," Lady Fitzherbert twinkled at the older couple, introducing them as Lord and Lady Coristand, and the brunette as their daughter, Clarice, who acknowledged the introductions in a bored tone.

"Annabel Maitland is quite the toast of Bath, you know," Lady Fitzherbert informed the trio naughtily, having a suspicion that Clarice did not welcome competition, accustomed as she was to being hailed as an Incomparable.

"Oh, Aunt Sarah, you put me to the blush. We are the veriest dowds compared to all these fashionable ladies you have assembled," Annabel protested, well aware of what her hostess intended. Sarah Fitzherbert delighted in stirring up controversy.

"Do you mean to make your come-out in London, Miss Maitland?" the austere gray-haired Lady Coristand asked, prepared to put this little provincial in her place. She despaired of Clarice finding a man to suit her, and although her daughter was an accredited beauty, she had not taken. Now in her second season Clarice had decided that perhaps Charles Fitzherbert might satisfy as an acceptable husband. Hence this journey to spy out the land.

"I am afraid not, Lady Coristand. The project would be too much for my grandmother, and besides I am very happy in Bath," Annabel replied politely and cheerfully. Before any more barbed comments could be exchanged, Charles joined the group, greeting Annabel and her grandmother with enthusiasm.

"Thank you for wearing my flowers, Annabel," he said, noticing at once the tuzzy-muzzy she had tied to her wrist.

"I find flowers wilt so easily at dances. I never wear them," Clarice commented scornfully, ignoring a warning look from her mother.

Annabel, swiftly deciding that Clarice Coristand was quite unlikable, smiled sunnily and made no reply. Her grandmother took up the challenge instead.

"Of course, you will know all about the latest fashions, but here we enjoy flowers and especially tonight, a celebration of Valentine's Day," Lady Clifton-More replied smoothly. She then turned to Clarice's father and asked him about the latest attempt in the Lords to put down the Corn Bill agitators. If Clarice felt snubbed she did not show it, instead batting her eyes at Charles and drawing him aside as if for a special confidence. Annabel paid no attention as she was claimed immediately by Charles's father, who beamed on her approvingly and gave her a welcoming kiss on her cheek.

"You are a treat, my dear. Do my old eyes good to have you lovely young things brightening up a winter evening." Lord Fitzherbert, in his late fifties, was a handsome man with a shock of gray hair, a stalwart carriage, and kind, glowing gray eyes. His son resembled him in both looks and temperament. He was a devoted husband viewing the foibles of his mercurial wife with a tolerant and proud air.

"Charles, you must introduce Annabel and her grandmother to our other guests," he advised, interrupting his son's tête-à-tête with the smoldering Clarice. Nothing loathe, Charles escorted Annabel and her grandmother across the room to meet the rest of the house party, which numbered some attractive men among the company.

However, when dinner was announced, it was Charles who led Annabel into the dining room. As they took their seats around the large mahogany table with its impressive decor of silver epergnes holding red roses and ferns, Charles whispered, "What do you think of the Incomparable? Quite fond of herself, isn't she?" he said cheerfully, as if he found Clarice nothing exceptional.

"She's gorgeous, Charles. Don't you think so?" Annabel quizzed, wondering for a moment if Charles really was impressed by this gazetted beauty who found him to her taste.

"She's all right but a bit overblown. Takes herself too seriously. And she doesn't ride," he confided. Annabel knew then that Clarice was damned in his eyes. Charles was a true countryman and had no use for languishing ladies who could not enjoy a brisk gallop.

Dinner was a simple affair, for a lavish supper had been planned for later that evening. In honor of the day, Lady Fitzherbert had ordered crème de coeur with raspberry puree, which climaxed the menu of saddle of mutton and partridges. Annabel's partner on her left was a sophisticated Guardsman accustomed to entertaining ladies, and once she managed to discount his rather blasé air, she found him agreeable. When he asked her eagerly if she would grant him several dances, her *amour-propre* received a fine boost, and the temporary depression induced by Clarice Coristand vanished.

Charles, although he appeared to be listening with every evidence of attention to his partner on his left, heard the exchange and leaned across to warn the young man. "Annabel is promised to me for the opening dance, Giles, so you will have to wait your turn," he insisted firmly.

Annabel, not entirely displeased with this display of possessiveness, still was not about to let Charles have his way without demur.

"But, Charles, you have all your London guests to see to."

"There are plenty of chaps to do that duty, and I want you to open the ball with me, Annabel." Then, as if the matter were settled, he turned back to his other guest. Impressed in spite of herself by this masterfulness on the part of the usually easygoing Charles, Annabel decided that she had no recourse but to obey since Charles was her host. She would deal with Colin later.

Finally, Lady Fitzherbert signaled that the ladies would

leave the gentlemen to their port, and Annabel trailed her grandmother and the others out of the room. To her surprise Lady Clifton-More immediately engaged Lady Coristand in conversation when they reached the drawing room. Knowing her grandmother capable of gathering from that austere lady all she wanted to know, Annabel decided she would leave her to it, and at a signal from Lady Fitzherbert joined her hostess on the settee.

"I see you enjoyed your dinner partner, young Giles Smedley, a very likable lad. He's in the Coldstreams and expects to go out to the Peninsula before too long. His parents tried to get him posted in London, but he would have none of it." Lady Fitzherbert darted a knowing glance at Annabel.

"Good for him. I would not think much of a soldier who tried to avoid his duty."

"Even when he is an only son? I suppose we were hasty in not allowing Charles to buy a commission, but we really need him here. I'm afraid my husband is not up to running the estate alone these days, and Charles is such a tower of strength. Do you think less of him for not fighting?" Lady Fitzherbert asked with a sudden perception.

"Of course not. Charles is not a soldier."

"No, he's a farmer, and we certainly need his expertise these days. He has some rather startling ideas on crop rotation which have proved to be most efficacious."

Lady Fitzherbert continually surprised Annabel with her practical grasp of affairs, which was hidden behind that facade of insouciance. And then there was her habit of masking the shrewd question in a veritable deluge of frivolous meanderings. Lady Fitzherbert was a clever woman, and Annabel had learned long ago to respect that quality in her neighbor.

Before Annabel could frame a question about Clarice Coristand, Lady Fitzherbert anticipated her. "How do you find Clarice? Such a sophisticated young woman, up to every rig and start. Her mother tells me she is quite the rage but also her despair, for no young man seems to suit. She has very demanding standards, I feel. Always a mistake because while she is dithering, various less well-endowed ladies will make off with the prize."

Was this Charles's mother's way of letting her know that she herself was in danger of falling into Clarice's mistake, taking Charles for granted? Or was she warning Annabel that Charles had a decided interest in the London visitor? Annabel smiled. She suspected that Lady Fitzherbert knew full well that Charles had already proposed, and this was her clever way of sounding out Annabel's feelings.

"Yes, often accredited beauties make indifferent matches. I wonder why?" Annabel replied, interested if her hostess would commit herself. But she should have known better. Lady Fitzherbert appeared to forget her interest in Clarice and wandered off into a tale of past Valentine's Day balls.

After a suitable interval the gentlemen appeared and the Fitzherberts indicated that they must repair to the ballroom to receive their guests as the sounds of carriages arriving could be heard in the driveway.

Annabel went over to see how her grandmother was standing up to the evening and found the old lady still engaged in animated conversation with Clarice's mother. Whatever the subject of their discussion they did not reveal it, and after a few minutes Giles Smedley joined them to make his obeisances to Lady Clifton-More and remind Annabel of his request for a dance. Charles did not appear, but Annabel granted Giles only one country dance and an extra after supper. By now she was eager to meet Colin. Doing the polite to the Fitzherberts' guests and parrying her grandmother's conversation as well as that of Charles' mother was fatiguing. She had come here to enjoy herself, and all these undercurrents spoiled the impact of the evening.

But before long she had forgotten her malaise as she and the rest of the company were escorted to the ballroom at the rear of the house. A folly his great-grandfather had added to the manor house and much scorned by Lord Fitzherbert, tonight the great room had come into its own, beautifully decorated with swags of red velvet and potted shrubs from the greenhouses. The three chandeliers had been cleaned and the white tapers tied with small red ribbons. At one end of the room was a huge paper heart pierced with a white arrow, and behind this romantic symbol the orchestra had begun to play as the Fitzherberts formed into a line to receive their guests, now coming in a steady stream, for it had just chimed ten o'clock.

Among the first arrivals were the officers of the Fifth Fusiliers, Colin Armistead among them. He made straight for Annabel. How handsome he was, she thought, in his regimentals. And he looked so intent, so eager to claim her, she could not help but be stirred by his persistence and his obvious devotion. Many of the guests, local county people, watched with interest, realizing that here was a possible romance suitable for the day which honored it.

Old Mrs. Sheridan, who missed little and purveyed all the gossip in the neighborhood, cocked her purple-turbaned head to her crony, Mrs. Whitefield, and nodded sagely. "That Maitland girl is quite taken with the uniform. She's a minx, that one, leading on Charles Fitzherbert and then flirting with the regimental," she cackled, her button-bright eyes watching the young pair avidly.

"An attractive couple. Most girls find a uniform fascinating," Mrs. Whitefield, a small jolly woman more charitably inclined, conceded. "He's certainly a handsome one, so who could blame her. She's the catch of the county, I hear, with a tidy amount in the funds and a beauty beside."

"Her father would never let her marry some line officer from an inferior regiment, and who knows what his family is. We've made a big mistake in receiving all these military without knowing anything about them."

"I'm sure he is a gentleman, Liza."

"More probably a scoundrel looking out for his best interests. He has a spoiled mouth and a shifty eye. I wouldn't trust my daughter to him."

Since Meg Sheridan was a matron of some thirty years married to a solicitor with a brood of rather unappealing children, Mrs. Whitefield made no comment on this rather specious remark. But, before any more gossip could be exchanged, the first set of the evening was beginning to form. Charles, seeing Annabel with his rival, marched up to the couple and reminded her that she must open the ball with him.

Annabel, a bit nervous that Colin might create a scene, turned to explain, but Colin was unwilling to challenge Charles's prior claim and gave way gracefully.

"Of course, if our host insists you must agree, Annabel, I absolve you from your prior arrangement with me," he said with a condescension which grated on Charles and caused Annabel to raise her eyebrows in amazement. What was Colin playing at, implying he had the governing of her actions? She had made no definite commitment to him, but she ventured no criticism. It would only take a few injudicious words for Colin and Charles to come to daggers drawn, and that would never do at the Valentine's Ball.

Charles and Annabel took their places in the set, and Annabel noticed that Colin had claimed Susan Pettigrew, sulky but stunning in her new eau de nile silk gown, the very one which had caused her father to raise his eyes at the bill. Annabel gave a fleeting thought that if Susan insisted she disliked Colin, it was odd that she was dancing with him.

Charles, clever enough not to disparage his rival, made no comment about Colin but talked randomly about the company, pointing out that Clarice had accepted Giles as a partner and suggesting that they were well-suited. The movements of the dance prevented any sustained conversation.

Susan had been correct in her belief that Annabel would have a surfeit of partners. After the opening dance she was besieged with beaux but managed to keep the supper dance for Colin and another for Charles. Despite her popularity Annabel was concerned. She knew Colin would be pressuring her for an answer to his suggestion that they elope, and she had made up her mind to refuse, although she could not deny that the young officer stirred her senses.

Just before supper a clumsy partner stepped heavily on her dress during a quadrille, and Annabel decided she would have to repair the damages. She excused herself to her next partner and began to make her way up the stairs to seek some maid who would help her pin up the offending tear. She noticed that Susan was again dancing with Colin. As she reached the hallway, she ran into Charles again.

"You are not sitting this out, Annabel?" she queried. She explained her reason for leaving the ballroom, noticing that he was eyeing her with a worried expression. But he accepted her excuse and escorted her to the stair, watching her wistfully as she made her way up to the first story. Then he returned to his host's responsibilities, a dance with a rather dowdy member of the house party.

Annabel found a maid on duty who was happy to mend her gown and, after dismissing the girl, sank down tiredly on one of the large winged Queen Anne chairs by the window. She needed a few moments respite from the party.

But she was not to remain undisturbed for long. The door to her sanctuary opened and a couple entered. Annabel was about to declare herself when she heard Colin's voice complaining. "This is hardly the time or place for a private conversation, Susan."

Annabel tucked her feet under her skirts and sank down farther in the concealing chair. For some reason she did not want to make her presence known. She knew it was unladylike to eavesdrop on what she sensed was to be an intimate conversation, but she excused her breach of manners by an inordinate curiosity. Why would Colin and Susan have to indulge in a private conversation? As far as she knew they disliked each other.

"Since you ignore my messages and refuse to see me, this is the only opportunity I have to call you to account, Colin," Susan said sharply.

Annabel sensed that the two were about to quarrel and thought she had best let them know they were not unobserved, but Colin's next words surprised her into silence. "We have nothing to say to each other. I told you it was all over."

"Yes, since you discovered that Annabel Maitland was an heiress and a much better match than an estate manager's daughter," Susan sneered. "I doubt if Annabel would enjoy hearing of our association in Salisbury."

Annabel bit back a gasp. She had no idea that these two had a prior relationship but remembered that Susan had some time ago spent several months in Salisbury visiting her cousin.

"That was a fleeting flirtation. Neither one of us took it seriously," Colin muttered angrily.

"I think that afternoon we met in your rooms was hardly a fleeting flirtation. You seduced me and promised to marry me. Then I was called home by Mother's illness and never heard another word from you until you turned up here with the Fusiliers," Susan reminded him, her tone bitter.

Annabel, shocked, could restrain herself no longer. She stood up suddenly, crossing the room to where the two were facing each other by the fireplace, Colin flushed and furious, Susan calm but determined.

"Is this true, Colin?" she asked, ignoring the amazed look on both Colin and Susan's faces.

"Spying, Annabel?" Susan said contemptuously. "Well, you heard more than you bargained for. And now I will tell you the rest about this precious beau of yours. Yes, he seduced me, and then deserted me. But he will not get away with such caddish behavior. He will marry me or pay the consequences. Your dashing cavalier is a rogue, a fortune hunter, and a liar," Susan spit out.

"Surely if what you claim is true, Susan, you can't want to marry him now," Annabel responded naively, uncertain of her reaction.

"Don't believe this jealous harpy, Annabel. I might have paid her some attention in Salisbury, but it meant little," Colin blustered, seeing his chances of securing the lovely and rich Miss Maitland evaporate.

"Not only did he seduce me, he borrowed money to give a

barmaid at the Nag's Head in Salisbury whom he had put in a family way," Susan accused coldly, not at all embarrassed by Annabel's question. "And of course I want to marry him. Who else would have me if they thought I were used goods," she added rather coarsely. "And I doubt if his commanding officer would like to learn about the gallant lieutenant's transgressions. I have postponed telling the truth to his colonel, but I will not keep silent while he persuades you to elope with him. Your grandmother is quite correct in her suspicions that he is not a paragon of virtue. Quite the contrary, in fact."

Annabel was stunned by this revelation and could not quite comprehend the infamy of Colin's actions. But she had to believe Susan. Surely the girl would not admit to losing her virtue if it were false. Turning to Colin, Annabel asked simply, "Is Susan correct in her accusation that you promised to marry her and then basely deserted her?"

"It was not like that at all. I paid her some attention in Salisbury, a damned dull post, and she made most of the running. I do not love her, you know that. It is you I care for, Annabel." He put his hand on her shoulders and looked into her eyes with every evidence of sincerity, and Annabel wavered. Could Susan be lying—jealous, frustrated because Colin preferred Annabel to herself?

"What about the barmaid?" she asked succinctly.

"All a lie. I needed the money to send to my sick sister in Northumberland," he insisted, his eyes meeting hers with appeal.

"If you believe that, Annabel, you are more of an innocent than I took you for," Susan scoffed, her chin set stubbornly.

"Surely, since you think Colin is capable of such heinous betrayal, you would not want to wed him. Your parents would be horrified." Annabel shook her head in dismay. What chance would such a marriage have? Her own disillusionment could not be denied. She remembered her grandmother's story and realized she had been within an ace of repeating that tragic folly. In that moment Annabel grew up, facing the iniquities of human behavior that she had never imagined.

"Listen to me, Annabel. Susan is romancing. She is desperate to be wed, but she will not blackmail me by such tactics. We would lead a dog's life, and I am not about to sacrifice my freedom to a frantic girl with delusions. Don't be taken in by her wild imaginings. You have as much as promised to be my wife," he insisted in desperation.

"Charles knows about you, Colin," Susan responded with telling simplicity.

"Then why has he kept silent?"

"Because I told him you would marry me and then he would have a chance with Annabel."

Annabel gasped. How hateful. And why had Charles said nothing to her?

As if on cue, Charles stepped into the room saying, "Here you are, Annabel. Had you forgotten our dance?"

"Never mind that, Charles. Did you know that Colin had promised to marry Susan and then abandoned her?" Annabel turned to Charles with dismay evident in her face.

"Oh, dear, I was afraid this would happen." Charles crossed to Annabel and took her hand, ignoring the two staring at him with disbelief. "Listen to me, Annabel. Susan did tell me her sad story and revealed the wickedness of this rogue, but I could not bear to disillusion you. I hoped you would discover his chicanery yourself. You would have only despised me for breaking a confidence and attacking a rival. It would have been dishonorable. But I would never have allowed you to marry such a man," he assured her quietly.

"I will call you out, sir, for impugning my reputation," Colin blustered, completely befuddled by the direction of events. Pulling Annabel away from Charles, he pleaded, "Pay no attention to these canards. Come with me now. We will ride to Gretna Green and you will be my wife. I promise you all this will seem like a bad dream."

Before Annabel could struggle from his hold in horror, Charles had pushed her aside and knocked Colin to the floor with an expert blow to the chin. Colin lay there stunned for a time, then groaned, but made no move to return the attack.

Charles looked at him with disgust.

"You are no longer welcome here, Armistead. Please leave as soon as you are capable." Turning to Susan who had stood by disdainfully while the sordid scene was enacted, he said firmly, "We will not mention this deplorable situation to anyone, Susan. You may do what you wish, but I would advise you wash your hands of the fellow. Come, Annabel, this is no place for you." And without further ado he shepherded the dazed and appalled Annabel from the room. In the hall outside he paused, gazing up and down to make sure they were not seen.

"I am sorry, Annabel, that you should have been subjected to such a performance, but the man is a bounder. Here, let us just repair into this bedroom for a moment so you can regain your composure," he advised calmly, just as if the horrid encounter had never happened. Meekly she allowed herself to be commandeered.

"I can't believe it, Charles. How could I have been so deceived. It is a nightmare," Annabel confided once they were alone beyond prying eyes. Then she remembered her dream, the nightmare come to life.

"Forget it all, Annabel. You should never have been exposed to the varlet. Let Susan make what she can of the cad. Surely you realize I could not tell you what she confided in me although I was tempted. I did not want all your dreams shattered. I love you and want to protect and cherish you, keep you safe from all the nastiness of the world," he insisted gently, holding her in his arms and looking at her with a gentle scrutiny that reassured her.

"Oh, Charles, I have been such a fool, mistaking the dross for the gold, just as Grandmother warned. How can you love anyone who has been such a ninny?" Annabel replied, not far from tears.

"I don't know. St. Valentine must have worked his magic," he teased, eager to lighten the atmosphere and restore her to happy reality.

"I don't deserve such a gallant cavalier." Annabel choked a

bit but managed a slight smile.

"Perhaps not, but you have him." And unwilling to listen to any more nonsense, Charles took her into his arms and kissed her with all the force and persuasion of which he was capable. Annabel, responding, felt a glowing sense of warmth and security. Nestling closer, she returned his kiss with a passion which surprised him. Looking down into her blue eyes, he teased, "And now I have compromised you, dragging you into this room and pressing my attentions on you. You will have to marry me, you know."

"Yes, I know, Charles. And thank goodness I have come to my senses in time. I was quite afraid that Clarice Coristand might capture you, and that would have been a real nightmare. I dreamt it all last night, you know. And in my dream you rescued me just like you did this evening."

"I will always be on hand now to rescue you, my dearest. Come, we must tell my parents and your grandmother. It will be a fitting climax to the Valentine's Ball," he said happily, certain at last that Annabel returned his love. "One more kiss before we share the news."

Suiting his action to the words, he gave his sentiments full rein. Annabel, content to surrender, fleetingly thought of Dorrie and her bay leaves, then forgot them both in the ecstasy of the moment. It was a long time before they returned to the ball, and watching them cross the floor to Lady Clifton-More, few of the guests were in doubt that another pair had been claimed by St. Valentine.

A Play of Hearts

by Valerie King

O Love, O fire! once he drew
With one long kiss my whole soul thro'
My lips, as sunlight drinketh dew.

—Alfred, Lord Tennyson

"Molland's grays. Whatever is he doing in Newton Bovey!"

Lord Brenton was only vaguely aware he had spoken aloud as he strained his neck to look out the window of his traveling chariot. A pair of matched gray horses, harnessed as they were to a shiny black curricle, threw up their heads and stamped their feet in protest. They were standing outside the Cob Inn, taking the force of a cold February wind deep in the chest and registering their discontent by snorting. Molland was nowhere to be seen.

Brenton had recognized the horses at once. They belonged to Henry Molland, a man of dubious birth, though considerable airs, skilled at beguiling the hearts of widows and known to be hanging out for an heiress. It was just like Molland, he thought, to risk his exceptional cattle by letting them take the brunt of a blustery St. Valentine's Day.

He had only one thought as he lifted a bored brow: he wished with all his soul that *good* Mr. Molland might take a fancy to Miss Ferrers and remove from his house the pollution it was now enduring by her presence there.

He smiled a very wicked smile of pure self-satisfaction as he gripped his ebony walking stick and gave it a hearty smack on the floor of the carriage. He was returning to Brentwood Court considerably beforetimes, unbeknownst to any of the inmates currently residing within the sandstone walls of the house. Miss Ferrers would undoubtedly receive a shock by his arrival. Certainly her schemes would be overset. His sister, his hopelessly featherheaded sibling, had let it slip in her last missive that Miss Ferrers was getting up a play for the general amusement of the children. A play!

The very thought of it brought such a sense of outrage to his concept of decorum and propriety that he again smote the floor of the coach with his cane. Dorinda had foolishly invited Miss Ferrers to spend several weeks at his house, Brentwood Court, against his wishes or approval. Her announcement of the impending visit had been accompanied by the uproarious, and rather unexpected, enthusiasm of his wards. "Auntie Beth is coming!" young Tristan had cried, his face alight with joy. Even stoic Charles, destined to become a man of the cloth, had cried, "What famous fun!"

Lord Brenton had been stunned. When had Miss Ferrers squirmed her way into the good graces of his nieces and nephews?

Dorinda's response to his dislike of the plan was entirely inadequate. He remembered her words now, each syllable a stinging slap to his self-consequence. "When was it," Dorinda had cried, setting aside the several shawls with which she was draped to rise unsteadily from her couch and confront him, "that you became such a dreadful bore! I have never heard more fustian in all my life! Beth Ferrers may be a touch beneath your station, and she may have an unusual mode of conduct upon occasion, but I find her amusing, agreeable, and the most generous-hearted creature in the world. And if I recall correctly, I remember there was a time, brother dearest, when you were much struck with her yourself! But what I don't understand is why, with all her extraordinary beauty, Beth has dwindled into a veritable ape-leader—though I begin to think you must somehow be the cause of it!" She had clutched her bosom after this long, extraordinary speech and fell back into a sea of cashmere and silk shawls. "Oh, dear, now I am grown excessively fatigued. How weak my poor heart has become since Jack succumbed to an inflammation of the lungs. I am not used to feeling peevish and ill-tempered. Where is my pug? There you are my precious sweet-cakes! Go away Geoffrey! You are bringing on a spasm. Oh, my nerves, my poor, poor nerves." She closed her eyes, settling deeply into her well-cushioned sofa. With Pug curled up at her feet, she pulled a shawl over her shoulders and drifted into one of her several daily slumbers but not before she murmured that he ought to stop being so high in the instep, otherwise he was likely to fall from his self-consequence and twist his ankle!

Lord Brenton shifted slightly to stare out the window of his carriage. Had he become *a dreadful bore?* He didn't think so, and if Claire Lydbury was to be believed, he was, how had she phrased it? *the most brilliant light in the firmament of their Bath acquaintances.* He would have taken more pleasure in her words had he not for so long a time known that she had set her cap for him. Besides, he could not forget Miss Ferrers opinion of Miss Lydbury. "I should admire her exceedingly if she did not speak through her nose! In general I do not mind such an affectation, but in her case, she looks *down* her nose as well! I do not hesitate to tell you I find the combination intolerable!"

Lord Brenton had been amused despite his efforts not to be. Even now, he smiled at the memory. Miss Ferrers had imitated Miss Lydbury's nasal voice to perfection. Had he not been in the habit of holding Miss Ferrers in disesteem, he would have been enchanted with her since he could not help but admire her abilities, the sharp twists of her mind, and her sense of humor. As it was, he had held his laughter in check only to hear her tease him for permitting his amusement to reach his eyes. She was nothing if not perceptive! He had turned on his heel and stalked away, though he had to admit that limping as he did from an ancient wound to his knee received while serving on the Peninsula hardly served to create quite the effect he had hoped to achieve. He remembered having turned back slightly—why, he could not remember—only to catch the strangest glimpse of sad blue eyes, and had her hand really been stretched out to him? He wasn't sure. How melancholy he had felt for several days afterward.

As the carriage rolled past the village of Newton Bovey, Lord Brenton surveyed the Devonshire landscape. In February, with a recent snow melted but the land still bleak with frost and skeletal trees not yet budded, he frequently felt as cold as the land about him. He was past thirty and had for several years known an intense longing to bring a wife to Brentwood Court. Indeed, he had almost offered for Miss Lydbury until he actually heard her snort while she laughed. She speaks and laughs through her nose. Detestable!

He wished it were summer. He always knew a sense of serenity during the summer in his home county. Winter, bah! He wanted to see the fuschia hedge near the stream alive with bobbing vermillion bells chasing ferns into the water, to recline on the banks and fish lazily for equally lazy trout.

As the horses of his traveling chariot struck the stone cobbles of the bridge, his mind turned a brilliant yellow. He leaned toward the window and gazed out and could see the stream as it would be in July. Time rolled back several years. He heard a young woman giggle, and when he turned the direction of her laughter, he saw several lads clearly up to mischief. He glanced from face to face and noticed one lit with unholy pleasure, most certainly the source of the giggling. A boy? Impossible. He watched the sunlight reflecting off the water and touching the youth's face—only it was Beth's face, though he didn't know it at the time. How that first glimpse of her had pursued him down the years! Out for a lark!

Beth! he murmured, caught up in the memory of meeting Miss Ferrers for the first time. She had been a mere chit, playing a boyish prank as she slung mud all over him and two of his friends, all fresh from Oxford and very full of themselves. She had been one of four madcap striplings, and he and his friends had easily run them to earth since they were astride their restless mounts. He had caught Beth, pulling the farmer's hat from her head, stunned to find he had a young woman in his arms. She had been as lively and warm as the sun itself, her blue eyes dancing merrily with excitement. The others were so far away. He recognized her as the daughter of a neighboring country squire. He still didn't know why, but he had drawn her into his arms and kissed her. To this day he could feel the softness of her young lips, the eager body that leaned into his, the confusion on her face when he let her go. She had been all of sixteen.

She was so readily kissed, so *easily* kissed, as she had proven again in London three years later.

But not by him.

A gust of wind rattled the glass and he turned away, the starkness of the land invading his heart and dimming the bright memory that always haunted him when he crossed this bridge.

She had gone too far this time, however. As soon as he reached Brentwood Court, he would eject her from his house.

"There, there, Tris!" Beth whispered, trying to soothe the little boy cuddled on her lap. He was hiccupping and crying at the same time.

"But it hurts, Auntie Beth!"

"And it will, too, for some time to come," she responded softly, wincing at the sight of a large bruise welling up into a purple plum on his cheekbone. "So you must be very brave. You took a nasty spill, though I think once your uncle returns from Bath I will mention to him that St. George ought to be moved to a different part of the house." Tristan had stumbled over the large feet of a suit of armor, christened St. George by the boys, which had inhabited the landing at the top of the stairs for centuries. The narrow walkway would have been an awkward place for anything large, not to mention the gleaming uniform of a knight, but tradition had ruled the fine old house instead of common sense.

"Take him to the attics now!" Tristan wailed.

"Well, we shall see what Lord Brenton decrees once he is come home," Beth countered firmly. "I shall strongly recommend St. George be moved to the library, but the decision must be your uncle's!" If Beth thought somewhat bitterly that Lord Brenton was more likely to attend to St. George's opinion as to where he belonged rather than her own, she refrained from expressing as much to the child on her lap.

Tristan had been following his two elder brothers in a fast-paced game of running from the housekeeper, ostensibly a harmless occupation which Beth had just learned was also known by the unhandsome appellation of "Taunting Mrs. Tibbs." Charles, who was standing nearby, had just returned slightly out of breath from spying on the inhabitants of the billiard room and was impatiently tapping his foot, his arms folded across his chest. James was nowhere to be seen, though Beth suspected he had returned to the kitchens to steal a brambleberry tart since Cook was making them up special today.

"Oh, do stop squawking!" Charles Hatherleigh cried at last, addressing his younger brother. He was a boy of eight, four years Tristan's senior and was of a serious and moral tone of mind. "You've had your cry and if you must know, Auntie Beth has something of far greater importance to attend to than your trifling wounds!"

"My wounds are not *truffling,*" Tristan responded, firing up instantly. "Are they, Auntie Beth?"

"No, of course they are not, dearest," she returned, petting his head and kissing his cheek. She frowned at Charles, who was now pulling anxiously on the sleeve of her round gown of blue sprigged muslin, and shook her head. She would have set about reminding him that Tristan was still a very small boy and ought to be treated a little more kindly, but as she glanced at the rather twisted grimace on Charles's face, she became aware that something untoward had occurred. "What is it?" she asked.

Having garnered her attention, Charles's entire body seemed to draw to a state of alertness in the manner of the faithful watchdog he had become for Beth. "It's—*the tutor!*" he responded gravely.

"Oh, dear," Beth whispered. "Has he tried to—I mean, has he crossed any of the bounds of propriety?" Could Charles, as young as he was, possibly understand what she meant?

"Yes!" he cried with a curt nod. "He kissed Sukey's hand. And not just her fingers! This part!" He pointed to his palm, his large, serious eyes open in astonishment. "Why would he do such a thing?"

"I don't know," Beth lied, blinking her eyes quickly and hoping that Charles would not realize she was telling a whisker. "Only tell me what Susan did. Was she in the least distressed?"

Charles appeared disgusted. "She giggled the entire time and looked like a simpering toad, ogling Mr. Chagford with her round eyes, and making her eyelashes move like butterfly wings! But what was worse, she was smiling so broadly up into his face, one could see all her teeth! What a cake she was making of herself! If I were Mr. Chagford I would have cast up my accounts!"

Beth repressed the laughter which Charles's remarks had occasioned and instead breathed a heavy sigh of relief, an emotion she had not experienced for a long time. Part of her could not help but feel grateful for Susan's blossoming interest in Charles's and James's tutor since the *tendre* she was forming for the quite ineligible though handsome young man meant that the difficulty with which she had been grappling for three tedious, exasperating weeks would soon be at an end. But the other, more long-sighted part of her knew very well that the young, high-spirited, and ridiculously romantic Susan Hatherleigh was about to tumble into yet another disagreeable scrape. "Is your mama anywhere abouts?" Beth asked, ever hopeful but certain to be disappointed.

"She is sleeping, I'm 'fraid. She's in the drawing room. I

tried to wake her, but Pug growled at me, and the last time I disturbed Mama, he bit me. Only what can be done? Do you remember that one scene of the play you most particularly told Susan not to rehearse?" When Beth nodded, he pinched his lips tightly together before saying, "They are whispering the lines to one another—something about 'It is the lark, no, no, it is the heron.' "

"You mean 'the nightingale.' "

"Yes, yes, that's it, 'the nightingale.' "

Beth gathered Tristan up in her arms, wondering if she could possibly traverse the distance from the landing, down the stairs and to the billiard room where the play was being staged, and still keep hold of the sturdy lad in her arms. "Come, Tris," she said. "We must see to your sister. Charles, why don't you find Priscilla and beg her to come to the billiard room. Perhaps I can persuade her to give Trissy here a cuddle."

At the mere mention of his other sister, who was three years younger than Susan, Tristan threatened to set up a wail. He was not nearly so fond of Prissy as he was of Beth—or Susan, for that matter—and she immediately relinquished any notion she might have had of being released from the charge of her poor little patient. Tristan had grown uncommonly attached to her.

As the unlikely threesome descended the stairs, Beth inquired of Charles as to whether Mr. Molland's curricle could be seen in the avenue yet. Letting out a horrified shriek, Charles bolted back up the stairs saying that he had forgot all about it. If Beth felt a prickle of her conscience at training a young boy to serve as a spy to his sister's comings and goings as well as to any of her beaux who might choose to rob Brentwood Court of one of its heiresses, she set her guilt aside. Perhaps once Lord Brenton returned from Bath, he could begin redressing the lesser of the evils she was creating in her own countermachinations to Susan's reprehensible desire to elope with Mr. Molland—she intended for the tutor to replace the wretched fortune hunter in Sukey's affections! Until then, she felt all she could do was somehow muddle through to the end.

Four weeks earlier, Susan had chanced to make the acquaintance of Mr. Molland, who had been traveling through the small thatched village of Newton Bovey, situated only a mile and a half from Brentwood Court. His wild blond locks, the Belcher kerchief tied negligently about his throat, his provocative mode of address—all spoke instantly to the vanity of Brentwood Court's reigning miss. He wooed her, tickled her girlish heart with fanciful compliments, inveigled himself into Dorinda's good graces, and brought the boys sweets with every visit until Susan firmly believed she had found her prince. The only members of the household not bewitched by the golden promises of the golden haired boy, were Charles, Colyton the butler, and herself. Of course she was hardly a part of the household, merely a neighbor and friend of long-standing—at least to Susan's mother. However, given the fact that Susan's mother, Dorinda, slept away the greater part of Mr. Molland's flirtations with her daughter, it was not to be wondered that Beth felt obliged to keep a watchful eye.

What made matters nearly intolerable for Beth was the fact that the only way in which she could keep an eye on Susan was by becoming her confidante and promising to aid her in an elopement with *dear, dear* Mr. Molland. *Dear* Mr. Molland, however, was a man Beth knew to be one of London's worst scapegraces, a profligate dallier with the feminine heart, a rake of the meanest order, in short a fortune hunter and nothing less.

With Tristan still held in her arms, Beth threw open the door to the billiard room. She saw to her dismay that the green baize used to form a curtain for the stage was drawn tightly shut, and Susan's laughter could be heard in a series of delighted chortles from somewhere behind the cloth.

Where was Dorinda?

"Susan, dearest?" Beth called out in a friendly way. "Are you ready to rehearse the second scene with Mr. Chagford? I'm sorry it took me so long to return to you, but as you can see, poor Tristan has hurt his cheek."

Susan emerged quickly from between the two widths of pleated baize and gave each side a shove revealing the stage. The color on her cheeks was considerably heightened as she said, "We, that is, Sylvestre—I mean, Mr. Chagford and I were just reviewing our lines. Oh, poor, poor Trissy! Come, darling, let me have a look at you!"

Much to Beth's relief, Tristan plunged from her arms, landing on the floor in what seemed to Beth a dead run, and hurled himself into Susan's outstretched arms. Beth could not keep from smiling at the sweet embrace that followed and the tender way in which Susan seated herself upon the edge of the stage, her legs dangling as she gathered Tristan into her arms. She was a tenderhearted girl, one who deserved all the love in the world. If only she had been given even a measure of discernment with which to choose her beaux more wisely. Dorinda ought to have seen to it herself, but Beth knew well indeed how imperfectly Dorinda Hatherleigh's own choices had been made. Her marriage to Jack Hatherleigh—also a fortune hunter and gamester—had been unpropitious in the extreme, save for the rather curious fact that Dorinda had loved him. No one, not even Beth would deny that Jack had been a man of great charm and ability. How well he had imitated Lord Brenton's halting walk that infamous night of the masquerade!

Shaking off these unhappy reminiscences, she turned her attention instead toward Susan. She ought to be brought out this Season, Beth thought. Susan was in great need of the diversion which a larger world could provide as well as the exposure to a score of disapproving matrons who kept their own daughters well in tow. Sukey, for all her spiritedness, was not beyond instruction. A gentle word from one or two knowledgeable tonnish ladies would go far to setting her feet on a proper path.

Well, there was nothing for that! Lord Brenton wouldn't hear of it! Susan would have to wait another year when she would be almost eighteen. She had tried several months earlier to give the viscount a hint concerning the waywardness of Susan's heart, suggesting that a young lady of Susan's temperament would benefit enormously from an early introduction into the *beau monde.* But he had cut her off with a mere sardonic lifting of his brow and a short reply that she ought to tend to her own affairs and not to those belonging more nearly to Susan's mama.

How hard Beth had bitten her tongue! How desperately she had longed to point out to his lordship that Dorinda behaved more like a careless sister to her children than a firm, concerned parent. But he did not have ears to hear anything she might have to say to him. How stubborn the man was. In her opinion, he was one of the most mulish, irascible creatures she had ever known. And if she could have torn the memory of having shared her very first kiss with him straight out of her heart, she would undoubtedly even now be a contented matron herself, with perhaps her own brood of chicks gamboling about her knees, instead of playing nursemaid to Dorinda's. Somehow, Brenton's kiss, so full of sunshine and mischief, had spoiled her for other, perfectly eligible men. Perhaps that was why she could forgive Dorinda for having loved Jack Hatherleigh, because for all of Brenton's disinterest in her, Beth still loved him, though for the life of her she could not say why!

As for the children, she certainly didn't mind playing the role of dutiful aunt. She had formed an easy bond with each and took sincere delight in their obvious affection for her.

From the shadows of the stage, Beth could hear Mr. Chagford speaking his lines aloud, attempting to create the illusion he had been busy about the play instead of flirting with Susan. Beth was not fooled for a moment, though she could hardly blame Mr. Chagford for his interest in Susan. He was quite young, not yet nineteen, and how was he supposed to resist the large emerald eyes which dominated Sukey's beautiful face? They were thickly lashed, glittering with her high spirits, and had fairly taunted him to tumble in love with her! No, it would have been impossible for such an untried stripling to have ignored the vibrant speech and manners of Susan

Hatherleigh. Beth could not truly fault him. If anything, her conscience again fluttered about erratically with the thought that she was making considerable use of Mr. Chagford's vulnerability in setting him in opposition to Susan's desire to elope with Mr. Molland.

Beth could only hope that all her devious machinations and subterfuge would coalesce this very afternoon—that Susan would jilt Mr. Molland's intriguingly wild locks for Mr. Chagford's recitations of Byron at every turn. If she did not, the future looked bleak indeed, with nothing short of a scandal destined to ensue.

As soon as Tristan's four-year-old sensibilities were quieted with the aid of a wooden sword thrust into his hand, Beth announced her desire to hear the flowery balcony scene from *Romeo and Juliet.* The billiard room had been stripped of its large, pocketed table, and in the center of the chamber, a small settee had been placed in preparation for the final performance at which Dorinda would comprise the whole of the children's audience. Beth sat down on the settee, and after bidding Tristan to practice his sword thrusts quietly at the back of the room, she commanded the fledgling actress and actor to begin.

Susan climbed to the third rung of a short ladder and gazed sweetly down upon the tutor, who remained at the bottom staring up at her. Beth bit her lip, trying not to smile at the mooncalf expression on Mr. Chagford's face. They began their dialogue, and it was quickly evident that both young persons had learned their lines well. As each word replaced the next, she watched in growing amusement the hallmarks of love which began altering poor Sylvestre's face. His eyes drooped lower and lower; he blinked slowly; his mouth remained perpetually open as he released sigh after sigh, his complexion rising with each word his Juliet spoke.

Beth felt a well of laughter strive within her chest for release at the sight of his evident infatuation with Susan. She would have failed to hold back a rising peal of mirth had not Charles suddenly burst into the billiard room. Beth turned around to find he was completely out of breath and his face was ashen in hue. At first she thought he must have seen Mr. Molland in the lane, but she realized immediately that something else had overset him.

Knowing his duty to keep his activities a secret from Susan, Charles said nothing until he had reached the settee at which time he leaned well over the back and whispered frantically into Beth's ear. "It is—it is my uncle!" he cried in gasps. "He has come home. Oh, Auntie Beth, you don't think he will take my sword away, do you, just because Sukey wished to elope with Mr. Molland? It wouldn't be fair!"

Beth remained seated, her entire being stilled with fright as she stared into Charles's horrified eyes. Her mind raced wildly about. Whatever was she going to do? Brenton was here!

"Are you certain?" she asked in a desperate whisper.

Charles nodded. "I heard a carriage in the drive and saw my uncle's traveling chariot heading toward the stables. He was still in the coach when it passed by. I saw him from the window. What are you going to do?"

"I don't know, but never fear. I shall contrive something, only let me think!" She turned away from Charles and stared down at her hands, which to her amazement were actually trembling. She could not remember being this frightened before. Of the moment, she did not know which she dreaded most—coming to cuffs with Brenton herself or the knowledge that his return could somehow precipitate Susan's flight with Molland! Beth sensed that should Sukey learn of her uncle's untimely arrival, the chit might take it into her head to elope with Mr. Molland after all!

But why had Lord Brenton returned so early? Dorinda, of course! She had written to him a sennight ago and must have told him about the play.

There was only one thing to be done in order to keep Susan's attention diverted from Mr. Molland. The play must be enacted immediately thereby preventing Susan from thinking of anything other than her Romeo. But how was she to get rid of Molland when Brenton would be stomping about his ancestral home, kicking up such a dust about the improper nature of the play as would make it impossible for her to do little more than occupy her time fending off his attacks?

On the stage, Mr. Chagford and Susan were still speaking their lines, the tutor touching the ladder and gazing up devotedly into his Juliet's face.

Beth rose from the settee and set her counterscheme in motion. "Why, it is absolutely perfect!" she cried enthusiastically. "I see no reason to delay a performance. Susan, we have but to inform your mama and begin! Why should we put off until tomorrow what may be delightfully accomplished today, especially since it is clear to me that the inspiration of the remarkable Siddons and Kean are upon you both!"

Mr. Chagford appeared startled, and Susan immediately began to protest, saying that though this particular scene was well in hand, she hadn't yet learned all her lines for the third one.

Beth waved aside her concerns, saying that Priscilla could prompt them both from the wings if she liked. She glanced around suddenly and realized that Prissy had been gone from the family circle for almost the entire morning, a circumstance unusual for her. Beth felt her stomach twist itself up nervously. Priscilla was the gentlest of Dorinda's children and had suffered acutely from Jack Hatherleigh's death only two years earlier. More than once of late, particularly living in the shadow of Susan's proposed elopement, Beth had watched the young girl's eyes fill with tears at the mere mention of either her papa or Mr. Molland. Trouble was brewing on that front, but Beth could hardly tend to it now, not with Lord Brenton just arrived!

Reiterating to Susan that the play would go on and brooking no argument, Beth turned to Charles and told him to bring his mama to the billiard room, *at once!*

"But what about Pug?" Charles asked, startled.

Beth cast about in her mind for an answer to this terrifying dilemma, knowing Charles had reason to fear his mother's pet. Swallowing hard, she walked toward the back of the chamber, where Tristan was parrying and thrusting with every particle of strength to be found in a young child's awkward arm and without hesitation wrested the wooden sword from him.

Even though Trissy set up an instant wail, Beth held him away from the sword with an arm slung about his waist and addressed Charles. "Make use of this!" she cried. "Do what you must, but get your mother here in good time—before your uncle discovers our whereabouts! Oh, and bid Colyton to find James and send him to the billiard room."

Beth wasn't certain Charles had heard all of her commands, since the moment she handed him the sword, his face had become lit with a broad, almost devilish grin. He hefted the makeshift weapon in his hand and cast several imaginary but violent thrusts toward the carpet, afterward mimicking Pug's wounded yelp in response to his attack.

"Poor Pug," Beth murmured with a smile as she watched Charles dash from the chamber.

Once she had calmed Tristan's seriously offended sense of fair play by promising him he could have James's sword once it was found, she began giving her orders for the presentation of three abbreviated scenes from *Romeo and Juliet,* to be enacted in no less than ten minutes.

Lord Brenton walked up from the stables on a slow tread. He was rehearsing precisely what he meant to say to Miss Ferrers. He chose each word carefully. He practiced his intonations, building to a most forceful directive requiring she vacate his house immediately, and even going so far as to see in his mind the gesture he would employ—the flinging of his arm toward the door—as he spoke the last line of his speech. He couldn't decide, however, whether he ought to call her a hoyden or not. It was a strong word, but then, she was an awfully strong-willed female. Stubborn! Deucedly so!

By the time he had handed over his hat, his gloves, and his many caped greatcoat to Colyton, he was well-satisfied with his speech and begged only to be shown to her current location within the sundry, august chambers of his house.

"Ah," Colyton responded with a curiously warm smile on his face. "I don't know how we would have gone on without Miss Ferrers in attendance upon your sister these several weeks and more. Poor Mrs. Hatherleigh has been suffering terribly from the vapors and has relied upon Miss Ferrers in everything. I don't need to tell you that Miss is a very competent young woman." He slipped the gloves within the crown of the viscount's hat and added politely, "To my knowledge, she is at present in the billiard room."

Lord Brenton had only one reaction to his butler's flattering speech—the *hoyden* had somehow deceived even wise, old Colyton. Evidently there was no end to her guile. "The billiard room?" he cried, refusing to comment upon Colyton's praise of Miss Ferrers. "Has she dared staged a *play* within *my* billiard room?"

If Colyton was distressed by the apparent disapproval with which Lord Brenton had spoken these words, he did not betray his feelings except by a slight narrowing of his rather piercing gray eyes. "Yes, m'lord, and making use of your library next to the billiard room as well."

"My library!" he bellowed. "How—how—dare—" He was unable to move any further words beyond his lips. They had gotten stuck in the ire that rose from within his chest. Taking a deep breath, he set his cane harshly on the black-and-white tile as he marched in tapping cadence toward the billiard room.

"Charles!" James Hatherleigh cried. "You must practice with me before we are to enact our scene."

"Well, if you hadn't spent the past fifteen minutes hiding in the buttery and cramming Cook's tarts into your mouth—"

"Charles!" Beth interjected in a stern whisper, with one eye fixed upon the performers on stage and the other overseeing the three, sometimes tiresome boys at her elbow. "I won't permit you to speak to your brother so unkindly, not in my presence!"

James, who was Charles's elder by two years, pulled a face at his provoking sibling and swiped his wooden sword—found beneath the settee in the billiard room—through the air several times. He was a pudgy child and oddly enough the same height as Charles. Of all of Dorinda's children, he was the least likable, except that when he smiled even the sun seemed to shine brighter. Getting him to smile, however, was a bird of a different feather.

Tristan clung to her skirts, munching a biscuit from a plate of warm macaroons he had charmed from Cook only a few minutes earlier. He was still unhappy about not having a sword of his own, but since James promised to teach him how to fence once the play was all behind them, he had quieted down.

"Charles," Beth called over her shoulder while her gaze remained fixed upon the tutor. She watched him climb the first rung of the ladder and begin the line, "Shall I hear more." "Is your finger still bleeding?"

"No, Auntie. It was the merest scratch!" he responded, grunting. The sound of wooden swords meeting with a firm whack struck her ears and she jumped. Earlier, a slightly protruding nail at the hilt of James's sword had caught Charles' finger when the combatants' weapons had brought them together in a close battle. Not thinking, he had wiped the ensuing blood on his white shirtfront. What would Brenton think of that, Beth wondered, glancing at Charles and James. No doubt he would accuse her of trying to murder his nephews. Again the wooden swords came together in a blistering crack.

"By all that's wonderful!" Charles cried. "I say, did you feel that?"

"We've never done half so well. My hand is still tingling!" The swords again began clattering and singing as the boys leapt into the air and danced wildly about.

Had Beth not been quite so distressed by her approaching confrontation with Brenton, she would have taken great pleasure in watching the boys actually playing together. They were cut from such different bolts of cloth that it was unusual for them to find anything to like or admire or enjoy in the other. As it was, she could only suppress the butterflies running riot in her stomach as she turned her attention back to the play.

Juliet finished her speech and Romeo began, "I take thee at thy word," when Dorinda called out suddenly, "Word? What word? Oh, oh dear. No, please go on, dearest one. I do beg your pardon. I was just—I thought you was speaking to me! Pray continue!"

From where Beth was standing, she could just see her friend, who had apparently drifted off, then awoken suddenly, her large eyes blinking rapidly as she stared at the players on the stage. Beth clapped a hand to her mouth to keep from laughing and just as she did so James let loose with a very loud shriek.

"You did that on purpose, you little beast!" he cried.

"I did not!" Charles countered. "You were just too slow and didn't move out of the way!"

By the time Beth turned around, the little darlings were engaged in a hearty bout of fisticuffs, their swords lying abandoned on the floor in favor of a more immediate and decidedly more satisfying form of mortal combat. She was just separating them when Lord Brenton's voice boomed clear to the rafters. "What manner of conduct is this? James! Charles! Stop your fighting at once or I'll have Colyton lock you both in the shed—for the night!"

"Uncle Geoffrey!" the boys chimed in unison, relaxing their hold on one another and turning expectantly toward the viscount.

For some reason, Beth expected the ruffians to start quaking in their boots at the sight of their formidable uncle. She was not precisely prepared to see them each dart eagerly forward and cast themselves upon his person, worrying his neatly tied neckcloth and begging favors of him. With mock severity, he bade them both cease their nonsense and to stand before him so that he might have a look at them. When they had grown quiet, he told them in no uncertain terms that they should first offer an apology to Miss Ferrers for behaving so atrociously in her presence.

"Oh, she doesn't give a fig for that," James exclaimed with considerable pride. "She's a right one and says a boy ought to kick up a lark now and again."

"Oh, she does, does she?" he glanced at Beth, a martial light in his eye. "Well, I don't care how accommodating she might be, you still must apologize and promise not to quarrel in the future."

Both boys promptly turned toward Beth and very politely offered their apologies along with a presentation of their very best bows.

Beth took a step toward the viscount wondering where she ought to begin in justifying the play to him. And how on earth was she to explain Mr. Molland and the proposed elopement? Her heart felt rather unsteady in her breast as it always did when she first met Geoffrey after a few weeks or months of separation. It would seem that she could never completely reconcile herself to how tall and fine-looking he was, how blue his eyes were, how they could glimmer irrepressibly when he was amused. He was attired in his usual meticulous fashion with a neat coat of blue superfine stretched to perfection over broad shoulders, a pair of pale fawn pantaloons encasing muscular legs, gleaming, tasseled Hessians molded to his feet, and a gold seal dangling from his waistcoat. His hair was trimmed and brushed à la Brutus, and he bore himself as he had for many years past, with the proud bearing and straight spine of a soldier.

She noticed his ebony walking stick and could not keep from cringing inwardly. A certain painful memory would always be permanently attached to his cane as well as to the mild limp which characterized his otherwise easy gait. Though she tried desperately to keep the image from taking possession of her mind, it came, nevertheless, of a man dressed in a black domino and mask, limping toward her in the subdued lighting of a conservatory, his interest in her visible in the hurried way he crossed the room, his cane beating against the polished wood of the floor in quick rhythm to his halting step as he whispered her name and took her in his arms. How fully she had given herself to be kissed! How desperately she had clung to the tall figure, masked and cloaked! How much she had delighted in the sweetness of his lips until his embrace grew rough and the awful truth of his identity was made known to her. She had been shocked, horrified, dismayed to learn how badly she had been deceived. All the while, she had thought herself held and loved by Brenton, when in fact, another man, whose laughter chased her hard down the hallways as she ran from the conservatory, had taken grievous advantage of her. And worse, before she had wrested herself from the deceiver's arms, she had seen Brenton and had known he had watched her kiss the masquerader.

Afterward, she had been bound by the laws of friendship not to expose her assailant. She knew him, she knew him too well since he resided in Devonshire and was married to a dear friend and was father to a houseful of hopeful children. How miserably she had wanted to tell someone, yet how impossible her circumstances were. Had she revealed the truth, she would have brought a horrible scandal down upon the heads of those she loved, not to mention risking the possibility of a duel.

Even as she looked at Brenton, however, she knew she would have changed nothing about the moment, save the man. Had Geoffrey kissed her she would have considered herself "blessed among women." She had loved him since first she had met and been kissed by him. And she believed in him, hopelessly, she always would, even when he behaved like a perfect idiot—which he was wont to do frequently in her company.

She addressed the boys. "You are giving your uncle a very sad notion of me," she said. "Since when have I ever condoned your coming to fisticuffs, at least, *in the house.*"

James, apparently feeling he had been chastised enough, ignored her entirely. "Uncle," he cried. "Have you come to see our play? Though it is not really a play, just three scenes, and Charles and I are to have a swordfight in the second!"

Tristan chose just this moment, before Lord Brenton could respond to the question, to pull on the tails of the peer's coat and demand to know if Uncle Geoff had brought him a present from Bath.

Lord Brenton looked down at Tristan. "What's this?" he exclaimed, his eyes opening wide with surprise as he surveyed the purple bruise on the child's face. "You've been hurt!"

"No I haven't," Tristan retorted with a scowl. Once Tristan got his cuddle, he did not like to be reminded of his wounds.

"No, of course not," Brenton responded quickly, picking Tristan up and holding him in his arms. He glanced over at Beth and cast her a scathing look, replete with recrimination. "I see you have taken a great interest in my sister's children," he said, sweeping his gaze in a purposeful manner over the blood on Charles's shirtfront and back to the bruise on Tristan's cheek.

Beth returned his expression with one of her own which she hoped he would surmise to mean that she had taken great delight in beating and torturing his nephews while he was away. He clearly had not softened one whit in his opinions of her. She therefore turned away from him and resumed her station by the door.

When she did, she caught sight of Mr. Chagford pressing his lips fervidly to the fingers of Juliet. "Oh, dear," she murmured. She could see from the corner of her eye that Brenton was crossing the room to join her, and she attempted to shut the door. She was not quick enough, however, and even with Tristan still couched in his arm, Brenton took up a place behind Beth, caught the door in his free hand, and pressed it easily out of her grasp.

Beth moaned slightly. Mr. Chagford had not as yet released Sukey's hand, and though he was no longer saluting Juliet's fingers, he was gazing rapturously into her eyes. Susan, naturally, leaned toward her Romeo, her own expression charmingly mooncalf, and for a long moment, the play stopped, though Dorinda's gentle snores could be heard cresting over the star-crossed lovers.

"Who the devil is that!" Brenton cried.

"Mr. Chagford, the new tutor," Beth replied cheerfully, at the same time jerking the door from the viscount's hold and closing it with an abrupt snap. Both Brenton and Tristan protested vehemently. The latter wanted to know why Mr. Chagford looked so sick, and the former expressed a strong desire to wring the young man's neck. The viscount then took a step forward, with Tristan still held snugly in his arms, as though he meant to speedily dispatch the enamored youth. But Beth placed herself firmly in his way, her palms flattened against the carved wood panels of the door. "I must speak with you, *privately*," she cried. "At once, before you ruin everything!"

When he took a second and quite menacing step toward her, Charles ran up to him and quickly intervened, "You must listen, Uncle! You must! Auntie Beth has tried ever so hard to sort things out while you were away! You must listen to her."

Lord Brenton looked down at his nephew, a thoroughly confused expression on his face. He shook his head and glanced toward James for enlightenment. But the eldest nephew had become intent upon the plate of macaroons and with his recently retrieved sword held at an awkward angle under his arm was busy shoving several of the biscuits into an already bulging coat pocket.

"Please, Geoff," Beth implored quietly as she gently took Tristan from him. Since he appeared to have acquiesced, or at the least to have become momentarily stunned by Charles's beseeching expression, she bid the boys leave her to speak with their uncle, *alone*.

Tristan did not at first oblige her until Charles lured him away with the one remaining macaroon. She heard Charles address his elder brother with words she was certain would set up James's back. "How could you take all of Trissy's macaroons, you care-for-nobody! What a devilish snatch-pastry you've become!"

James had already begun to retaliate by mumbling through a biscuit stuffed into his mouth that he thought Charles was a pompous idiot. Fortunately at this moment, the door closed and the remainder of what would undoubtedly become a battle of words, could not be heard.

Once Beth was finally alone with Lord Brenton, she blurted out, "Why did you have to come back now! I would have had everything settled. The one thing you have always suffered from, my lord Brenton, was the worst timing in the world! Were you an actor, there is not a company in England who would hire you!"

"Thank God I am not, then," he responded, taking several steps away from her toward the center of the chamber. "For it would seem that I must spend my days protecting my nieces and nephews from being introduced by you to that vulgar trade!"

It was not a propitious beginning.

Beth knew how the quarrel would progress. He would condemn her actions as he frequently did without knowing the entire truth; she would grow steadily more and more silent, her heart turning in stages to the hardness of sandstone; he would end by accusing her of a great and horrible wickedness which her own pride had for years forbade her to refute.

She could not do it, she thought. She would not be part of another argument with Lord Brenton. Instead of engaging the battle, she folded her hands primly in front of her and said, "I apologize for taking you to task about arriving beforetimes. The past three weeks have been a sore trial to me. But now that you are here, I shall place everything in your capable hands. The fact is, Juliet—I mean Susan has planned an elopement for today—ostensibly with my aid—with Mr. Molland. You know of him, of course!" The viscount appeared stunned, undoubtedly as much by her immediate surrender as by the horrible facts she was laying before him. When he nodded, she continued. "He should be in the lane to the north of your property right now, awaiting Susan's arrival. Do what you will. I shall pack my belongings and will have Jeremy Coachman drive me to the inn within the hour." She strode past him, taking several steps before she remembered one significant detail. Turning back to him, she added, "I almost forgot. I think you ought to know that your sister was in favor of a little church wedding. I told Susan it would not be half as romantic as an elopement."

She whirled around, the blue muslin of her gown catching slightly about her ankles as she moved forward on a brisk step.

She was a little surprised that he followed hard on her heels. If anything, she would have supposed the shock she had just delivered to him would have halted his cogitations for at least one minute so that she could take her leave without further incident. She did not want to exchange another painful word with him or to see yet again the accusing light in his eye. Instead, she felt his hand grasp her elbow.

"What the devil do you mean?" he cried.

"Pray, m'lord," she responded curtly, stopping in obedience to the pressure of his hand on her arm. "Will you not lower your voice? Or do you wish your entire staff to be privy to the dreadful scrape your niece has fallen into?"

Beneath his breath he muttered, "You are the most insufferable woman I have ever known."

Her heart seemed to stop dead in her breast as she looked into his eyes. She could not quite make out his features since her own gaze was blurred with tears. "If I am the most insufferable," she retorted, "you are the most despicable, the most hateful, by far the most hypocritical man I have ever known. I despise you more than words can express." She did not wait for a reply but pulled her arm from his clasp and set her feet in motion down the hall, heading toward the stairs.

He caught up with her again, whispering and fuming. "How can you say that when I have always been honest and straightforward with you on every score. My principles have been above reproach; I live by what I believe in my heart is right. While you—!"

"While I what?" she interjected in a hoarse whisper, tears still brimming full in her eyes. She did not cease walking but threw her words over her shoulder. "While I *what?* Take to kissing every man in England. That is what you meant to say, isn't it?"

By this time, she had reached the bottom of the stairs. With one hand on the rail, she paused, whirled around, and after taking a deep breath, confronted the issue which had lain solidly between them for ten years. "You kissed me once," she began, her heart constricted in her breast. "Do you remember? Do you remember how it felt? I had never been kissed before, and my life was never the same afterward. I don't know what that moment was like for you, but I'll tell you what it was like for me. You turned the sky green and the grass red and the roses blue. The earth became the sky and the sky the earth, the stream started moving backward, and the trout sprouted wings and flew away. I— oh, what's the use!"

She started to head up the stairs, but he caught her arm, holding it fast, and forced her to stop. "What are you saying?" he asked, his voice low and earnest. His face had taken on a strange appearance, his blue eyes had become dark but not with anger. Beth felt her arm tremble beneath the touch of his hand. She felt queer and disoriented as he continued to gaze into her eyes.

"I must ask you something," he said. "I must know—"

"Auntie Beth!" Charles cried, his voice pitched high as it echoed loudly down the stairs and through the vaulted entrance hall.

Beth's attention was instantly drawn away from Brenton. She looked up to the top of the stairs and saw Charles beckoning her forward in a wild manner. "Come quickly! You must hurry!"

Picking up her skirts, she ran lightly up the stairs and heard Brenton grumble, "Oh, the devil take it!" as he, too, mounted the steps.

When she was close enough to Charles, she called to him, "What is it, dearest?"

Charles, his loyalty to her brimming over and excluding the viscount, cast a disparaging look in the direction of his uncle. He was clearly uncertain as to whether or not Lord Brenton ought to be included in their schemes.

"It's all right, Charles," Beth said, arriving at the top of the landing, her heart beating in her ears. "I think your uncle should hear what you have to tell me."

"If you're certain it's all right, only the way you were quarrelling just now—"

"Never mind that," Beth said quickly. "We—we could not decide on whether to invite the vicar for dinner tonight or tomorrow. We'll probably let your mother decide. Now tell me, what is it? What has happened!"

"Mr. Molland has arrived," Charles replied with a worried frown. "You must come and see! He's in the lane, just as he said he would be. I saw him from your bedchamber."

"You have even got the children spying for you?" Brenton asked incredulously.

Beth glanced at him and said, "I am a desperate woman with a schoolgirl on my hands who has not been properly attended to for *years*. If you could have done better, I would like to have seen it."

"Mr. Molland would not have dared come around had I been here."

"Well, you weren't here, were you!" Beth returned hotly.

For the first time since she had known Geoffrey, an arrested expression stole over his features, the truth of her words sinking deeply. "You have a point," he admitted, much to Beth's astonishment.

"But there's more!" Charles interjected. "I saw Priscilla running across the fields—that was what I wanted you to see, for I wasn't certain you would believe me!—with a bandbox on one arm and her other hand pressed to her poke bonnet to keep it from flying off."

"Priscilla!" both Beth and the viscount cried together.

"Beth," Lord Brenton cried, taking hold of her hand and clasping it gently. "Whatever does this mean? I thought you said Susan—"

Beth turned to look into his eyes and saw that his features had been softened with genuine concern for his niece. She felt his fingers touching hers, and she was nearly overcome with wild hope. Shaking her head, she turned her thoughts to the difficult matter at hand, trying to make sense of it. "I don't know, unless—! Oh, good lord in heaven. I fear she has lacked terribly for a little attention. She misses her father very much, you see, and when Mr. Molland came round—Oh, Geoff, you have no idea the sort of flattery and nonsense he spilt all over this house! He quite turned Dorinda's head, Susan's as well, yet I never suspected Priscilla! She is but a child of thirteen! I never thought she might be in danger! Never! But now that I think on it, she has been so quiet, so withdrawn of late. I can't imagine Molland taking advantage of her youth, but he spoke his lies so charmingly. Geoff, you must stop her!"

Brenton did not hesitate to respond to her entreaty but retraced his steps down the stairs, his progress slowed only by the stiffness of his left knee. By the time he had reached the bottom, Beth bethought herself of his tendency to march headlong into battle, even if the enemy was an errant child, and ran after him. "Brenton!" she cried. "One moment!"

He was almost down the hall but stopped to wait for her, his face drawn up into a knot of anxiety.

"Don't wound her sensibilities!" she said, approaching him on a hurried tread.

He offered in response a sardonic twisting of his lip as he cried, "I am afraid I shall wound a great deal more than her sensibilities, if you please!"

She had by this time reached his side. Catching one of his hands in hers, just as he had done a few minutes earlier, she pressed it hard. "Do but listen to me," she pleaded. "Prissy has a delicate heart and worships you! She will do anything you tell her to do if only you will try for a little tact, a speck of kindness!"

"I shall do, Miss Ferrers," he responded quietly, "precisely as I deem fit!"

Beth released his hand immediately and resigned herself to the fact that his stubbornness would rule the day. She could only trust that her words might have greater effect when he had reached Prissy's side and saw for himself the state she was in. He did not look back at her as he headed down the hall, but she had the distinct impression he was plotting her murder once he had dispatched Mr. Molland and returned Priscilla to her home.

Geoffrey Ashburton, sixth Viscount Lord Brenton, slipped into an uneasy trot as he made his way across a roughly plowed field that ran the length of his property at the back of the manor. He knew quite well his leg would be stiff for a full sennight after this unhappy trek to prevent his younger niece from ruining herself in the eyes of the world. A country lane, blocked by an ancient hedgerow, marked the end of the field. Through a slight break in the hedge, he was able to see the curricle in the distance and, with no small degree of relief, noted that while Priscilla was standing beside the carriage, Mr. Molland was still seated, keeping a tight hold on the reins. The unlikely pair appeared to be arguing, which would indicate Molland was showing some sense in rejecting the younger heiress.

When he reached the hedgerow, he watched Priscilla pull her bandbox off the seat next to the would-be husband. "But I thought you liked me!" she said mournfully. "And I wouldn't be a terrible nuisance for you and Sukey. I should keep house for you, if you like! I'm exceedingly clever at needlework and can repair any of the linens. I even know a receipt for a poultice and Papa taught me one for rum punch!"

"We wouldn't hear of employing you so ungenerously," Molland returned handsomely. "And you do not truly wish to become our housekeeper, do you? Why, in a very few years I'm certain you will have beaux beyond numbering and shall find a husband of your own. No! No! It is far better that you stay here with your mama! Besides, you know you cannot accompany us to Gretna Green! It just wouldn't be the thing!"

So that was it, Brenton thought angrily. *Gretna Green,* of all the heinous exploits! He stepped through the break in the hedge and with a twist to his lips, said, "When I saw your grays outside the inn as I passed through the village just a few moments ago, I couldn't imagine what had brought you to Newton Bovey! Of course finding you in the lane behind my home and speaking to one of my nieces regarding a flight to Gretna Green somehow clarifies the point, wouldn't you agree?"

"Uncle!" Priscilla cried, turning a tear-stained face toward him. Her freckled cheeks were still flushed from her jaunt across the field and her brown hair, inexpertly dressed, was already escaping her poke bonnet. She looked like a waif.

He ignored the trembling schoolgirl entirely and addressed his remarks to Molland. "I'm afraid you'll have to excuse Miss Hatherleigh from joining you just yet. She has suffered a grave indisposition and cannot accept your hand in marriage at this time. Though I do suggest you wait a few more years, let us say a hundred, before you come calling again—and even then, only if you dare!"

Mr. Molland's mouth had fallen agape upon the mere sight of Lord Brenton. His response to the viscount's speech, however, was wholly imprudent. "Good God!" he exclaimed, his eyes nearly popping from his head. "I thought you was in Bath!"

"You scurrilous beast!" Brenton cried. "If I did not have an entire house of children to attend to, I swear I would drag you from this carriage and tear your heart clean out of your breast. I give you this warning only—if I ever see you within fifty miles of this house, I will call you to book! Swords or pistols, I will have your head, so help me God! I suggest you give your horses the offices to start! Come, Priscilla!"

He held out his hand to her, but to his astonishment, the young lady refused to budge. "I will not!" she cried, her large green eyes, so very like Susan's, still brimming with tears. "I intend to wait here until Susan arrives to elope with our dear Mr. Molland—and he is *not* a scurrilous beast! Mama dotes on him and I do, too! Mama wanted a little church wedding! If you must blame someone, then you ought to blame Auntie Beth! She is the one who insisted on Gretna Green!"

"Priscilla!" Brenton cried, turning bodily toward her and fixing an angry stare upon her person. "I will brook no argument. I don't give a fig who's to blame. You will come with me at once and no caterwauling!" Eight years earlier, such a tone of voice accompanied in particular with a glare more than one foot soldier had called "colder than a hard frost" would have caused to tremble the heart of the bravest soldier in His Majesty's Army. For that reason, Brenton did not expect biddable Priscilla to stand her ground, but that she did.

"You are not my papa," she announced with a decided lift of her chin. "And I will not do as you say! You have no right to order me about—or Susan, for that matter!"

Brenton might have been startled by her suddenly mulish behavior, but he was by no means deterred from his intent. When Molland gave no indication that he meant to remove himself from the lane, Brenton approached the curricle, and though it went quite against his respect for the fine grays harnessed to the carriage, he gave the nearest horse a hard slap, on his flank. The gray bolted forward, nearly unseating Molland from the curricle. Brenton turned swiftly to catch Priscilla in his arms in order to keep her from getting hurt by the large, spinning wheels of the curricle as the horses jumped into an unsteady gallop. In the process he wrenched his knee and only with the strongest of efforts kept from crying out at the pain which burned in agonizing, quick pulses up and down his leg.

He heard Molland shouting at his team, the dust flying up behind the carriage as it disappeared down the rutted lane.

"Oh, how could you!" Priscilla cried, struggling to tear herself from his arms. Brenton had to let her go as he worked to place all of his weight on his good leg. He felt sweat beading up on his forehead, the pain in his knee throbbing madly.

Priscilla dropped her bandbox at her feet and, covering her face with her hands, promptly burst into tears.

After a few seconds had passed, Lord Brenton felt able to give his niece the severe dressing down he believed she needed. The child had been without discipline far too long, a wrong he meant to begin redressing immediately. It seemed, however, that the moment he opened his mouth to speak, Beth's words swept down upon him as though she was standing in his ear. *Prissy has a delicate heart and worships you. Pray be gentle with her.*

Pray be gentle. Of the moment all he wanted to do was strangle the child! Yet, as he stared at his niece, watching her shoulders bounce with unhappiness, he knew a sudden compassion for her which surprised him. Her father had been a rascal, not unlike Mr. Molland, and had died an early death of perfectly unexceptionable causes. Brenton had not been surprised by his demise, only that *nature* had decided to take him first instead of one of his creditors! Somehow in his dislike of Jack Hatherleigh, he had not realized the breach his absence had occasioned in the lives of his surviving children.

Limping the short distance between himself and Priscilla, he stooped down slightly to accommodate their difference in height and placed his arm about her shoulder. Speaking softly, he offered, "Mr. Molland does have considerable charm, doesn't he?"

"He is the most wonderful man I have ever known," she exclaimed between sobs. "Save for Papa, of course,"

"Of course," Brenton responded sympathetically. "I hope you realize I was not being a complete brute in ending this, er, elopement. It's just that—that I feel I ought to tell you that I think Susan has formed a—a *tendre* for the, er, tutor."

Priscilla looked up from her crying and swallowed hard. "I knew she would," she responded with a sad sniff. "Poor Mr. Molland. Susan is the most inconstant creature. I only wish I had been sixteen instead of her! I should have made Mr. Molland an exemplary wife!" Her tears resurfaced, and she again buried her face in her hands.

For the first time since Beth had informed him of the impending elopement, Brenton realized that his wards' education had not only been lacking in scope but in general principle as well. He knew Dorinda was a somewhat indifferent parent, but until this moment he had not truly understood how disastrous the consequences of her indolence had been. He felt a sudden, and very powerful, respect for Beth, who had been able to achieve so much given the wholly ineligible thinking of the young ladies involved. Her inventions had been entirely unorthodox, of course, even dangerous, but she had at least succeeded in diverting Susan's attention completely away from Mr. Molland. He had no need to be further concerned on that score. As for the tutor—well, perhaps he ought to ask Beth what she thought might answer! He intuited that to dismiss the enamored young man would only set up Susan's back and go a long way, he was sure, to precipitating a second elopement.

"There, there, Pris," he said, patting her shoulder. "It shall all work out for the best, you'll see." Pulling his kerchief from his coat pocket, he tucked it into one of her hands which was still pressed to her face. He was a little stunned when, instead of making use of the linen, she turned immediately into his neckcloth and proceeded to ruin the elegant folds of the *trone d'amour* with a renewed flood of her girlish tears, all the while clutching the lapel of his coat.

But what surprised him more was that he rather liked the thought that he could offer comfort to his unfortunate niece. He had never known quite how to go on with the young ladies. He had always been able to romp with the boys, but the girls . . . !

As he guided Priscilla back through the hedge, he felt his knee nearly give way beneath him. He stumbled slightly and was startled when Priscilla cried out, "Uncle! You've hurt yourself! Oh, do let me help you! It is your bad knee, isn't it?" When she slipped her thin and rather useless arm about his waist, he did not demur but instead let her think that she was the sole reason he was able to cross the field at all. If it was more work than having been left to his own devices, he made no mention of it but instead began teasing Priscilla about the handsome young men who would soon be courting her if she could but wait to grow up a trifle.

Dorinda Hatherleigh cast sleepy eyes upon her brother. "And pray tell me—what objection could you have possibly had to Susan marrying Mr. Molland, though I daresay it was poor spirited of him to have just driven off like that!" Not expecting an answer, she sighed, "How very romantic it would have been, and on St. Valentine's day, too—an elopement! You ought not to have sent him away. Beth had arranged it to a nicety! She will be very much distressed at your odious, interfering conduct!"

Lord Brenton had only one response as he seated himself on the settee. "Go back to sleep, Dorinda!"

Easing himself carefully onto the cushions beside Pug, he stretched out his weakened leg before him and sighed with relief. Pug, however, took decided exception to his presence, baring his teeth and growling. Brenton lifted a bored brow as he gazed down upon the fat beast curled up at Dorinda's feet.

"Such an ill-mannered pet!" he said, then set about rubbing Pug's ears and soon had the spoiled dog whining contentedly.

Dorinda chided her brother for calling her beloved Pugsy anything so atrocious as "ill-mannered," afterward protesting at the very thought of going to sleep! How could he think such a thing of her! Especially since, being the devoted mother that she was, she was taking great delight in the play her darlings were enacting so enchantingly before her.

Brenton glanced at the stage where James and Charles were busy demonstrating their newly acquired fencing prowess. He almost credited his sister with a proper maternal feeling until she ruined the effect her former words had created by adding irritably, "Besides, how could I possibly sleep with the boys clacking about with their wooden swords. It is the most monstrous noise!"

Brenton could not help himself. He laughed aloud. Dorinda was quite one of the most useless females he had ever known. She had been far too much indulged as a child by her own mother, and the results were less than happy. He watched his nephews playing out their roles as Mercutio and Tybalt. They feinted and parried in crude but recognizable fencing patterns, and he found himself duly impressed, deciding it would serve them well to study with a fencing master in a year or two.

As for Susan, she had quite properly torn herself from Mr. Chagford's side and was now seated to the right of the stage, holding Tristan on her lap. She had given the youngest Hatherleigh boy his uncle's cane to play with in place of one of the swords. Tris was busy thrusting and waving the stick about in imitation of the loud, enthusiastic movements on the stage, grunting everytime pudgy James grunted. Priscilla had refused to join the family party but had retired instead to her bedchamber exclaiming she had the headache. This much Brenton could well understand, though he also believed her red, swollen eyes might have increased her reluctance to attend the performance.

"Look at my little Tristan," Dorinda cried. "Isn't he clever! Do you know your walking stick quite puts me in mind of the night Jack kissed Beth? Do you remember, Geoffrey? Of course you do, you were there! It was Beth's first season, and my horrid husband had formed the most ineligible *tendre* for her. He had dressed up just like you for the masquerade at Lady Simmons house. He even bought a cane like yours! I didn't know what he was about, else I would have stopped him. He had taken sore advantage of the poor girl's love for you! He told me later he had never been so delightfully kissed in his life! What a strange man he was. Would it be too unkind of me to say that I'm glad he is my husband no longer? Not that I wasn't very much in love with him and I do miss him at times, but he was a rather wild man, wasn't he?"

Lord Brenton turned to stare at his sister. "Yes, he was," he replied, stunned. "I always thought him a dreadful scapegrace, but I didn't know, until this very moment, how right I was. Are you telling me he bought a walking stick, dressed up for the masquerade with the sole purpose of looking like me, then kissed Beth in my stead?" Brenton now realized he had arrived at the conservatory at the worst possible moment—perhaps the reason Beth had complained bitterly of his unfortunate *timing*—and therefore had not been witness to Hatherleigh's initial performance with the deceitful walking stick. He had only seen Beth embracing Jack with utter abandon. Seconds later—another, equally disastrous choice of timing—he had turned away feeling nothing but disgust and disillusionment.

"Oh!" Dorinda cried, misunderstanding him. "Had you meant to kiss her that night as well? Did Jack take your place on purpose? I didn't know. I had supposed my husband to have arranged it for his own pleasure! How abominable you gentlemen are!"

"Of course I hadn't meant to kiss her!" Brenton snapped. "Jack must have lured her to the conservatory somehow!" Ignoring the pain in his knee, he rose to his feet, much to the complaint of Pug, who had thoroughly enjoyed the viscount's companionship.

When he had gained his footing, he remained standing over his sister and asked, "But what I wish to know is why you didn't tell me of this before?"

"I don't know," she responded, with a negligent wave of her hand as she adjusted her pale green cashmere shawl. "I suppose I thought it was of little consequence. It was just a trifling kiss, after all!"

"A trifling kiss!" he exclaimed.

"Yes, and what's more, Jack said Beth quite enjoyed it, or so it seemed to him. Was he wrong?"

For a long moment, Brenton stared at his sister in both horror and amazement.

"Why do you look at me in that terrifying manner?" she cried. "You are making my heart beat in little fits and starts! I vow I feel a spasm coming on. If I didn't know better I would suppose you had become angry with me!"

He shook his head. "I would box your ears, Dorinda, if I thought there was the least possibility you would comprehend why."

The steady striking of wood against wood rang through the small room as Charles and James continued to enhance their dramatic roles. Brenton quit his sister's presence, moving blindly past the door, into the hall, and through the open doorway of the library.

He found Beth talking in a low voice to a very subdued Mr. Chagford and supposed she was representing to him the impropriety of his flirting with any of the young ladies of the house. He had his suspicions confirmed when, upon catching sight of the viscount, the tutor jumped, his ears turning a bright red. He rose abruptly and cried, "Sir! I—I don't know what to say. Of course, I shall be taking my leave of your house immediately!"

Brenton took in Beth's troubled expression as she looked up at Mr. Chagford, a hand lifted toward him. He knew her thoughts and therefore addressed the tutor in an easy manner. "Whatever for?" he asked. "Did not my sister engage you with a large enough salary? I assure you, I would be most happy to renegotiate."

"It is not that! Indeed, a most handsome wage! I—it is just that . . . !"

The unhappy young man glanced beseechingly at Beth who rose quickly to her feet and took the tutor's part. "Mr. Chagford has become convinced that your sister no longer desires him in her employ."

"Eh, what's that?" Mr. Chagford cried. He then attempted to argue with his protectress, telling her he would not add to his crimes by trying to deceive Lord Brenton, but she bid him *hush!*

"I suggest you attend to Miss Ferrers," the viscount said, smiling in what he hoped was an amiable fashion. "After all, it is hardly proper to contradict a lady."

Mr. Chagford's face grew pinker by the second. "No! No! I certainly meant no such impertinence! Indeed, no—"

"And as for my sister," Brenton continued, enjoying the complete look of astonishment on Mr. Chagford's face. "You may leave her to me. She will do my bidding, of that you may rest assured. And now, if you please, I must speak with Miss Ferrers."

Mr. Chagford swallowed hard, evidently unable to believe his good fortune at not having been called to account for his behavior toward Susan. He fairly ran from the room, backwards of course, bowing several times in the manner of an obsequious court jester. Just before he was able to make good his escape, however, Brenton turned toward him and said, "One moment, Mr. Chagford! I nearly forgot! Do you fence?"

The tutor's face turned a chalky white in marked contrast to the glorious crimson which had characterized his features but moments earlier. "Y-yes, I do, but only a very little!"

"I'm sure that will be sufficient for my needs."

"I see," the tutor breathed, resigning himself to his fate. Greatly to his credit, he drew himself up ramrod straight and with the expression of one who was facing the gallows, said, "As you wish. You have but to name your seconds."

"My seconds?" Lord Brenton queried, vastly amused. "I suppose if that is the way you wish to express yourself, then I suppose I will have to name *Charles* and *James* to support me!" He heard a chuckle of laughter catch in Beth's throat and knew she was sharing in his truly despicable joke.

"Your—your nephews?" Mr. Chagford cried. "But aren't they a trifle *young!* I mean, it would be considered not quite the thing!"

"Oh, I don't know. I believe I was James's age when I first made use of my sword!"

"You were ten years old?" he asked, dumbfounded. "Well, it is no wonder you are accounted a Nonpareil!"

"You flatter me. Only give me an answer straight out—will you, or will you not instruct my nephews on the rudiments of fencing? I realize it will be adding to your duties here, but I think they will make quite remarkable pupils if their current—and still rather noisy—efforts are an indication of their respective abilities."

A look of comprehension dawned upon the features of poor Mr. Chagford. "Oh!" he cried, taking his kerchief out of his pocket and mopping his face. "Are you saying, then, that you wish me to instruct your nephews in the art of fencing?"

"Whatever did you think I meant?"

"Nothing!" Mr. Chagford assured him quickly, backing through the doorway and proffering another string of absurd bows. "I should be most happy to teach the boys what skill I possess with regard to the sword. But if you would excuse me, I believe the exigencies of the play have quite taken a toll on my—my heart. A rheumatic complaint since childhood! Nothing to be alarmed about, though I—I think a turn in the gardens would be quite beneficial . . ." His mumblings continued until they disappeared, along with his person, down the hall.

"Reprehensible!" Beth murmured.

Brenton turned toward her and caught the wicked glimmer in her blue eyes and knew she was teasing him. How pretty she looked with her wispy blond hair dancing in curls about her face, her soft, blue gown clinging to her womanly figure, her pretty features alive with laughter.

A warm, yellow light seemed to surround her suddenly, and he saw again the young woman he had held in his arms and kissed so many years ago. He should have enjoyed hundreds of kisses since then, only he had been a complete idiot and had truly believed her guilty of having shared a passionate kiss with Dorinda's husband. How could he have been so blind, so stupid! Why had he refused to believe her innocent?

He just couldn't say. He only knew that he had a great deal to say to her now, to try to make up for the past, but he didn't know where to begin.

"Geoffrey, are you well?"

He heard her through dizzy thoughts. "Yes," he answered quietly. "That is, not precisely."

Beth looked hard at Lord Brenton. Something untoward had occurred: she could read as much in the distressed way he was looking at her. A dart of fear pierced her heart. "Then is it Priscilla? Is she all right?" she asked quickly, taking a step toward him. "Molland didn't—"

"Priscilla?" Brenton queried, distracted. "No, no. She's perfectly well, I assure you. She is upstairs resting from having indulged in a bout of tears. I wanted you to know that I did as you bid me—I was gentle with her." He touched his neckcloth, adding, "I think she ruined my linen, though! It is still damp!"

Beth felt inordinately pleased with him as well as relieved that Prissy had not come to grief. Smiling faintly, she said, "She is something of a watering pot, isn't she? But I am glad you let her cry on your shoulder. She is a very lonely child! For all her papa's faults, Mr. Hatherleigh did treat his children with affection. He used to take Prissy riding every afternoon—when he was home, that is. A young girl doesn't forget that sort of attention easily."

"I suppose not. The truth is, until this past year, I have not been well acquainted with my nieces and nephews, though I fully intend to do better. I was able to send Mr. Molland away, and unless he is an addlebrained nodcock, besides being devoid of principle, I don't think he will come back."

"It hardly matters anymore, at least where Susan is concerned. To all appearances she has tumbled desperately in love with Mr. Chagford."

"I surmised as much," he said, and with a smile added, "Were you planning *their* elopement just now?"

"Oh, no! Of course not! How could you think—"

"I didn't think anything of the kind," he interjected quickly, closing the distance between them and catching one of her hands in his. "I was only teasing you a little."

He watched a blush suffuse her cheeks as she tried to pull her hand out of his, but he wouldn't have it.

"I only did what I thought best where Molland was concerned," she explained, trying to ignore the sweet feelings which rose in her breast at the feel of his hand possessing hers.

"I know it was wrong of me—"

"It was not wrong at all, not with Dorinda half in love with him herself!"

At that, Beth looked up at him, her eyes again dancing with laughter. "I don't know which I feared more, that Susan would elope with him or that Dorinda would cut out her own daughter and steal Mr. Molland for herself!"

Brenton laughed outright. "Knowing all that I know now, I would have shared the same concern."

An awkward silence fell between them for a moment until Beth bethought herself of the coming Season. "Brenton, pray don't eat me for suggesting this to you, but having been acquainted with Susan for such a long time and having observed her most particularly over the past several months, I have come to believe that nothing could be better for her—especially now that we—that is now that you have Mr. Chagford to consider—than to bring her out this Season. I believe with all my heart she would respond quite well to the demands our London hostesses would place upon her behavior."

She waited anxiously, still feeling conscious of the hand which held hers so tightly. She didn't know what answer he might return, and she feared he might not take kindly to a suggestion he had spurned once already.

"I can foresee only one difficulty," he responded gravely but with a decided twinkle in his eye.

Beth breathed a quick sigh of relief. He wasn't angry and by the devilish look in his eye she knew he meant only to tease her. "And what is that, pray tell?" she queried.

He shook his head in mock seriousness. "Why, transporting Dorinda's sofa to London, of course!"

Beth let out a peal of laughter. How long she had waited for this day, when his easy camaraderie might be returned to her.

Brenton smiled down into the face of the prettiest lady he'd ever had the pleasure to make laugh. So much needed to be said, but where to begin? He felt his heart warming toward her in quick degrees. She had stopped laughing and now returned his gaze steadfastly, though a delightful blush had deepened on her cheek. "All these years," he said, "everytime I came close to offering for this female or the other, I would end up comparing her to you. I had gone to Bath in part to offer for Miss Lydbury, but I couldn't, especially not when I recalled your opinion of her."

Beth felt a song swell in her heart, one she was afraid to sing. Was Lord Brenton truly standing before her, possessed of her hand, speaking such wondrous things to her? It seemed utterly impossible.

"Dare I hope," he continued, taking her other hand and catching both to his chest where he placed a kiss upon each in turn, "that you have in your heart the smallest place for me? Or has my idiocy put me beyond the pale?"

Beth felt overwhelmed and for the moment quite unable to speak.

"If you cannot answer that question then will you at least explain to me why you didn't reveal the horrendous trick Hatherleigh played off on you the night of the masquerade?"

Beth felt her throat constrict with tears. "It was my pride," she whispered. "And—and because Dorinda was my friend. I was afraid to hurt her or her family by exposing Jack's treachery. I didn't know what to do, so I remained silent."

"You could have told me. Surely you knew how I felt about you."

"I was afraid if I told you, you would call him out and later, when you behaved so abominably, believing I had *enjoyed* kissing him—which was not at all the case—I was too angry to speak!"

"Dorinda seemed to think you had enjoyed Jack's kiss very much, and from where I stood, I believed as much as well."

Beth felt tears prick her eyes. Her gaze fell from his as she responded, "I was never more humiliated in all my life! You and Dorinda are both greatly mistaken. If I took any pleasure in his embrace, it was only because for the longest moment I thought—" She could not continue.

He lifted her chin with his finger and as he did so, tears that had been brimming on her lashes drifted down her cheeks. He kissed them away very gently and said, "You thought what, my dearest Beth?"

His lips were warm and loving on her skin as they continued in a gentle sweep toward her lips. When he was but a mere breath from kissing her, she whispered, "I thought I was kissing you."

He drew her into the safe embrace of his arms and covered her lips in a tender kiss. Beth felt like she had some ten years earlier, when a handsome young buck had chased her on horseback into a thicket of wineberries, dismounted, chased her again, caught her, and kissed her. She could even remember how the sun had warmed her hair, how exquisite was the feel of his mouth upon hers, how the kiss they had shared had wrapped her up in a feeling of love so intense that she had known, from that day forward, she could never love another.

And now he was holding her and kissing her again.

Tattered Valentine

by Irene Loyd Black

At Clarendon, the late Earl of Clarendon's London town house, in the rose and blue salon adjoining her bedchamber, Dowager Countess Lucinda Rose Grey looked down at the wide gold band on the third finger of her left hand and felt ill. For the life of her, she could not understand those women who enjoyed the title of Dowager, especially when their late husbands had only used them to produce heirs, and then went traipsing off to their mistresses' houses, never to darken the doorway of their wives' bedchambers again.

Having been brought up within the bounds of propriety, the countess refrained from venting her anger and, instead, twisted the ring from her finger. Feeling the greatest amount of pleasure, she dropped it into the nearest wastebasket, which was full of scraps of paper she had discarded while cutting valentines for the children's party, less than an hour away.

The countess worked a while longer on the valentines, and when she was satisfied and had no more paper to discard, she summoned a house maid and ordered the contents of the basket to be taken to the burning pit.

"Essie, see that everything in the basket is burned," she said, "and I had better not hear of your searching through the contents for anything valuable."

Essie bobbed a curtsy. Black bombazine rustled. "Yes, m'lady."

The look on Essie's face told the countess the curious maid could not be trusted. "Here, I shall burn it myself. You may go, Essie."

The maid bobbed again, then quit the room. Lucinda hurried down the stairs and out back to the burning pit. She smiled as the flames flickered, and when she smelled the heat melting the gold, tremendous relief washed over her. The ring, with its intricate, symbolic designs, had been worn by every Grey bride for three centuries. Lucinda found this singularly disturbing.

"Well," she mused. "My son will not foist the ring off onto *his* bride, for she shall be happy." Up until now, Lucinda had never heard of a happy Countess Grey. In truth, she recalled, according to the chronicles hidden away in the bookroom, several of them had committed suicide. And little wonder, she thought. If she had been prone to such behavior, she might have followed in their footsteps.

Lucinda, who prided herself on being no milk-and-water miss, accounted her escape from such fate to her three precious children, eleven-year-old twin girls, Heather and Elizabeth, who were perfect darlings, and a son, now five.

And she had kept herself busy, lobbying the House of Lords against the employment of climbing boys, and other worthy causes.

Lucinda found herself smiling. With the twins independent spirits much like her own, they would most likely cause frowns of disapproval from England's society and furnish plenty of grist for the quidnunc's mill.

But little Luther, called Luke for short, would always be the perfect gentleman. His father, the sixth Earl of Clarendon, had reminded him almost from the day he was born that he was heir to the earldom and that he must live up to that noble heritage. And he must, as soon as possible, produce a son, an heir.

After making certain that the ring was totally melted into an unrecognizable blob, Countess Grey returned to her bedchamber, where she laboriously unbuttoned the row of tiny buttons that started below her waist and followed a path to her throat. She then pushed the black mourning dress from her shoulders, letting it drop to the floor. With the toe of her right foot, she kicked it onto the smoldering coals in the fireplace. Orange flames licked upward towards the chimney.

The countess watched pensively while the hateful dress was reduced to a pile of gray ashes. Turning her face to the handsomely carved ceiling, complete with dancing cherubs, she gave thanks that her year of mourning was over. "Mourning, faugh," she said. She had only worn the widow's weeds out of respect for her children.

Without summoning Josephine, her lady's maid, to help her dress, Lucinda donned over her white chemise and pantalettes a claret red velvet gown which she thought suitable for the party. Standing straight and tall, she checked her appearance in the looking glass and was pleased. She had never worried overmuch about her appearance. If she had been guilty of that, she thought, her life would have been in shambles, growing up in the shadow of a sister who was beautiful beyond measure.

This day, the countess's hair was wound around her head in thick braids. Josephine had done a superb job. The twins said it was her golden crown, declaring that it made her gray eyes big and wide, so that she could see everything they did when they did not want her to. This had made the countess chuckle.

Turning her attention back to their valentines, she wrote a lovely poem on each one, in flowing script. Tears sprang to her eyes, and her chest pulsed with pain. Another place, another time, she had received a valentine with a lovely poem, one of Lord Byron's, except the words the poet had written to Caroline had been written as James's own. "To his Lucinda," he had said.

Even though she fought with all her might, the memory would not go away, and the countess's thoughts moved back in time. He was there, standing before her, his deep hazel eyes probing hers, a lock of tawny brown hair falling onto his forehead.

As if caught in a faraway dream, Lucinda took the key from its hiding place behind the chiffonnier, went through the door to the copper-bound trunk at the foot of the canopied bed, and unlocked it. Crouched on her knees, she dug through the mementoes of her past, drawings from her children, her dead mother's picture, and finally took from beneath it all the valentine.

Holding it to her breast, she imagined that she felt warmth and love flow from the hand-painted rose and from the neatly inked lines etched deeply into the cheap paper.

Fourteen years of handling had yellowed the paper and made it fragile; fourteen years of secret tears had faded the red rose to a mottled pink. Even the words on the back had changed color. But that did not matter, for they were printed indelibly on her heart. She whispered them into the silence broken only by an occasional pop and crackle from the dying fire.

The words, Lucinda now knew, had been James's farewell to her; although, at the time she had not known he was saying goodbye. From the start, it had been a misalliance, she a member of the nobility, he the nephew of the housekeeper.

Tears came uncontrollably to the countess. Suddenly, without ceremony, the twins burst through the door.

Quickly, Lucinda placed James's valentine under a fold in her red velvet skirt. She did not want her children to see her sorrow or to know its cause. After all, they knew little of her past, and it was such a minute part of her life where they were concerned.

Looking into their young faces framed with golden curls, she smiled brightly and held out her arms. Never would she think of scolding them for entering her room without an invitation or without being announced. "Darlings," she said laughingly, "how naughty of you to come crashing in here when I'm making ready for your St. Valentine's party."

"Mama, why are you crying?" asked Heather, the older of the two by six minutes, a truth she never let her "younger" sister, Elizabeth, forget.

Heather reached up and, with her hand, wiped at the tears that lay damp on the countess's cheeks. Elizabeth, as she always did, followed her sister's lead. Both faces had turned somber. Lucinda gathered them into her arms and held their slight bodies tightly against her breast. For a moment, she could not speak; for a moment she imagined that they were James's children.

But wishing did not make it so, she silently scolded. The past was immutable. Telling herself that for this occasion a little lie would not hurt, she crossed her fingers behind the girls' back and said, "They are tears of joy. While making your valentines, I was thinking of how fortunate I am to have such wonderful little girls to receive them."

"Mama," Heather scolded, "I saw you hide the old valentine, and Elizabeth and I have seen you sit and stare at it . . . when you didn't know we were watching. Will you not tell us who gave it to you? Did Papa . . . before he went away?"

"No, the valentine was not given to me by your father." She tried again for levity. "Stuff, it doesn't signify. It was long ago and such a silly thing. I was thinking that I was not too much older than the two of you when a young man gave it to me. As you grow older, you will find that one keeps things that remind one of youthful experiences."

Then, like a raging river out of control, memories engulfed the countess, probing deeper into her soul. *If Elanora had not died . . . if James had not left without a word . . .*

Once again Dowager Countess Grey was Lady Lucinda Avervich, with five and ten summers behind her.

The Avervich carriage tooled its way through the Kent

countryside. The sound of the four bays' hooves hitting the hard-packed road resounded into the quietness. It was February, and hot bricks warmed their feet. Lucinda was anxious to be home. The journey from London had been long and laborious. She had not wanted to go in the first place, but her father, Lord Avervich, had insisted.

"You are fifteen," he had said, "approaching womanhood, and you must learn how to go on in society. Going with your sister to choose her come-out wardrobe will be a learning experience for you. When your time comes—"

"I'm not having a come-out, Father. I care not a fig for your wonderful London society. When I come of age, I shall marry James Elston."

"The housekeeper's nephew! Demme if that's so. Have you gone queer in the attic, gel?"

"Oh, Father," exclaimed Elanora, "Lucinda is only funning. She is a mere fifteen. When I was her age I was in love with Cook's son." She laughed a tiny laugh, waved her fan in front of her face, and gave Lucinda one of her condescending looks, which Lucinda hated. So Elanora was approaching eighteen. Did that make her wise and worldly? Of course not, Lucinda decided. If she had a brain to spare she would not set her cap to marry Lord Grey.

Curling her lips in a half smile, Lucinda said, sotto voce, "Lord Steven Devon Grey, the sixth Earl of Clarendon."

Lucinda knew what her father wanted from the marriage of Elanora to Lord Grey: guineas to fill the near-empty family coffers. The Grey wealth was massive. But for the life of Lucinda, she could not fathom why Lord Grey wanted to get leg-shackled to Elanora, who was ill-tempered and self-centered.

Her brother Malcolm was spoiled, Lucinda thought, and she supposed that one had to be the oldest in the Avervich family to be spoiled . . . or even noticed. Most of the time her father totally ignored her. It had come as a surprise to her when he had insisted that she go to London with them.

Lucinda looked at her sister and thought how beautiful she was, with her shiny chestnut hair, violet-blue eyes, long, slender neck, and well-developed bosom. This day, under her palatine, she wore a purple traveling dress which showed her décolletage to advantage. Lucinda's dress was a plain blue muslin, and her long cape a gray wool. Her bonnet was made from the same fabric as the cape.

"The beauty of the family." That's what their father often said about Elanora. And Lucinda was glad, else Lord Grey might have offered for her. Lord Grey did not look anything like James.

Lucinda felt her heart quicken. The two weeks in London had been the longest of her life. She could not wait to see James's smile, to hear his laughter, which was a happy sound coming from deep within his chest, as if it came from his soul. He had not told her he loved her, but he would soon, she just knew.

Malcolm, asleep on the opposite banquette, beside Lord Avervich, began snoring, interrupting Lucinda's ruminations. His head rested in the corner of the carriage. In Malcolm's five and twenty years he had managed to spend the family fortune at the gaming tables in London or anywhere else he could find to place a wager. Lucinda looked at his crumpled cravat, his Weston coat, which was twisted askew, and felt pity. Once he had been a handsome lad with the same chestnut hair and blue eyes as Elanora.

They both look like Father, Lucinda thought. *I have Mama's blond hair and gray eyes.* She wondered if her father had really loved her mother. Lucinda could hardly remember Lady Avervich, but she often studied her portrait hanging in the bookroom behind her father's desk.

"If we just didn't have to wait for the Season to be over before you marry Lord Grey, Elanora," Lord Avervich said, "Malcolm was forced to go to the moneylenders this time." He shook his head. "We must needs find a way to keep him away from London until the marriage—"

"You might consider a rope, Father," Lucinda said, thinking that the only way to stop Malcolm's gambling was to tie him up.

"Lucy," exclaimed Elanora in a haughty manner, "you make the most ridiculous suggestions. Brother must needs have his freedom." And then she went on talking about her coming marriage, telling about the touch of royalty from which the Avervichs had descended. "I'm certain the blending of the Grey and Avervich bloods is the one reason Lord Grey chose me from all the other ladies of quality."

"That, and your beauty," Lord Avervich said, smiling and looking fondly at Elanora.

Lucinda felt ill. The royal blood the Avervichs could honestly claim was worth hardly a pence on the market. Sometime in the past an Avervich had married a fourth cousin to King Henry VIII's fourth cousin. And Lord Grey was impressed by *that!*

They were passing by Folkstone where Caesar had camped. Lucinda looked out the carriage window. In her opinion, the Kent countryside was the most beautiful part of England. A winter sun shone on the dormant hopfields and cowled-coast houses. In the distance, the white shoreline was startling against the green sea. She heard the crack of leather over the four bays backs and felt the carriage jerk as the horses speeded up. She supposed even the coachman was anxious to be home.

Lucinda let down the window and sucked in a breath of salt air wafting in from the sea. She craned her neck in preparation for a glimpse of the manor, which she knew would come into view around the next curve in the road.

Visibly shuddering, Elanora pulled the hood of her fur-lined palatine closer around her face. She scolded: "Lucinda, you are freezing me to death."

"Put the window up," Lord Avervich added, not too pleasantly. "We do not need illness at this time."

Malcolm squirmed and lifted his head from the corner of

the carriage, then shook it as if to clear his brain. At least the cool air had awakened him, Lucinda thought as she shut the carriage window. But she would not let a mere scolding keep her from being happy, for in only a few moments she would see James.

The carriage rounded that last curve and Winfield was in plain view. Perched on a rise, the stone manor house, with its many chimneys and row after row of mullioned windows, glistened and shimmered in the lowering sun. The carriage quickly ascended the rise and pulled under the portico where footmen waited to help them alight.

James, tall, lean, and without doubt the most handsome man Lucinda had ever seen, stepped forward to hold the lead horse's head. With his other hand he raked at the lock of brown hair that fell onto his forehead and smiled directly at Lucinda.

She smiled back at him and, uncommonly, drew the attention of Lord Avervich. A frown creased his dark brow, and his eyes were darker than usual, the way they were when he was angry. Immediately Lucinda regretted having told him she was going to marry James. She sensed trouble.

And she was not sure James wanted to marry her. He had not asked her, she reminded herself, and he had not actually said he loved her. But he did. She could feel it when they talked, especially when he accompanied her on her morning rides. Sometimes he accidently touched her, setting her skin afire.

It was during those rides that James told her about himself. He had been away in school when his family had succumbed to a strange illness. Unfortunately, after expenses of the illness and the funerals, there was no estate. His only living relative was his Aunt Ellen, the head housekeeper at Winfield. She had secured his position as groomsman from Lord Avervich.

Not waiting for a footman to help her, Lucinda quickly alighted from the carriage and dashed through the huge double doors the butler held open, through the great hall, the kitchen, and out the back entrance. On the slope of the hill, which dropped to the sea, were the stables. She knew that if she moved quickly enough her father would think she had gone to her rooms. She had made up her mind; she would not wait for her morning ride to talk with James.

When she reached the carriage house entrance, she watched as James unhitched the horses. He looked round and gave her another big smile. Lucinda felt her heart leap to her throat. He had beautiful white teeth, and, even from the distance, she felt his piercing hazel eyes burning into her own. "I've missed you," he said.

"I've missed you, too," she answered, and then she went to walk with him as he led the four bays to the stables. No one else was around, and she assumed the coachman had repaired to his quarters.

"How was London?" he asked.

"Boring. Elanora visited the modiste every day, and I was forced to go along—"

James cocked an eyebrow. "Forced? I can't imagine your being forced to do anything you did not want to do."

"This time Father was adamant. I like being ignored better."

"And I can't imagine anyone ignoring you," James replied.

Lucinda felt her face flush. James had never spoken to her in such a familiar way. Maybe, just maybe, this day he would tell her he loved her. Oh, she prayed that he would. It would be awful to love someone who did not love you.

They had reached the stables, where James turned the horses over to two stableboys. After giving strict instructions that the horses be rubbed down, he turned to Lucinda. "Let's go down to the shore. Do you think we will be seen?"

"I imagine Father, sister, and brother are all in their rooms preparing for a long nap. The journey was very tiring."

"Are you not tired?"

"I was until I saw you," she said, feeling brazen. But she did not care. She believed one should be open about one's feelings. After all, she was fifteen, and James was eighteen. Friends her same age were already spoken for. James must needs speak to her father about paying his addresses to her.

James took her hand and they walked down the slope toward the sea. The wind hurled huge waves against the cliffs; silver spray melted into the air. Lucinda wished that everyone in the world could be as happy as she was at that moment.

They found a large rock on which to sit, out of sight of the manor house and far enough away from the spray to keep dry. With the sun almost gone, Lucinda felt chilled and pulled her cape close around her.

"Are you cold?" Concern showed in James's voice.

"Not really," Lucinda answered.

James looked at her and grinned. "I was hoping you would say that you were freezing to death."

"Why—"

"I would have an excuse to put my arm around you."

"Then, I am nigh to freezing to death."

Laughter, happy laughter, rang out. The pounding of the surf against the rocks drowned out the sound. James put his arm around her and held her close to his side; he pushed the gray bonnet from her head and ran his long fingers through her hair. "You are so beautiful," he said.

Lucinda heard the catch in his voice. A chill danced up and down her spine. "Stuff! Everyone knows that Elanora is the beauty in the family."

"Elanora is beautiful on the outside, but inside she has a vain heart. Your goodness comes through when you smile. I've watched you these three years I've been at Winfield."

Lucinda never dreamed she would be told she was beautiful. She feared James could hear her heart sing to his words.

"Elanora and I *are* different."

"As night and day."

She felt James's arm tighten around her; she felt warmth emanate from his hard, lean body. Her own body responded in kind, a new and strange feeling, and she just knew that she would explode with longing.

Longing for what, Lucinda did not know. "James, I told Father that we, you and I, would marry."

"You what! Oh, my darling Lucy, you should not have done that."

"Why not? I took a chance that you felt for me what I felt for you, and under those circumstances there was nothing for us to do but marry." After a pause: "Are you afraid of becoming leg-shackled . . .?"

James turned his head away and Lucinda's eyes followed his gaze. A sea gull, its white wings spread to maximum, its long neck stretched forward, guiding its graceful body, floated above the green-black sea.

"Isn't the gull beautiful, so quiet and peaceful in its own world?" James asked, almost in a whisper.

Lucinda looked into his handsome face and saw pain registered there. The dark lashes that fringed his eyes were damp, as if the sea had sprayed its mist on them.

"Share your thoughts with me, James," she said. "You seem so faraway."

"I'll never be far from you, Lucinda. But . . ."

"But what, James."

For a moment a deep silence held them, then James jumped to his feet and pulled Lucinda up to stand beside him. "This day we shall be happy. Do you not think so, my love?"

My love. Surely she had not heard him correctly, she thought, and then James turned her to face him, wrapped his long arms around her and held her body to his. He towered over her; her head rested on his chest where she felt his heart pounding. Gently he pulled the bonnet back up onto her head and pushed her hair back under its folds. "I love you, Lucinda," he said. "Don't ever doubt that I do."

Lucinda lifted her head to look into his face. The dampness still clung to his eyelashes, and his hazel eyes had turned as dark as the sea stretched out from them, beyond forever.

"Never, never forget that my heart belongs to you," he added.

Lucinda spoke firmly and truthfully. "I love you, James. have for three years since first you came to Winfield."

"But you have had only five and ten summers; you're still a mere child."

"Don't say that, James. I'm no longer a schoolroom miss, and I'm old enough to know what I feel."

A wave splashed; the sea gull faded into the dusk.

James jumped from the rock, and, reaching up, lifted Lucinda down. Holding her hand, he started walking back up the slope toward the stables. "I have something to give you," he said. "I made it for you while you were gone."

"James, what—"

"Shh, it's to be a surprise."

When they reached the stables, they climbed the stairs to James's room, which was as dark as a cave. Lucinda knew that it was against propriety to be in a man's room unchaperoned, but rules were made to be broken, she quickly determined. Besides, it could hardly be called a room. A loft was more like it.

"Stand here," he said.

A lucifer scraped against the stone wall; a circle of light from an oil lamp spread dimly into the windowless room. Shadows danced on a narrow bed pushed against the wall and on a desk made from stacked boxes. Clothes hung from a line stretched from corner to corner.

Books covered the top of the desk, and Lucinda could imagine James sitting there reading. She watched as he took from under a book a folded sheet of paper.

"I made a valentine for you, " he said.

Lucinda could hardly speak, so full of love was her heart.

A lump formed in her throat. "James, I am such an addle-brain. I completely forgot that St. Valentine's Day came in February. I did not—"

"Don't feel badly. I did not expect one from you."

She took the valentine and held it where the light would fall on the heart he had drawn, inside of which was a beautifully sculpted rose, every petal perfect, as were the stem and leaves.

"Not an arrow," he said. "An arrow cuts through the heart, breaking it. A rose is forever." Then he avowed, "Lucinda, my love for you will last *beyond* forever."

Lucinda held the folded paper to her heart, and James took her in his arms and kissed her, pressing her to his long, hard, lean body, the valentine pressed between them. She twined her arms around his neck and returned his kiss with the fervor with which it was given. She felt his body tremble against hers; she felt his breath warm against her face.

Lucinda's own body flamed. She wanted him with her whole body, and she knew that, even though she was supposed to be too young to know, she would never love another man.

"You must speak to Father," she whispered between kisses.

As if the words had cleared his mind, James released her and stepped back, letting the valentine fall to the wood floor. He stooped to retrieve it. "I wrote a poem on the back, one of Byron's. He wrote it to Carolyn, but I wrote it to you. Read it tomorrow. There isn't time now. I must needs let you return to the manor before they come looking for you."

He kissed her again, a long, lingering kiss filled with tenderness. Gone was the passion which, just moments before, had flamed between them. Lucinda knew that something was troubling him, and she resolved to learn what it was. "James—"

He pressed a finger to her lips. "Hush, my love, some things are best left unsaid. What cannot be changed must be accepted."

They went down the narrow stairs, he in front reaching back to hold her hand. When they were out in the dim glow of dusk, he said again, "I will see you tomorrow."

Lucinda smiled at him. "Good night for now, and thank you so very much for the beautiful valentine. I shall treasure it forever."

Hoping no one had missed her, Lucinda, with the valentine hidden in her bosom, returned to the manor house where supper was being served.

"Where have you been?" Elanora asked, not waiting for an answer before turning to her father to say something to him.

Lucinda gave her cloak and bonnet to a maid, then sat down at the table. She ate in solitude, not caring what the others were saying, and later, when she was alone in her bedchamber, she took the valentine from her bosom and read Lord Byron's poem that James had written on the back:

But when our cheeks with anguish glow'd,
  When thy sweet lips were join'd to mine,
The tears that from my eyelids flow'd
  Were lost with those that fell with thine.

And yet, my girl, we weep in vain,
  In vain our fate in sighs deplore;
Remembrance only can remain,—
  But that will make us weep the more.

A portent swept over Lucinda of something bad to come. What did the words mean? Had James chosen this way to say to her what he could not say when they were together?

The next morning, Lucinda, dressed in her best riding dress, a deep purple trimmed in green, went early to the stables. Ian, a small man with a wrinkled face and graying hair, stood between two horses, one Lucinda's chestnut mare, the other a dappled gray stallion, the horse James rode on their morning rides. Both were saddled. When Lucinda approached, Ian looked up but did not smile. He seemed ancient to Lucinda, and she could not remember when he had not worked at Winfield. Stepping from between the two horses, he gave a half-bow. "Good morning, Lady Lucinda."

Lucinda forced a smile. "Good morning, Ian." Her brow wrinkled questioningly. "Where's James? We were to ride together—"

"I be riding with ye."

"How can that be? Is James ill?"

"No, m'lady," Ian answered. He looked away, then brought his gaze back to meet Lucinda's. Pity showed in his eyes, and his voice trembled when he spoke. "Lady Lucinda, the boy James be gone."

Lucinda felt her heart plummet. "Gone? What do you mean?"

"He left at first light—"

"Where . . . where did he go?"

Ian stepped closer. "Ye'll be learning that from Lord Avervich."

"When will he return?" she asked.

Ian dropped his chin and looked to the ground. "I fear he won't, m'lady."

Lucinda whipped around and started running. Over her shoulder, she called to Ian, "I won't be riding this day." The distance back to the manor house seemed interminable. Her heart pounded in her throat and in her head. Would James leave without a word to her?

Obviously he has, she told herself. Behind her the wind blew from the sea, grabbing her riding skirt and twisting it around her legs. As she ran, she untied her bonnet and held it in her hand. Her long blond hair moved with the wind.

Reaching up, she pulled strands from her face and touched the tears that streamed from her eyes.

Upon reaching the manor house, Lucinda went directly to the bookroom, where she knew she would find her father. He sat in a red leather, high-back chair, smoking a cheroot. The odor of burning tobacco was heavy in the air.

Behind Lord Avervich a fire burned in the fireplace, and shadows danced on Lady Avervich's life-size portrait, on floor-to-ceiling bookcases, and on the spines of the leather-bound books that filled them.

Lord Avervich was immaculately dressed in a coat of blue superfine, moleskin trousers, and his perfectly folded cravat glistened white against his dark skin. He gave Lucinda a friendly smile.

Lucinda felt anything but friendly. Her breath came in short spurts; her voice was barely a whisper. "Father—"

"What is it, my pet? Is it about the stable hand?"

"Where's James?" she managed.

Lord Avervich stood. "James is gone," he said, "along with his aunt."

"Gone?" Lucinda repeated. "Is that all anyone can say? Ian told me as much. Where has he gone? Why—"

"Why are you so upset?" Lord Avervich asked, "James was a common stablehand. I imagine the only course open to him now is His Majesty's Service."

Lucinda stifled a sob and asked: "Why did he leave?"

"How should I know? He came to me at early dawn to give his notice of leaving, which he did, taking the best housekeeper Winfield ever had with him. They walked to the main road and caught a mail cart."

"Did . . . did he mention me? Did he leave something for me . . .?"

"Why should he? Oh, I know, Pet, you said you were going to marry him, but I knew that was only a child's infatuation. He was tall and handsome but of the lower orders. I assure you that he had no notion of marrying you." After a long pause, he added: "I do not wish to speak of this further. He's gone, and that is that."

Lucinda hated being treated as if she were a child, and at that moment she hated her father. Turning, she stumbled from the room. Why should she stay? The look on her father's face told her he felt nothing for her. She returned to stables and spoke again with Ian.

At least, she told herself, the old groomsman held pity in his eyes when he told her James was gone. But Ian could tell her no more than he had told her earlier.

"Did he mention my name—"

"No, child, he never did, but I know'd. Many times I saw the look in yer eyes when yer looked at him."

"What about when he looked at me? Did you not see love in his eyes when he looked at me?"

"Thet, too, Lady Lucinda, and I always cringed. Knowing as I did how hopeless it was. Upper orders and lower orders don't marry. I think yer young man knew that . . ."

Lucinda turned away and slowly made her way back to the manor house, going to her bedchamber. There she held the valentine James had given her and read again Lord Byron's prophetic poem: "And yet, my girl, we weep in vain. In vain our fate in sighs deplore. Remembrance only can remain—but that will make us weep the more."

Tears fell from Lucinda's cheek, staining the paper on which James had etched the heart and the rose. She whispered: "I will remember, James, I will remember . . ."

As the months went slowly by, Lucinda was true to her promise. She did remember. At first she watched the post for a letter which never came. Anger because he had left without a word was often her companion, but that did not diminish her love for the housekeeper's nephew. She knew not where he had gone, or why he had left without saying goodbye; she knew only that no one would fill the place in her heart that he held. When she slept, the valentine was under her pillow.

Elanora laughed, calling her a child and scolding her for her moping. "Why are you so down in the dismals? Love is not for the upper orders; one marries for convenience and a place in society."

Then Elanora went to London for her come-out. This time Lucinda was not allowed to go, and she knew why. They were afraid she would find James.

Elanora's season was short, for her marriage to Lord Grey was imminent. And then a horrible thing happened. Two days before the wedding was to take place, Elanora was thrown from a horse and killed. They said that she had been riding at breakneck speed.

Lucinda was devastated. Although Elanora was self-centered and haughty, she was Lucinda's sister, and at the funeral copious tears dampened the lace-edged handkerchief she carried. Shortly thereafter, however, in a small morning room at Winfield, shock dried the tears and put a much heavier burden on her youthful shoulders.

"You will marry Lord Grey," Lord Avervich said, his eyes, for the first time looking into hers. Before this, he had always looked past her or over her as if she did not exist or did not matter.

Hearing the shocking words, Lucinda wished that were still so. "Father, I will not marry Lord Grey. Surely he will need a time of mourning as will I."

Lord Avervich sank into a chair and heaved a deep sigh. "You have no choice, Lucinda, since we are near to losing Winfield. Malcolm is in to the money-lenders in London. Winfield came to Malcolm through your mother. It was her home, and it is for her that I ask that you marry a man whom you do not love. Lord Grey does not want a marriage of love; he wants to marry for convenience. As you know, he has a mistress of which he is quite fond. But that has nothing to do with his wanting to marry. He believes the Avervich blood to be of suitable lineage. After you produce an heir—"

"I will not—"

"Then Malcolm will go to debtor's prison, and we will be reduced to a life of penury. Winfield will be gone . . ."

Lucinda saw a brokenness about her father she had not noticed before. She remembered when his shoulders were held straight with pride. *Losing Elanora has taken its toll,* she thought, *and if Malcolm should go to debtor's prison . . .*

She, too, could not bear it, Lucinda told herself. If only she could circumvent her father's plan that she marry Lord Grey, she would think of a way to pay Malcolm's debts.

But first things must come first, she told herself. She loved James, and the thought of being another man's wife in the Biblical sense was beyond bearing.

Another thought crept into Lucinda's mind. The quidnuncs also had it that Lord Grey demanded an innocent for his wife. Perhaps if she told him that she had belonged to James in *that way* he would refuse to marry her . . .

Lucinda's plan did not work. Grinning incongruously, Lord Grey scoffed at her. "Of course, at fifteen, you are virginal," he said. "These thoughts might have gone through your mind, but you, being an Avervich, would have never acted upon them." His silly grin broadened as he added: "Not with a common stable hand."

Lucinda wanted to slap the grin from his face but knew that it would only increase his mirth. She knew what he was thinking—that, at fifteen, she was not old enough to know her own mind. "You know that this is bartering, do you not? Me for payment of my brother's gambling debts and to save Winfield."

Lord Grey laughed. "Many marriages are for such reasons."

Lady Lucinda sat for hours in her bedchamber and stared through the window at the tumbling sea. But she could not come up with a plan, other than marrying Lord Grey, to pay her brother Malcolm's gaming debts and to save Winfield. That, to her, was the most important. She could not imagine not having Winfield to come home to, no matter to whom she was married.

The wedding date was set for one month from the date of Elanora's death, and, because the Avervich family was in mourning, a simple affair was planned, all without any help or cooperation from Lucinda. When she saw his lordship, which was not often, she managed to look her ugliest, and if she knew of his arrival beforehand, she hid in the attic, watching for his departure from a small hole she had torn in the slanting roof. She did have the presence of mind to place a bucket beneath the hole should it rain.

Finally, having given up on circumventing the marriage, she went to her father, and, in the presence of Malcolm, the culprit who had gotten her into the fix she was in, demanded that her brother sign upon their dead mother's grave that he would stay away from the gaming tables. Lifting her chin, she stated in an unequivocal manner: "Furthermore, before the ceremony Grey will pay all encumbrances against Winfield and deed it to me."

"What a farrago of nonsense," Lord Avervich said, anger showing in his voice. "You are in no position to bargain. Besides, women cannot own property—"

"Oh, but I am in a position to bargain, Father," retorted Lucinda. "If I must needs get leg-shackled to Lord Grey at least I will own Winfield. If I seal my lips and do not promise to do my duty by Lord Grey, the rector will not declare me his lawfully wedded wife to do with as he pleases, most especially bear an heir to inherit the earldom and the entailed estates."

Lucinda could not keep the scorn from her voice. The thought of marrying Lord Grey made her want to run away to a convent. But that would never do, she told herself. Someday she would see her beloved James again, and should she be dressed in a black habit he surely would refrain from kissing her.

Lucinda remembered with painful pleasure the love that had welled up inside her when James kissed her. At night she dreamed of him holding her again, of him kissing her in the delicious way that, she was sure, no one else would ever, ever do.

In the village she inquired of James's whereabouts, but it seemed as though he had dropped from the face of the earth.

As the days went quickly by and Lucinda could not see a way out of her dilemma, she determined that when she lived in London, which she would do when she became Countess Grey, she would learn where James had gone, even if she had to hire the Bow Street Runners. She consoled herself by sitting for hours and staring at the valentine he had given her. She would never believe that he had not meant it when he had promised to love her beyond forever.

Lucinda also had another consolation; Winfield now belonged to her. Malcolm could never again borrow against it to pay his gaming debts. At least she had won *that* battle. Even though her brother had signed the agreement to stop his excessive gambling, she held little hope that he would stay away from the green baize tables at White's, his favorite place to gamble away the Avervich assets.

"But you will save us, my pet," Lord Avervich said. "You will learn to love Lord Grey . . . enough to warm his bed and bear an heir." After a moment he added, "Then, if you desire to take a lover . . ."

"Never, never," Lucinda avowed. "I will never love anyone but James."

Lord Avervich went on: "After you produce an heir, if you wish, you may take a lover."

Unable to look at him, Lucinda turned away. They were in the bookroom where she had gone to plead her case for the last time. Short of running away, which she was tempted to do, she had been left no recourse short of begging. She hated begging.

"Father, did Mama come to you as a chattel? Did she love a man of the lower orders but was forced to marry an Avervich? Is that why you are so cold? Did she take a lover?"

"I am not cold! It is the way of society—"

Lucinda knew she had struck upon the truth. *Mama was forced to marry him. And she died young, most likely from a broken heart.*

Well, Lucinda determined silently, I shall not die young. I will live to find James. And then she reminded herself that her beloved James had left her without a word. She pushed the thought from her mind. Time enough to settle *that* when she saw James, she told herself.

Turning to leave the bookroom, Lucinda declared in a clear voice: "Father, it seems I cannot stop this unholy alliance. So I shall marry your Lord Grey, but I promise that I will be a very reluctant bride."

And she was. One week before Lady Lucinda's sixteenth birthday, she was awakened by blinding blades of sunshine hitting her in the face. Josephine, her French lady's maid and companion, had opened the curtains, and she was making matters worse by humming a merry tune. From a silver tray, which rested on a table near Lucinda's bed, came the smell of hot tea, eggs, stewed kidneys, and hot bread.

Lucinda opened one eye to stare at the room and at Josephine, who was smiling like a Cheshire cat.

"Wake up, little one," she said. "Today is the most important day of your life . . . your wedding day."

Scooting deeper into the feather mattress and pulling the coverlet over her head, Lucinda let out a loud groan.

"Now, m'lady, 'tis not as bad as all that. After the first night, which is oh so-o-o bad, things will right themselves and the first thing you know you will be with child."

The thought of having a child of her own—even if it could not be James's—did not seem so terrible to Lucinda, but that oh, so-o-o bad first night frightened her to death. She could only hope that she could find a hiding place where Lord Grey could not find her.

Thinking she would smother to death if she did not come out from under the comforter, Lucinda emerged from the bed and picked up a silver bell, ringing it as loudly as she could. When the downstairs maid came Lucinda told her to take the tray away.

"Hurry, Cora, before I'm sick," she added.

The maid shook her head from side to side. " 'Tis bad, I know, and me pity goes out to yer, m'lady." She dropped a half-bob. Tears misted her huge, perfectly round, brown eyes, which glared at Lucinda from a perfectly round face. Lucinda hid a smile. Cora always looked for a reason to cry.

So as lively and carefree as she could manage Lucinda tossed her head and declared: "Cora, it will soon be over. Just think, tomorrow, I shall be a countess."

"And you will be leaving Winfield forever." Tears filled the maid's eyes and almost instantly they were dripping from her chin.

Lucinda said quickly: "No, no, Cora, not forever. I shall return to Winfield sooner than you think."

Lucinda had no idea what she meant, but the promise dried the maid's tears and it planted unexpected hope in Lucinda's heart. She did not know how, but she would return to Winfield.

Josephine stepped forward and took Cora's arm, leading her to the door. "Cora, you are upsetting Lady Lucinda with your tears. Take the tray below stairs and be done with you."

Cora jerked her arm free, retrieved the breakfast tray, and left, taking the smell of unwanted food with her.

Lucinda raised the window to let in fresh air. She refused to look toward the stables or at the restless sea she would soon be leaving behind. She could not imagine what living in London would be like. The visit there when Elanora had been choosing her wardrobe for her come-out had been dreadful. She thought the ladies of the *ton* nothing but a bunch of jaded gossips and tattlemongers. How could she ever have anything in common with them? She heard Josephine speaking to her but tried to shut out the words.

"M'lady," Josephine said, "we must needs get you into your wedding dress. 'Twas fortunate that Elanora's dress could be altered to fit you. Such delicate white lace and satin." She went to the chiffonnier and pulled forth the dress. "Look at the beautiful pearls that adorn the bodice and they are at the hemline as well—"

"Put the dress back, Josephine. It is bad enough that I must needs take Elanora's left-over bridegroom—"

"But, m'lady—"

"Don't m'lady me, Josephine. I know what I am doing. I refuse to wear white for Lord Grey. I will save that for when I marry James and then it will be a dress of my own choosing, not Elanora's."

The look on Josephine's face made Lucinda smile. The poor thing looked as if she might at any moment have a spell of the vapors. "Don't pull such a long face, Josephine. What do you think Lord Grey will say when he sees his bride in a blood-red dress or do you think that, under the circumstances, I should wear black?"

With that, Josephine swooned dead away. Lucinda sat on the side of the bed and waited. She was in no hurry to become Countess Grey and she prayed that this night she would find a safe hiding place. She looked in the mirror; pale, gray eyes looked back at her.

And then a smile played around her mouth as an excellent plan formed in her mind.

Taking a vial of vinaigrette from the dressing table, Lucinda waved it under Josephine's nose. The maid sniffed and coughed, then sat up. "What happened?" And then, as if she remembered Lucinda was this day to be married, she asked, "You were only funning, were you not, Lady Lucinda? You would not wear red on your wedding day—"

"No, not red," Lucinda said. She went to the chiffonnier and pulled out a dress made of black muslin. She'd only had two mourning dresses made when Elanora died. This one had a high neck, long sleeves, and hung limply over her straight, undeveloped fifteen-year-old body. Quickly she took scissors and cut a heart from a skirt made of red velvet. With needle and thread she began whipping it to the sleeve of the black dress.

"What . . . what are you doing?" Josephine asked, now sitting up and leaning back on her hands.

Lucinda whipped away. "I'm preparing to dress for my wedding to Lord Grey."

"What . . . why—"

"The black is to show that I am mourning the occasion, and the red heart on the left sleeve is to show that my heart belongs to James."

With that the maid fainted again, hitting the floor with a plop while Lucinda whipped away.

Lucinda's memory stopped there. The rustling of the valentine she had hidden in the folds of her red velvet skirt brought her back to the present. In a minuscule of time she had visited Winfield and passed through her youth.

It was a youth full of dreams of seeing James again. Now she had seen almost thirty summers, and she no longer dreamed. After removing to London she had learned that James had indeed entered His Majesty's Service when he left Winfield, and later, for his bravery in battle, he had been awarded a dukedom along with a beautiful country estate. He was now His Grace James Elston.

And rumor has it that he is affianced to be married.

She gave the twins another hug and then, taking the valentine from Heather, stared at it for a long, silent moment. "It's time I threw this old valentine away."

"Mama, do you have to?" Heather asked.

"It's beautiful, even if it is quite tattered," Elizabeth added.

"Yes, my darlings, it is time to let go of the past." Turning, Lucinda dropped the valentine with the red heart and sculpted rose into the wastebasket, the same one she had earlier dropped the gold band that had bound her to Lord Grey for fourteen years. Taking each of the twins by a hand, she rose from her chair. "Come, we must needs go find your brother. It's time for your Valentine Day party."

"Mama, why are you weeping?" Heather asked.

"Yes, Mama, why does the valentine make you weep?" Elizabeth asked.

"Perhaps it is not the valentine that is making me weep," the countess said. "Perhaps I am crying because I am without a mate on St. Valentine's Day. You know, years ago, many held the belief that birds chose their mates on Valentine's Day."

At the door the countess stopped and looked back at the wastebasket, then quickly jerked her head around and moved forward down a long hall, still holding the twins' hands.

That part of her life was over she told herself, for she no longer believed in youth's foolish dreams.

Although Countess Grey did not care a fig for London's society, she did enjoy the theater, and two nights after her children's Valentine Day party, she went to King's Theater in the Haymarket to hear English tenor John Braham, whose voice, the critics said, compared favorably with Tramezzani, Ambrogetti, and other singers from Italy.

Lucinda agreed with the critics and was enjoying herself immensely until she saw below the Grey's box His Grace James Elston. Beside him sat a lady whom Lucinda assumed was his future wife.

Anger roiled up inside the countess, and she was immensely glad that she had had the fortitude to destroy the valentine he once had given her so many years ago. Moreover she was immensely pleased that she no longer cared for James Elston.

Not caring was one thing but curiosity was another, she told herself. She lifted her lorgnette and blatantly stared. Hair as black as a raven's wing fell to the woman's shoulders.

Lucinda could not stop staring, and eventually the lady turned and their eyes met. The black hair framed an extraordinarily beautiful face; her eyes were deep violet and her complexion that of the belly of a pink rose petal. *She looks like Elanora.*

When the woman turned her attention back to the stage, Lucinda's gaze focused on the back of James's head. His once brown hair was now streaked with gray.

The countess felt her heart move to her throat where it throbbed unmercifully. Inclining her head toward Josephine, who had accompanied her to the theater, she whispered, "James and his affianced are seated in a box directly below us. We will leave at intermission."

"Don't be foolish, m'lady," Josephine said. "After you have seen him face-to-face, you will see that the dream you've carried these many years is only that—a dream."

How Lucinda prayed that that be so, but the raw pain of James's leaving her without saying goodbye ripped agonizingly across her brain, and she felt that any moment she would have a spell of the vapors. Never in her life had she succumbed to such nonsense. "We will leave; I have no desire to see him face-to-face." In truth, the countess was consumed by jealousy of the beautiful woman who sat beside *her* James.

Josephine shrugged her shoulders in compliance, making Lucinda feel guilty for denying her the joy of listening to the English tenor. "We will come another time," the countess whispered. "When *he* is not here."

It was difficult for Lucinda to think that the nephew of

Winfield's housekeeper was now a duke. What a strange trick fate had played. Had he been titled fourteen years ago and had had the means to pay Malcolm's debt, her father would have thought him worthy of an Avervich.

Having lost interest in the English tenor, Lucinda looked around at the fabulously bejeweled ladies; the Duchess of Argyll, Lady Melbourne, and Lady Jersey were among the boxholders.

She forced her attention to the pit where the Beau and his following were strolling about to show off the fine cut of their clothes. They rattled their canes, the lids of their flowered snuffboxes, and chattered loudly to each other, seemingly not the least disturbed when patrons in the boxes shouted at them to be quiet.

For the first time in her life Lucinda joined in the shouting at the detractors. When she realized what she was doing, she felt her face flush with embarrassment, which grew when James turned to stare at her.

Even in the dim lighting Lucinda immediately saw that he was no longer the boy of eighteen, the vision she had carried for these fourteen years. His face was lined and brown; a frown creased his brow, and the infectious smile was missing. But his hazel eyes had not changed. They were still deep, penetrating. He was splendidly dressed.

His gaze never wavered until Lucinda tossed her head to one side and looked away. She felt that James was scolding her for her outburst, and she seethed with indignation. Standing, she gathered her skirt around her. "Come, Josephine, we are leaving *now.*"

"M'lady," Josephine protested, to no avail.

Lucinda, begging the pardon of those who sat in boxes she passed, determinedly made her way to the door of the theater, with Josephine in her wake.

Outside she ordered the Grey carriage brought round. "With great haste," she added. She wanted nothing more than to remove to Clarendon House to her precious children, and when she reached home, cold and anxious, she quickly ascended the stairs and asked that the children be brought to her bedchamber.

Josephine struck flints to light candles, and the countess quickly donned a sleeping gown and crawled up into the high bed, placing plump pillows behind her back. When Josephine offered her help, Lucinda waved her away.

Josephine dutifully rang for the children's nanny. She appeared wearing a long gown and a lace sleeping cap with a look of disbelief on her face. "What's wrong, m'lady? The children are asleep."

"Does something have to be wrong for me to want to see my children?" the countess asked. "Wake them. They won't mind."

To Josephine she said, "Have someone restart the fire. The room is frigid."

A lackey came to chunk the fire and add more coal, and by the time the children had gained the bedchamber, flames licked at the chimney, sending warmth out into the room.

Luke was the first to mount the bed and land in his mother's arms. He wore a flannel gown that covered his small, bare feet. Unlike his sisters he was small for his years, and was the image of his father—in looks and in actions. His dark, straight hair covered his ears and his eyes were dark like Lord Grey's. She loved him dearly, and, hugging him fiercely, she told him so.

"Can we sleep with you, Mama?" he asked.

"Of course you can. That is why I sent for you."

"Us, too?" the twins chimed in unison as they climbed onto the bed, clamoring for their space by Lucinda.

"Of course, darlings. There's room for all my chicks." The twins were her precious darlings also; blond curls crept from under lace sleep-caps, framing their young faces. The twins were very forthright in their jealousy of their younger brother. When Lucinda told them that she was to be blessed with another child, they had declared it was sure to be ugly.

Lucinda had smiled and assured them that they would love their sibling.

Secretly she had prayed that the expected baby would be a boy, an heir, for then her duty to Lord Grey would be finished.

The Lord had answered her prayers.

"I want all three of you here with me," Lucinda said again. When they were settled, each head on a pillow, she dismissed Josephine, asking that she extinguish the candles before leaving. "But open the curtains so light from the moon can shine through the windows."

She remembered another night when moonlight laced the dusk with twinkling stars and surf pounded the Kent seashore.

This night, with her babies gathered around her, memories of mist sprayed high into the air and filled her senses. The fresh smell of salt air floated around her, invading her nostrils.

Homesickness suddenly overtook the countess; she wanted to go home to Winfield. Since marrying Lord Grey, she had returned to her home only once, and that was to attend her father's funeral. The visit had proved painful. The rock where she and James had sat was there; the loft where he had given her the valentine still held his presence.

After Lord Grey had been laid to rest in a tiny graveyard between Lady Avervich and Elanora, Lucinda had told Malcolm that he would always be welcome at Clarendon house but that she would not be coming back to Winfield. *Not until I'm too old to remember,* she had silently promised herself.

Now she wanted to return.

"How would you children like to go to Winfield?" she asked.

"Oh, Mama, could we?" Heather asked.

"Would you tell us about it . . . again," Elizabeth asked in a sleepy voice.

So, as moonlight danced across the faces of her three children and shadows of tree boughs played on the walls, Lucinda talked about Winfield: "It's a huge manor house perched on a mound above the sea. One can hear the waves pounding the rocks . . ."

She prosed on of her youth at Winfield, leaving out only that about her love for the handsome groomsman. "We will go there right away," she said, then smiled. Her little ones were asleep.

But sleep did not come easily for the countess. For hours she lay and stared at the scrolled ceiling, thinking of James, of the valentine he had given her so long ago, the promise he had broken . . .

The next morning, Clarendon house was at sixes and sevens, for when the countess decided she would do something, she did not tarry. Before first light three carriages awaited under the portico, one for Lucinda and the children and the other two for servants and boxes of clothing. Sleepy-eyed children, the girls with dolls under their arms and carrying small satchels for the dolls' clothes in their hands, were handed up by a footmen.

"Give the driver office to be off," the countess told one of the footman.

The driver cracked a whip over the four bays. A tiger rode the lead horse, and two liveried footmen rode the back. "May I ride on the box with the driver?" Luke asked.

"Absolutely not," the countess answered.

"Don't be a slowtop," Heather told him, and Elizabeth reminded him that *he* was the seventh Earl of Clarendon, that it would be foolish to endanger his life. She also told him that their dear Mama had had him only because their papa wanted an heir.

Lucinda wondered where in the world Elizabeth had learned *that,* but of course servants gossiped, she told herself, and they thought children did not have ears to hear with or brains to think with. "Elizabeth!" she scolded. "Luke was a welcome member to the Clarendon household."

"See there, Lizabet, you don't know what you are talking about," Luke said.

The countess's voice was firm. "Children, stop your squabbling. I love all of you equally."

Heather reached to give her brother a pat. "Of course we wanted you. Now Elizabeth nor I will be forced into a marriage of convenience; that is, unless you grow up and gamble away our wealth. Uncle Malcolm—"

"Hush, Heather," the countess told her, this time her voice sharp. After that the children settled down.

The carriage wheels rolled out onto the cobbled street. Lucinda gathered Luke up onto her lap and held him to her heaving breast. *I'm going home. I'm at last returning to Winfield.*

Tears misted the countess's eyes.

Three hours after the Grey entourage left London, there was a morning caller at Clarendon House. Greaves, the butler, lifted a quizzical brow at the imposingly tall man who stood before him. With one arm he held what looked to the butler like dozens of roses; the other hand held a black cane on which he leaned heavily. "I'm James Elston," the stranger said. "Fourteen years ago, I worked at Winfield . . . as a groomsman. I wish to see Dowager Countess Lucinda Grey . . ."

Winfield looked the same. Of course it would not have changed, Lucinda thought. Late sunlight sparked the many mullioned windows; she smelled the fresh air from the sea. "Wake up, children," she said, "We have arrived."

Small fists rubbed sleepy eyes as necks craned. "Mama, 'tis beautiful," Heather said, and Elizabeth parroted her.

Little Luke raised his head and looked, then went back to sleep. Under the portico the countess kissed the children, then gladly let the servants she had brought with her take charge of them. Since she had arrived unexpectantly, Malcolm did not wait to greet them. "This night they will take their meal in the nursery on the third floor," she told Nanny and the footman who was carrying Luke. "It has been a tiresome journey. On the morrow they can explore."

That the children offered no objection to the countess's orders attested to their tiredness. Heather and Elizabeth scrambled down the carriage steps without help, and then Heather climbed back up, declaring, "I forgot my satchel."

"Uh-oh, don't do that," Elizabeth said, while looking up into her mother's face.

Guilt, the countess thought, smiling. She could not imagine why, but she knew the twins quite well, and guilt was there in both their countenances. She bent for their goodbye kisses as she told them, "Sleep well, and I will see you on the morrow."

Both satchels now secured in young fists, dolls under arms, the twins followed Nanny through the side door.

"I'll see that your old rooms are made ready, m'lady," Josephine said.

"Thank you," Lucinda answered attentively. She could not help it, but the memory of that fateful day when the Avervich carriage returned from London floated through her mind. James, dressed as a groomsman, waited under the portico . . . and later he had given her the valentine.

Silently the countess scolded herself: *Will I never stop thinking of him?* She swept up the steps and rattled the brass knocker. Two wide doors opened almost immediately.

"M'lady, you've come home," Maximilian said, a twinkle in his eyes.

Lucinda noticed that his livery was new—black tails and high collar points pristine white and stiff as a board. He had grown older, she thought, adding under her breath, "And so have I."

"M'lord and m'lady are in the withdrawing room on the second floor," the butler said. "They'll be surprised to see you, m'lady."

"I know, Max. I should have sent a missive. But there wasn't time . . . once I decided to come."

"It has been a long time. We've missed you. But I'm happy to tell you that the household is very fond of the new Lady Avervich."

"I'm pleased to hear that," Lucinda told him.

"I will announce you."

"No, please don't," Lucinda quickly said. "I am wont to surprise them."

He gave a slight bow. "As you wish, m'lady."

Lucinda walked the length of the great hall and noticed as she did so that the crystal prisms dangling from the chandeliers glistened from proper care; the stairs that curved upward shone from recent polishing and smelled of beeswax. Three years ago, Malcolm, at thirty and two, had very quietly married a young Russian princess. Lucinda had been informed by an intelligence from Malcolm himself . . . after the wedding. And he had not brought his bride to London.

That the new Lady Avervich had been good for Winfield was evident. Fresh flowers spilled out of a Wedgwood vase resting on a table at the top of the stairs. Lucinda stopped to smell them, then moved on. To the right was the withdrawing room. She stood unobtrusively in the doorway and, for a long moment, looked at the room so familiar to her yet so strangely different.

Heavy red draperies framed the many windows; a new colorful Turkish carpet covered the floor.

A cheerful fire burned in the fireplace before which Malcolm sat in a newly covered begère chair, gazing at the beautiful woman who sat opposite him in a matching chair. Hair the color of umber spilled down her back, her youthful skin was the color of warm milk, and love emanated warmly from large brown eyes framed by long, black lashes. She was smiling at her husband, obviously unaware of the figure standing in the doorway. Lucinda was reluctant to invade their private moment and waited a moment longer.

Malcolm looks younger . . . and happier, Lucinda thought as she walked softly across the carpet. Standing by Malcolm's chair, she bent and kissed him on the cheek. "I've missed you, Malcolm."

As if she had jerked him from another world, Malcolm jumped to his feet. "Welcome home, Lucinda," he said in a chocked voice. "This is Lady Avervich . . . Sasha, my wife."

When Sasha stood, her Grecian-style gown of sapphire silk clung to every curve of her full body. Lucinda wondered if she were enceinte. Little wonder Malcolm was so smitten. Sasha exuded warmth and smiling she dropped into a throne-room curtsy.

Embarrassed at such homage at Winfield, Lucinda told her quickly that she did not wish to be curtsied to. "We are family," she told her. She then kissed her sister-in-law as she had her brother.

"I shall order tea," Sasha said. She went to pull a bellrope. "There's so much I wish to know about you, Lady Grey. Malcolm has spoken lovingly of you."

"I've told Sasha about your marriage to Lord Grey, about your saving Winfield."

"Yes," Sasha said, "we know it is your home, and we shall remove to another place should you wish to return."

Lucinda laughed. "I believe there is room enough for all should I decide to return permanently. As for right now I am merely visiting." Her voice tight in her throat, she continued almost inaudibly, "I wanted to come home. London suddenly became too much for me."

She did not add that seeing James with his affianced had been too much for her. A maid brought a steaming pot of tea on a large silver tray. Scones and tiny cakes were piled high on a delicate china plate. "Thank you, Melba," Sasha said. When the maid did not immediately leave, Lady Avervich said in a kind voice, "That will be all."

Lucinda asked about Cora, the maid who had cried the night she married Lord Grey because she thought Lucinda would never return to Winfield. "She has retired" Malcolm explained. "She married a boy from the village and I believe she is expecting her first child."

Sasha poured, and, after the three of them had settled comfortably in chairs, sipping tea and eating scones and cakes, Lucinda inquired of the former groomsman.

Malcolm grinned sheepishly. "As you know, I am not in London overmuch these days. After meeting Sasha the gaming tables lost their lure." He favored his wife with a dazzling smile before going on, "But even here, we hear *on-dits*. It seems he made quite a name for himself fighting alongside Wellington, and his name is on every village quidnunc's tongue."

Lucinda's cup shook in her hand. "Why the village? What would they know of James Elston."

"His Grace's estate which was awarded to him by His Majesty, joins Winfield."

For sure, Lucinda thought, she would have a spell of the vapors. Her breath came in short waves and the room swam before her eyes.

"Lucinda, you look goosish," Malcolm exclaimed. "The independent Lucy I remember would never swoon."

"I've mellowed with age," the countess answered, still shaking inwardly. It was obvious to her that Malcolm did not remember—if he ever knew—that she had once loved James Elston.

Trying in vain to steady her cup, she instead knocked it to the floor.

"I'll call for a maid to take the tray and to clean the tea from the rug," Sasha said, now hovering solicitously over Lucinda's chair. "I fear you've ruined your beautiful traveling dress."

"Cold water will remove the stain." Lucinda hardly recognized her own voice.

"Well, a new gown can be ordered," Malcolm said. "You will be needing something beautiful to wear to His Grace's Valentine's ball. The invitation came yesterday. After I send word that you have come to Winfield, I'm sure an invitation for you to attend will be forthcoming."

With that, the countess fainted dead away.

"The devil take me," exclaimed Malcolm. "What did I say . . .?"

"Of course I shan't go," Lucinda told Josephine, "even if the invitation does come." They were in her old bedchamber, the one where she had dressed for her wedding to Lord Grey.

"Of course you will go," Josephine told her. "You've worn your heart on your sleeve long enough." She gave a little laugh. "And the good Lord knows that you stared at his valentine long enough. Time for you to meet that dream man face-to-face—"

"You've said that before," the countess retorted. "I met him face-to-face at the theatre, and a beautiful woman flanked his right side. Remember? I'm glad that I finally had the good sense to throw the silly valentine in the trash where it should have belonged from the day he left Winfield without a word to me."

"Mayhaps you don't know the full story."

Lucinda turned her head. She absolutely refused to look at the sea. There might be a sea gull. . . . "I know enough of the story. He left, and that is that. Not a goodbye, never an intelligence, and now he is betrothed to *that* woman. Who is she anyway?"

"Winfield gossip has it that she's a sister of a soldier who fought in the war with His Grace."

"How perfectly charming," Lucinda said. *And how perfectly*

charming that his estate runs with Winfield.

This newly learned fact rankled the countess. Always she had desired to return to Winfield to rear her children. She hated London with its false society and the *ton's* ridiculous strictures. Now it would be impossible to live at Winfield. "How can I live at Winfield expecting each morning *that* woman to call?"

Josephine shot her a sideways glance. "Since when have you made morning calls?"

"Well, I might—"

Just then there was a soft rap on the door. "Come in," Lucinda said, and was not surprised that it was Sasha.

"Lucinda, there is a gentleman caller who wishes to see you." She handed Lucinda a card which read simply "James Elston."

"I will not see him . . ."

Josephine grabbed the countess's arm. "Now don't you start swooning. I'm tired of waving vinaigrette under your nose."

Lucinda jerked her arm loose. "I'm not prone to swooning, and don't you dare stick that horrible stuff under my nose again."

Sasha, standing quietly by, finally said, "What shall I tell His Grace? I took the card from Maximilian thinking that, by your earlier reaction when you heard His Grace lived nearby, I could reason with you." She stopped to give a slow smile. "James Elston is a handsome man. He awaits down stairs in the receiving room."

"A betrothed man," was the countess's rejoinder, and then silence engulfed the room. She went to sit in a chair by the window. Now, her anger in place, she stared out at the sea. All these years she had secretly longed for James Elston—and now she was angry for that longing, for his leaving without saying goodbye, and for his not writing. Josephine was right, she told herself, smiling with relief. She had escaped into a dream, an unrealistic dream that had begun in a fifteen-year-old's heart. With that thought, the countess immediately calmed herself and began planning what she would do.

Outside the bedchamber two ears pressed hard against the door. "Mama is thinking," Heather whispered.

"How do you know?" Elizabeth asked.

"It's too still in there."

Heather grabbed Elizabeth's hand and started running down the hall as quietly as possible. "Come on, Lizzie, we'd best hurry else Mama will catch us."

James Elston struggled to his feet when the twins entered the room and dropped into a deep curtsy. Leaning on his cane, he lifted the hand of the one most forward to him and kissed it and then did the same for the other, smiling down at them. Tousled blond curls framed their faces, and huge gray eyes, the color of Lucinda's, looked up at him somberly.

"Your Grace, I am Heather and this is Elizabeth. We are Lady Grey's twin daughters. We have something for you, and we must needs hurry with giving it to you, else Mama will know and have our hides. She is so terribly angry with you, and she says she is not coming to receive you, but she might change her mind."

"Then by all means hurry. I would not have anyone take your beautiful hides."

These are Lucinda's twin girls of whom I've heard, His Grace thought, a lump rising in his throat. He wanted to bend and hug them to him, and he wanted to ask them why their Mama was so terribly angry with him. But time was of essence.

Heather held out a crudely wrapped package tied with a blue ribbon. "Here, this is for you. I believe you gave it to Mama when you were quite young."

"She calls it a youthful experience, and she says it was nothing important," Elizabeth added.

"But we know better." Heather looked at her twin and bobbed her head. "Don't we, Elizabeth. After you look at it, Your Grace, you will see that it is all tattered from so much handling and faded from her tears."

"Yes," Elizabeth said, "we know better and we don't like to see Mama cry."

When Elston untied the ribbon, he thought his heart would burst inside of him, and he felt his eyes mist with tears, blurring his vision. But it was not necessary for him to see. All that mattered was that she had kept his valentine. And it was not necessary for him to read the poem, for he knew it by heart. He fingered the tattered edges and felt the cheap paper. Faded by her tears, the girls had said. He looked into their upturned faces. "How did you come by this?"

"Mama threw it in the trash, and we went back later when she didn't know and got it," piped up Elizabeth. We've carried it in one of our satchels ever since, hoping that we might encounter you."

Heather gave her sister a scolding look as if to say that *she* was the spokesman for the two, and then she added, "But she didn't mean it when she said it was just a youthful experience. We happen to know that when she married Papa she wore a black dress with a red heart on the sleeve—"

"The red heart was for you, Your Grace," Elizabeth explained. "And she kept hiding from Papa. It took him all of three nights to find her so they could order an heir to his title and wealth."

It was difficult for His Grace to digest all that the girls were telling him. Elation suddenly filled him; his Lucinda *had* loved him. She had not married Lord Grey willingly.

"They told the stork to bring a boy, but he brought Elizabeth and me. Me first, I'm the oldest. It took the stork a long time to finally bring little Luke. He's five."

His Grace smothered a laugh. "And how did you girls learn all this?"

"By listening at doors," Heather said, "but don't tell Mama."

"Servants are terrible gossips," Elizabeth explained.

"I'm sure your mother would hide you plenty if she knew you did that. Only servants put their ears to the doors."

"Mama never hided us in our life, but she would scold us if she knew," Heather said.

"But mostly Mama laughs and tells us how much she loves us."

James Elston could imagine this being true. He could still hear Lucinda's youthful laughter . . . and he knew she was capable of loving without constraint, for he remembered her blatantly declaring her love for him, the housekeeper's nephew, and he remembered too vividly holding her in his arms. Desire to see her overwhelmed him. Did she still look the same? Of course not, he told himself. Fourteen years had passed.

From the table beside the chair he had sat in before the girls made their appearance, His Grace took a delicately wrapped package and held it out to Heather. "Will you give this to your mother? And tell her, pray, that I expect to see her at Stanton Manor for a Valentine's ball two days hence."

"But, Your Grace, St. Valentine's Day has passed," Heather said.

"I know, but I only recently returned from Paris." He looked down at the cane that supported his weak leg. "I was in the hospital there."

Upstairs, Josephine looked out the window and exclaimed, "He's leaving; His Grace is leaving, m'lady."

"Let him leave," the countess countered, but she jumped to her feet and ran to the window. Already the crested carriage was headed down the hill, away from Winfield. At least this day she could see him leave, she thought, not like before when he sneaked off before first light.

Before Lucinda could assess her feelings, the fast beating

of her heart, and the whirling in her head, the twins bounded through the door. "Mama, Mama," they said in unison.

Elizabeth turned to her sister. "Give her the package and have done with it." A twinge of nervousness showed in her voice.

"His Grace left this for you," Heather said. "He waited ever so long for you to receive him. We had a nice long coze."

Elizabeth looked earnestly up into her mother's face. "He said that he prayed you would come to his St. Valentine's ball."

Hardly hearing the twins, Lucinda took the package and gingerly untied the ribbon, her hands shaking in a manner they had never shook before. She found her way to a chair and sat down. A replica of the valentine that her precious James had given her over fourteen years ago lay in her lap staring up at her. This time it was on fine paper; inside the heart was the beautifully sculpted rose, every petal perfect.

"Not an arrow," he had said. "An arrow cuts through the heart, breaking it. A rose is forever." And then he had avowed, "Lucinda, my love for you will last *beyond* forever."

She turned the valentine over, and there she found another poem by Lord Byron. In a soft, almost inaudible voice, she read aloud:

> As some lone bird, without a mate,
> My weary heart is desolate;
> I look around, and cannot trace
> One friendly smile or welcome face,
> And ev'n in crowds am still alone,
> Because I cannot love but one.

In his own flowing script, His Grace had written: "My Lucinda, my love for you will last beyond forever."

"From a man betrothed," the countess said, sotto voce, and, after hugging, then dismissing the twins, she declared again that she was *not* going to His Grace's Valentine's ball.

"Oh, but you must needs go, Josephine said. "How else will you learn why he left Winfield without a word. I'll wager he has a good excuse."

"Don't all men have excuses for their indiscretions?"

The countess did not know why she said that; she knew very little about men and their excuses. Unless it was her deceased Papa who had rationalized everything he did.

Sasha, who had been standing silently by stepped forward. "Sometimes their excuses are well formed. Lucinda, do you realize that Malcolm's rakehell ways were brought on by his father's trying to live in his pocket. There are those who say I changed my husband, but that is not so. He changed after his papa died. Perhaps your anger at James does not signify. As Josephine says, you must needs learn the truth."

The countess could find no argument. She looked at her sister-in-law, who seemed more a celestial vision than a mere person made of flesh and blood, and thanked God that she had come into Malcolm's life. "I don't have an appropriate gown, and it's too late to have a modiste—"

"Oh, but I have a beautiful gown that has never been worn," Sasha countered. "With a little stitching it will fit perfectly."

How can I watch James with that *woman?* the countess asked her heart, not receiving an answer. And then true confusion set in. Why did James bring her the valentine when he was betrothed to another woman. Was he out to punish her? But for what? Had he not, years ago, left her?

Good sense told the countess that she should not attend James's Valentine's ball, but her heart told her she must. For her own sanity, she told herself, she must needs look one more time into those piercing hazel eyes to entirely expunge him from her mind, from her heart, and from her soul.

When the truth is known, truth of which only James is cognizant, then the pain will go away, the countess whispered unconvincingly to herself.

The countess dressed for the ball without much concern. Although Josephine and Sasha exclaimed with great forcefulness how beautiful she looked in Sasha's made-over gown, Lucinda hardly allowed herself a glance in the tall looking glass that hung on the wall of her dressing room. She had never thought of herself as beautiful, and that was that. She did, however, allow Josephine to braid her hair into what the twins called her golden crown.

Looking down, her ladyship saw plainly that the décolletage of the gown was entirely too revealing. White flesh showed above rows of delicate French lace. From the empire waist, which fit snugly under her breasts, soft gray silk fell to cover her feet. Despite having given birth to three children, she had kept herself slender for which she was, this night, especially thankful, and she could not help wondering what James would look like. At the theater she had only seen his eyes and his graying hair. Accepting the fan Josephine held out to her, the countess picked up her skirt, then announced in a clear voice, "I'm ready . . . as ready as I shall ever be."

"You are positively beautiful," Sasha said, and Josephine nodded her head in agreement.

This night Josephine would attend both ladies, but her thoughts were on the countess and the paleness of her skin, the pain in her huge gray eyes.

The three rode with Malcolm in the Avervich carriage, and as they neared Stanton Manor, which was on the coast as Winfield was, Lucinda listened to the waves breaking against the rocks. A pale moon illumined a black velvet sky, and a thousand stars sparkled like glittering diamonds. It was as if something reached inside her and squeezed her heart until she could not breathe, and once inside the manor she was seized with panic. Pausing in the foyer, she looked around her, trying at the same time to breathe normally.

Giant pots of airy ferns and huge baskets of red roses were everywhere, like a garden in full bloom.

Footmen, dressed in formal livery of blue with gold braid, stood at attention at the foot of a curving staircase, beside which stood elegant stands holding urns of more red roses.

Not realizing the others in her party were trailing long behind her, the countess climbed the stairs to the ballroom. She could hear the din of clamoring voices and the strains of soft music being played by the orchestra. And then the butler was announcing her in: "The Countess Lucinda Rose Grey."

Lucinda's eyes quickly traversed the crowd, looking, not for His Grace but for the beautiful woman who had flanked his side at the theatre, for she suddenly realized that it did not matter *why* James had left her without saying goodbye when she was five and ten years. What signified was that he had declared, by way of another valentine, that his love for her had not died even when he was affianced to another. Behind her she heard the butler announcing Lord Malcolm and his lady in.

Looking up, she saw James coming towards her, walking not as he used to, in long, fluid strides, but leaning heavily on a black cane. She sucked in a breath. In full light, she could see that twenty years, not fourteen, had been added to that long-ago youthful face. As he neared, she dropped into a formal curtsy.

"Lucinda," he said, his voice low and guttural, as if he were choking on her name. With his free hand he reached for hers, lifting it to his lips. For a long moment he held it thus, and when her hand left his lips, Lucinda could feel the trembling as his fingers twined hers. "Let's get the hell out of here," he said, leading her to the nearest door.

"But, Your Grace, your guests. . . . 'Tis against propriety to leave."

"The guests be demmed. I only have one guest, and that

is you. The ball was for one purpose, and that was to lure you into my home. It would have been given on the appropriate day, exactly fourteen years from that other Valentine's Day, had I not been detained in Paris."

"But what about *her?*"

"Who?"

By now they were through the door, standing in a garden of climbing rose bushes and sprawling vines with blossoms from which emanated a tangy odor of jasmine. James, with assistance from his cane, started walking in front, reaching back to hold Lucinda's hand as he led her along a well-trodden path, away from the sound of music, away from voices of strangers. "Where are we going?" she queried.

"To find a sea gull," His Grace answered.

Slowly they twined their way through the garden, gaining an open space and then a ledge, where they stopped. Below was the rocky shore, and beyond that stretched the sea, green turning black as moonlight and silver stars sparkled upon the waves. Silver mist sprayed high in the air, and waves beat rhythmically against the rocks, just as they had fourteen years ago.

But we have changed, Lucinda thought. *We're no longer fifteen and eighteen. James is betrothed . . .*

She asked again: "What about *her?*" And James asked again, "Who?"

"Your betrothed, the beautiful woman you were with at the theater."

James threw his head back and laughed. It sounded so sweet, so natural to Lucinda. But he had not answered her question. She jerked her hand from his, and he immediately reclaimed it, declaring: "I will not lose you again, my love."

"You lost me when you left without telling me goodbye . . . after falsely declaring your love for me. Do you take me for a fool, James Elston?"

There was nothing petulant in the countess's voice, for she made sure that her anger came through in a direct manner.

They were standing side by side, and James clasped her hand tightly. They looked out at the sea, fresh salt air blowing in their faces.

"I'm happy that you did not call me 'Your Grace.' I've hardly become accustomed to such honor."

Lucinda turned to look at him. "James, you are talking of everything except what I am addressing. I wish to know about *that woman*. Why am I here with you when you are betrothed? Why did you leave me without saying goodbye and never an intelligence. Surely you must know that my love for you died—"

She couldn't go on.

James, smiling down at her in that old familiar way, reached inside his waistcoat pocket and produced the tattered valentine, stained with tears, the edges ragged from handling. Lucinda vividly recalled the many times she had clasped it to a heaving breast. "Where did you get that?" she asked in an almost inaudible voice.

"The twins gave it to me. It seems they retrieved it from the wastebasket where you tossed it. They told me about your tears, and they told me you still cared. My feet have hardly touched the ground since, and I find myself laughing over the silliest things. Forgive me—"

"That doesn't mean I still care—"

The expression on James's face went serious and tender. "I want you to care, for I care deeply about you." Again he reached inside his waistcoat pocket, this time bringing forth a small packet of letters tied with a ribbon. "Malcolm gave these to me, missives I wrote which your father confiscated. Yesterday, after hearing my story of how Lord Avervich ordered me from Winfield saying no Avervich would marry a stablehand, refusing to even let me say goodbye, he searched the attic at Winfield and found these."

Lucinda recognized James's handwriting, and it was not difficult for her to believe Lord Avervich would keep the letters from her, justifying the deed in his own mind. "But what about *that woman?* And why did you wait a whole year after I was widowed to call on me?"

"That woman you speak of is the sister of the man who saved my life in battle at the cost of his own. Her husband was also killed. She is not my affianced. She came to see me when I was in the hospital in Paris, which, by the bye, is why I did not call on you the first year you were widowed. An excellent physician there says that one more bout with surgery will make my leg as good as new. A bullet caught me in the knee."

"I'm sorry," Lucinda said.

His Grace returned the valentine and packet of letters to his waistcoat pocket. "Because Meredith—that woman—has no one else with whom she can speak of her tragedy, she came to visit me at Stanton Manor. And the quidnuncs have had a field day with their speculative *on-dits,* even in London. She knows of my deep love for you."

The countess's questions had all been answered as Sasha had predicted they would be. Josephine had said that when Lucinda saw James again she would realize that she had carried in her heart a youthful dream, but that was not so. Her love for James was not a dream; it was real. "I love you, James," she whispered against the wind.

"And I love you, Lucinda. Will you marry me?"

Lucinda answered quickly, "Yes."

He opened his arms and she stepped into them, feeling as if she had never been away, and when his lips claimed hers, a quickening invaded her body, a feeling she thought long dead but now revived. As the kiss deepened her heart began to beat faster and her body felt afire. She whispered between kisses: "We'll have lots of children . . ."

"You promise not to hide from me on our wedding night? The twins told me—"

"I promise."

He chuckled. "Then the banns will be read this Sabbath."

Silently they turned to look out at the sea, to smell the

fresh air, to bask in their happiness. A huge wave climbed high into the air and came down to pound the rocks, resounding loudly in the stillness of the night.

Above the shimmering water, through the silver mist, a sea gull in graceful flight, its white wings unfurled, its long neck stretched forward, faded into the night's blackness, beyond forever.

"A good omen," James said, and then he turned to again take his future bride into his arms, holding her tightly and feeling his own desire roiling inside of him. His kiss was deeper, more demanding, and he felt her body come to his promisingly.

"Yes, m'lady," he said with a small smile, "I believe there will be many children."

A Valentine Bride

by Teresa DesJardien

The butler McCane looked at the young woman sitting in the nearest corner, her hands held serenely in front of her, her face fixed into what might have been a vague smile or a suppressed grimace, he could not tell which. She was finely dressed, though the slippers that peeked out under her satin gown were sadly scuffed and dirtied. Her hat was of the latest mode, her gloves were unmended and crisply white, and there was an air about her that spoke of quality. That was absurd, of course, for no lady of quality would be in his master's parlor this day. Still, it was time to call her forward, and "You, there!" was clearly not appropriate in this case. In the normal way of things he would have ventured to call her attention his way by murmuring, "My lady?" but now he settled on, "Miss?"

She turned her fine-boned face his way, gave a simple nod, and rose. He thought for a moment that she might swoon, but she recovered herself and stepped forward with all the grace and serenity of a well-bred lady. He led her across the parlor, through the connecting door, down a hall to its far end, and through that door into his master's library.

Lord Whittham sat behind a large mahogany desk, much as the lady had expected to find him. He was, she knew, somewhere between twenty-five and thirty years of age. He looked up from his notes, registering for a moment a flicker of surprise at the refinement of her dress, and waved her into the chair that was set before the desk. He turned his attention back to the sheet of paper before him, making quick notes. The butler left, quietly closing the door to leave the two—most improper, but then wasn't the entire day just so?—alone together.

"Name?" Lord Whittham inquired, not looking up.

"Christine Jordan."

He looked up at that, frowning a little. She saw the gray eyes she remembered, the dark unruly hair, the prominent cheekbones.

"*Lady* Christine Jordan," he said. It sounded rather like an accusation. "Why have you come here today? I pray it is not to scold me or tell me how I may manage my life. You must trust that I have heard it all already."

"I have not," she said quietly.

He sat back then, looking at her fully. It was clear he was trying to decide whether or not he was going to be curt with her. She met his gaze coolly, hopeful that he could not see the way she trembled inside.

"Lady Jordan—"

"I have come to apply for the advertised position," she interrupted him, her clear voice ringing in the room a little too loudly, a reflection of her nervous state.

"You cannot be serious."

"I am very serious, sir."

He stood and came around the desk. He crossed his arms and leaned back so that his thigh rested against the top of the desk. "We have met before, I think."

"Once or twice, at parties."

He nodded. "Your family . . . ?"

She blinked slowly, once, to force back tears. "Dead," she said simply. Reports of the carriage accident had been in all the papers. Lord Whittham had undoubtedly heard of it at the time. It had been months since, yet the pain of her loss was quite fresh to Christine, for she had lost not only her parents but so much more.

He circled around the desk, resuming his seat as he said dismissively, "My dear lady, I am sure your guardian, whomever that might be, is fully capable of finding you a husband."

"I have no guardian," she said past a tight throat. "I have no family at all. My brother died at Salamanca, and my sister of childbirth, three years ago."

"Then you should apply to her husband."

"He is somewhere in the Americas, my lord. I have no notion of where. The last known location was a place called Virginia. I wrote. A woman wrote back and said Stephen had gone west. She did not know where. She said she would hold my letter for the time, if ever, he returned."

"Perhaps patience is the key here. Give it a little more time, to allow him to receive your missive. Now if you will excuse me, I have many—"

"My lord, I cannot wait!" she cried. Her fingers tightened on the straps of her reticule so tightly that one of the strings snapped audibly.

He looked at her coolly, but his silence was enough to urge her to go on.

She rallied, speaking quietly and firmly, not allowing a tremor to enter her voice. "My parents left me almost nothing. The house sold at once, that I might afford the costs to bury them. It went with everything in it—the paintings, the furniture. I had to move to a hotel. I have sold my mother's few jewels, the carriages, Papa's watch and fob, and even their clothes. Even most of my own clothes. I have nothing left, my lord, not a single ha'penny. I have no idea how I shall buy my next meal."

She met his eyes levelly, ignoring the single tear that fell down her cheek.

"Have you tried to find employment?" he asked, but even as the words came out of his mouth he knew she would have no success in that quarter. She was so young, perhaps eighteen, and very pretty. There was not a mama in London that would have such a one in the house—for Lady Christine Jordan would outshine most daughters and would certainly tempt most sons.

"Of course. I was told it would be very difficult to place me," she said, the pain and hurt he heard in her voice causing her moist eyes to dry now. "I thought I was to have a position as a seamstress, but the lady changed her mind."

Lord Whittham did not ask, for regardless of why she was turned down, it would be the same wherever she went. She was too pretty for servitude in a household, too well-born for menial work—the lower classes were often mistrusting of one who "stooped"—and too delicate for hard labor. There was no place in the working world for such a one.

"An aunt? An uncle? A cousin? Is there no one?" he asked, not unkindly.

She shook her head. "No one."

"A friend?"

"They wrote some recommendations for me. Some advised me to sail to America to search for Stephen."

He waited for her to break into noisy tears and pleadings for assistance. Here was the time she was supposed to declare dramatically that she was completely orphaned and must throw herself on his mercy. She ought to be asking outright for funds or assistance in being placed.

This woman did none of those things. She had lost everything, everything except her ability to hold her head up.

Despite the uncomfortableness of having her here in his home, describing her situation in such a way as to tweak the hardest heart, he could only commend her self-possession. He said, "So you saw my advertisement and decided to come here."

She nodded and gave a sound that was almost a laugh, self-deprecating. "I could not even afford the price of the paper, my lord. I found the sheet on the street and picked it up to see if anyone needed some kind of a servant, any kind of task that I might perform . . . well, that does not matter. Obviously I read the advertisement and have come here, among all the others, to see if I might do."

He ran the feather of his writing nib through his fingers, staring at her. Hundreds of ladies had assembled in his home today. McCane had weeded out the obviously inferior ones—the prostitutes, the drunkards, the mentally unbalanced, and then had brought the fifty or so remaining to his master, one at a time, for a brief interview. They had been mostly shopgirls, governesses, or companions who were looking for a way out of their dreary lives. Some had the gleam of ambition in their eyes and had been ruled out at once. Some were poor, cringing creatures who may or may not have been ill-used. A few had been mostly just curious, intrigued by his advertisement.

It was shocking, horribly shocking, that advertisement, for it said that the Baron Whittham was looking for a wife. A member of the blood had chosen to solicit a wife, not by means of the routs and assemblies of such correct places as Almack's, but by the direct course of interviewing for her. It stated clearly: "Applicants must be healthy, quiet, and willing to marry posthaste. You must apply today, February 14th, between the hours of 8:00 A.M. and 4:00 P.M., at the residence of Lord Oliver Whittham of Duke Street."

He rubbed the feather over his clean-shaven upper lip, then sat forward suddenly. "Age?" he asked as he dipped the nib into a jar of India ink.

"Eighteen."

He did not smile or in any other way acknowledge that he had guessed correctly as he marked her responses upon the paper before him. "Parentage . . . ? No, I already know." He read aloud as he wrote it down, "Lord and Lady Quincy Jordan, deceased." He hesitated for a moment, only a quick movement of his eyes acknowledging the pain he may have unthinkingly caused her. "State of health?" He looked up then, assessingly.

She felt her face grow a little warm, but she answered as calmly as he asked. "My health is good, my lord."

"You are thin."

"I have not been eating a great deal of late."

"Any diseases, past or present?"

"I had measles when I was a child."

"No female diseases?"

"I do not know what those might be," she said, but there was that in her voice that said she had a thought as to the matter.

Lord Whittham hesitated a moment, then asked instead, "Are you a virgin, Lady Jordan?"

She closed her eyes, finding the interview even more difficult than she had imagined. "Yes," she whispered.

"You would be willing to allow a doctor to determine that as fact?"

"Yes."

"Pardon me, but can you speak up?"

"I said 'yes,' my lord."

"That's better. Now, let me explain, in case you have not seen it for yourself, that if we were to marry, you would be cast out entirely from the *ton*. The entire social world is fully aware that I have advertised for my wife. We will not be welcome anywhere. You could expect to spend your life in the country. Is that clear to you?"

"Yes."

"Is that acceptable?"

"Yes."

"Lady Jordan, you will pardon me for saying that surely this is not what you expected in your life, and it is therefore somewhat difficult to believe you would be contented with such." He spoke a trifle harshly.

"Neither did I expect to become orphaned and destitute," she answered him flatly.

"Ah." He ran the feathered nib through his fingers again. There was something faintly approving in the gesture as he did it now. "There is one other thing I have brought to the attention of all applicants."

She waited for him to continue, not knowing what was coming.

"I want it clearly understood that I intend to execute my conjugal rights as I see fit. I do not mean to offend the sensibilities, but the truth of the matter is that this marriage *will* be made to hold solid and that progeny are expected. Is that clear as well, my lady?"

Colored lights danced in front of her eyes, perhaps because her breathing had become very shallow. "Yes," she whispered, but despite the dizzy feeling she did not let her chin drop, not even a little.

He laid down the quill, clapped his hands together once, and stood. "Very well then, Lady Jordan. It seems we have an agreement." He extended his hand across the desk to her.

She leaned forward, not trusting her knees to stand, and took his warm hand in her own slightly shaking one. They shook, and he withdrew his hand at once, coming around the desk to take her elbow and assist her to her feet.

Before he could lead her forward she asked, "My lord, may I ask one question?"

"That seems only fair," he smiled faintly.

"Why? Why a *wife?* Why this way?"

"That is actually three questions, my lady," he smiled again, and this time it reached his gray eyes. "It is very simple and, I am afraid, very mercenary. I stand to lose my entire inheritance if I am not married by the date specified in my father's will. All my money, this house, everything that is not entailed for my mother will go to charity. I prefer to keep it, you see, my dear."

"But you must have known the date was coming! Why not find a wife in the conventional manner?"

He pulled gently on her elbow, leading her toward the door of the den. "I tried to fight it legally as I did not either care to marry just yet, nor did I care to have my father lording it over me even now as the man is in his grave. Unfortunately, my efforts in that regard were unsuccessful. And so you see, I have found myself on the verge of losing it all and must make haste to see that does not happen. Are you ready to see the doctor? He awaits upstairs."

Her mouth twitched down. "You are very efficient, my lord."

"At times."

"When is the wedding to take place?" she asked, wondering if her landlord would let her stay a while longer at the hotel if she could promise to pay him later. Surely Lord Whittham would settle that one small account for her?

"Tonight. No later than seven o'clock."

She stopped, absolutely stunned, but his hand on her arm urged her past the door he opened, into the hall. "Tonight? Valentine's Day?" she echoed, the thought coming into her mind that the date was a kind of sick joke. On Valentine's Day, the day set aside for lovers? How much farther from lovers could any two persons be than they?

"Is it? Why, yes, I believe you are quite right, Lady Jordan. It is just like my father to make Valentine's Day his deadline. I am surprised I had not thought of it myself. This way, please."

He pulled her toward a long staircase. She heard and answered his questions about where to send for her pitiful few remaining things, and did she feel the need to await the arrival of one of her other gowns before the ceremony? . . . and a dozen others questions. Only one part of her mind heard it, for the other part was desperately working to keep her from crying and panicking and lamenting the loss of all she had known. Yes, she would not cry before this man. He was, after a fashion, her savior. Because of him, this night she would have food to eat and a bed to sleep in . . . a bed that she must share with him. As difficult as that thought was, it was still preferable to starving to death . . . or worse. She had seen the miserable creatures that stood just beyond the lights of the theatre, waiting with their consumptive coughs or their hungry eyes or a whimpering babe in arms. She thought, perhaps, this was not far above that kind of desperation, but, no, this could only be better than that, for her and for any children she might have. It was not a joyous bargain, but it was certainly better than the fate she had faced all alone in the world.

Her only reaction to the wedding ceremony was a sense of relief when it was over. There had been only the two witnesses: McCane and the reverend's wife. She signed the documents, pleased to see that her hand did not shake, and allowed herself to be escorted outside. Lord Whittham began to follow his butler into the carriage only to pause. He turned to ask her, "Is it too cold to walk back, do you think?"

It was cold but mild for February. The thought of being inside the small space of the darkened carriage with this man held no particular appeal for Christine, and so she answered at once, "No."

"No, it's not too cold, or no, you don't wish to do so?" he gave that faint smile again.

She liked to see it, for it was a kind of proof that he was not a stern man, or at least given to some forms of humor. It would be difficult to reside with someone who could not laugh a little. She managed a weak smile herself. "I mean to say, no, I cannot see why we should not walk. It is not far."

She raised her eyes, seeing the darkened street with its large, elegant houses, lamps flickering like golden eyes in the windows that looked out upon the street. She could not see his home from where she stood, but she knew it was only three short streets away. The ride to the church had been over almost before it began as had the ceremony itself. No flowers, no special dress, no family to smile down upon them. Their wedding had been as deserted as this street now was.

He waved away the carriage and offered her his arm, upon which she lightly laid her hand. They walked in silence for a minute, he apparently as lost to his thoughts as she was to hers.

At length he spoke. "How may I call you?" At the way she frowned a little, he added, "I will call you Lady Whittham in such public as we shall encounter, of course, but is that what you wish in private as well?"

"No. Christine will be fine."

"Then you must call me Oliver. I could not care to be 'Lord Whittham' during every waking moment." The reference to slumber seemed to disconcert him for a moment, but he recovered quickly. "So, is there anything you wish to know about me or the household?"

She shrugged, but she did have a question. "Am I to plan the menus? Shall I have access to funds for the household expenses?"

"Yes to both. Mrs. Harringdon has managed all that for me for some years now. You shall meet her tomorrow. Most of the staff is gone home by this time of evening, she among them. I am sure she will be amenable to whatever you desire."

"How long shall we live in London?"

"Not long. When the weather is better, less likely to snow, we shall go to the country. My estate there is called Pottershead, for no reason that I have been able to determine."

She noticed how he said "mine," not "ours," but what could she expect, after all? He had married her for a warm body and a signature on a form, that was all. Still, she could not help but smile just a little at the way he drawled "Pottershead" in a manner that said he had meant to amuse either her or himself.

It was his turn to ask a question. "I find myself thinking you are a rather brave young woman, my la—Christine. Are you not wondering what manner of fellow I am? What would you do if it turns out that I were to beat you?"

Again she shrugged. She did not say that she would count herself lucky merely because it was one brute and not a different one every night. Instead she said, "I would probably avoid your company as much as possible."

"And if I should be the kind to beat our children?"

She ceased walking, to look up at him, wondering what it was she saw on his face as he stopped before her as well. Was this some kind of test? What was he looking for in her answers? *Was* he that kind of man? She could not know; all she could do was give an honest answer.

She said slowly and distinctly, "My lord, I would kill you."

He startled visibly at that, but then he was laughing. "By heaven, I think you would!"

She said nothing, merely beginning to walk on again. He joined her, still chuckling to himself. "I'm afraid I must tell you that although I take you seriously, it has not given me a fright of you," he said, swinging his cane as he walked.

Did he think she meant to hold him at arm's length with stupid games, insipid tales?

"I am not frightened of you either, my lord," she said calmly.

"Oliver. I insist." He was still laughing with his eyes if not out loud.

"Oliver then. Is this the house?" She pointed up at the painted white bricks of a large faintly Roman-style facade. She had only seen it the once, in daylight. Like everything else at night, it looked a little different. Like this decision she had made, now irrevocable.

"This is it," he agreed. He swung open the gate for her and waved her through.

They were met inside by the butler, who took their coats and reported that their rooms were ready.

"Very good, McCane," Oliver said, slipping his watch out of his vest pocket for a quick glance at its surface. "Could you please have some hot tea and scones sent up to my room?"

"Of course, sir. May I show Lady Whittham to her room?"

"I'll escort her myself." He picked up a candelabrum from the top of a large chest and turned to Christine, again offering her his arm. He led the way back up the stairs, past the room where the doctor had confirmed her answers as to her physical state of being. She shivered as she passed it and hoped he did not feel the palsy course through her. He passed several doors, stopping before one, which he opened without knocking. Her bags sat in the middle of the floor, apparently still packed.

"This will be your room," he said. She followed him in, and he closed the door behind them. He handed her the candelabrum he carried and crossed to her bags. He gathered them up, the two small cases looking weightless and pathetic in his hands, the meager remnants of her once-plentiful life. "This way," he said, and indicated a door on the wall to their left.

She moved before him and took his lead by not bothering to knock before she pushed it open. She held the candelabrum aloft and saw another bedchamber. He pressed close behind her, silently urging her in. She moved forward to get out of his way. He came in, set down her cases, and closed the door behind them again.

He removed a candle from its holder and crossed the room, where he soon had two lamps glowing softly. Christine set the candelabrum above the fireplace and looked around the room. It only took her a minute to realize this was his personal bedchamber.

He crossed to her side again, bending down before the fireplace to start the fire that had been laid there. When it appeared to be going well enough, he stood and returned the candle to the candelabrum. It was only then that he turned to look at her fully, and for a brief moment she thought she saw a tightening around his mouth that said he would have been better pleased to be spending his evening elsewhere also. Instead of being insulted, it almost made her like him for a moment.

"I am not normally a crude man," he said, and now his eyes moved down to the fire to avoid her own penetrating gaze. "But I'm afraid I must be quite honest with you. According to the terms of my father's will, I must be 'duly and irretrievably wed before midnight of February 14th.' " He dragged out his pocketwatch, flipping open the cover to show her its face. "As you can see, 'tis after eleven already."

"I see," she said, turning away from him, her hands buried deep in her skirts to keep them from fluttering like foolish butterflies around her pounding heart. "May I have a few moments alone to change?"

"Of course." He left without another word through another door, obviously the one that led to the hall.

She had grown adept at unhooking the many buttons of her gowns by herself since she had been forced to let her maid go on to an employer who could pay for the girl's services. It only took a minute to do so now. She found it seemed best to stick to an old pattern, so she laid her clothing carefully over the back of a chair as she had all her life. Servants used to take them away in the morning. It was only of late that she had learned to care for her own clothing. She slipped out of the tattered slippers that had not served her well as she trod from the agency to her few appointments with prospective employers. She removed her stockings and her other underthings, all of which methodically were added to the pile on the chair. She slipped into the one fine lawn nightgown that she had not sold, took down her long blond hair, braided it, and tied on her nightcap. Then she bit her lip, frowned furiously at her reflection in a mirror above the dressing table, and stood in the middle of the room, willing herself not to cry or scream.

When he knocked, she jumped and gave a little squeak. She found that her voice would not work, so instead, after a pause of indecision, she crossed to the door and opened it for him. His eyes roamed over her, taking in her attire, but only briefly, not insultingly. Her hands had been steady when she signed the marriage license, but now they shook like leaves in the wind. She did not know what to do with herself, so she moved before the fire, thinking its warmth might invade and still her shaking limbs.

Oliver took out the pin holding the folds of his cravat. Just as the snowy fabric was pulled away from his neck, another knock sounded. He crossed to the door and waved the person inside.

Christine turned her back to them, mortified to be seen by the butler dressed as she was. She heard the sounds of the tray he carried being set on a low table, smelled the scones and the fragrant tea. She heard Oliver murmur, "Thank you. That will be all."

She turned, her eyes going to the tray, her mouth watering at once even though she willed it not to. She swallowed uneasily and crossed her arms, hugging herself. Oliver crossed to the tray, looked over the scones, and absently selected one. He looked up at her then and saw her shivering. "Come, come, have some tea. Something to eat. The scones are still warm."

She crossed to the tray, ashamed at how her hand trembled as she picked up the treat, rich with clotted cream and jam. She scarcely tasted the first bite, so full of hunger was she, but then the delicious taste overrode everything else. She closed her eyes and suddenly hands were on her elbows. The room was swaying, but she was still conscious enough that she swallowed the delicious bite, refusing to surrender the tidbit. "Here now!" someone said near her ear.

"I'm all right," she said.

She was helped to the chair, the one with all her clothes over the back, and a half-full cup of tea was pressed into her hands. "Are you well?" someone asked, and it brought her back, made her aware that it was Oliver Whittham who was asking.

"I'm well, truly. I was . . . it is just that I have not had anything to eat in three days. I got a little light-headed—"

"Three days! Are you joking?" he cried, even though he knew she was not.

He plied her with three more scones until she declared they were starting to make her feel a trifle ill. However, the warm tea he poured for her spread to all her limbs and, combined with the food, gave her a sense of well-being restored, so that even the nervous shaking was calmed.

"Thank you," she said to the floor, brushing crumbs from her lap.

"You're welcome, of course. I will speak to Mrs. Harringdon. She will see that you receive any kind of food you might wish. And she has a knack for restorative remedies."

"Pray don't bother yourself."

He frowned a little and made a dismissive gesture. "I assure you, it will be no bother."

She sat in her gentle fog of contentment for a minute longer, but then she could hide from the moment no longer. She raised her face to look at him fully. She did not try to hide the deep blush that crept over her skin, and she did not demur from saying the obvious. "We are running out of time, my lo—Oliver."

He did not consult his pocketwatch as he nodded, his expression annoyed. "Oh, what does it matter? Who is to know but us if we miss the deadline?"

"You do not mean to troop in the courtiers at midnight to see the proof?" she asked, making the words less caustic by giving him her first true smile since they struck their bargain ten hours earlier, even if it was a crooked one. "No, we struck a bargain, my lord. I could offer you only the last thing I had, and that was my word, and I shall uphold it."

He pursed his lips quickly, then glanced at the ceiling. "Ah, Father, will you cease to haunt me then?" he asked up into the gloom of the evening. He did not wait for an answer from either his father or her, but turned from her and began to remove his coat.

She crawled into the bed, pleased to find a bedwarmer had been run through the sheets and lay near the end, its interior cargo of coals more inviting than even the heat cast by the logs in the fireplace. As she waited for him to join her, she allowed her mind to slip over all the events of the day, lastly his comment to his father's spirit. Well, perhaps he would be putting a ghost to rest this night, but so would she. The black-cowled specter of penury was at her shoulder no more, and so it was that among the other emotions she experienced there was a small measure of gratitude mixed in as she shared a bed for the first time in her life.

Morning brought introductions. There were not many servants to be met, for Oliver had been helping those that wished it to find positions, anticipating the need to move. Some would go with them to the country, but most preferred to stay in London. Mrs. Harringdon was one who meant to travel with them, and she proved to be an amiable sort. She could have stood on her laurels and refused to be dictated to, especially by the likes of a woman who married via the papers, but she did not. On the contrary, she seemed to expect Christine to begin her wifely prerogatives at once.

"And as to the butterman, what shall I tell 'im we'll be needing?"

Christine looked to Oliver, who merely looked back. "I've no notion," he pointed out.

"Perhaps a pound for now, Mrs. Harringdon?" Christine ventured.

"Would leek soup and roast pigeon serve for supper, m'lady?"

"I'm sure that would be lovely," Christine said.

There was also a chambermaid, Rita, and a groom, Roger, who were married. Christine met the gardener, who would stay on in the London house toward some unspecified event, as well as Mrs. Harringdon's two underlings, Gilly and Katie. The tweeny was gone to new employment as were the other chambermaids, grooms, and gardeners.

"I am sorry we have no one to act as your maid. Perhaps someone can be found," Oliver offered as he led her on a tour through the house.

"She might not be willing to travel to the country. No, do not concern yourself. We are not receiving," she stumbled over the words a little, for it was impossible to receive if no one would come, "and I am quite capable."

"As you wish."

After the tour he bid her adieu, giving no explanation as to where he was going.

She found her way back to the library. It had been a long time since she had read, for she dared not squander the money for the fee at the lending library. But try as she might to concentrate on the book in her hands, her mind kept wandering back to single moments, like paintings etched on her mind, from the night before. There had been the image of him in only his breeches, standing near the bed and looking at least nine feet tall in the wavering candlelight. There had been the strange, half-angry look on his face when he told her how thin she was. She recalled the texture of the velvet canopy over her head and the feel of the real feather tick, so unlike the harsh fabrics that made up the bedding at her hotel. There was the eerie silence, broken by only small, furtive sounds. Too, the strangeness of a hand touching where she had never been touched before and the flash of an eye poised in the darkness just above her own. There was the pain, acute but not as bad as the fears of her imagination, not as cruel as the cramping of a stomach too long without food. But overriding everything was a comment he had made when all was done. "Well, that was awkward," he had said. She had laughed, just at the moment when she had least thought she could laugh, and he had joined her briefly, for it was so true. "I want to stay the night," he said then, his voice drifting to her ears through the deep cover of night. "I want the servants to find us together, for the look of it, of course."

She had nodded her acquiescence, wondering silently if he would have left had she refused him or if he would have sent her to the connecting room.

"Let us get some sleep," he had said then, and his voice had been so understanding, even kind, and the night so dark and inviting to slumber, that it had been easy to do so in very short order.

She settled the book in her hand again and tried to read, but those images, plus a fervent wish that her mother could be alive that she might ask her a few pertinent questions, kept her eyes from really seeing the pages before her.

Oliver disdained the carriage, choosing instead to ride his favorite seat over to his mother's house. He was admitted at once, but he could not miss the speculative glance that his mother's butler gave him out of the corner of his eye.

He cooled his heels in the front parlor, but it was not a long wait. Mother might pretend otherwise, but she was anxious to see him. That was proved when he entered her sitting room and the first word from her mouth was, "Well?"

"It is done. I am married."

Her upset was clear to see. "How could you, Oliver? Whatever possessed you—?"

"Better to ask whatever possessed Father? You knew what the will said."

"No less than you! You've had three years to find an acceptable parti."

"What difference now, Mother? It is done," he said with the cold logic of fact.

She took a deep breath. "Who is she? I vow I'll not see you again if she is some common baggage."

At this his tense face relaxed a little, and he replied, "In that we are somewhat fortunate. Her name is Christine Jordan."

"Lord Jordan's girl?" his mother cried, but now it was more from surprise than outrage.

"Yes."

"Howsoever did you arrange *that?*"

"I'll tell you no lies, Mother: she came because of the advertisement. Her parents left her penniless. She was as desperate as I."

"You'll have to leave London."

"Yes, when the roads are clear. I hear that Cumberland is a frozen wasteland now."

"I wish you could go at once. Perhaps people would forget. Perhaps they would not care so much after a few years. . . . You could leave now, stay at a hotel as far north as you can go. What about that?"

"Perhaps. I have business to finish first. And . . . my," he formed the word on his lips for a moment before it came out, sounding stiff, "my wife ought to have a few days to . . . recover." He looked at his mother, letting down his guard for a moment. "She is . . . very thin. Starved, almost. I think it best to let her build up her strength a little."

"Oh, Oliver!" Lady Whittham cried, filled anew with horror to think of her son doing this terrible thing, bringing shame down upon their heads, on their good name.

"Goodbye, Mother. I'll bring her to meet you. Tomorrow, if she's well enough." He did not linger, and showed himself out.

He looked at the lady opposite him at table. He noted her table manners, the unfamiliar gown she wore, the way she had twisted her hair up into a cascading knot.

"Where did we meet before?" he asked suddenly into the silence.

She looked up from her plate and set her fork aside. "Let me think," she said. "I knew your name, of course, from the advertisement, and your face was familiar to me when I saw you again."

"Yes, I recognized you also, but I do not know from where."

She looked at him without seeing him. "It was . . ." she said slowly, touching a hand to her temple as though to draw out the memory. "Ah yes! At Lady MacAlbee's youngest daughter's betrothal party. It was you with whom I was back to back, you at one table and I at the other, wasn't it?"

He frowned, striving to remember. "I'm sorry," he said. "I don't recall. I was thinking that it was something to do with horses . . ."

"Yes, I remember that. Some of the gentlemen joined the Garden Society ladies after the races at Ascot."

His brow cleared. "Ah yes, I recall! You were serving tea. I remember because we teased you terribly."

"I was given the pot that was not rinsed properly. Everything tasted of soap. Yes, and I recall your hair kept escaping from under your beaver." After the words came out of her lips, she raised her napkin from her lap to dab at her mouth, hoping to cover the blush that her too-particular comment brought on.

"It always does. No amount of pomade will keep it in place, so I do not try any longer." He sliced another piece of beef and chewed it meditatively. After a rather awkward silence had gone on too long, he cleared his throat and asked, "Do you care for more gowns? I do not mean to pry, but it seems to me that you cannot have many."

She fought to keep back the tears. She was not even sure why they had suddenly leapt into her eyes. Perhaps it was the sense of being a charity case, or perhaps it was the way he asked, trying to be delicate. Either way it was embarrassing, but she would be a fool to deny the truth just to assuage her own feelings for a moment's time.

She nodded and gulped out, "I need some. Not many."

He waved his fork in the air. "Get as many as you want. Because of you, I now have plenty of blunt. Make use of it."

He paused and added, "Within reason, of course."

"I'll go to the shops as soon as I may."

"Have them come to you."

"I . . . I'm sure there are some that would," she said, looking down at the meal for which she had just lost any appetite.

"Oh," he said, wishing he had stuck the fork in his leg instead of putting his foot in his mouth. "There are businesses who know good coin when they see it. We will make our purchases there."

"I can sew a little, my lord. There is much I could do myself—"

"Nonsense. Order them made," he said, his face growing flushed. He had known this was going to happen, but the fact of confronting the beginning of the ostracism smarted despite himself. Perhaps it was his mother's outcries that had unsettled him, or perhaps it was this other lady's bowed head. Either way, he was uncomfortable to find that his father had succeeded so well in controlling his life for him that it had brought him to this moment. He threw down his napkin beside his plate and scraped back his chair that he might stand. "Whatever you choose, do it soon. I am thinking of leaving for the north soon."

When he had left the room, she raised her head and said bitterly into the silent room, "All right then, I shall. They will be my bridal gift from my new husband."

She went up to her room and prepared for bed. She had unpacked her own bags, a fact which Gilly protested when she discovered it. The maid had whisked away the two other gowns Christine owned, one to launder, one to press.

In her room Christine found a fire already burning and a lamp lighted against the night. After a while she heard sounds in the adjoining room. She dressed in her nightgown and crawled under the covers of her bed to stay warm and waited, not knowing what to do.

When an hour had gone by and there was still a light shining under the door, she crawled out of the bed and crossed to give a small knock upon its surface. "Come in," Oliver called.

She opened the door and stuck her head in. "My lo—Oliver, I . . . I am afraid I do not quite know what is expected of me. Should I come here every night? At what time?"

He might have smiled just a little—it was hard to tell in the shadowplay of the candlelight. He leaned forward and patted a chair opposite the one he sat in before the fire. She came into the room and took the indicated chair, looking at him with large brown eyes, but he was looking into the fire.

"You have no mother. You ought to have had a mother to talk to you," he said, as if he were talking to himself.

"Of course not," she replied.

If he had been talking to himself, he did not do so now as he turned to her. "She would have told you some of what to expect."

"I know a little . . ."

He lifted a decanter filled with an amber fluid from the small table at his elbow and enquired of her, "Brandy?"

"Yes, please," she said, although she had never had brandy before. Ratafia and champagne were the limits of her experience.

He poured her a finger's width in the bottom of a round-bellied snifter and handed it across to her after he also replenished his own. He raised his glass in the manner of a toast and said, "Let us drink to ourselves. I can think of no better cause than we."

She lifted her glass a little in response and took a tiny sip. It burned, and for a moment she did not like it at all, but then the taste mellowed and she sensed a little of why gentlemen might care for it.

He sighed and stared back into the fire. "In the normal way of things," he said, his voice sounding like a professor reciting a history lesson, "we should come together whenever it pleased us to do so. There would be no schedule, no demands."

He took a sip of the brandy. "You should know that it is not always as it was last night; you may take some small pleasure from the act in time. That is to say, you may actually welcome me . . . someday."

She sipped her brandy again, now actually relishing its sting, the physical bite that distracted her a little from his awkward words.

He looked at her then, causing her heart to plummet into her stomach for a moment, but then she saw he meant to speak on, not reach across for her as she had thought. "There is one other fact I have not revealed to you. I have not done so because it gnaws at me and fills me full of foul temper. Here it is then in simple language: there was one additional codicil to the will. I am to 'produce a legitimate heir within a span of eighteen months following the wedding.' "

He sipped his brandy, gazing at her, assessing her reaction, as she gazed back, unblinking. He did not know what it meant when she looked at him this way, so calmly, so levelly. It disconcerted him a trifle, made him speak a little more gruffly than he might have otherwise. "So you see, we cannot avoid one another a great deal, or we shall lose all that we have sought to gain by marrying."

She sat back in the chair to support her strengthless limbs perhaps or maybe to show a measure of indifference. Even she was not sure which. She said, "So, I ask again: should I come here every night? And at what time?"

He stood then, his shoulders moving under his jacket like an angry cat in a sack. His jaw clenched, but then he leaned one arm on the mantelpiece, watching the flames of the fire through the glass of brandy. "No, no, not that, not every night. Not every week, for that matter."

She blushed anew, realizing he was not ignorant of a

woman's cycles.

"And not at any certain time either, I think. We are not a stud and brood mare, are we? Much as it may feel that way, I insist we are not. I tell you what, my dear, to make it very simple for us both, I shall come to you when I think the time is right." He laughed a little then, without real mirth, and said dryly, "Like a real married couple."

She left him soon after that, returning to her room alone. That phrase "like a real married couple" passed vaguely, just out of reach, through her thoughts as she tumbled toward sleep.

Alone before his fire, Oliver poured himself another brandy. He was glad to be free of the heavy weight of her company. He realized, too late, that he had made an error in accepting this particular lady for his wife. Better to have chosen a simple, common girl. One who was meek and as easy to see through as the surface of a still lake. This one had some depth hidden behind brown, unblinking eyes, exposing so little of herself even when he looked directly at her trying to see if what reflected below the surface was truly there or merely a reflection of other things that she wanted him to see. Neither was she meek for all that she had never opened her lips to a single protest. She had readily understood the bargain he had offered her and seemed content to follow its dictates. But was she truly content, after the fashion of their agreement? It was too early to tell, of course. It seemed quite likely that with time she would be less so. He had never known a woman yet who was content with her lot, not a woman of her position and station in life. There was no reason to expect anything better from this stranger.

He pushed aside the snifter, for the brandy had served to make him feel soured. Well, she could be anything she wanted, for soon he would take her to the country and undoubtedly leave her there once she was with child. Perhaps he could return to London when some time had come and gone. People were so forgetful of one's follies if those same follies were then well hidden away. The hard-edged thought did not make him proud, and that, more than anything, assured him he had made a mistake in accepting this lady to wife.

He cursed softly as he rose to his feet, slightly drunk. Whether she was content or no, he had no need to feel guilty for the plans he had made . . . plans he was sure were still quite valid, despite the lady's refinement. He knew full well that his sins might be forgiven, but hers would not. It was the way of the world that a woman could not be forgiven any indiscretion. . . . But at least he had saved her from starvation! Yes, he need not feel guilty for making a lady of quality a party to his disgrace. She had been informed, had been warned.

He found his bed, his drink-shrouded mind welcoming its expanse, entirely contented to be its sole inhabitant this night.

"How do you do," Christine said, the corners of her mouth turning up a little, but not much. Her mother-in-law presented her with a very sober countenance, one that did not respond to Christine's smile.

"Fine, thank you. How are you?" that lady asked stiffly.

"Fine, thank you."

"Do you care for tea?"

"Yes, please." Christine turned her head a little, looking out from under her lashes toward Oliver.

"Your people are from Hertfordshire I understand," said Lady Whittham as she passed a delicate china teacup to Christine.

"They were, yes." Christine turned the cup so the handle was properly placed for ease, hiding the spark that came into her eyes. Oliver turned his head slightly, giving her to believe that if his mother had missed the flash of anger, he had not.

Christine was neither stupid nor naive. It had taken her no more than one minute to recognize this banter as a match, a feminine version of dueling. She knew it well from many a tea in many a parlor. Lady Whittham was trying to politely dampen any or all of her possible expectations, tell her exactly where she fit into the scheme of things, which was to say not at all.

It was now the time when Christine was to be cowed, to be as silent as a mouse unless spoken to, and to have absolutely no opinions but those that matched the hostess's. Christine had seen many a young girl behave exactly so, but Christine was no longer a young girl despite her chronological age. Deprivation and despair had been far more harsh a mistress than ever Lady Whittham could be.

"May I bother you for a lump of sugar?" she asked, as blandly as that.

"Sugar? You like your tea sweetened?" Lady Whittham asked, sniffing as though Christine had said something vulgar.

"And a little milk, if you please."

Eye met eye, brown one to gray, and after a long silence the gray turned away first. "Allow me," Lady Whittham said, accepting back the saucer to apply a lump from the sugar loaf and a dollop of milk from the tiny silver pitcher on the tea cart.

"Perfect," Christine said as she accepted the cup in return, although she had not tasted the offering.

Oliver said nothing, but both ladies sensed he was watching the silent drama with some interest. His mother threw him an exasperated look, but he did not bestir himself in any fashion to respond to her silent entreaties.

"Miss . . . ? I mean to say Lady . . . ?" Lady Whittham began, as two bright pink spots grew on her cheeks. It was apparent to all that she was reluctant to call Christine by her newly married name. "May we dispense with titles? I shall call you . . . ?" she looked to her son.

"Christine," he supplied with a small nod of his head and perhaps the ghost of a smile.

"Christine. And you may call me Divinia."

"What an unusual name. Do you like it?" Christine asked, taking a carefully planned sip of tea to hide a rather wicked smile.

"Do I—!" Lady Whittham sputtered, but then she recovered herself. "It is not relevant whether I like it or not. It is my name."

"Well, I like it very well. 'Tis very elegant, don't you think so, Oliver?" She turned a sunny smile his way.

"Yes, quite," he drawled, placing one finger across his upper lip as he settled back in his chair.

"Divinia," Christine went on at once as she set aside her tea, "I know you can only be upset by the circumstances surrounding the marriage of Oliver and myself. I know I should be so, were our situations reversed. I bring this up merely to say that I have no intention of intruding myself upon you. I can only respect your sensibilities. We will await your visits to us as you choose. Oliver tells me that we are to leave for the country soon, and that is where I plan to live my life. It will be pleasant, actually, to be away from wagging tongues, don't you think?"

"Well, I . . . that is to say—"

"And of course you may see the grandchildren whenever you wish, should you choose to acknowledge them, of course." She stood, though they had only been there a few minutes, tugging on her gloves. "That said, I think it best we leave. Oliver?"

He rose and gathered up his hat and cane and many-caped coat, not offering a single word of protest or denial. However, he did say, "Go ahead to the carriage, Christine. I wish to speak with Mother for a moment."

"Of course you do," she answered pertly. "Lady Whittham," she acknowledged her hostess, "farewell. Pray do not

hesitate to call upon us. You shall always be welcome wher
ever we reside." She left the room without so much as a
backward glance.

Oliver turned to his mother, a grave kind of amusemen
dancing in the depths of his eyes. His mother was com
pletely baffled, that much was clear at a glance. "What an
extraordinary creature," she said, staring up at her son.

"Yes," he said, turning to gaze out the door by which
Christine had just left. "Yes, she is that." He had not ex
pected her tart tongue either. It had been, he had to admit
a very effective way of handling his mother's stiff disap
proval.

He turned back to her, asking, "May we call again for as
long as we remain in London?"

She noted the use of the plural "we," but she nodded a
once anyway. She could not approve of the marriage, o
course, but that did not mean she had to completely isolate
herself from her son.

"Thank you, Mother," he said, bending to press a kiss to
her cheek. The act surprised them both.

On the carriage ride home, they did not have much to say
to one another. He studied the mixed feelings he had: on the
one hand he rather wished Christine were more dismissable
and on the other he could only chortle to himself that she
refused to be so.

For her part she pondered over the expressions that had
crossed his face this evening: from regret that she must mee
his mother to a kind of diversion to outright amusement
She did not know what was taking place behind those gray
eyes of his, but she had no doubts he was working as dili
gently as she toward understanding the nature of his future
life, whatever that might entail.

He escorted her to her room and did not leave until wel
after midnight. He laughed aloud once, obviously at a
thought or a memory, briefly. She did not laugh, but she
sighed with a kind of appreciation that his physical approach

was not so painful as that first time. When he left, he said nothing, though he did look to see that she must be sleeping before he walked out on quiet, bare feet. She had not been sleeping, however, but merely pretending.

For several days she did not see him at breakfast, though they always sat down at Mrs. Harringdon's appointed supper hour of eight o'clock together. They were both surprised when McCane came into the room with a calling card on his small silver salver. Oliver read it and murmured, "Kilkarry, by heaven!" He glanced at Christine, and then up at the butler. "Show him in, McCane. And bring another setting. If I know Victor, he'll care to join us."

Christine did not ask, and Oliver did not offer. She continued to eat quietly, sedately, not unaware that her husband had been pretending for several days that she was invisible. It was not an entirely terrible experience, for it meant he did not claim her company at night either.

A gentleman was shown in, and Christine could tell by the set of Oliver's shoulders that it was someone of importance to him. He leapt to his feet, a hand beckoning the visitor into the room.

"Victor!" he called. "By Jove, it's good to see you. Will you join us?"

The gentleman, well-tailored in black evening silk and hose, approached the table and said, "Not until I've met the lady of the house, Oliver, lad."

She looked up into kind blue eyes and liked him instantly. Here, in his gaze, she became visible again.

"This is, as you may well guess, my wife. Christine, please meet Lord Victor Kilkarry. Victor, Christine."

He took her hand and bowed over it, saying, "It is my pleasure, my lady." He stood upright and declared with an appreciative glance at the foodstuffs that graced the table, "And now I'll join you!"

He chose a seat which was on the same side of the table as Christine, causing her to like him even more, as the simple gesture indicated a lack of disapproval. It was clear by his very manner, his presence, that he knew the hows and whys of this marriage but chose to treat the matter lightly. He waited for his place setting to be settled before him, but as soon as the butler had retreated he looked at Oliver and said, "I'm quite upset with you, you scoundrel."

"Are you? And what was my offense?" Oliver raised his eyebrows as he passed a platter of sole in béchamel sauce.

"You got married without inviting me!" Victor cried. "And I'm your best friend."

Oliver's mouth twitched, not happily. "It was, as you well know, a hurried affair."

"No excuse. I ought to have been sent a note. You know I'd have come at once. Isn't that right, my lady?" he turned to Christine for support.

"Quite right," she agreed calmly, not knowing the man from Adam, much less his likelihood to behave any one way over the other. But he was so obviously intent on being generous to her, the wife who had been all but purchased, that she would have supported him had he suggested they strip naked and dance in the moonlight. It was not that she felt the need to be accepted by his world, his society—such needs were as nothing next to the need for sustenance—it was more that she simply felt the need for a friend. Oliver was a husband, strange and unknown in every way but the most intimate. Those who had known her before would cross the street before they would speak to her now, of that she had no doubt. Lord Kilkarry presented her with the chance to make a new friend, to sustain her in her new life.

"Why are you here?" Oliver asked tersely, but the anger was hollow, insincere.

"Oh, that's a fine way to treat a friend, that is!" Victor cried. "I came to meet the missis, of course, and pleased I am to do so." He turned to Christine, "Did you know we had met before?"

"Was it over a pot of soapy tea by chance?" Christine asked, ignoring her meal to enjoy the attention. If she could have this, this little bit of company, an occasional friendly face, then she knew she could be content enough.

"It was! You remember."

"Well, a little. It is how Oliver and I first met, but I'm sorry to say I don't truly recall you."

He frowned at that, but very theatrically, so that she found a bubble of laughter burst from her lips.

He spent the evening with them. He taught them how to play three-handed pinochle and persuaded them to play for points. Christine had looked up with alarm at that, in time to see Oliver sliding several bills over the tabletop toward her. "Your pin money," he said, his serene gaze informing her it was hers to accept.

"Thank you," she said in a voice that she tried to make sound casual.

At length, when she had lost half the bills before her, their guest arose and stated it was time to go on to his club. For the first time he looked a little uncomfortable, having forgotten that Oliver was unlikely to attempt his club these days.

"Lay a large sum at faro for me, will you, old chap?" Oliver said. Victor smiled, the awkward moment past, and he was gone after bowing again over Christine's hand.

She sat at the table, sorting the cards with no particular haste until Oliver walked back into the room. "He's a good fellow," he said, leaning against the mantelpiece in a manner that was becoming familiar to her, watching her arrange the sorted cards into neat piles in their lacquered ebony box.

"I liked him. He is very kind, I think."

Oliver nodded, and she thought she had pleased him with the observation. She rose and took the two steps to be within arms reach of him. She held up the few small remaining bills. "Thank you," she said.

"There is a carved box on my desk in my library. It has

funds for whatever needs might arise. You must feel free to make use of it."

"I thank you again. As for now, I shall return these to that box, and then I think I am for bed."

"Is that an invitation?" he heard himself ask, mildly shocked at the words, not sure why they had slipped out. Perhaps for a moment he had thought it was going to come out sounding humorous.

She blinked, but her polite expression did not change. "You are welcome whenever you care to come, my lord. I thought that was understood."

The coolness of her regard stung him, made him flush with displeasure. Still, it was not a reprimand or a scold that came to his lips; it was an apology. "Yes. I beg your pardon. I've had a little too much port perhaps. . . ." His words wound away, leaving them standing in silence.

"Good night, my lord," she said.

He watched her go and experienced a mild annoyance. It would be boorish of him to go to her room now, and he had been half of a mind earlier today to do just that. Well, if it was not to be, it was his own fault for speaking out of turn. Like it or not, he could not will away the truth that he had married a lady. She expected to be treated as such, and in truth it was only her right. If he felt like a clod for a misplaced word or two, then he ought to remember to match her refinement with his own.

As he headed upstairs to his own room, he thought back to the visit paid by his friend. It had been very good of Victor to make the effort. Oliver had not invited him, had not wanted to be turned down. There were not many that would care to be stained by the brush that was this marriage. Victor had proved himself a true friend, coming as he had, and being so agreeable to Christine, including her in the evening. It cheered Oliver a little to think that they need not be completely isolated from the world they both knew, even if they must only remain upon its very fringes. That made him think again of the desired move to the country, and he determined that tomorrow he would speak with someone from the mails to see how the roads north were faring.

A week later he knocked on her door and received a call to come in. He found her sitting on the bed, a dozen gowns spread out on the comforter around her. Her pretty face, lighted by smiles, gazed up at him. "Oh, Oliver," she said breathlessly, "How can I thank you?"

He looked at the bounty and shrugged, though he smiled a little as he leaned against a bedpost. "What did I do?"

"I didn't order all of these! And I certainly didn't order all the other things—the shoes and stockings and the matching ribbons. It had to have been you, wasn't it?"

He could not resist the pleasure on her face, so he nodded. "Madam Oprée let it slip, rather conveniently I suppose, that your order was not 'complete.' She made the selections. I had no more to do with it than to nod at the bill she presented."

She gathered a rose satin evening gown into her arms, careful not to crush the fabric, and rose to her feet to execute a turn for him, to demonstrate the quality of the work. "You are so generous!" she said.

"I am glad it pleases you."

She laid down the gown, her face still lighted with pleasure, but now there was a serious set underscoring it. "You don't have to, you know."

"What? Buy you gowns? You must have clothes to wear."

"A few is all a person needs, really."

"But you must enjoy having more!"

"Oh, I do, and please do not mistake my words for ingratitude. It is just that I do not want you to feel you need to 'keep me,' in any kind of style. It seems so unnecessary, in the circumstances."

Some of his satisfaction at her response to the gowns was

taken away by this reminder of the facts. His words were less warm as he said, "It is good they have come, for I have word that we may travel north now, as we desire. If Katie and Gilly are yours for a day, can you be ready by the morning after tomorrow?"

"Of course," she said, her smile gone, replaced by her usual collected look. There was nothing disapproving in the way she said it, as he had expected. She did not ask for more time or suggest that perhaps it was too soon to remove themselves. So then, Victor's visit had not emboldened her to believe they might yet find a place in Londontown. She was too shrewd, as he was coming to know, to believe in such fairy tales.

He did not see her for the rest of the next day, not until dinner, when she calmly announced she was ready to go.

"Early tomorrow, then," he told her.

He watched her on the carriage ride. She evinced nothing except a curiosity as to where they were going, asking a few questions on what to expect of the house and grounds of Pottershead.

He watched her as she settled into the new household, saw her delight at the domed entrance, the large stained-glass windows that rained flashes of color down on her blond head. He watched as she interviewed new servants, saw her organize the kitchen alongside the staff, clear in how things ought to be arranged, which was to say according to Mrs. Harringdon's beaming approval.

He watched as she ventured forth to meet the neighbors, to meet the vicar, to join the Woman's Society. He saw the fans that hid whispered words, knew the tales had followed them to Cumberland. He knew the slight hesitation before the local squire took his hand to shake it in greeting. He saw Christine refuse to bat an eye, to look away, not even when blushes stained her cheeks.

"Yes, it is quite true." He heard her answer the question as to how their marriage began a dozen times, and though the first few times he cringed inside, by the sixth or seventh he began to notice that the rumor was losing its strength, that Christine's refusal to be cowed was having an effect, a startlingly positive effect. Instead of being shunned as he had dreaded and expected, it seemed these country folk liked an honest answer, for they took Christine to their hearts. Her acts of charity were not unnoted, her patience and ability to listen to and act upon a complaint appreciated. Before long he heard the commoners referring to her as the "good Lady Whittham." He found himself laughing out loud, alone in his library one day, when he realized that even he had deferred to one of her opinions regarding increasing the pension of the old retired vicar.

He saw, too, the contentment growing in Christine rather than waning. He was astonished when he realized it was serenity he read in her features. He would never have thought a woman of the blood should find such gratification so far from the teeming, bustling life of London.

Here they found easy acceptance, taken as they were at face value due to Christine's insistence that she would not hide in the house just to spare a few blushes. He was asked to join the Hunters Club. She was asked to lead the gathering of Christmas foodstuffs for the poor. They were invited to a small house party, then a come-out ball, and soon found any number of invitations on McCane's salver of a week. It was gratifying, he could not deny, to have actually to refuse an engagement because they had too many to attend of a week.

One evening Christine did not return until it was nearly suppertime. She greeted him as she pulled off her bonnet, saying, "Reverend Thompson kept us until the light failed, unaware of the time until it grew quite gloomy." She referred to her work with the Women's Society, who had been given the task of decorating the church for Easter services.

They had a leisurely dinner, for once not expected to make an appearance at a neighbor's this evening. After the meal, they adjourned to his library, where he worked on the papers his solicitors posted from London as she sat curled in a chair before the fire, reading a book.

She had nodded off, he saw as he glanced up once, making an occasional sleeping noise as he worked.

At length he put his wax and seal to the small pile of correspondence to be posted the next day and rose. He crossed to her side and started to reach for her shoulder to give her a little shake to wake her. His hand hesitated, and then he merely stood and looked down at her as she lay sleeping. She was so pretty and delicate, but it was not that which he saw now. He saw the dirt on her pattens which sat next to the chair on which she slept, the dusty hem of her gown, evidence of the hours she spent traveling from one tenant's house to the next seeing how she might aid them, even if it was with only a kind word or two. He saw the form, no longer spare to the point of starvation, saw the bloom of health in the pink of her cheeks. He saw the slight stain of green on her long, slender fingers, proof that she had spent the better part of her afternoon clipping flower stems for arrangements for the church. He knew she gave extra money and help to Mrs. Harringdon so that foodstuffs could be sent to the disabled and old, knew that she had hired an extra gardener they didn't need merely to give one-armed David Hutchen a place of employment. He had seen her reach into the pockets of her pelisse a hundred times to pull out a boiled sweet just to see and laugh gaily at the light that came into a child's eyes. He had seen all these things, and even his skeptical heart had eventually been touched, enough so that he wanted to believe she was actually and truly content in what he had thought of as a limited role, the role to which fate, and he, had brought her.

Even so, it had not been these acts so much that had slowly convinced him she was what she seemed to be. No, it was their times in bed together. She was, as they had both been raised to believe she ought to be, a passive partner, never a word of protest from her lips, never an act to put him off. But, too, there was the occasional light, the small sound, the way she had bit her lower lip that had proved to him, more than anything else could, that guile was not her natural way. That she stifled her own responses, responses that had grown, he knew, as she came to understand the physical act, showed him that the lady was no actress. He had begun to lose the resentment he had felt at first, forced into the union with her, had begun to look forward to their lovemaking with a kind of eagerness he had not known in years. He began to look for, to try to solicit, the reactions that proved she was not indifferent to the pleasures he tried to bring her body. If there was a disappointment, it was that she never asked for him. She received him complacently, but she did not seek him out. He found he was of late dallying more and more in her company, waiting, wondering if she might run a finger down his arm or bend to press her soft lips to his ear if only he stayed long enough, amused her enough.

He looked down at her a minute longer, then found himself stooping beside her, sliding his arms under her, lifting her into his arms.

She came awake at once, blinking the sleep from her eyes. "Oh, Oliver," she said, her smile lopsided. "I fell asleep. But you may put me down. I'm fine to walk to bed."

"I want to carry you," he said, his voice husky.

She blinked the sleep from her eyes, seeing the dark fire in his. "All the way upstairs?" she said a little breathlessly, her heart beginning to pound. She never knew when he would want her, but it seemed to her of late it had been more and more frequently. She could not mistake the timbre of his voice now.

"Not necessarily," he said, lightning flashing through his eyes as he glanced toward the desk top.

"Oliver!" she squeaked, wiggling so that he lost his grip enough that he had to set her on her feet. She took a step away from him, but that was suddenly so wrong, all wrong. She was rattled for a moment longer, abandoning the effects of slumber swiftly, something in her responding to the way his hand half-raised as though to summon her. So she stepped back into the circle of his arms, a boldness she had never done until now. She did it more from instinct than thought, but then reason took over and quite deliberately she found she leaned into him and raised her face to his with an unforeseen and acute need to feel his lips on hers. He complied with a kiss, a warm kiss that said nothing of duty, nothing of obligation.

Her pounding heart seemed to be sending a lot of blood to her head, making her giddy. She stepped away again to catch her breath, and their arms stretched between them until their fingers separated and they stood apart, not touching. Regret flickered over his face, and an echo of disappointment shivered through her as well.

He said very quietly, "Could you invite me, this once?" She saw that he actually trembled.

It was important, though she was not sure how and in what way it would change things between them, but she heard the urgency, the request in his words, for they echoed inside herself. It was not her way to be overt, she had not been trained to such boldness. A lady was never forward. A lady would sooner die then ask for that which she was not supposed to want. But she did want him, in a way that shocked her to her core and made her tremble in return, in a way that dared her to forget her upbringing, dared her to respond to the need in his eyes. But how to form the words, to make them come from her lips? She could not, not directly. So instead she gave a funny hiccup-giggle and cried, "Last one to the room is a rotten egg!"

She turned and dashed from the room, and it only took him a minute longer to laugh as well and shout a protest and dash after her. She heard her heart pounding, the sound of his boots over the tiles at the base of the stairs, his laughter rising to mingle with hers. She ran up the stairs, given over to the thrill of the contest, the chase, the fire in the gray eyes that blazed up at her as she glanced back with another squeal of laughter.

He caught her at the top of the stairs, and they laughed together breathlessly for a moment. He caught her to him, his hands sliding around her back, pulling her into his embrace. His lips lowered to hers, hungrily, and she responded in kind, her hands slipping around his neck. After a few too-brief moments, he raised his head, the gray eyes looking as dark as storm clouds, and he lifted her into his arms again. It was quick work to stride through the doorway, to set her down, close the door, and turn around only to clasp her closely to him again for another passionate kiss. For it was passion, on her part as well as his, and there was no more room for manners or pretenses, there was room only for the touching, the kissing, the shedding of clothing.

She had begun to know there could be pleasure in the act of laying together, had been forced to hide it well from him. Now she could hide nothing, and the depth of her response to his touch surprised her, brought tears to her eyes. She understood at last why he could seek her out, why he had not turned away despite awkward moments and what had been cool receptions. Now she was incapable of coolness, warmed to the center of her being by the fire of his desire, of her own desire for him.

When they lay still and silent, stunned by their impulsiveness, he ran a hand down her length, making her shiver, as he did some quick math in his head. Somberly he said; "I think you must be increasing. It's been a long time since . . ."

"Yes," she answered. "I think so, too."

They were silent, the passion cooling between them, leaving the awkwardness of unspoken words. In the clearer light of satiation, he thought: *this moment has been, after all, only passion.* Their bodies had come together, blended for a while, but it could not mean that all was understood, all was well between them, could it? It did not seem likely, and yet. . . . He sought to dispel the feeling of incompleteness, resenting it suddenly, fiercely. He said, "I am happy about the child, of course." He went on quickly, not looking at her, "But not just for the inheritance. I . . . that is to say . . . it is just that I can imagine you as a mother. I believe you will be a good one."

"Promise me something, Oliver."

"Yes," he said, thinking he might as well have said "anything," for he had been changed, changed by her need of him. Changed by the way she had come into his life. The way she had accepted this simple country life, had made it her own. Changed by the way she filled up his home and made it seem empty when she was gone from it. The revelation of change stunned him anew, so that he must force his mind to hear her words.

"Promise me that, regardless of gender, you will set up a fund for the child. For any children. That they need never be penniless. I don't care if I ever have another new gown, not if that money is put aside for the children."

"I promise," he said, and meant it.

"Thank you."

He wanted to thank her back, but his newfound emotions were too delicate, too unsure, too undetermined. Instead he made love to her again and hoped that said something of what was locked inside his heart.

He looked up to see her out in the main hallway just returned from some errand or other. He could not miss the way her gown now rounded out in front.

"Christine!" he called, rising as he spoke to come toward her.

She turned, tugging at a glove, and smiled at him. If it had not been for the missive in his hand, he would no doubt have smiled back. As it was, his serious expression caused her to step toward him, shutting the parlor door behind herself. "What is it?" she asked at once.

"I thought we had left most of the . . . unpleasantness behind us," he said uncertainly. He passed her the vellum that was in his hand, the seal already broken. She read it swiftly.

"Lady Jersey!" she cried as she looked up, startled. "What could Lady Jersey want to do with us?"

"I don't know," he said, wondering if he looked as nonplussed as she.

"I see nothing for it," Christine said, her chin coming up in the manner which he knew meant she was preparing to give her best in a fight. "We'll have to receive her, of course."

"Of course. Even if she means to cut us to ribbons, it would be worse should we refuse her entrance. She arrives at nine tonight."

It was a measure of their disturbance that they both dressed in some of their finest clothing, more elegant than was their usual wont of an evening. He asked her if his cravat was straight; she asked him if her hair looked all right. They looked away from their toilettes, glancing at each other with misgiving as they heard the sound of carriage wheels in the drive. To erase the frown on his face, she went up on tiptoe and kissed him quickly. He caught her hand, pulled her close enough for her to protest about the state of her gown, and kissed her back. "For good luck," he said.

They came downstairs and settled in the front parlor, he with a newspaper and she with a bit of stitchery. They did not care to be found waiting with a show of what was, in truth, agitation.

McCane made the announcement of their guest's arrival and held the door open for Lady Jersey to enter the room. Their projects put aside quickly, each rose, and Lady Jersey found them thus, Oliver standing behind with a hand on Christine's shoulder. Lady Jersey glided forward as though they had both welcomed her warmly and said with a cool smile, "Whittham, well met!"

"Lady Jersey," he said, taking the hand she offered him and bowing over it. "May I introduce to you my wife, Lady Whittham."

The patroness turned with the same cool smile and said to Christine, "How do you do, Lady Whittham. I feel as though I know you. I was quite fond of your mama."

Christine felt a tiny smile pass over her mouth at the words, and she said in sudden warmth, "You knew Mama?"

"She was a delightful lady. I was so sad to hear the news of the accident."

"Thank you. I miss her terribly. Would you care to be seated?"

"Indeed, yes. I have just come from the soiree at the Stillman place. You know them, I am assured. Lady Stillman is a crony of mine and asked specifically that I might attend her little gathering."

Christine felt the smile flicker into being again, for she knew full well that the "little gathering" had included over fifty guests. She and Oliver had been invited, but had turned down the offer, her pregnancy now so noticeable as to limit her outings.

"Would you care for something to eat?" Christine offered.

"No, thank you. The party fare was too tempting, I fear." She looked at them with her sharp, clever eyes and said, "You are no doubt wondering why I came to call."

Oliver and Christine resisted the impulse to exchange glances, and he replied, "We are."

"Because I wanted to," she said, and laughed heartily even when they did not join her. Lady Jersey was used to doing as she pleased, and if she noted the lack, it did not disturb her. " 'Tis true that Lady Jordan was a friend of mine. It was never my intention to neglect her daughter. It will surprise you to know that I was trying to discover what had become of you, Lady Whittham, when I heard the news through the tattlemongers of your marriage. You were gone from your family home within a week of the accident, and when I applied at the hotel where you were said to be staying, I was assured you had gone. They did not know where. There was only a handful of rumors after that, until Whittham here pulled his little peccadillo."

Christine stared at the great lady, amazed. "The hotel was so expensive . . . I had to move to another. . . . I . . . I never knew. Mama spoke of you, but it never occurred to me—!"

"All water under the bridge now, isn't it, my girl? I can't very well 'save you' now you are already settled, but I can do something else for you."

"Yes?" Christine said, shaking her head in wonderment.

"Time and a few well-placed words can work miracles, my dears. If you wish it, I believe I may open the doors of London to you once more."

"It isn't necessary." They might have been Christine's words, but she heard them come from Oliver instead. She turned to ask him what he meant, but Lady Jersey spoke first. "Pardon me?"

"I mean to say that it is appreciated, but we have no need to return. Or, at least," he said, a flush creeping up his face, "*I* do not."

"And why is that?" Lady Jersey again echoed Christine's unspoken question.

Oliver did not answer for a moment, the words not coming easily, especially not in front of a witness, but the time had come to speak, to dare to expose his secret heart. He had not at first meant to say his thoughts aloud, but now that they were made public, he must speak to them.

"Because I have found all I need here," he said quietly as his hand stole over the top of Christine's as she sat beside him. She looked down at his large hand over hers, up at him, and back at Lady Jersey, her expression bemused. She wanted to say something, but she was not sure what, for she was filled with astonishment to hear such caressing words in front of their guest.

"You feel no need of companions, Whittham?" Lady Jersey now sounded distinctly amused, but her smile had warmed to reflect that the question was kindly asked. "What of London's refinements—the fine wines, the sophisticated entertainments, the exceptional company?"

Oliver looked from the patroness to his wife and smiled slowly, encouraged by the wide-eyed hope he saw there. Looking into her astonished eyes, he said, "Here is the fine wine, the sophisticated entertainment, and most especially the exceptional company. Here is the finest being I have ever met."

Christine's mouth was parted in wonder, and a dawning happiness brought sudden, glad tears to her eyes. She had to blink, and smiled brightly that he not misunderstand the misting in her eyes.

Lady Jersey made a sound that was somewhere between a cluck and a snort. "Time to tell him how you feel later, my girl," she said, coming to her feet, "when I am not here to get in the way. I declare you two would scorch my ears.

"And despite your protests to the contrary, Whittham, I mean to do what I can to smooth the waters for your possible return. Someday you may wish to indulge me with a visit. Please know that howsoever the rest of the world goes, you may be assured that at my home, at least, you are always welcome." She extended her hand to Christine, who took it in a preoccupied fashion. Lady Jersey went on, "I am so pleased to have met you at last. Had your mama lived, I have no doubt we should have been presented at Almack's. Perhaps we still shall, eh?"

She turned to Oliver. "My lord," she said, smiling in the superior fashion that had not always served to make her popular, "I must inform you that it is simply not done to fall in love with one's wife. Very vulgar. But you have already proven you can be that, with this whole nasty advertisement business. I daresay, if we are clever we can turn that fault into a virtue. Everyone loves an eccentric, as long as they are not a member of one's family, of course. We shall see. Now, show me out, my dears."

They waited with her for the time it took her driver to return from walking the horses, during which time Christine commented on how kind the lady had been.

"Ha!" she gave a shout of laughter. "I wish Mrs. Drummond-Burrell could hear you say that. She'd quite disagree, I vow."

"I'm glad I know better," Christine said, and received a kiss on the cheek for her sincerity.

Lady Jersey waved to them from the window she had lowered just as the horses began to pull her carriage away. "I did not ask: when is the child due?" she called.

"Mid-February," Christine called back, also waving.

"I shall expect to be the child's god-mama!" Lady Jersey declared, speaking into cupped hands that the words might carry to their ears.

As the carriage disappeared into the night, Oliver turned to Christine. She slid into his arms, raising her face for a kiss and to murmur sweet words that she had never hoped to share with the man who had married her. "Is it true? Do you love me, Oliver?"

He might have asked her the same question, might have tried to shield himself from the possibility of hurt, but instead he did not hesitate to answer, "Yes."

"I love you, too."

He kissed her again and then smiled when he raised his head to look down into her face. "February, is it? Perhaps this child will be born on St. Valentine's Day—our anniversary, as we both well know."

"That would be lovely."

It would be lovely indeed: to celebrate the start of their new life with the start of another. The life they had created, the living proof of the love St. Valentine's Day had brought them, despite the odds against it. She recalled from her history lessons the tales of the sainted man who had defied the law that kept Roman soldiers from marrying, because once married they were reluctant to leave their wives and families for long wars in foreign places. St. Valentine had married the sweethearts secretly and for his efforts had been imprisoned and eventually killed. Now he was the patron saint of lovers, and she could almost believe the tales, could believe that it had been his intervention that had prompted a lord of the realm to place an advertisement and that had made the paper wherein it was printed blow into her hands. She offered a small prayer of thanks, for it was easy to believe the saint smiled down upon them as they stood in silent joy, their arms entwined, as were their hopes and their dreams and their hearts.

ELEGANCE AND CHARM WITH ZEBRA'S REGENCY ROMANCES

A LOGICAL LADY (3277, $3.95)
by Janice Bennett

When Mr. Frederick Ashfield arrived at Halliford Castle after two years on the continent, Elizabeth could not keep her heart from fluttering uncontrollably. But things were in a dreadful state. Frederick had come straight from the Grange, his ancestral home, where he argued with his cousin, Viscount St. Vincent. After his sudden departure, the Viscount had been found murdered.

After an attempt on his life Frederick knew what must be done: he must risk his very life, and Lizzie's dearest hopes, to trap a deadly killer!

AN UNQUESTIONABLE LADY (3151, $3.95)
by Rosina Pyatt

Too proud to apply for financial assistance, Miss Claudia Tallon was desperate enough to answer the advertisement. But why would any man of wealth and position need to advertise for a wife? Then she saw his name and understood why. *Giles Veryland.* No decent lady would dream of associating with such a rake.

This was to be a marriage of convenience—Giles convenience. Claudia was hardly in a position to expect a love match, and Giles could not be bothered. The two were thus eminently suited to one another, if only they could stop arguing long enough to find out!

FOREVER IN TIME (3129, $3.95)
by Janice Bennett

Erika Von Hamel had been living on a tiny British island for two years when the stranger Gilbert Randall was up on her shore after a boating accident. Erika had little patience for his game of pretending that the year was 1812 and he was somehow lost in time. But she found him examining in detail her models of the Napoleonic battles, and she wanted to believe that he really was from Regency England—a romantic hero that she thought only existed in romance books . . .

Gilbert Randall was quite sure the outcome of the war depended on information he was carrying—but he was no longer there to deliver it. He must get back to his own time to insure that history would not be irrevocably altered. And that meant he must take Erika with him, although he shuddered to think of the havoc she would cause in Regency England—and in his own heart!

Available wherever paperbacks are sold, or order direct from the Publisher. Send cover price plus 50¢ per copy for mailing and handling to Zebra Books, Dept. 3641, 475 Park Avenue South, New York, N.Y. 10016. Residents of New York and Tennessee must include sales tax. DO NOT SEND CASH. For a free Zebra/Pinnacle catalog please write to the above address.

REGENCIES BY JANICE BENNETT

TANGLED WEB (2281, $3.95)

Miss Celia Marcombe's dark eyes flashed with righteous indignation. She was not a commodity to be traded or bartered to a man as insufferably arrogant as Trevor Ryde, despite what her high-handed grandfather decreed! If Lord Ryde thought she would let herself be married for any reason other than true love, he was sadly mistaken. He'd never get his hands on her fortune—let alone her person—no matter how disturbingly handsome he was . . .

MIDNIGHT MASQUE (2512, $3.95)

It was nothing unusual for Lady Ashton to transport government documents to her father from the Home Office. But on this particular afternoon a gust of wind scattered the papers, and suddenly an important page was lost. A document desperately wanted by more than one determined gentleman—one of whom would murder to get his way . . .

AN INTRIGUING DESIRE (2579, $3.95)

The British secret agent, Charles Marcombe, had done his bit against that blasted Bonaparte. Now it was time to nurse his wounds and come to terms with the fact that that part of his life was over. He certainly did not need the likes of Mademoiselle Therese de Bourgerre darkening his door, warning of dire emergencies and dread consequences, forcing him to remember things best forgotten. She was a delightful minx, to be sure, but it would take more than a pair of pleading emerald eyes and a woebegone smile to drag him back into the fray!

Available wherever paperbacks are sold, or order direct from the Publisher. Send cover price plus 50¢ per copy for mailing and handling to Zebra Books, Dept. 3641, 475 Park Avenue South, New York, N.Y. 10016. Residents of New York and Tennessee must include sales tax. DO NOT SEND CASH. For a free Zebra/Pinnacle catalog please write to the above address.

DISCOVER THE MAGIC OF REGENCY ROMANCES

ROMANTIC MASQUERADE (3221, $3.95)
by Lois Stewart

Sabrina Latimer had come to London incognito on a fortune hunt. Disguised as a Hungarian countess, the young widow had to secure the ten thousand pounds her brother needed to pay a gambling debt. His debtor was the notorious ladies' man, Lord Jareth Tremayne. Her scheme would work if she did not fall prey to the charms of the devilish aristocrat. For Jareth was an expert at gambling and always played to win everything—and *everyone*—he could.

RETURN TO CHEYNE SPA (3247, $2.95)
by Daisy Vivian

Very poor but ever-virtuous Elinor Hardy had to become a dealer in a London gambling house to be able to pay her rent. Her future looked dismal until Lady Augusta invited her to be her guest at the exclusive resort, Cheyne Spa. The one condition: Elinor must woo the unsuitable rogue who was in pursuit of the Duchess's pampered niece.

The unsuitable young man was enraptured with Elinor, but *she* had been struck by the devilishly handsome Tyger Dobyn. Elinor knew that Tyger was hardly the respectable, marrying kind, but unfortunately her heart did not agree!

A CRUEL DECEPTION (3246, $3.95)
by Cathryn Huntington Chadwick

Lady Margaret Willoughby had resisted marriage for years, knowing that no man could replace her departed childhood love. But the time had come to produce an heir to the vast Willoughby holdings. First she would get her business affairs in order with the help of the new steward, the disturbingly attractive and infuriatingly capable Mr. Frank Watson; *then* she would begin the search for a man she could tolerate. If only she could find a mate with a *fraction* of the scandalously handsome Mr. Watson's appeal. . . .

Available wherever paperbacks are sold, or order direct from the Publisher. Send cover price plus 50¢ per copy for mailing and handling to Zebra Books, Dept. 3641, 475 Park Avenue South, New York, N.Y. 10016. Residents of New York and Tennessee must include sales tax. DO NOT SEND CASH. For a free Zebra/Pinnacle catalog please write to the above address.

THE ROMANCE OF LORDS AND LADIES IN JANIS LADEN'S REGENCIES

BEWITCHING MINX (2532, $3.95)

From her first encounter with the Marquis of Pender-leigh when he had mistaken her for a common trollop, Penelope had been incensed with the darkly handsome lord. Miss Penelope Larchmont was undoubtedly the most outspoken young lady Penderleigh had ever known, and the most tempting.

A NOBLE MISTRESS (2169, $3.95)

Moriah Landon had always been a singularly practical young lady. So when her father lost the family estate over a game of picquet, she paid the winner, the notorious Vis-count Roane, a visit. And when he suggested the means of payment—that she become Roane's mistress—she agreed without a blink of her eyes.

SAPPHIRE TEMPTATION (3054, $3.95)

Lady Serena was commonly held to be an unusual young girl—outspoken when she should have been reticent, lively when she should have been demure. But there was one tra-dition she had not been allowed to break: a Wexley must marry a Gower. Richard Gower intended to teach his wife her duties—in every way.

SCOTTISH ROSE (2750, $3.95)

The Duke of Milburne returned to Milburne Hall trust-ing that the new governess, Miss Rose Beacham, had in-stilled the fear of God into his harum-scarum brood of siblings. But she romped with the children, refused to be cowed by his stern admonitions, and was so pretty that he had the devil of a time keeping his hands off her.

Available wherever paperbacks are sold, or order direct from the Publisher. Send cover price plus 50¢ per copy for mailing and handling to Zebra Books, Dept. 3641, 475 Park Avenue South, New York, N.Y. 10016. Residents of New York and Tennessee must include sales tax. DO NOT SEND CASH. For a free Zebra/Pinnacle catalog please write to the above address.